Respectfully dedicated to James Hervey Macomber,
Naval Surgeon, U.S.S. Honeysuckle, 1864, East Gulf
Blockading Squadron of the United States Navy,
who died in the service of his country and was the
inspiration for this novel

At the Edge of Honor

Robert N. Macomber

Pineapple Press, Inc.
Sarasota, Florida

Inquiries should be addressed to:

Pineapple Press, Inc.
P.O. Box 3889
Sarasota, Florida 34230

www.pineapplepress.com

Library of Congress Cataloging in Publication Data

Macomber, Robert N.
    At the edge of honor / Robert N. Macomber.—1st ed.
        p.   cm.
    ISBN 1-56164-252-5 (alk. paper) (hb.) — ISBN 1-56164-272-X (p.b.)
1. Florida—History—Civil War, 1861–1865—Fiction. 2. United States—History, Naval—19th century—Fiction. 3. United States. Navy—Officers—Fiction. I. Title.

PS3613.A345 A8 2002
813'.6—dc21
                                                                      2001052090

First Edition
10 9 8 7 6 5 4 3 2

Design by Shé Sicks
Printed in the United States of America

Preface

This book is a novel about a real squadron of men in the United States Navy who fought in the American Civil War. Their war was unlike that on the Mississippi River or the Carolina coast. No glory could be attained where these men fought. No entourage of correspondents were with them to disseminate and immortalize their deeds. Only a dirty, personal, and frustrating ordeal awaited the officers and sailors who were ordered to the East Gulf Blockading Squadron on the tropical coasts, islands, and rivers of Florida, Cuba, and the Bahamas.

Like their descendants one hundred years later on the coasts of Southeast Asia, they fought a war without lines, enemy uniforms, or clear rules and goals. It was a war in which the person in the gun sight could be an enemy, a refugee fleeing from the enemy, or one of their own irregular troops. In fact, the enemy spoke their language, worshipped their God, appreciated their songs and humor, and shared many of their political views. Many of the new enemy had been their comrades in arms just three years before during the Third Seminole War in southwestern Florida.

The naval Civil War in Florida was a war in which the geography, flora, and fauna were against them also. Jungle insects, various types of carnivores, and poisonous plants and snakes were every bit as deadly as enemy bullets. Mind-numbing heat and humidity competed with unseen diseases, like malaria and yellow fever, to terrorize even the strongest men. The badly charted coast of Florida was a maze of islands and rivers that led into a forbidding interior. Shallow waters and tropical storms and a landmarkless coast added to their troubles and strains.

On top of these problems, the British and Spanish had territory only a few days' sail away. Many of the vessels on the southwestern Florida coast were foreign, which brought international law and serious repercussions into every encounter with them. Patrolling the coasts and islands of Cuba and the Bahamas increased the tension and the potential for unwanted conflict with the imperial might of Spain and Britain. Communication with the squadron commander at Key West was very difficult at the best of times, and the ships' commanding officers were frequently left to their own devices and judgment.

And yet, in spite of all of these handicaps and obstacles, they did it. They maintained the blockade, porous at first, but increasing in its strength so that by 1863 they could go on the offensive and bring Union control to the coast. These men, who fought against so much in addition to the enemy, closed down the Confederate coastal supply routes. They then assisted the army in disrupting the interior supply lines, which had been giving the main Confederate armies further north the beef and foodstuffs to prolong their operations and thus the conflict. The Anaconda Plan, devised in 1861 and the primary mission of the U.S. Navy in the Civil War, had finally extended its mortal squeeze even to the jungle coasts of Florida.

The main character of this book, Peter Wake, commands an armed sloop named the *Rosalie* on those coasts. Already an experienced merchant marine officer, he now goes through the tough process of becoming a naval officer and combat commander. Wake and the other characters in the book are constructions of my own. Many ships mentioned in the book actually were with the East Gulf Blockading Squadron. Several of the events are based loosely on real incidents documented from the Official Naval Records.

Your most humble servant,
Robert N. Macomber

Acknowledgments

This book is the product of years of work and there are many to thank. First, my gratitude goes to Dena Sue Macomber, my wife and co-adventurer of twenty-one years, a true believer from the start, enduring and encouraging when times got tough. My thanks also to Randy Wayne White, famous Florida author, fellow Islander, and seaman, a gifted teacher who enlightened me in the ways of storytelling, and the one who introduced me to the two most important writers it has been my privilege to know— Dian Wehrle and Roothee Gabay. These two Parrot Hillians were aboard for the entire voyage, sharing all the frustrations and exhaustions of this adventure. They gave far more than they got from this old sailor, became my good friends and have my great appreciation. I must also thank that other Island legend, Sheba, the Wonder Dog, my writing companion and morale officer, who made me laugh when I needed it most. And finally, thanks also to June Cussen, my editor at Pineapple Press. About a hundred times I've thanked the Lord for giving me a *writer's editor*. Peter Wake would be honored to have them all in his crew.

—Bob Macomber
Off the coast of Florida
31 August 2001

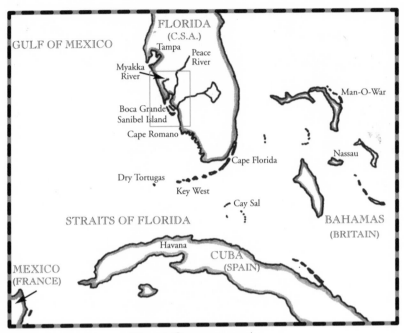

Naval Operations Area
Florida/Bahamas/Cuba
(Charlotte Harbor—inset)

MYAKKA RIVER

PEACE RIVER

Punta Gorda

CHARLOTTE HARBOR

BOCA GRANDE

Pine Island

CALOOSAHATCHEE RIVER

Useppa

Captiva Island

Punta Rassa

GULF OF MEXICO

Sanibel Island

Naval Operations Area
Charlotte Harbor

1

Bound for the War

Peter Wake stood near the gumbo limbo tree at the back gate of a modest house on Whitehead Street, vaguely aware that the town of Key West was starting to come to life around him, his attention focused on an upstairs windowpane as it turned pink with the coming sunrise. He felt the winds shift around to the east even before the moving air brought him the smooth feminine scent of jasmine, the scent he would now forever associate with Linda, who watched him from the window.

He had managed to tell her, this green-eyed girl with whom he had fallen hopelessly, and foolishly, in love during the weeks he had been in Key West, that he could not say when he would see her again as he had been assigned a ship and would be sailing soon. He'd told her of his feelings and she'd professed her own, and they now knew their lives would be intertwined, whatever that might mean in this time of war. His gaze did not leave hers until the wind rose further with sound and movement in the swaying limbs of the gumbo limbo.

His mind then shifted to that other female that had arrived in his life, the *Rosalie*, the sloop he would command starting today. She'd be hove short and needing to catch the ebb. He began to think of the many things he was responsible for accomplishing in the next few hours.

Linda blew him a kiss, and he had another brief moment of deciding to abandon his duty and go back to her. But then, in the way of a sailor, he turned and left her. He did not look back at her in the window of her father's house on the shaded street, on the gentle side of town.

Moments later, as the young naval officer walked toward the harbor, home of the East Gulf Blockading Squadron, he thought of his situation and winced. He was more than just a little concerned at how close he had come to not leaving her world. It would have been very dangerous to stay here in Key West and be around Linda Donahue. His decisions had not been very logical lately. As he turned onto Duval Street he started to return to his usual demeanor, carefully observing the sky for signs of what could be expected, watching the streets of the port as they began to convey various types of early morning persons on their errands. He was confident of his experience on the sea, but he knew little of the business of war and had plunged into his temporary staff duties with a will to learn. He found that being a United States naval officer carried with it expected duties and attitudes he had not known during his years as a schooner's mate along the New England coast. Used to the small shipping firm owned by his family, he was astounded at the bureaucratic chaos of the nationwide naval organization that had sprung up over the last few years. But then he had finally received his orders. Not only was he going to sea, but because of his experience he was commanding a small armed sloop that had been brought into the navy just a few weeks earlier. It was more than he had dared hope for. The excitement of anticipation became stronger with each step away from Linda—not that his love was diminishing with distance, just that the overwhelming stimulation of a new command filled him with a positive energy that fairly propelled him along the street.

When he made the officers' landing at the seawall, the sun

was just starting to emerge from the horizon. In the clearing light, Wake confirmed what he had felt earlier as he left Linda. The wind was a steady trade breeze out of the rising sun, with not a cloud in sight. Another beautiful May day, in this, the third year of a very ugly war. A broad reach to the north, he thought as he looked out over the congested anchorage that contained a diverse selection of vessels. Every type of warship, except for those new-fangled monitors he had seen when passing through the Charleston squadron, competed with merchant and local fishing vessels for space to swing on their hooks. The tide was starting to ebb now. Time was not to be wasted on pipe dreams of lives that were not to be. It was time to be the naval officer that he had become, and to go meet the *Rosalie*. She would be his world now. His life, and the lives of other men, would depend on her.

The young seaman in the dinghy at the landing had been trying to get his attention for some time now, Wake suddenly realized.

"Pardon me, sir, but is ya Master Wake, the new cap'nin of the Rosey, sir? I'm meanin' the *Rosalie*, pardon, sir."

The boy was obviously attempting to be extremely polite while daring to question a dreaded officer, hoping not incur the wrath of someone who could have him disciplined without recourse.

"Yes, I am, boy. Are you from her?"

"That I am, sir. The bosun sent me for ya, sir. Said that Master Wake would be here, sir. She's a fair pull out yonder, sir," the boy said, without adding that it would be he who would be doing the pulling and he wanted to shove off and use the tide to assist him rather than fight it.

The boy was trying so hard to look competent that Wake almost started to laugh at the sight, but he pulled himself togeth-er and assumed the look of command that captains have worn since men first went to sea.

"Very well, boy. Bear a hand with my bags and gear, and shove off for her."

Well, he thought, a proper ship would have a whole boat's crew of four or five men, in a real ship's boat and not a dinghy, to bring me to my first naval command. But then, this was pretty much in keeping with how things had gone for the last several months.

As the boy struggled to row the cramped dinghy away from the landing and through the anchorage, Wake thought about his life before the navy. A life on the sea, to be sure, but with the comparative freedom of a mate in the merchant service. Born and raised into a family of seafaring men and strong-willed women, Peter Wake had been at sea since the age of ten. His brothers, James, Luke, and John, had all gone on to command schooners. But his father had other plans for Peter, whom he recognized as having a different constitution from his other sons, with some aptitude for the intellectual side of carrying trade on the sea. He had sent his youngest son ashore at age thirteen to receive the necessary education to someday run the offices of the family business.

At the hands of the dull-demeanored instructors at the Teignmouth Classical School, Peter had excelled in the musty world of the great thinkers of history, science, and mathematics, but he spent every spare moment available to him at the docks of the small coastal village three miles from the institution. Talking with the fishermen, watching the small craft sail into and out of the port, and many times just sitting on the cliffs staring out to sea, Peter dreamed of life at sea. Three years dragged by.

A week after his sixteenth birthday, he summoned the courage to speak to his father and tell him of his desire to return to the freedom of the sea. To his surprise, his father had nodded and said that he, more than many, certainly understood his son's feelings. Two days later he was a seaman in a schooner bound for Maine and a cargo of spar lumber. Wake had not been ashore for more than two months since that voyage, sailing as a seaman, next a bosun, and finally the mate on the biggest of the family's six schooners. He was looking forward to his own command when one of the older captains would retire ashore and a position would be available. Wake's life was moving along the predictable course of a fifth-generation New England sea captain when events far to the south finally made themselves felt even in the cold reaches of the coast of Massachusetts.

War had come to the United States. States were squaring off against each other like school boys whose taunts had finally gotten to the point of fisticuffs. The South's threats of the previous fifteen years were no longer dismissed by New Englanders as a problem far away.

Thousands of young men flocked to the regimental recruiters, but the commerce of the coast continued as before and the Wake family schooners still sailed their routes. By early 1863, even this facet of normality changed though, as Confederate ocean raiders' successes struck fear into the American merchant marine and intimidated many of the insurers of ships and cargoes. Even the coastal trade suffered. No insurance meant no cargo, and therefore no ships, so hundreds of sailors were thrown onto the beach. Many owners sold ships to the rapidly expanding navy or to the army as transports, but the senior Captain Wake refused to sell even when the price was better than average. For generations the family had been building up their fleet, with a ship only leaving the company when she was old and worn out, and always replaced by a newer vessel.

But finally old Captain Wake had no choice but to make the tough decision that would send his youngest son to war. The family laid up three of their schooners, with the senior siblings commanding the three remaining. Peter was without a job and knew he would soon have to decide, not if, but how, he would become involved in the war that was engulfing every part of his world. To stay connected with something he understood, he chose the sea and volunteered for the navy.

"If you've got to die, then die clean, son," his father had told him. "Soldiers always live and die in the mud." The year before, 1862, had provided the nation with enough examples of soldiers dying in the mud. Fewer and fewer maintained the illusion that this would be a short war.

So he had taken his father's advice and ended up here, in a nearly-awash dinghy, rowed by a terrified boy through the crowded harbor at Key West—leaving the woman of his dreams and going to war.

The boy was heaving hard now, glancing over his shoulder at the *Magnolia*, a five-gun sidewheel steamer captured from the Rebels off New Orleans the year before and soon to be the flagship of the East Gulf Blockading Squadron, which was based at this harbor. The boy swung the dinghy away from the stern of the steamer and passed along her starboard side. Wake could see the officers lounging on the afterdeck and watching him. He thought he could see the smirks on their faces as he tried to look dignified while the boy struggled onward around the tough-looking steamer.

Next ahead was the *Dale*, the squadron's aging ordnance ship. The boy swung wide around her as well, reflecting the sailor's age-old fear of ordnance ships. Thank God I'm not on her, thought Wake as he inspected her weather decks. She was a bit slack in the rigging, the officer of the deck apparently not paying attention to his duties. Better the lowly *Rosalie* than that vessel of slow death by boredom or much quicker death by mishandling the powder and ammunition aboard.

And then he saw her. Anchored out beyond the ordnance ship, the *Rosalie* was not imposing or beautiful. Just another small vessel attached to the squadron for inshore patrol, she lay in the shallower water by the Frankfort Bank close to the schooner *Ariel*. He could see some activity on *Rosalie* now. Several figures were looking his way. The boy was still heaving away at the oars with a steadily increasing stroke. He now had to impress the men of the crew as well as his new captain. Wake stared ahead and let the lad do his job, for he could remember times like this in his own youth.

As they got closer, Wake cast his sailor's eye over his new command. She appeared to be set up well in the rigging—a sloop rig, relatively high freeboard, wide beam and shallow draft of a coaster used to the Southern sandbars and inlets. She was obviously a centerboarder—still, he wondered how she would point into the wind. He could see now the twelve-pounder howitzer set up on her deck just abaft the mast and hoped that they had strengthened her deck beams for it. At forty-five feet long, she was the smallest ship in the squadron. But she was his.

The dinghy was approaching the starboard side of the sloop, and Wake could see what appeared to be the bosun standing at the stern giving orders to some seamen forward. The boy startled Wake by giving the traditional shout for a naval captain coming to his own ship, "*Rosalie!*"

Suddenly they were alongside and the boy tossed his oars in a sailorlike fashion, impressing his new commander. Wake immediately went up the side at the chains as the boy struggled to hold the dinghy and get the gear lifted up.

"Welcome to *Rosalie*, sir. I'm Hardin, the bosun."

Wake turned to look at the eyes that were boring into him and saw a muscular man about fifteen years older than himself. The man had the air of a hunter who was examining his freshly trapped catch. The New York accent and the obviously broken nose did nothing to diminish the image. Wake knew immediately that Hardin was the type of man who disdained kindness as weakness and judged men only from their ability to steer, reef, row, drink, and fight. He had known many such men in his life on the sea.

"Very well, Hardin, see that my baggage is put below. Muster the crew for the reading of my orders."

"Aye aye, sir," Hardin replied in the carefully neutral voice of the veteran sailor to an unknown officer.

When the tiny crew of eight had mustered into line before him, Wake read aloud his orders from the admiral commanding the East Gulf Blockading Squadron, Cantwell Barkley, directing him to assume command of the United States naval vessel *Rosalie*, take care of her condition and that of her men, and proceed to the southwest coast of the peninsula of Florida to blockade and take action against the Rebel enemy in that area, in concert with the bark U.S.S. *Gem of the Sea*, to which the *Rosalie* was now attached. The crew stood in mute apathy as he completed his duty of reading the orders. He stared at the men for a moment, wondering how they had come to this place and time. The bumping of the dinghy alongside reminded him of the ebb tide and the need to get through the required procedures.

"Hardin, I will now inspect the crew."

"Aye, sir."

In the freshening breeze the line of men swayed easily. Wake looked at each in the eye and tried to gauge his ability to accomplish what was expected of him. He could detect no sign of surliness, drunkenness, or stupidity in the line of men. It appeared that all, except the boy, had served for a while in the fleet. They certainly had the look of seamen. That was a blessing. With the fleet expanding so rapidly, many ships were forced to go undermanned, with a large percentage of their crew being untrained landsmen. Wake thought it very strange that he should have so many veteran seamen, until he thought of what might be the reason for this windfall: an opportunity for the captains of the ships anchored around him to get rid of their less than desirables? Time would tell. . . .

Next came the inspection of the vessel herself, with Hardin beside him. Wake assumed Hardin's intent demeanor was due to his responsibility for the condition of the sloop as well as wondering how much his new captain would know to ask about and look at. *Rosalie* appeared in good shape, with the rigging, spars, sails, and deck gear in proper condition.

The twelve-pounder was a bit large for the vessel, and Wake wondered how her weight would affect the sloop when she heeled. He knew she had been built in 1858, recently captured from the Rebels off Charleston, and brought here to be taken into the navy. During the last three weeks Hardin had been given the duty of arming and provisioning her—and waiting for his new captain, who had been waiting himself at the squadron office for two weeks for orders to a ship. Either *Rosalie* was already well found or Hardin had done a good job of refitting her. Time would tell on that issue also. . . .

Below decks the inspection worked aft from the forepeak, through the magazine and the crews' berthing, until he and Hardin came to his own cabin, a crude and miserable affair set against the transom that might measure ten feet abeam by five feet forward along the deck. The deck was five feet overhead. A scuttle hatch above provided the only daylight, and a small and rather shoddy door led forward into the crews' berthing space. Wake's sea bag and other gear competed with a rough-hewn bunk and tiny chart table to fill the space so that he could hardly move about. Well, not the great cabin of the captain on a regular man-of-war, but I've been in worse, he thought. Out of the corner of his eye, Wake caught Hardin staring at him.

"Well, this will do fine, Hardin. Heave her up short and prepare to get under way immediately. I will be up on deck directly."

After Hardin's departure Wake unpacked his sea bag and stowed some of his possessions as neatly as he could. He would leave the rest of his belongings packed for now. His immediate duty was to get *Rosalie* under way and moving out of the channel with what ebb tide remained. He took a deep breath, and a last look around at his place of refuge and privacy on this small warship, and climbed the ladder up and out of the scuttle hatch.

The sun was making itself felt when Wake returned to the deck and noted that the ship was ready to get under way. It didn't take long on a vessel of this size. Hardin reported to him that the anchor was hove short, the mainsail was ready for hoisting, and the ship was ready for sea. Wake looked out across the harbor and, seeing no vessels close enough to warrant danger, quietly told Hardin to haul the mainsail up. After the ponderous sail was lifted, thundering in protest along the mast, the gaff peak was hauled taut and belayed. Six of the crew then took hold of the anchor rode and walked away with it aft, their bodies straining against the line as the anchor slowly ascended off the bottom of the harbor. As her head swung off to the west, Hardin took the large tiller himself and steered her out of the harbor. He called out to the men on the mast to set the jib, and the men at the waist hauled in the sheets. Wake, standing at the windward rail to the right of Hardin, noted that all of this was accomplished quietly and with no confusion or loud oaths. Indeed, the crew had not uttered any words during the entire process. As they now coiled and stowed the various lines they had just hauled, Wake noticed them casting occasional glances at him.

Rosalie, her main and foresail up and drawing well, was surging along the edge of the Frankfort Bank bound out of the harbor through the Northwest Channel. On several of the nearby ships men stopped and looked out at her, and Wake felt a bit of sympathy for the sailors who were cooped up in this harbor on some of these ships like the *Dale* and the *Magnolia*. What his vessel lacked in power, image, and comfort, she made up for in freedom. She was heading out to do the job they were all there for, to go to war and end the Rebellion as soon as possible, not sit in harbor and waste away. Wake took in a deep draught of fresh sea air and reveled for a moment, in the way of so many captains before him, in the obvious envy of those watching from the other ships, who were condemned to sit and rot at the hook in this harbor.

As he watched the houses of Key West getting smaller and more indistinct, he thought of Linda. She was probably having breakfast right now. He could picture her in his mind, sitting at the table conversing with her mother and father about the day's news in the Key West newspaper, the pro-Union *New Era*. Her father would be raging about the "Yankee lies" about victories won in Virginia and Tennessee, and her mother would be cautioning her father against getting too upset about the war when there was nothing he could do to change the outcome. Linda was probably acting ever so innocent during the family morning meal, he thought wickedly, and never giving any indication that she loved a despicable Yankee sailor. If her father only knew the truth of the matter he would be absolutely outraged. Linda's beautiful image swam back into his vision and replaced the harsher one of her father. He could see her green eyes and feel her soft auburn hair. Her voice, its Southern accent tinged with an Irish lilt, called to him. Wake realized that he was probably smiling as he thought of Linda and her considerable charms. He frowned and turned to Hardin.

"Hardin, that departure was well done. The crew appears to be about their wits and know their jobs."

"Aye, sir, that they do," Hardin said with what Wake imagined was the slightest hint of pride in his voice.

"Well, we're bound up the coast to the war, so they'll get their chance to show it some more. Set the watches and follow the channel until the light ship, then close-haul in to the northeast. Any questions?"

"Where are we bound for exactly, sir?"

"The Rebel haven by a place called Sanibel Island. We're to assist the *Gem of the Sea* in shutting down the supply route through there. I don't know that coast. Have you been there?"

The voice turned neutral again, "Aye, sir, I know that damned coast."

"Well Hardin, I shall rely upon your local knowledge then. But you don't sound pleased to see action there again."

"You've not been there, sir. I have. You'll understand when you've been there."

Wake turned from Hardin's look, suddenly unnerved by the man's negative demeanor. As Wake gazed out over the water to the massive structure of Fort Taylor receding in the distance, he spoke loudly for the crew's benefit.

"Well, at least it's better than rotting afloat here in port. The sooner we get this damned war over, the better. Put the scoundrel Rebs in their places, and we can get back to our lives."

The crew, who had heard the entire dialogue, were now silently looking at Wake and Hardin from the foredeck.

"Aye, sir, we'll put 'em in their places and get it over with."

Hardin thoughtfully regarded the island of Key West on the horizon, then turned and walked away to the gun carriage.

"Nor' by west . . . and mind ya steer small," he muttered to the duty helmsman as he passed him.

As the *Rosalie* slid along the quartering seas, Wake stared off to windward and barely heard the helmsman, Conner, a short, thin man of indeterminate age over thirty and below fifty, quietly speak to him.

"Beggin' your pardon, sir, but is we bound fer that jungle coast agin, sir? We all been there afore, in other ships. We thought maybe in *Rosalie* we'd be a guardship for the channels at Key West, sir. That was the scuttlebutt amongst them idlers on the docks. Liberty ashore every week, they said, sir. Dockside yeoman clerk of the boiler shop, him own self told me that, sir, an' that's no lie."

"No, Conner. The idlers and clerks told you wrong. We're not stationed at Key West. *Rosalie* is bound for the jungle coast. We're bound for the war."

At that, Conner turned and stared at the luff of the jib and busied himself in steering the sloop. The dutiful manner of his voice eerily echoed Hardin's. "Aye, sir. Bound for the war. . . ."

2

A Question of Identity

The day progressed in the way of the sea, through the endless changes of the watch. The wind held steady in strength but began to veer to the south. Soon *Rosalie* was not sliding along the waves as before. Now she was surging along and rolling with the wind further aft. Wake ordered the centerboard lowered completely in an effort to dampen the roll. It was moderately successful, but still she rolled. They held course to the northeast, where Wake hoped to make a landfall to the south of his destination and then work his way up the coast to this place called Sanibel Island.

That night the first clouds started to arrive from the south. The air started to feel more humid and tense. Wake had the mainsail reefed and the jib taken in as precaution for arriving at the coast in the dark. He had made many a landfall in his time, but never on this low coast. The cast of the lead showed a shallow bottom of eight to ten fathoms, and they were still about forty miles off the coast. The seas were steep and short, with very little length to the trough. Wake started to think about the currents in the area and pondered whether he should stand further offshore.

The motion of *Rosalie* was such that most of the crew was sleeping up on the deck. Below decks was a chaos of creaking joints, falling gear, moaning rigging, and stinking bilge water sloshing around in the rhythmic ritual of a rolling ship. Only the dead could sleep in there, Wake thought as he came out on deck and lay down, braced against the raised transom board across the stern.

There were only three men aboard who could stand watch as officer of the deck: Wake, Hardin, and the gunner's mate, Durlon, a short, thin man of maybe thirty years, who had shown a positive demeanor so far on this voyage. Durlon was an unknown to Wake, but Hardin had informed the captain that Durlon could do duty as a deck officer, so Wake had him put on the watch bill. As he lay on the rolling deck, Wake's mind reeled from watch bills to mysterious coasts and the multitude of other thoughts competing for attention and decision. They all faded, however, when he remembered the last time he had lain down. It now seemed as if Linda and Key West were from another life. He wondered what she was doing now, and immediately put the thought out of his mind. Forget her and pay attention to keeping your men alive and your ship afloat, the captain of the *Rosalie* admonished himself. He finally started to feel the mental and physical exhaustion of the last eighteen hours and slowly succumbed to sleep, one hand unconsciously gripping the transom for security against the constant movement of the ship around him.

When the first light of the coming day filtered through the black of the night, Wake was back on watch. The lead now showed the bottom at five fathoms with more shell in the tallow, so he told the helmsman to steer northerly to keep further off the coast. That order had the effect of increasing the roll so that occasionally the end of the large main boom would dive into the seas alongside. She was sailing by the lee now. Wake worried about an accidental jibe and watched the helmsman, a man named Smith, struggle to keep her from slewing around. *Rosalie* was making very good time and was bound to see the coast at any moment, somewhere around the Romano Cape.

He tried to put a confident look in his appearance for the first landfall with a new crew. Since the night and morning had been cloudy, he had had no opportunity for a celestial sight and had been dead reckoning, hoping they would sight land before the Cape Romano Shoals would wreck them. Wake had no idea of the state of the tide or strength of the current and so could only hope his navigation was correct.

Suddenly the bow lookout yelled against the wind, "Land ahead, sharp on the starboard bow! Looks like 'bout three or four miles off, sir."

Wake couldn't see the dark line on the horizon yet, but he wasn't going to wait.

"All hands on deck to wear ship! Time to stay off the coast, men. We've got to get the mainsail over to the starboard tack!"

The crew came awake at Wake's yell and began to rouse themselves up and to their sail handling positions along the deck. Hardin came striding aft and asked, "Sir, wear the ship, or tack her?"

"Well, Hardin, how's she handle when wearing in a sea and wind like this?"

"It's a bit much, sir. I'd like to tack her through the wind to save the strain on the spars."

"Very well, Hardin. Let's get her around through the wind," Wake yelled against the increasing breeze.

Moments later, the *Rosalie* slowly turned to starboard, her huge mainsail of thick canvas thundering in protest as her turn became a circle back into the wind and seas from the south. The moment of truth came when she continued turning, seas smashing over her bows, around to the west and then the northwest, the mainsail abruptly announcing with a loud crack that it was full of wind again. *Rosalie* quickly heeled over on the starboard tack and surged forward, having completed a full circle with the mainsail on the other side of the ship.

Throughout it all Hardin was watching and directing the men in their duty, from the man on the tiller to the men on the sheets. Wake did not have to intervene at all. Part of him appreciated the smooth evolution of a very dangerous maneuver, and part of him wondered at Hardin's control of the crew. Wake was definitely getting the impression that he was on Hardin's ship, as opposed to the other way around.

After the ship was secured on the new tack, the off watches were sent to their breakfast, a cold porridge and salt beef junk because no galley fire could be lit in these sea conditions. The seas continued to build and were moving with the wind from the southwest. It certainly looked as if a storm was heading their way.

"Hardin, do you recognize that coast yonder?"

"Sir, the coast all looks pretty much the same from this far off. From the size of the beaches I'd guess that we're somewhere around Cape Romano. I think definitely not to the south of the Cape. There's fewer beaches along that stretch of the coast, and the soundin's would be far less. I'd suggest stayin' off this far and running up the coast till we see an island in front of us, sir. That'd be Sanibel Island. About forty miles from here I'd venture. Should see it afore dark at this speed."

And so they sped along up the coast, staying about three miles from the white beaches of the islands that formed a barrier to the bays and rivers that wound their way up through the jungle into the interior of the peninsula. Before taking over his new command, Wake had spent his time at the squadron offices at Key West asking for information about this coast. The various officers he came in contact with could not tell him much about the interior. Some told him that the coast was full of renegades, Rebels, and refugees. The renegades were common criminals who preyed on anyone who came within their grasp. The Rebels were Confederates, on both the land and the sea, who were determined to keep this coast open for supplies to move through. And the refugees were civilians who were pro-Union and hiding among the islands of the coast. Rumor had it that there were hundreds, if not thousands, of refugees.

The officers had told Wake that the main trouble with all

these people was that there was no way to tell who was who. There were no battle lines. A Rebel one day could be a refugee the next. And the renegades could portray themselves as anyone if it served them at the moment. Mistakes had been made by other captains. Innocent people had been put into prison, and scoundrels had been let go. Blockade runners had been captured and paroled, only to be captured again on their ships that had been seized and sold back to them. Of course, the Northern papers had not reported on this aspect of the war.

Admiral Barkley had told him to use good judgment based on common sense. All of this had served to depress and confuse Wake even before he had gone aboard *Rosalie,* for prior to his arrival in Key West from Boston he had imagined an orderly war where progress could be measured and known. Instead, Wake and the *Rosalie* were sailing into an area where a guerrilla war was being fought. To top it all off, storms were frequent here in the winter and diseases were rampant in the summer. Wake had heard about the dreaded yellow fever of this coast. All this pre-amble to his arrival here was not made better by Hardin's reluctant attitude about returning.

Five hours into the new day Wake was in his cabin when he heard the bow lookout call out to Durlon, "Sail on the bow, hull down, dead ahead 'bout four miles, I think. Looks that she is headin' this way."

Seconds later Durlon lowered his head below the scuttle hatch and told Wake of the sighting. The captain had been sitting at his tiny chart table trying to memorize the features of the coast on the scanty chart he had. It was an 1851 coastal survey chart showing very little detail. Wake climbed the ladder and found Hardin standing by the cannon staring ahead. Wake, with the only telescope aboard, checked out the approaching vessel. The closing speed of the two ships was very fast in these conditions, another twenty minutes and she would be within gun range.

"Hardin, all hands to quarters. Stand by on the twelve-pounder. Do you recognize that sail?"

"No, sir. She looks a schooner. There are several schooners the Rebs are using on this coast."

"Send up the colors, Hardin. We're going to stop her."

As the men of *Rosalie* transformed their home into a fighting ship, Wake kept focused on the approaching vessel. She was a schooner, all right. About sixty feet or so.

She was close-hauled on the port tack and making a fair amount of leeway, causing her to slide ever further west offshore as she fought the wind to go south. Soon he would have to make a decision as to how to stop and search her. In these seas he couldn't come alongside and board her. No, he would have her heave to and send the dinghy, as dangerous as that was.

As the national ensign went up to the peak and streamed out to port, Wake and Hardin looked for the reaction from the schooner's crew. They could clearly see several men looking and gesturing among themselves and back at the sloop, for the range was now only a couple hundred yards. They were caught by surprise, Wake suddenly saw. The *Rosalie* was new on this coast, and the navy had had nothing like her before. The schooner had not turned and flown before the wind on sighting the sloop, because they had no fear of a vessel like her.

In the time that it took Wake to form those thoughts, the schooner had doused her jib and backed her staysail, with her foresail down and main strapped in. She was now lying hove to in the seas and rolling like a dead whale. Her crew was apparently having an argument while they struggled to hold on as she rolled.

"Hardin, take two men and board her. Find out what she is about and send word back to me by one man in the dinghy."

"Aye aye, sir." Hardin looked forward to the crew. "Conner, you and Wilson man the dinghy. Cutlasses and pistols. But *do not* cock the damned things, is that clear?"

Conner and Wilson took their weapons from the ready chest kept on the after deck and pulled the dinghy up to the transom. Hardin followed them down into the tossing dinghy. They shoved off and slowly negotiated the hundred feet between the schooner and the sloop, both of which were now hove to with their jibs aback. Wake watched as Hardin was the first to climb up onto the deck of the schooner, with no assistance from the crew. He was followed by Conner, with Wilson holding the dinghy alongside. An intense discussion was going on, but Wake could not make out the words since they were to windward of the schooner. The crew of the *Rosalie* also watched their shipmates on the other vessel. Durlon stood by the loaded cannon, and several others had muskets ready.

In a few minutes Wilson was back alongside the sloop and made his report to Wake.

"Sir, Hardin presents his respects and says the following to tell ya. He says that she is the schooner *Victoria* out of Nassau, sir. He says that she has six men aboard and that one is the cap'in, one is the mate, three is the crew and one's a passenger like, sir. Hardin says, sir, that the cargo hold is empty. He says that the last port was New Orleans and that they are bound for Havana. I thinks that's 'bout all, sir, 'cept that Hardin says to tell ya that he thinks it's all a bunch a dung, and that they're runnin' the blockade."

With the strain of his recital completed, Wilson looked over at the grinning gun crew and replied with a maniacal grin himself.

"Wilson, did he say what nationality they were?"

"Aye, sir. Ya have me there, sir. I forgot to tell ya. Sorry, sir." The grin vanished and a look of fright replaced it, which only led the gun crew to greater mirth.

"Stand easy on that, gun crew. Durlon, control your men." Wake, his annoyance clear to all, turned back to the reporting sailor. "Now, Wilson, tell me what he said about their nationality."

"Aye, sir. Hardin said that they said that they was all limeys. Even the black uns. Said they said they was neutrals in our war, an' subjects o' the limey queen, sir."

"Row me over there, Wilson," said Wake as he climbed down into the dinghy. He looked forward and quietly said to Durlon, "You're in charge of the sloop. Keep watch over the schooner."

The crew still aboard the sloop lost their look of amusement at the proceedings and stared as their officer boarded the schooner.

Hardin met Wake at the rail and led him aft, where they could talk away from the schooner crew huddled on the foredeck. Hardin advised him that he thought that the passenger was a Reb, and that the schooner had probably come from the Sanibel Island area. With the winds and seas what they are, that could very well be, thought Wake as he looked over the supposed Britishers. Hardin further advised that all had identity papers except the black crewmen and the passenger, who had a Southern accent.

The passenger was brought aft to Wake. His name was John Saunders and he appeared to be a middle-aged gentleman by his clothing and demeanor. His build was slight and his accent was that of the middle Atlantic coast, possibly Virginia or Maryland. He told Wake that he was a British citizen from Abaco Island in the Bahamas and that his family had lived there for generations since they had fled the American colonies after the Revolution. It seemed that they were loyal to the crown of England and the Bahamas was the closest place to go in their flight from their fellow former colonists.

Saunders then stated that he booked passage on the schooner to and from New Orleans to ascertain if the Union forces then in control of the city were in need of salt from the Bahamas. No written confirmation of being in New Orleans was available, Saunders explained. The authorities in New Orleans were not working when the schooner left the city hurriedly in the night due to a rumor that Confederate river gunboats were getting ready to attack. Therefore, no clearance papers were on board. The port arrival papers for New Orleans were still on some clerk's desk there.

Wake had heard of loyalists settling in the Bahamas, but he had never actually met one before. He had also read in the newspapers that the Rebs had gunboats building on the Mississippi in an attempt to regain control of the river. Hardin, standing next to him during the conversation, could hardly control his disbelief of the story told by Saunders. Wake knew he had to make a decision. He remembered Admiral Barkley in Key West telling him to be very polite with neutrals. There had already been several incidents on this and other coasts with Spanish and British ships and citizens that had nearly led to war with those countries.

"Very well, Hardin, if you are sure that there is no contraband of war aboard her, then we will let her go."

This last was said as the schooner lurched and slewed down a wave, nearly throwing Wake off his feet. Hardin looked disgusted.

"Captain, there's no cargo 'cause they've already unloaded it on this coast. This here is a Rebel, and this schooner is a runner. Captain, sir, we'll see 'em again sure as hell, but next time maybe we won't catch up to her. Let's take her into Key West now and let the prize court judge it. She'd be worth every bit o' two thousand dollars."

And that was another factor to be taken into account—the prize money. Every sailor in Uncle Sam's navy wanted his share of prize money. The recruiting placards had promised thousands of dollars of prize money to men who enlisted. It made the intolerable conditions a little more worth it. *Rosalie* herself had been sold into the navy for fifteen hundred dollars with most of it divided among the sailors who had captured her off Charleston just three months ago. Wake could see Hardin's mind at work calculating his share of two thousand dollars.

"No, Hardin. I will return now to *Rosalie* and send Wilson back for you and Conner. We will let them go. They are neutrals and I cannot prove anything otherwise."

Wake swayed across the deck and dropped down into the dinghy, telling Wilson to shove off and get him back to the *Rosalie*. As the dinghy fought her way back to the sloop, he could see Hardin speaking to the passenger, Saunders. Wake had a sick feeling that maybe Hardin was right and his own decision was wrong. So far, this new command had not gone as he had hoped it would.

Ten minutes later both vessels were on their way. *Rosalie* again was surging northward along the coast, and the schooner was slowly slogging her way south against the wind and seas. The crew was secured from quarters, and the watch routine again took over.

It was several hours later when Hardin and Wake had occasion to speak again, at a watch change. Wake was studying the bosun's face for signs of problems as they formally made the relief of the officer of the deck, but he saw nothing but the inscrutable façade that was becoming the norm with Hardin.

"I'm sorry you won't get your prize money, Hardin, or your time in Key West. But you see, it was a question of proof of identity."

"Aye, sir," came a low moan in reply. "It is always that. A question of identity. They try to fool us, an' we try to catch them. I just hope you're right, sir, on this particular question of identity. . . ."

Hardin saluted, for the first time since the cruise started, and walked away to the foredeck, leaving his captain alone with his thoughts. Wake gazed off behind the sloop to the southern horizon, where the schooner was already long gone.

Renegades and Scoundrels

ake looked around the anchorage at Punta Rassa in the early morning light. A light and already warm land breeze could be felt from the east. Three miles to the southwest the island of Sanibel lay tranquil in a sea turning jade as the sun rose higher in the sky. The flood tide was surging along past the hull of the sloop as she lay at her anchor. Other than the crude trader's camp on the beach close by, there was no sign of anything on land or water. Another quiet day, he thought with a shudder.

On a morning just like this a week ago, at this same spot, his crew had been working on repairing chafe on the sails and were sitting around on the deck, canvas in hand. Without any warning a shot rang out and a musket ball thudded into the mast. It missed Conner by a few inches, and scared them all. Nobody had seen where the shot came from. There was no place to return fire. In fact, there was nothing to actually do. Hardin had said that sharpshooters usually only shoot once and then leave the area, but nobody felt safe for days after that.

Lookouts posted to scan the mangrove jungle shoreline when they anchored or sailed close in had not spotted anyone since then, but the crew knew they were out there. Wake knew the sharpshooters had accomplished their mission—making everyone edgy and adding one more damned thing for him to worry about.

The *Rosalie* had been on station on this coast for a month now. In that time she had stopped and boarded five more vessels, none of which was seized. She had run after three others but failed to close with them. Wake's little ship had also run supplies twice for the *Gem of the Sea* and other ships in this area of the coast. That meant sailing back to Key West, usually a two-day sail, spending one day loading at Key West and leaving that day or early the next.

Supervising the loading, dealing with the dock workers, making his reports to the staff at the admiral's office, and guarding against the crew getting ahold of the cheap and abundant rum that seemed to be everywhere in Key West, he hadn't had a spare moment to see Linda. He wondered if she had heard that *Rosalie* had been in port those two times. He wondered if she thought he was intentionally avoiding her. He dared not try to send a note to her for fear that it might end up in the hands of her father, whose rabid Confederate views were well known.

It had been a relatively busy month for *Rosalie* and her crew. But the summer heat and windless days were coming upon them. Wake had heard stories from the crew about the fevers of the coast, of drifting with no wind, of the sudden tropical gales and hurricanes that came without warning, and of the ever-present vicious insects that could drive the sanest man mad with their incessant attacks. The crew told him that in the summer most of the ships of the squadron would lie further off the coast to keep away from the diseases and insects and currents when the wind died. For the hundredth time, Wake wondered just what he had gotten himself into by volunteering for the navy.

It was with a mixture of curiosity and apprehension that Wake turned and followed the lookout's pointing arm one Sunday while sailing off the beach at Estero Island. The subject of the alert was a small sloop of maybe twenty-five feet sailing out of Carlos Passage at the southern end of the island. She was moving fast in the afternoon sea breeze and bound southerly, with several people visible sitting or standing on her low flush deck.

Hardin came up from below at the shout and inspected the vessel through Wake's glass. By this time *Rosalie* had come about and trimmed her sails to go after the lively little sailer. The whole crew was staring ahead at the stranger vessel and making comments about whether the old Rosey could catch her. As some of the men were hoisting the topsail and others were sending up the large balloon jib, Hardin said to his captain, "Sir, I don't know her. There's several small sloops hidden in the backs of these islands along here. Some are refugees, but most are runners. I'd wager that there is a blockade runner, sir."

"Well, Hardin, I believe we'll soon find out. Do you suppose that Durlon could hit her from a couple hundred yards if she doesn't stop?"

"In this sea, I don't know, sir. But he could surely try. Maybe it'd scare 'em enough to heave to."

"Very well. All hands to quarters. Send up the ensign and prepare to open fire for a warning shot."

Within a few minutes the crew had manned the gun and the sheets and were now speculating on Durlon's ability as a gunner. Wake had never fired even so much as a warning shot in his encounters so far with ships at sea, and he wondered if this potential enemy vessel was big enough to justify a cannon shot. Perhaps he should just use a musket?

The chase lasted over an hour. *Rosalie* had ideal wind and sea conditions, surfing along on a broad reach with a steady wind. Nothing carried away aloft and the canvas held, so it was up to the helmsman, Conner, to gain every yard he could to get closer to their prey. When they were near enough, Wake ordered Durlon to first fire a musket shot close alongside the suspect vessel. When this had no effect, he told Durlon to fire a warning shot from the cannon whenever he was ready.

All hands aboard *Rosalie* became silent. The banter and speculation ended. Every man stared at the fleeing vessel and looked at Durlon, trying to will through their minds a good shot from the cannon. Not a kill shot, of course. No, there just might be something about that little sloop that would have value in an admiralty court. That was the real reward of the chase. Wake could see them adding up the prize money in their minds.

Boom! The cloud of smoke blew away from the gun and everyone watched the sloop ahead. Twenty feet off their bow! The cheering of the crew overcame all other noise as the small boat ahead immediately turned into the wind and dropped its sails. Durlon was now shaking hands and reciting the various bets made in his favor just a few minutes earlier.

Wake returned everyone to his duty. "Hardin, stand by to go over with two men to inspect that vessel."

"Durlon, that was a fine shot, man."

"Thankee, sir. It *was* a bit of a piece of timing, sir," Durlon responded with a grin, to the accompaniment of guffaws from his shipmates.

As they came close by the strange boat, Durlon and his men manned the gun again and trained it upon the potential enemies, while Hardin and his detail went aboard her. Wake could hardly wait for information. He watched the interactions on the other deck intently. Finally Hardin came back and climbed up on the deck. His face told Wake that this was not like the other boardings that they had done so far.

"Don't like the looks a this, Captain. Sloop is the *Betty* of Estero Bay. Twenty-five feet with only one ton of cargo space. No papers and no cargo aboard. Only a skipper and three men. Two of the men are crew and one is a cattle trader from up the Caloosahatchee River. They're tellin' me that they hates the Rebs and are refugees from middle Florida. Say they're sailin' down to Key West to do a deal with the navy for some beef cattle they got hidden inland. Say they will sell 'em to the navy to feed our ships here."

"Do you know them, Hardin?"

"No, sir. But I thinks they're up to no good. Got no papers and look like scoundrels, sir. There is cattle up that river, sir. But the stories are that they are driven north to the Reb armies, or sometimes sold to the Cuban Spanish for contraband war supplies. I think we should seize 'em all and take 'em to Key West."

Wake thought over the situation. A vessel with no papers. A crew with no papers. Bound from the place where blockade running had been rampant. She was heading south, which could mean Key West . . . or it could mean Havana or Nassau. Plus, *Rosalie* was due to return to Key West soon anyway to resupply. He made his decision. This one would be different from the others.

"Very well, Hardin. Inform them that they are to come to this vessel and that we all are going to Key West for adjudication on their sloop and themselves. They and their boat will be released shortly if the admiralty court believes their story. Hardin, you are appointed prize master of their sloop."

"Aye aye, sir. I'll take Wilson and the boy Sommer with me. We'll leave directly and meet you at Key West."

"Very well, Hardin. Transfer the prisoners to this vessel. As soon as that is done, set sail for the south."

Seizing the prize vessel, transferring the prisoners, and setting sail took little more than half an hour. Hardin drove everyone to get it accomplished as soon as possible. Wake noticed that Hardin appeared to want to be away from him as fast as he could be. It struck Wake also that it was odd that Hardin would want to take Sommer and Wilson with him. Neither of them would be much help to him. Sommer was just a boy learning the ropes, and Wilson was a bit dim-witted, did everything by rote and could not be trusted to make a competent seamanlike decision on his own initiative. Still, Hardin could obviously handle the task, as simple as it was.

The prize sloop got under way first and sailed off to the south on a broad reach. *Rosalie* followed as soon as the prisoners were secured on the foredeck. With a shorthanded crew, Wake was taking no chances and had the prisoners tied to a line at the mast. They could move about, but not too far away from their tether. The prisoners' demeanor was anything but polite and they repeatedly reminded Wake and his crew that when they got to Key West the crew of the *Rosalie* could expect retribution from the authorities in charge. Wake urged his men to carry as much sail as she could take, as much to get the carping prisoners off his ship as soon as possible as to keep up with the *Betty*.

As the day darkened into night, the prize sloop was lost in the darkness. One of the crew was armed and detailed to keep watch over the suspect men at all times, for Wake had heard of prisoners taking over a ship and he wanted none of that here. The sailing was fast and wet for crew and prisoners alike through the night and early morning hours. A moon lit the way for them and under other circumstances it might have been pleasant for Wake. But the nagging doubt of the correctness of his decision, the security of the prisoners, and an odd feeling about Hardin and the prize vessel kept Wake from enjoying the sail or getting much sleep.

The opposite emotion was prevailing among the crew, however. They merrily added up their portion of the prize money from the anticipated sale of the *Betty* and spent hours debating aloud how they would spend their share. Since he couldn't sleep anyway, Wake listened to his men and learned about many places in Key West with which he was not acquainted. He put them all in the back of his mind for future reference in case he should ever have to find his happy warriors and return them to the *Rosalie* the morning after a night of liberty.

As the sun rose out of the sea later that morning, the prize vessel was nowhere in sight. Durlon woke up Wake, who had finally gotten to sleep out of exhaustion an hour before, and told him the news. It did not unduly alarm the captain since frequently vessels separated at sea and later met at rendezvous. The possibly counterfeit cattlemen decided to offer unhelpful comments about it though, until Wake explained to them that he would have them gagged if he heard any more sounds from them.

The tone of his voice and the look in his eye were enough to silence the prisoners and make his own crew wary of him. Even though the *Rosalie* was but a ship of forty-five feet in length, the discipline of the navy was such that no one doubted that Wake, as her captain, had absolute power over their lives.

By mid-afternoon that day the lookout spotted the rooftop observatories of the Tift and O'Hara buildings along the waterfront of Key West. Half an hour later he spotted the brown walls of Fort Taylor rising out of the harbor waters with the trees of the island behind them. Sails were seen moving every which way, and the wharves at the northwest corner of the island came to life as they got closer.

Wake sailed the sloop through the anchorage looking for the prize with no luck. Finally, he anchored his ship off the wharves and went ashore in the dinghy to make his report, leaving the prisoners in the care of Durlon. Wake was not feeling very good about his situation when he entered the offices of the admiral and reported into the staff yeoman's desk.

The staff yeoman passed him along to Commander Johnson, the chief of staff for the admiral and the man who usually kept track of ship movements and reports in the squadron. Since the squadron's area of responsibility covered almost a thousand miles of coast and islands in Florida alone, with the Bahamas and Cuba in addition, Commander Johnson was a busy man with little time for a junior officer with the grade of master who was captain of a mere forty-five-foot armed sloop. The commander looked Wake in the eye and waited silently. Wake got to the point immediately and told the story of the preceding day's boarding and seizure.

Johnson was one of those men who made decisions quickly. Within ten minutes of Wake's entering his office, Johnson had told him to put the prisoners in the brig at Fort Taylor, wait one day for the prize sloop, and tomorrow set sail to find the *Betty* if she did not come in. He added that the crew of the *Rosalie* had to be back in five days' time since that was when the next admiralty court would sit and they would have to testify against the crew of the seized vessel. Johnson's demeanor indicated that he was not impressed by Wake or his report.

When the guard detail from the Forty-seventh Pennsylvania Volunteer Infantry Regiment, which was garrisoning Fort Taylor, arrived at the landing two hours later and took the prisoners away, Wake was relieved to at least have the obnoxious carpers gone from his responsibility. Throughout their captivity, the men from the suspect sloop had complained that they were not Rebel sympathizers. However, Wake had noticed that they had gotten much quieter once they had arrived at Key West. He felt in his gut that he was right in seizing the vessel and crew, a feeling that grew as time went by. But where was Hardin and the *Betty*? His feeling about that was growing worse.

The *Rosalie* lay at anchor with lookouts scanning for the *Betty* throughout the remainder of the day and during the night, with no success. Early the next morning, Wake went ashore to the squadron offices to check for any sightings or new information on the missing vessel. Finding no new intelligence on her, he returned to the *Rosalie* by the harbor duty boat. Even from a distance he could see that things were amiss aboard his ship by the movements of the crew. When he climbed aboard he instantly knew what had happened. No interrogation was necessary. In his short absence ashore they had gotten rum, probably purchased from one of the many bumboats in the harbor.

The gunner's mate and the crew left aboard were already under the effects of rum. Wake could smell it and see it in their faces. His curt orders to weigh anchor and get under way were met with apathetic labor as the men hauled away on the anchor rode and the halyards. It still amazed Wake how fast sailors could get rum, drink it, and get drunk. He had been gone no more than forty minutes. Conner, who had accompanied him, was every bit as upset as his captain, but only because he had missed out on the "sailor's nectar" himself.

The *Rosalie* sailed back out the Northwest Channel into the Gulf of Mexico. Course was set for the coast that lay by Cape Sable and the Shark River, at the southern end of the peninsula of Florida, in case the *Betty* had been driven down to a lee shore there. Lookouts were doubled and the men went watch on watch because of the shorthanded crew. They sailed through the night with all sail set in the gentle westerly wind, constantly looking, wondering, worrying.

This was a very dangerous coast to shipwreck on. The Confederates were just one problem. The Third Seminole War had ended only three years before this war had begun. It was the Seminoles who controlled this part of the coast, and they had no love for the men in the uniforms of the Navy or Army of the United States. In addition to the Indians, the diseases of this area were legendary. The insects at this time of the year would swarm and crawl all over a man, looking for exposed flesh to attack. And there were other dangerous creatures of the jungle, such as poisonous snakes and alligators, lying in wait for an unwary victim. Wake found himself praying that he would find Hardin and the *Betty* at sea and not have to search the coastline.

At the next dawn Durlon was on watch, with the impressive ability of the veteran sailor to be no worse for the wear after his fast drunk on bad rum. It was he who roused Wake with the news that a boat was sighted up on the beach several miles ahead. At that news all hands came on deck and stared at the dark object that Colman and Smith insisted was the *Betty.* Wake couldn't tell, even with the glass, but went along with the crew's enthusiasm.

It took an hour to get up to the shipwreck. It was the prize sloop all right, half on the beach and half awash. Hardin, Sommer, and Wilson were on the beach jumping up and down to attract *Rosalie's* attention. When Wake got ashore, Hardin told him the story.

The bosun explained that the crew of the *Betty* had evidently surreptitiously holed the vessel in the bilge under the quarter when they went below to collect their belongings, just before they were transferred to the armed sloop. Hardin had noticed her getting sluggish after sunset that first day but had not found the source of the leak until later that night. They had bailed all night to keep her up and had run her ashore at the first land they saw the next morning.

Hardin told Wake and the listening crew that the insects at their place of landing had been unbearable. None of them had been able to sleep in the night. Only during a breeze in the daytime could anyone relax and rest. At night, creatures walked and slithered through the mangrove jungle behind the beach and further frightened the shipwrecked sailors. Sommer and Wilson echoed the bosun throughout his story, and all exhibited mosquito and other insect bites everywhere on their bodies. They looked exhausted. For the first time that Wake could recall, Hardin looked pleased to see him.

But Hardin had other news that he said was the best that could be hoped for. He went to the beached boat and returned carrying a small box. He related that while shipwrecked on the beach, they'd had time to thoroughly inspect the *Betty*. In the tiny bilge spaces he found a Confederate ten-dollar bank note from Virginia. The bank note had been tucked away in a box of Cuban cigars down in the bilge. The cigars were completely ruined by the bilge water, but an address had been carved into the wooden box:

John A. Saunders
Richmond, Virginia
Confederate States Army

Now Wake knew the reason for Hardin's apparent change in attitude toward him. Hardin now had proof that the man Wake had let go on the *Victoria* was a Rebel. Wake looked at Hardin and said, "Well, Hardin, it is a pity that we didn't know this when we had Saunders, for this is evidence and not supposition, which is all that we had at that time."

"Whatever, sir," came the smiling reply as Hardin looked right into the eyes of his captain. Wake took possession of the box and told Hardin to refloat his prize vessel and follow them to Key West, which would be a slog to windward from this place.

Tar and a plug from *Rosalie*'s supplies made quick work of patching the hole in the *Betty*. They bailed out her insides and refloated the hull. Two men with muskets guarded against Indians or other threats, while the rest of the crew, Wake included, worked on the *Betty* to make her ready for sea.

At last, the two vessels were able to take their departure from that forbidden coast and get out to sea. This time they stayed together, tacking every four hours and slowly gaining distance toward Key West. By the time Wake was able to lie down for three hours' rest that night, he didn't care what Commander Johnson would think about the Saunders affair. He was just glad that his men were alive and well and the prize sloop was back in his possession.

The tropical dawn found them sailing leisurely down the Northwest Channel into the anchorage. The *Betty* went directly to the wharf and tied up, with Wake arriving by dinghy from the anchored *Rosalie*. He brought Hardin along to the admiral's offices for his meeting with Commander Johnson. Aside from personal implications, the box and its contents had an intelligence value for the squadron and the chain of command.

Commander Johnson was watching a steamer in the channel from the window of his office as they entered. He turned as they saluted and listened to Wake narrate the story of the beaching and refloating of the *Betty*. He listened even more intently as Hardin described with triumph finding the Rebel money and cigar box, and how it related to the boarding of the British schooner earlier. Then, after several minutes' silent inspection of the evidence that was put into his hands, Johnson declared that this was indeed important information. The squadron had heard from the steamer assigned to patrol around the islands of the Bahamas that the ships from those ports were using the west coast of Florida because the ports of its east coast and those in Georgia and South Carolina were closed by the blockade. Several had been captured. But this evidence had now provided some proof of the connection—and of a Rebel named Saunders who was posing as a neutral.

Johnson complimented Hardin on his insightful actions and told him that his name would be prominently mentioned in the report accompanying the evidence to Washington. After smiling for a fleeting moment at Hardin, Johnson dismissed him and bade him goodbye. Wake stood waiting as Hardin left the room.

After the bosun's departure Johnson looked at Wake and quietly said, "Mr. Wake, it appears that you have had fortune on your side in this affair with the *Betty.* One of them is a scoundrel cattle dealer who sold beef to the Reb army at Gainesville last year, according to our refugee partisans here, one of whom escaped from there a few months ago. There is no doubt in my mind that this scoundrel now wants to sell to us. Another is a renegade deserter from the Rebel Seventh Florida Infantry. The trial should be interesting."

"It would appear, sir, that the refugees provide good intelligence on who is who in this area."

"Only when it suits them, Mr. Wake. It also appears that Hardin has provided us with very valuable information concerning Saunders and the Bahamian connection."

"Yes, sir. Hardin has done a good job as bosun. He runs a sharp crew, sir."

"Yes indeed, Mr. Wake. He also looked like he was enjoying the moment while describing Saunders, the boarding, and your subsequent decision. Be careful of that man Hardin, Mr. Wake.

"But now, Mr. Wake, you have to get ready to act as prosecution witness against the crew of the *Betty.* It looks like you have the evidence to show her as a runner. You are authorized to remain at this port, in the anchorage, until the end of the trial. Confer with the United States Attorney and make sure all is prepared for the trial. You may send those men you trust on liberty ashore."

"Aye aye, sir." Wake saluted Commander Johnson and left the room. Upon his return to the sloop, he directed Hardin to secure the ship for at least three days' anchorage and set up two-man liberty parties to go ashore in rotation. Hardin maintained his neutral tone and proceeded to implement Wake's orders.

The trial was held two days later. The admiralty judge was a U.S. district judge who did double duty, a man without patience or humor. A lawyer represented the accused and their vessel, but he looked like he was better suited for the bar at Sibbald's Pub on Caroline Street than the bar of the court. His clients scowled as their attorney whined, and the judge fumed at his half-hearted delaying tactic of requesting time for additional information from witnesses who were in middle Florida. Finally the judge had heard enough and declared to the lawyer that the trial would be started and finished that very day.

After the naval contingent and the refugees had testified regarding the identity of the *Betty* and her crew, the defendants and their lawyer looked positively depressed. They had no defense, stated their attorney, without the other witnesses who had been denied to them and thus rested their case. The judge was not helpful.

"If you have no defense, sir," he intoned to the defense lawyer, "it is because you are defending a scoundrel who would profit from both sides in this sad war, and a traitorous renegade who has renounced even his Rebel brethren in order to side with a scoundrel. Men like these have no defense because they have no character."

The judge then declared that the seized vessel was contraband of war and that the men aboard her were prisoners of war to be taken to Fort Warren in Boston Harbor on the next ship northbound for further incarceration. Four hours after it started, the trial was over.

Wake breathed a sigh of relief at having survived this entire ordeal. As he walked out of the Customs House and through the palm trees toward Duval Street, he pondered the many turns of fate of the last week. They had made him richer from the sale of the *Betty* and provided valuable information for his side in this complex conflict. Those same turns of fate had made other men prisoners of war, bound for a dungeon fifteen hundred miles away, branded forever by their enemies as scoundrels and renegades.

4

Yellow Jack

As he stared at rivulets of sweat running down his arm, Wake decided that the August heat in Key West was the most pervasive he had ever known. The wind was nowhere to be found, and the humidity made everything wet all the time. It penetrated everywhere. No building ashore nor vessel afloat was impregnable against its effects. It made everyone move slowly and think even more slowly. Initiative ebbed away among the civilian population and even among the naval crews, making an order to do some task seem surreal and resented. Only in the early morning, and as the afternoon thunderstorm was brewing up its hour of wind, could any strenuous physical work be done.

It was even worse after the cooling wind of the afternoon storm had ended because then the wind died and the ground and decks actually steamed from the renewed heat. Tempers flared afloat below decks and ashore in the bars and hovels that were optimistically called hotels. Discipline suffered. Commanders despaired. And the month of August seemed to drag out far longer than the thirty-one days allocated in the calendar.

The anchorage at Key West rolled with the low swells that

swayed the *Rosalie*'s spars in a long, lazy arc. Her crew lay on deck under a sail awning, trying to move as little as possible. Swimming helped a bit, but the water was almost as warm as the air. Besides, many officers thought too much swimming was lazy behavior and bad for naval discipline.

Two days earlier Wake had been ordered back to the southwest coast of Florida after a supply run to Key West, but the *Rosalie* couldn't move out of the harbor without wind. So she lay at anchor and they waited, without even the usual afternoon storm to break the soul-draining monotony. The supplies had to be off-loaded into an army transport steamer and sent up to the blockade ships, so at least those crews, who had the same problems with the August heat as those at Key West, could get reasonably fresh provisions.

Wake stood in the corner of the office of the squadron yeoman, which was filled with the commanders of the other vessels in Key West at the time. They had all been summoned to a meeting that was to have started fifteen minutes earlier at two o'clock, but neither Commander Johnson nor anyone else had invited them into the meeting room. So, demonstrating discipline even in this heat, the sloop and schooner captains left the chairs for the senior vessel commanding officers and stood there, mute and unobtrusive, while their seniors pondered the reason for the meeting and the excuse for its tardiness.

Finally, after several more minutes of listening to inane gossip among his seniors, Wake saw Commander Johnson and Admiral Barkley walk in the front entrance and through the assembly to the large room used for meetings. Neither had a pleasant look about him. No greetings were exchanged as the admiral strode through the officers in the room. In fact, from their demeanor, Wake immediately thought that the Confederates had launched some unforeseen offensive and the squadron was going to be given fighting orders.

When everyone had assembled in the room and the speculative talk among the officers had subsided, Admiral Barkley spoke in a quiet and measured voice, his eyes studying each man before him in turn. Commander Johnson stood to his chief's right, holding a sheaf of papers and bearing the countenance of a man about to go into battle against overwhelming odds.

"Gentleman, the Rebels' greatest friend, and our greatest foe, has been found on this island. The yellow jack is here."

A collective gasp could be felt in the room as the officers mentally grappled with the worst possible intelligence they could have been presented. The dreaded yellow fever was in their midst. Commentary immediately rose among them as the admiral continued.

"The squadron surgeon has met with the doctors on the island and confirmed that there are five cases in the town. So far, we have not seen any among the naval people here, but that, as you know, is just a matter of time."

"Therefore, gentlemen, I am ordering all vessels away from this place, including the ones normally based here. Those will anchor no closer than three miles off the island. All others will weigh anchor by sunset and go to their stations on the coast. When we feel certain that you can return, that word will be sent out to the squadron. It will probably be at least several weeks."

Each officer was now calculating his ship's provisions aboard and how long he could make them last. Almost as one, they began to protest the order of making such an abrupt departure.

"Yes, I know what you are all thinking, gentlemen," said Commander Johnson. "However, you also know that this has to be done, and done now. There is safety at sea on this thing. Just be glad that you have the ability to leave. . . ."

At Johnson's last words the room grew quiet, every man knowing exactly what the commander meant. Those who stayed at the squadron headquarters in Key West were going to confront an unseen and unknown foe. There was little they could do against it—just work and wait and hope and pray. Many of them would become terribly sick and incapacitated. Some of them would die a horrible death.

Admiral Barkley concluded the morbid meeting. "Gentlemen, good luck. The main thing in all of our minds should, and will, be the safety and efficiency of the East Gulf Blockading Squadron. The war does not end when yellow jack appears. You will be on your own for a while, but I have every confidence in your ability to do your duty. I look forward to seeing you all again in about a month or so." As he said this, the admiral forced a smile to show on his face. "And at that conference you can report to me on your latest victories. Now, goodbye and God protect you."

The stunned officers muttered offers of good luck to the admiral and his staff as Barkley and Johnson exited the room and left them standing there. For a moment, the crowd of captains stood there gazing at each other. The heat and humidity of the room had been forgotten in the comprehension of the brutal news presented by their leader. But now they suddenly realized how beastly hot the room was, aggravated by their growing fear, and they made their way to the doorway while removing their uniform coats that were always worn for a meeting with the admiral.

Wake's first thoughts were for the *Rosalie* and her crew. The sloop was provisioned and ready to go, Wake knew, as he walked out of the building slowly. The rest of the captains had rushed out, trying to get done in the few hours before sunset what normally would take days to accomplish. The crew of *Rosalie* was aboard and ready to get under way. The lack of wind was not an obstacle anymore. Steamers would be ordered to tow the sailing vessels out away from the island. They would wait for wind out in the Gulf of Mexico rather than in the harbor.

That left Linda. His mind was racing with various plans to find her and spend those few remaining hours with her. It had been three weeks since he had last held her. And that rendezvous had only been for three hours in the early morning before dawn. Wake knew the relationship could not continue like that, and at some point it would either end or be accepted by her family. But now was not the time for those decisions.

He finally decided on the direct approach of going to her family cook at the back door of the house and asking if she was there. He thought that he could trust in her maid's loyalty to Linda. He wondered if Linda knew of the yellow fever since he had not heard of its arrival prior to the meeting. Judging by the response of the officers gathered there, neither had they. Therefore, it probably was not out among the population yet, he decided as he walked down Whitehead Street. But it soon would be, after that dramatic announcement by Admiral Barkley.

Mattie, the cook, was working in the cooking shed, set back in the gumbo limbo trees behind the main house. She listened and watched him intently as Wake asked her if Miss Linda was home and free to come to the kitchen. A few moments later Linda was there and in his arms, Mattie watching out toward the house for any oncomers.

"Darling, I've got to leave the harbor by sunset. I don't have much time. Linda, there is a fever in the town and we have all been ordered away."

"Peter, it is the fever season now. It has always been a danger. Everyone from here knows it. Is it yellow jack? That's the worst."

"From what I understand it is, my dear, and you and your family need to be very careful." After which he related in a general way the outcome of the meeting at headquarters. He reasoned that the news was already spreading over the town anyway.

He made her promise to be very careful: sleep under nets, fumigate the house frequently with smoke, stay away from strangers, and stay home as much as possible. As he recited the precautionary procedures, he became more anxious for her. He wished there was some way to take her away with him. If he had been a merchant ship captain, he could have.

They sat and talked while Mattie made the dinner for the family. The black cook pounded on conch meat with a mallet as Wake and Linda quietly exchanged tender kisses and conveyed their thoughts about what was about to come. Mattie's rhythmic pounding provided a subtle sense of time ebbing away. Long before they were ready for it, Mattie pronounced that dinner was soon to be served and that sunset was only a little ways off. She then stared at Wake without saying a word.

Mattie's departure to the main house with the dinner food jolted Wake to make his own exit. He felt a tremendous sense of cowardice fill him as he said goodbye to his lover. His sense of guilt almost destroyed his power to speak. There was so much he wanted to say, and so much he wanted to do. And yet they both knew that he was powerless to do anything.

Promises having been made and long, loving kisses having ended, Wake quietly walked away around the back of the property, feeling for all the world like a cad. It reminded him of the renegade from the Confederate army whom he had captured and who was now rotting in a prison somewhere. It was all so damned unfair.

He caught a ride on another ship's boat going his way. All across the harbor he could see ships moving and hear men calling out orders. He turned and looked at the squadron offices. In the second floor window of Commander Johnson's office he could see the flash of a reflection off a telescope. It now turned toward his direction, and Wake could only imagine the thoughts going through that veteran officer's mind as he watched the squadron escape from the island's sickness.

Hardin met him as Wake came aboard. He had already heard the news and had the anchor hove short and the crew standing by. The crew went about their work without the excitement shown all over the harbor. Wake was once more impressed with his small band of men. Anyone with any sense wanted to be away from this place, but at least they were going to do it in a seaman-like manner.

A steam tug soon came by, and her young ensign, one rank junior to Wake, rather abruptly said to be ready in ten minutes to receive a tow line from the schooner *Annie,* which would be under tow from the tug herself. The ensign then steered away to another sailing vessel. The young man appeared to be feeling the pressure of trying to assist so many ships at once.

Just then, Sommer pointed ashore to the signal mast at the squadron building. The men of the *Rosalie* were joined by the men of the other ships in the harbor in watching a large yellow flag ascend the mast and hang there in the deathly stillness. The golden yellow of the signal was accentuated by the spreading glow of the sunset. Wake felt an ice-cold chill run down his spine as he stood there drenched in sweat, mesmerized by that flag. The yellow jack . . .

Twenty minutes later they were under tow through the Northwest Channel and away from the island. The breeze felt by the forward motion of the tow was like a refreshing sweet drink to all hands. Almost all were bare-chested as they savored the movement of air that cooled the sweat on their bodies. At little more than steerage way, the tug and tows slowly moved along the channel between the shallows and coral patches to either side toward the open Gulf of Mexico. Two hours later the schooner and the sloop were anchored fifty yards from one another and the tug was heading back up the channel to the harbor in the darkness. Anchor watches were set, and Wake lay down exhausted on the deck, wondering when the wind would come and what Linda was doing at that moment.

Morning came and there was still no wind. Swimming was authorized for all hands of both vessels by the captains. The crews of the sloop and the schooner spent the day in the tepid water, mainly under the shade of the bow or the stern. Even here, in this heat and flaunting the customs of the old navy, the line between junior and senior was clear. The seaman and junior ratings stayed in the shade of the bows, and the senior petty officers and the commissioned officers treaded water under the sterns. Periodically, some competitive soul would try to organize a swimming race, but the general mood of laziness precluded any exertion.

Wake swam over to the schooner and floated under her countered stern with her captain, James Williams. As they lay on the calm surface, Wake listened to Williams tell of how four months earlier he had fired at a fleeing British schooner off the coast of Cuba, and then lost her as she went inshore to the territorial waters. The action had sparked an international incident among Spain, Britain, and the United States. Admiral Barkley had defended Williams' actions to Washington, but had privately lambasted him for being a hundred miles off his station at the Tortugas, and being near Cuban waters at all. But, Williams related, they couldn't officially discipline him because it would be an official admission of wrongdoing and get them all in trouble with the other countries. Now, however, Williams observed to his brother captain, he was not on the most favored list of Commander Johnson and the admiral.

Wake related his own history on the coast, with the diverse results that he had achieved. Both young captains then pondered the variables of international maritime law and decided that it was all a toss of the dice and not a well-ruled game. With the intellectual certainty of their age and position, they proposed that the powers to be in Washington could not even imagine the problems of the men making the decisions on the scene of these actions.

After the sun had crossed its apogee, the lookout stationed aboard the *Annie* cried out that he saw a wind line in the water to the south. He was greeted by the floating crewmen of both ships with comments about his eyesight and that of his ancestry. But when the lookout from the *Rosalie* confirmed the sighting a few minutes later, no one doubted it. Instead, all hands looked at the two captains to see what their decision would be. Wake and Williams looked at each other, then turned toward their crews and told them to get aboard and make ready to get under way. Technically, Williams was senior in grade by five months, but that kind of procedural strictness did not intrude at this moment. Within five minutes the crews were starting to weigh anchor and set sails.

The wind was very light at first, but it built steadily to a nice sailing breeze. The *Annie* set off to the west for the Dry Tortugas, as the *Rosalie* spread all sails wing and wing, bound north to the coast. As the wind built up, so did the clouds that would soon send one of the usual summer thunderstorms. In harbor at anchor, the cool winds they brought were a relief. However, out at sea they could be very dangerous, and Wake kept an eye on the mountainous clouds to the south. As the schooner sailed off westward, he called out good luck to Williams, who waved back the same.

The storm that afternoon was a quick succession of gale-force winds and nasty breaking seas, then driving rain followed by a calm where the sloop wallowed in the leftover seas. The entire storm took no more than an hour and a half. During the height of the rain all of the crew's clothing was tied into the rigging to wash out the body sweat and sea salt. The men stood on deck rejoicing in the God-given shower, reveling in being cool, knowing it would not last long since after the rain had subsided, they would have to work the pumps. In the heat of the summer the seams on deck would open and rain leaks would turn the deck below into a dark and humid cave where fungus would grow on anything not used for a day, and the lowly bilge demanded its tribute at the pumps.

On the third day after leaving the *Annie*, the sloop sighted the now familiar Sanibel Island. Wake decided to sail north to the anchorage at Boca Grande and meet with the *Gem of the Sea*, the vessel to which his sloop was attached. He wanted to tell Lt. Baxter, her captain and his superior, about the situation in Key West and the orders for the ships of the squadron.

It took all day to get the twenty miles up to Boca Grande. Wake found the *Gem of the Sea* at anchor just inside the pass in the wide expanse of Charlotte Harbor. This harbor, Wake knew, was the domain of the Rebels on land and on the water. Many of the blockade runners had come out of this twenty-mile-long by five-mile-wide bay. He and Baxter had conversed several times about extending their reach up into the bay and exploring the Myakka and Peace Rivers, both well known for being Rebel havens.

Once Wake had come alongside the larger ship, which had been a difficult maneuver in the fast currents and light winds, he reported his news to Baxter. But Baxter had more depressing news for him. The yellow jack had already been reported among the ships at Tampa Bay. Baxter had a crewman down sick with the symptoms. He had not yet confirmed it as the jack and had told his surgeon not to talk about it with the others. He was trying to stop any premature panic or speculation that always attended discovery of the disease. Baxter listened as Wake completed his narration of the squadron's affairs and then told him to leave the anchorage as soon as possible and patrol along the Gulf off the islands to the south. He was not to venture inshore until the fever was gone from the coast. Wake acknowledged his orders and returned to the sloop rafted up alongside.

His orders to Hardin to cast off and ride the ebb tide out through the pass in the almost nonexistent wind met with a questioning look but dutiful response. Wake didn't elaborate and went below to his cabin, where he studied the scanty charts of the pass once again. On deck a few moments later he personally took the helm, now essentially drifting with the outgoing tide, through the pass and out into the Gulf. Once they were about two miles offshore he gave the order to anchor, again without explanation. He thought about advising Hardin of the situation but decided against it. At dawn they would sail to the south, try to capture another runner, and get away from this place.

Dawn found them still sitting there, in sight of the larger ship anchored inside the pass. It was Durlon who quietly came aft in midmorning and told Wake that the other ship had hoisted the yellow flag a moment earlier. He stared at his captain with the knowing look of a man who is resigned to his fate and said nothing further.

Wake pivoted to go forward and check the anchor rode when he saw the entire crew on deck and looking at him.

"I know, men. Captain Baxter is not certain but is being cautious with the yellow jack flag, as he should be. We still have work to do, and as soon as the wind pipes up we will stand south offshore and patrol for runners."

No one replied.

"Now, get to work on the running backstays. And I want the sheet blocks set higher to improve the sheeting angles when we do get wind to sail. Hardin, if you please?"

"Aye aye, sir. All right, ya slack-eyed sons, ya heard the captain. Let's get that work started now. Both backstays at once. Conner, set up the halyards to take up the strain."

Four days later they were off Boca Grande again, having sailed to the south as far as Gullivan Bay with no sail sighted. This time they anchored in the pass and rowed in the dinghy a hundred yards to the windward of the *Gem of the Sea*. Wake and Baxter conversed, shouting through cupped hands, over the water between them. Wake told Baxter that he was very low on fresh water and getting low on food. He asked for orders.

"Sail to Key West, Mr. Wake. Stay off the port and speak to the guardship. Ask the situation of them. If all is well, then go in and reprovision and tell them of our problems. Ask for medicine to be sent here, along with regular supplies."

"If Key West is still under the quarantine, sir, what then?"

"Then, Mr. Wake, you are to use your own initiative, sir. God protect you all."

Wake hesitated a moment, then had the dinghy rowed back to the *Rosalie*. He had not expected Baxter to order him go to Key West. It must be getting worse on that ship, Wake thought, as he looked back at Lt. Baxter, who was on his afterdeck watching him row away.

The next morning, a strong land breeze came in from the southeast, the first they had had in many days. It was amazing how a good fair breeze could pick up the spirits of a sailor. *Rosalie* had all sail set on a close reach and acted as if she loved it. The wind, steady in strength and veering around into a nice sea breeze from the southwest as the day progressed, provided the energy to move the sloop smartly. *Rosalie* started to buck through the small waves on her bows. A light pattern of spray occasionally swept over the decks. The men were smiling and moving about with at least some semblance of enthusiasm. The main topic of discussion was what the guardship would tell them. The secondary topic was what they would do in Key West if they could go into port there.

Wake smiled as he heard the last, another constant in the world of the sailor. Not a thought of the wider implications or of future consequences. In the world of deck sailors next month was in the far-off future, not to be worried about or looked forward to. The turnabout in attitudes even diverted Wake's now constant worry about water and provisions. By tomorrow, with this wind, they would be off the port, with the answer to the sailors' primary question.

The *Annie* was sighted in midafternoon the next day. The two vessels converged about twelve miles off the island. All hands were by the shrouds and listening intently as Wake asked the dreaded words. The cheering of the *Rosalie's* crew at the answer took several minutes to quell, Hardin threatening dire punishment if they didn't shut up and let the captain continue. The captain of the *Annie* told Wake that the last sufferer of the yellow jack had recovered several days earlier, and the ships of the squadron were starting to come back to the port. He added that there were several ships on station that had not been heard from and fears were growing for their safety. At this last news, Wake told Williams of the situation of the *Gem of the Sea* so that he could pass it along to any ships northbound along the coast.

The Rosey's crew turned to with a purpose as they squared away for Key West after leaving *Annie*. Wake could sense the change as clearly as if a hood had been lifted from his head. The wind smelled cleaner, the sea looked greener, the ship felt livelier, and the crew sounded happier. It was amazing what a positive piece of information could do for a man's outlook. All hands had almost a glow about them as *Rosalie* arrived at the harbor anchorage at sunset and looked around themselves at the town and the ships.

The yellow jack signal was gone. The harbor was still not as crowded as it usually was, but vessels were coming in, even after dark. Sounds were coming from the streets of the town, and Wake could see his sailors anticipating the delights of the port.

He ordered Hardin to report in to the squadron office and then take two men on liberty until dawn. Wake would stay on board with the rest until Hardin's return. With a clamour of bragging about previous liberties and plans for this one, the liberty men departed. The rest of the crew gathered on the foredeck and yarned into the evening, with only one man on anchor watch.

Wake sat at the transom and watched the harbor and the night sky. Linda filled his mind. He wondered and feared and dreamed about what had happened to her and her family. The enormity of it all consumed him as he sat there listening to and watching the harbor at night. He could feel his heart beating in his chest with fear for her. It had taken all of the discipline in his character to allow Hardin that first liberty. Wake knew it was the proper thing to do, but he also knew that it prolonged his agony. Come sunrise he would know. His future was tied to the path and timing of the sun. Wake sighed and lay on deck, listening now to his crew talk about rum and women and gambling and beds ashore. His last waking thought was of Linda lying beside him, both of them slowly falling asleep.

The movement of the sloop woke him. A steamer had come though the harbor, sending a wave that had moved *Rosalie* enough to bring her captain to his senses. He looked forward along the deck and saw the lookout standing by the mast staring at the steam gunboat as she glided through the silent harbor, an apparition in the dark night. Above him, Wake saw the tropic stars in a carpet across the sky, with the moon a cold amber light just touching the eastern horizon.

He slowly got up from the deck, knowing the day would be a long and stressful one. He felt as if he had had too much to drink the night before, the effort of rising draining him of strength. The consequence without the pleasure, he thought. He crawled down the scuttle into his cabin and searched for his pocket watch in the darkness, a task he was well acquainted with by now. Four A.M. by the watch, with a flood tide and no wind. Wake started to remember the plan he had formed the night before and returned to the deck to have the seaman on watch call up the boy to row him ashore.

Twenty minutes later he was ashore at the officers' landing watching the boy row back to the sloop. Semi-refreshed by a salt-water rinse and in his number two uniform, he walked through the dark and quiet streets of the town, down Caroline Street to Whitehead and around to the back of the house that he knew so well by now, fanning away at a mosquito hovering around his face. He heard a provost patrol from the army garrison walk by, over on Duval Street, but nothing else was overtly stirring.

Moments later he was in the house through the back door and creeping silently up the stairs to Linda's room. Every creak of the house seemed like a gunshot aimed at him, and every moment he expected the challenge or the charge of Linda's father. The tension instantly faded as he saw that she was alive and sleeping soundly in her bed. As quietly as he could, he sat on the bed beside her. Linda looked up with a frightened face and was about to scream until she recognized his form.

In a voice filled with emotion that he hoped sounded soothing, he whispered to her in the darkness, "Shshhh . . . it won't do to have all your family walk in right now, my love. I've only an hour to be here before the sun will be arriving."

Linda said nothing but held onto him and buried her face in his chest, silently sobbing and trying to get the strength to tell him what had happened. Wake felt the conflict of sadness and anger rising inside him, desperate to know the cause of her sorrow.

"What is it? What happened?"

She first spoke so softly he could barely hear her, but then the words came in a flood, and he sat there, holding her, as she recounted the horror of the epidemic. The yellow jack had swept the island. Each day more people had come down with a fever and some were dying. Life in the town stopped as families huddled behind the doors of their homes, waiting for a sickness they did not understand and could not fight. It went on for two weeks, getting worse each day. People scanned each other for signs of the disease and prayed fervently to find none. But each day, more would get sick. She had seen the carts herself as they moved through the early morning hours collecting the dead from the homes.

Her home had not been spared. Through her sobs she told him of the day that her mother had come down with the aches and the fever, how her father and the cook had also had the symptoms. As her mother got worse and was confined to a bed, her father had somehow managed to hold his own and nurse his sick wife. But the efforts to help were of no avail for her mother, and she died one night with Linda and her father holding the frail hands of a woman who had done her best in life to build a family. The doctor had been there, but his feeble work had produced no effect. The cart came the next morning. The funeral was at noon that same day.

Mattie had died three days later. With his wife gone, Linda's father had sunk into a deep depression. Linda cared for Mattie by herself, not knowing when the dreaded sickness would attack her own body. As Mattie slid off into the fevered sleep that preceded death, Linda almost gave up hope in anything. Her father was not communicating or even coming out of his room. Her love was far away in this evil war. She was all alone in this house of death. Waiting for her father to start being her father again. Waiting for the sickness to stop. Waiting for her love to come back to her. Waiting, helplessly, for what would come no matter what she did.

Linda was emotionally and physically exhausted as she spoke these last words. Her summation of that time from hell told of how her father's brother, another widower since his wife had died many years earlier, had moved into the house last week. He and her father now stayed up late at night and spoke of how the damned Federal army and navy had let the town die. How they had withheld medicines that would have saved the people. How the Yankee beasts had no decency or shame. Their illogical anger grew into hate, which manifested itself in a form Linda had never seen before. Her father's whole being descended into a deep core of rage against all things that were connected with the U. S. government and the American flag.

Linda, scarred permanently by this ordeal, looked at Wake and said no more. They both knew their lives had changed, that an unseen force had increased beyond any limit the dangers of their relationship. Wake was sure now that Linda was the woman of his life. He knew now that they, one way or another, would be intertwined forever. However, he knew that any distant hope in his heart that he and her father could be reconciled had ended. And the hope that he and Linda could live a normal life together in Key West was now dashed.

And all because of an evil force that had moved among them and destroyed randomly. Yellow jack had done his malevolent work well.

The River of Peace

The autumn on this coast was certainly not like the ones in New England, Wake thought as he stood by the mast and swatted a mosquito on his face. Moving sluggishly in a light wind along the coast of Pine Island, northeast of Sanibel Island, the *Rosalie* was looking for blockade runners reported in the area the day before. Wake thought of the smell of the leaves burning in the crisp, clean air as his ship came to anchor at Boston after a fast and profitable voyage.

Letters recently arrived from his father added to his pining for the season, the real season, up north. Six of them, grimy from handling and covering five months, had been bundled together by various clerks who had received them and then searched for Wake down the coast to the squadron off Charleston and finally Key West. Each letter was read and reread for news of the family and the business and the war. Then Wake would swear to himself not to read them anymore for the pain of homesickness they caused. The next morning he would read them again, envisioning his family and former life.

Hardin brought him out of his daydream as he asked if they

should post a man with a musket by the mast now that they were closing in to the jungle. Instantly the dream was gone, replaced by the smell of vegetation rotting in the dank humidity and the squawk of a heron upset at the arrival of this giant, winged creature disturbing the bird's hunting. Wake replied affirmatively while swatting at still another of the buzzing little torturers that plagued them whenever they got close to the mangroves. Lord, how he missed New England.

Since the beginning of the summer, they had patrolled along the Gulf beaches of the islands, but now they had been given orders to penetrate up into the bays and rivers and bring the war to the Confederates' home bases. Wake wondered if the man who gave that order, Admiral Barkley, had ever actually been up in this area. He doubted it. If he had, he would have left it to the Rebs.

The morning was young, only three hours since sunrise. With the sun still low, the heat had not progressed to the point of overwhelming, but the humidity was already stifling. The easterly land breeze was a breeze in name only. Wake estimated their speed at maybe one knot at the most. At this rate it would take all day to get to Punta Gorda, twelve miles to the north at the mouth of the Peace River. The enemy was probably further up the river. His check of the tide showed a half flood, which was likely the main reason for his forward motion. Only about three hours of helpful tide left.

He looked at the crew, who looked back at him, knowing what was on his mind. Hardin stood up from his seat on the twelve-pounder gun and said the inevitable.

"Run out the sweep oars ta get her goin', Captain?"

A look at the sky and one at the water told Wake that no wind of any strength would come that day. Confederate lookouts at Punta Gorda would watch them approach, slowly and without surprise. Wake decided to wait.

"No, Hardin, we will wait until nightfall and then slide along the coast with the night wind and sweeps, if we need 'em. That way we will catch them unawares at dawn with a flood tide at the mouth of the river."

The crew, having heard all of the conversation, started to go back to their work. No cheering or appreciation came from them, only a grudging acknowledgment of the captain's orders that for once meant less exhaustive exertion.

"We hidin' for the day, sir? Get amongst the mangroves and they won't see us atall afore dark."

"Yes, make it so. Get her over into the mangroves."

At this last the crew glanced at Hardin with looks of disgust, for moving the sloop into the mangroves meant mosquitoes and maybe sharpshooters, but they got the sweep oars out and ran the ship in among the dense foliage of the mangrove jungle. The sounds of the men complaining of the heat, the lack of wind, and the mosquitoes soon became a background of noise to Wake as he sat down on the transom board and tried to think through his mission and how he would accomplish it.

Lt. Baxter had ordered him to investigate up the Peace River and try to ascertain exactly where the Confederate docks were. Those docks were one of the bases for the supplies that came in to this coast from outside the Confederacy. They were connected to the interior trails that wound north through the middle of the peninsula. Cattle, cotton, and other agricultural goods moved south. Munitions, medicines, and manufactured goods moved north from the coast. There were other bases along the coast, but the ones on the Peace River were reputed to be the most important to the enemy.

Baxter had promised him support, if it was available, in the form of his ship's boats. Propelled by oar and sail, they could provide reinforcements of about twenty to thirty men for the expedition. That promise had been made two days ago at the Boca Grande Passage, eight miles to the west. However, no boats had arrived and Wake had decided that he should go on ahead without waiting for reinforcements that might never arrive. The drone of the insects assisted him in making this decision, but he told himself that it was the element of surprise that was the real deciding factor.

The day was slow torture. The urge to get away from the jungle was overwhelming. The hours dragged by, Wake ordering the men to try to get as much sleep as possible since they would be moving all night and possibly fighting all the next day. Finally the sun started its slow descent to the west. Slowly and almost imperceptibly the day began its flaming final display.

Looking out to the islands to the west of the sloop, Wake saw the indescribable colors of a Florida sunset slowly paint the sky. The cottony clouds provided brighter islands in the sea of pastels that covered the world above. Birds of pink and blue and green glided through the sky as the sunset approached, apparently to add even more color to this beautiful scene. Wake thought that the beauty of this exotic place was cruelly expensive to behold, for one had to first brave the dangers that guarded that beauty. And he thought of the night and day to come. He wondered if he would die in a place ironically called Peace River. Then he thought of the one he always thought of while watching the sun set into the far-off sea.

Ten hours later they were off Alligator Creek, just a few miles from Punta Gorda. The men were very tired, having rowed with the sweeps for most of the way. The ponderous sloop had slowly moved along the coast of Charlotte Harbor, that vast twenty-mile bay that expanded east and north into the body of Florida. Wake ordered a rest and the crew collapsed over the looms of the oars, gasping in the humid, still night. Hardin was in the bow, searching for any movement or alarm on the coast ahead.

After a thirty-minute rest, they were back at it again, with Wake steering out and around the large point of land called Punta Gorda, or "fat point" as it translated into English. Slowly a land breeze came up from the east, and the men set the sails and gratefully stared to the gradually lightening horizon. Wake set a regular watch of men and told the rest to get as much sleep as they could. The off-duty crewmen sank down onto the deck where they stood and immediately were dozing, while the rest of the crew stared off around them in the growing light to catch a sight of an enemy vessel or land contingent.

As they turned northeasterly at the mouth of the Peace River, the sun started to make its arrival. The wind turned up a bit, and the sloop, now close-hauled on the starboard tack with all sail set, was moving fast on the smooth water. Wake, steering her himself into the river and relying on a hand-drawn diagram of the sandbars, had a fleeting thought of how beautiful this moment was and how much Linda would appreciate it were she there now.

Moments later, Wilson called out from the crosstrees that he saw a sloop and a schooner at anchor ahead, close by the northern shore. Instantly, the entire crew was awake and staring to the shoreline off the port bow near a point of land with live oaks growing prominently. Wake gave Hardin his glass and told him to go aloft and report, whereupon the bosun climbed the shrouds with surprising rapidity and turned his attention to the vessels anchored some two miles distant.

"Small sloop of about twenty-five feet, sir. Schooner of about forty feet, sir. Both have what may be bales a cotton on deck. Men're aboard and weighin' the anchors, I think, sir," came the call from aloft.

"Very well, Hardin. Durlon, please clear for action, send up the colors, and prepare to fire a shot near those vessels."

The rush of activity on deck was interrupted by another report from aloft. "Sir, their anchors are hove and sails bein' set. They gonna head upriver. It'll be a beat upwind for them 'n us, sure as hell."

The enemy craft were going to run for it—up a river they knew well. But *Rosalie* had the advantage of already being under way and moving fast. The distance between the two forces diminished quickly. They were now about a mile and a half away, almost in range.

The Rosey's twelve-pounder was set up on deck directly aft of the mast, so that any fire directly ahead was difficult. With all the sails, shrouds, stays, and halyards in front of the cannon, it was too dangerous to fire. Instead, the *Rosalie* would have to bear off or up a bit so that the gun could be aimed over the deck aft of the bow and past all the rigging. It made bow chases difficult. Still, it could be done.

"I will luff the ship up into the wind, Durlon. Fire your warning shot when they safely bear. You won't have much time before I have to fall back onto the course again."

Durlon's reply was muttered as he concentrated on his great metal pet. In addition to putting his gun crew through the prescribed regulation loading and aiming drill, he began to talk softly to the gun, stroking the barrel and looking forward to the enemy ships. Those ships now had all their sail set and were also heading upwind, about a mile ahead.

"Watch for shallow water, men. They know the river and we do not. Hardin, you will be crucial on that issue."

Wake was mentally doing the geometry, trying to figure out where the Rebel crafts would be before they would tack. He thought that it would be good to hit them when they were slowed down, making their turn through the wind.

"Durlon, fire when ready. The next one will be for effect in their rigging!"

The crew smiled at the thought that their captain was trying to save the vessels for seizure, but came back to their senses when the *Rosalie* slid to windward and started shaking her rig as the sails luffed. The noise of the slapping jib and the thundering mainsail was overcome by the deep boom of the cannon. The gun jumped backward on the recoil and the crew quickly went about reloading it.

The shot landed one hundred feet astern of the sloop, which was astern of the schooner. The bearing was right, but the mast and rigging still prevented a good aim toward the enemy. Wake's mind did more calculations.

"Got to get closer," came the useless observation from aloft. Durlon and the gun crew did not reply but instead gave the bosun dark looks that told of their thoughts.

"I will luff again when they slow and tack, Durlon, and when I do, then fire into their rigging," Wake said quietly.

"Aye aye, sir. Don't worry, I won't hole 'em," said a grinning Durlon as he stroked his gun again.

"And see that ya don't set the cotton afire also, ya crazy muzzle lover," yelled Hardin from the rigging. Everyone's voice was tense by now, and the men were silently imploring the enemy to stop and surrender their ships and cargo.

The sloop passed the schooner to windward and both Confederate vessels sailed up and across the river, now less than a mile from the *Rosalie*. Hardin reported that they were easing their sheets and starting to slow. Wake then made his move and brought the large tiller down to leeward, luffing the *Rosalie* even more than he had before.

The gun blasted again, and the rigging of the schooner suddenly went from being taut and orderly to loose and ragged. Her sails started to shudder, and they could hear her crew yelling at each other. The crew of the *Rosalie* promptly started cheering and hitting Durlon on the back. Even Hardin called down from his perch and offered a congratulatory word. Wake, still steering and holding her now back on course, decided to go after the schooner first. He would lay his vessel alongside her and board her with his crew armed to the teeth. The schooner had not surrendered yet and was still trying to sail away. The enemy sailors were staring at the image of death or capture fast surging towards them.

"Hardin, come down and arm the crew for boarding. Men, we will go alongside and capture her!" Wake found himself yelling and getting caught up in the enthusiasm of the crew, much to his surprise. His heart was beating faster and faster, and he knew that victory was close.

And then he felt it. . . .

He knew what that feeling was, and what came next. He felt the *Rosalie* slow a bit. The rudder got sluggish and the keel started to plow the mud below. Wake looked over the side to see the bottom in clear detail as his ship slowly ground to a halt on a sandbar.

It suddenly was very quiet. The sails were still full and drawing silently. She was still heeled. Everything was the same as before except that she was as still in the water as a rock. Wake looked at the schooner, slowly sailing away. He couldn't believe it. His disbelief turned to anger, and he ordered the sails hauled in even more and half the crew in the water to shove off with the other half on the leeward gunwale to heel her over even more. This attempt to lighten her worked a bit and they gained twenty feet but then took the ground once more. This time it was more solid.

It took the Rebels awhile to realize that their pursuer was no longer sailing forward. When they did, they let loose a yell that got louder as it progressed, until it sounded like what Wake thought an Indian war cry would sound like. Or it was more like a raging animal? After it ended in a shriek, several puffs of smoke could be seen on the deck of the schooner. They were firing symbolic shots from their muskets at him, Wake thought with a cold anger. The sloop, now far ahead, was followed slowly by the schooner up the river, Rebel flags at the peaks of their mainsails.

The tide was still on the flood and the wind served to heel them over, Wake observed with a little hope. He looked at Hardin, who was already getting the dinghy alongside to move the kedge anchor out forward of the ship.

"Durlon, please get your ammunition over to leeward, along with the crew. Hardin, good work on that kedge. The tide's a flood, lads, so we'll be off after 'em in a bit. We've got 'em bottled up in the river, so those vessels will be ours, by God!"

Wake hoped that this sounded inspiring. He certainly meant it to be. He also hoped that it would be true. Was it possible that Hardin's head shook just a bit?

"Aye, sir, we've got 'em where we want 'em now," said Durlon, who was silenced by Hardin yelling for slack in the anchor rode. The other sailors gave no clue to their thoughts and turned stone-faced to their duties.

As the enemy vessels were rounding a curve of the river far ahead, the tide finally lifted the *Rosalie* off the shoal. Wake immediately gave orders to trim the sloop for beating upwind and up the river. With a man aloft now, she sailed close-hauled to the east and northeast as the river narrowed from a mile wide to half that with islands and curves to deal with. The lookout could not see the Confederates ahead and searched the shoreline to see if they were hidden, for the crew desperately wanted to make the captures this time. They talked of nothing else, and Wake saw them turning to their work without verbal or silent complaint.

It was slow going, and by midday Wake decided that it was time to man the sweeps because the channel had become too narrow to tack. He kept the pace slow and deliberate, fighting the ebb tide, which had set, and the heat as the morning land breeze faded away into the noon calm.

When the afternoon thunderstorm started to build, the men rejoiced in its wind. On the fourth hour of working the sweep oars, the lookout called out two small vessels behind them, coming upriver from the mouth under sail. He thought they could be boats from the *Gem of the Sea*, but the distance was too great to be sure. For the first time since the grounding, Wake started to feel better. He was relatively sure that they had not passed the prey, hidden among the islands or shoreline, and so when the night finally fell on that eventful day he gave the order to anchor in midstream. Half the crew was put on watch, with muskets and cutlasses in their hands ready for action and the twelve-pounder loaded with grapeshot. The other half was instantly asleep, right on the deck, ready for action if needed. Wake took the first watch while Hardin snored away on the afterdeck.

As the clouds from the early evening sailed through the night off to the west and each of the on-watch crew peered out at his assigned sector, Wake sat down on the transom board and thought about the situation. He had no chart of the river, only a diagram that covered the first several miles. He was already upriver beyond that. He possibly had reinforcements coming upriver behind him. Or they could be the enemy, whose domain he was in the midst of. He didn't know their strength or location. The schooner and the sloop were probably further upriver. So the choices were: retreat down the river, go up the river after the enemy vessels, or stay put.

Wake knew the answer. Sighing, he looked aloft at the stars sprinkled randomly like silver dust on a black felt cloth. They seemed soft and gentle, bringing memories of Linda and their moments together. The thud of the twelve-pounder handspike on the deck, and the accompanying curse of Durlon, brought his thoughts back to the war and the decisions he had to make. Feeling far older than his twenty-five years and as if this war were his life, Wake thought of his previous life in the merchant marine as belonging to someone else, far away and long ago. That man who sailed schooners on the New England coast knew about sailors and the sea, but nothing about war and doing your best to kill other men before they killed you on a god-forsaken coast that few even wanted. That other man that he used to be had no understanding of the lethal consequences of command decisions in war, or even of the consequences of falling in love with an "enemy" girl, whose father would kill you in the beat of a heart if he knew of it. The stars above had no answers for him, just reminders of his past, as they glittered across the sky in disinterested witness to his dilemma.

Wake remembered that day in May when he'd met Linda. The hot, musty guard room at the entrance to the fort, where he had gone to pass on a message from the admiral to the colonel commanding the Forty-seventh Pennsylvania, had smelled of unwashed men and stale food. He had been waiting there when the girl came in, looking for an officer to speak with about her father, who had been arrested. She had started with Wake, not realizing that he wasn't an army officer, until he had gently introduced her to the officer of the day on duty at the fort. Wake had stood by while she explained her problem and her fears to the army first lieutenant, a rank equal to Wake's naval rank of master. The lieutenant had looked like he wasn't even listening to Linda's plea and then had had the arrogance to tell her that her father was lucky he had not been shot after pushing away a sergeant from the regiment who had demanded that he give way in the street to a patrol of soldiers. The lieutenant went on to suggest, with a leer on his face, that the girl might want to stay away from the fort because even though she was a Reb, she was exciting the soldiers there.

Wake had stood there in dumbfounded silence as the army lieutenant completed his show of superiority. Wake then asked the girl to follow him outside the room and to wait outside while he spoke to the young officer, who appeared to be all of about twenty-one, obviously a political appointee. Wake remembered his rage boiling up within when he confronted the little, arrogant, sniveling bastard of a boy. His quarterdeck voice came out as he ordered the army officer to take him immediately to his commanding officer, the colonel. The snide remarks of the onlooking orderly staff stopped, and they watched in terror while the formerly quiet naval officer's face transformed into something maniacal. The lieutenant started to talk but no sound came out. He gestured for Wake to follow him to the colonel's office.

Wake remembered striding through the adjutant's office, bringing the lieutenant along with him, straight into the colonel's office. As the surprised colonel looked up from his desk, Wake stated in a voice loud enough for half the soldiers in the fort to hear, "Sir, Naval Master Peter Wake requests permission to report the conduct, unbecoming of an officer, of this man here, to the colonel!"

The astonished regimental commander replied in the affirmative, more out of curiosity than anything else, and Wake related the events of the guard room. When he was done, Wake looked at the terrified lieutenant and asked him if the recital of his behavior was correct. He received a mumbled agreement.

One hour later the father of the beautiful girl was released pending trial, the lieutenant had disappeared, and he knew that he would see that girl again. For the next several days they had seen each other about the town, each time greeting and talking as if they were friends with no war separating their lives.

Then one evening Wake saw her at sunset at the northwest corner of the town, standing alone and staring at the horizon. He walked over to her and they embraced immediately, with no hesitation or awkwardness. He had held her for a long time until they kissed. They held that kiss while the sun set in a flaming crescendo, and Wake knew a peace as he held her that had eluded him for years. That was the real beginning of his hopeless yearning for her.

They made secret rendezvous in the evenings at places like the cemetery where no would see or report them. The rendezvous eventually became longer and more involved. Wake understood that Linda Donahue, unlike any other girl in his life, had come to completely possess his feelings. But it came as a surprise to his logical mind that this devotion posed no deep concern. Indeed, when they were together he came to know a happiness unknown to him so far in life.

He sighed again and realized again that he was remembering events months old and that the present had to be dealt with first. The stars had drifted to the west when he next looked up at them as the nightly breeze made its usual appearance. Once again he felt old, much older than his years. When Hardin and his half of the crew came on watch, Wake gratefully lay down on the deck and slid his cluttered mind into nothingness. Just remembering Linda and their love together had exhausted him.

The birds woke him just before dawn with a sound unlike any he had ever heard. Hundreds of birds, birds of all kinds, from the majestic great herons to the seagulls and the smaller birds whose names he did not know. They filled the sky and swooped close to the sloop. Their varying cries and squawks woke the crew and started an excited conversation among the men about the strange sight. Wake remembered his uncle back in New England telling him as a boy that the presence of men would disturb the animals of the woods and cause them to become agitated. Wake also remembered the many times he'd seen a predator fish startle a school of smaller fish. The frenzy below the water would soon extend above it, the hunters and the hunted both jumping and skimming the surface.

Wake peered through the gloom toward the southern shore of the river, a tangle of reeds and mangroves, where the birds seemed to be coming from. He called the attention of the crew to that shore and told them to scan it for the enemy just as the sky was starting to show the loom of the sun traversing the earth still far below the horizon. Wake then decided that the best thing to do was to get the whole crew to quarters and set some to scan both sides of the river. This done, he told Hardin to weigh the anchor and man the sweeps with only four men, the rest to be used as lookouts. From the strange sight of the birds and Wake's definitive orders, the crew was stimulated and the dialogues among them soon spoke of prize money and women and rum.

It was Wilson who first saw the vessels. They were not coming down the river, but upriver from the west. Two boats from the *Gem of the Sea* could be seen rowing up the channel about two miles away in the shadows of the lower river. Wake told the men to keep working the sweeps, but to slow down so the boats could catch up. He certainly was not going to forfeit progress upcurrent, and the relatively cool morning was the best time of day to use the physically demanding sweeps to make headway toward the enemy.

Wilson was receiving the accolades of his messmates when Durlon shouted out that the enemy vessels were along the southern shore on the starboard bow. A spontaneous cheer went up from the men of the *Rosalie*, and Wake felt an embarrassing surge of pride in his little ship and crew. By God, he thought, we will capture those vessels and take them back, right here, right now.

Since they knew they had been spotted, the Confederates were setting sail on the sloop and schooner as they had only to go downwind, and they knew the location of all the shoals and deep areas of the river. Once again Wake set his mind to work visualizing the geometry of the two opposing courses. The Rebs were moving fast now, with the last of an ebb tide and the easterly morning land breeze pushing them. He looked behind and saw that the boats from the *Gem of the Sea* had started to move at an angle toward the south shore. Wake knew at that point that he had the Rebs. If they did get past him, the boats astern would have a chance at them. He altered course for the shoreline also and told Hardin to prepare to set sail. They would cut off the enemy and board them, schooner first. The ship's boats could get the stragglers.

Just as he finished explaining his concept to Hardin and Durlon, Conner called out that the Rebs had turned around and were heading upriver again. Having doused their sails, they were now under sweeps like the *Rosalie*. Wake examined them by telescope, and then offered it to Hardin and Durlon for their perusal.

"'Bout a mile, I venture, sir. They're movin' pretty good under them sweeps. Bottoms are probably cleaner than ours. 'Course, they got some reason to be goin' fast too," reported Hardin as he handed the glass to the gunner.

"Extreme range, sir. I can try one for moral effect, if you'd like," said an enthusiastic Durlon. He always would have a reason to fire his beloved cannon.

"If we fire right now, it'll help to establish that the chase and the captures are ours. Those bastards from the *Gem* don't deserve a penny of our money. They'll only get the in-sight money. Just make sure you don't accidentally hit that Reb hull, gunner!" counseled Hardin to his captain and the gunner's mate.

Wake looked again at the Confederate ships, the Federal ship's boats coming up from behind, and the relative angle of his own vessel to the others.

"Very well. Durlon, fire a shot. Make sure you have the range and don't fire short of them. I don't want to encourage them!"

The boom of the ship's gun wasn't even noticed by the crew in their intensity to see the fall of the shot. It threw up a geyser just forward of the Rebel sloop, which was leading the schooner upriver. Another cheer rose from the men as Durlon accepted his congratulations from the crew. But the Confederates did not stop. Instead, a puff of musket smoke showed on the deck of the schooner, the flight or impact of the round not apparent.

"Wastin' a blank fire." Durlon shook his head with disapproval.

With the defiance of the Confederate crew, Wake knew that it would be a long chase up the river into the jungles known well by the enemy. It was obvious now that they were hoping to lure him into a trap. Good Lord, he thought, if I lose this ship I'll never be able to go anywhere in New England again. The disgrace would be complete and well known. No victory at this place would ever make the papers up north, but a defeat would be broadcast everywhere, and by the Reb papers as well. Linda would sympathize, and her father would rejoice. . . .

As the chase continued inexorably up the narrowing river, Wake stood by the mast and stared at the stern of the schooner, trying to will himself into the mind of her captain and his plan for escape. It was intensely personal with the men now. A quiet sense of commitment had settled over ol' Rosey and her men. The day progressed with the changing of the watches, the shoreline of the river slowly going by at two knots, a quarter mile away on either beam. Discussions periodically rose as to the distance between the *Rosalie* and the schooner, but it wasn't until almost noon that the space began to grow noticeably shorter.

The shorelines crept ever closer to the sloop, and now the crew had to watch for sharpshooters as well. Behind them, the other boats kept coming. With their lighter hulls they were gaining on the *Rosalie* and almost within shouting distance. Wake kept his course on the schooner since she obviously drew at least as much water as *Rosalie*.

But even with relieving the men at the sweeps every half hour, the crew was nearing exhaustion. The heat and humidity were taking their toll. Wake decided the only thing to do was to keep chasing them until close enough for an effective shot. It was time to end this. He didn't want to go too far upriver and into a trap.

As the day went on, Wake and Hardin took their turns at the

sweeps too. Hardin was not enthusiastic but could hardly protest when the captain took his place at a long oar. Still the chase continued, until the range was slowly closing down to an almost sure shot.

By this time the shoreline had changed from mangrove jungle to marshland, with an occasional palm thicket clumped on higher ground. Small creeks opened up more frequently along the shoreline and they saw people among the trees twice. Watching them. Waiting. Every man aboard was unnerved by the sight of the Rebs watching them. Imagining what was to come started to give way to verbal speculation among the men. Wake told them to save their breath for working the sweeps. He also told Durlon to check all the weapons to make sure they were ready for immediate use.

By sunset they were still at it, now more like dumb animals toiling at a simple but long-lasting job. The Confederates showed no sign of stopping, had not even slowed. It appeared in the half light that the distance to the enemy was starting to widen. The shoreline had become thick palm and bush, with overhanging oak limbs reaching downward and underwater snags reaching upward. The *Rosalie* seemed huge in the narrowing river, with jungle now only a couple hundred feet away on either beam. The men felt totally exposed on the flush deck with no shield from a rifleman on the river bank. And there was no way with all the dense forest to see that man until he fired and the smoke revealed his position.

As it started to get dark, Wake told the men to rest easy on their oars, set the anchor, and let the two ships' boats behind catch up with them. He wasn't going to continue onward in the dark after the enemy vessels. Instead, they would take the three naval craft and anchor in line across the river. There would be no way the Rebs could get past them in the night. Wake waited for the smaller boats to come alongside and invited their officer aboard the *Rosalie* for a conference.

Amidst the sounds of the crews gasping for air as they lay all over the decks of the vessels, Wake, Hardin, and the boat officer and petty officer sat down on the afterdeck and evaluated their situation. The ensign in charge of the boats was a tall, awkward-looking boy of around nineteen named Thorton. He acted nervous and constantly looked over at his second in command, a bosun named Moore. Moore had the appearance, like Hardin, of being a man who had seen a bit of life. Wake, who was now the ranking officer of a small flotilla, spoke first.

"All right, men, we will anchor in line abreast the river for the night. Watch on watch for lookouts, with all weapons loaded and ready. Any questions or suggestions on that part?"

After receiving the expected reply, Wake continued, "How much food and water do you have, Mr. Thorton?"

Thorton looked perplexed and then terrified. He glanced at Moore, who stared at the shoreline without acknowledgment. Thorton then started to cough and gasp. Wake waited a moment and looked at Moore. "Moore, do you have an idea of how many rations you may have?"

Moore turned to Wake and replied quietly, "Three days, sir. Got fifty rounds per man, too." As he ended, Thorton's coughs subsided and he mumbled something that sounded like, "Excuse me, sir." The boy then stared at Wake like a man awaiting his sentence before a judge. Hardin and Moore looked at each other and silently communicated their disgust for Thorton, their supposed superior officer. Wake ignored Thorton's misery.

"All right, get your boats anchored. Keep your men sharp tonight. An hour before sunup we will start upriver again. If we don't see the enemy vessels by dark tomorrow, we will turn back for the coast. We've spent two days chasing them and have got to come to the head of navigation on this river soon."

Hardin turned from staring at the almost teary Thorton and said in a challenging tone, "We'll get 'em in the morning. This river goes on for quite a ways, but that schooner can't carry her draft much farther. Bring a nice price at Key West too. Just you men from the *Gem* remember who started this chase and who's been firin' at 'em. The Rosey's got the main prize money and you bastards aren't gonna get your hands on it."

The crews from all three vessels heard *that* remark. According to regulations, all naval vessels and sailors in sight at the time of capture would share the prize money. Wake sensed the tension fill the air around him. The men from the *Gem of the Sea's* boats started to stir, and Moore stood up and said directly to Hardin, "Hardin, you always were a sea lawyer. Why don't we catch the Rebs first, and then you can argue over it."

"That's enough from both of you," Wake ordered as the two petty officers started to face each other and the other sailors, now alert and watching every move, got very quiet. "Mr. Thorton, take your boat crews and get anchored now. These men need all the rest they can get before the morning."

Thorton, who had slid back from the center of the action, answered meekly in the affirmative and got up to head for his boat. Moore turned his back on Hardin and proceeded to his own boat.

Ten minutes later, Wake had Hardin in his stifling and humid cabin. Wake was sitting on his bunk at the tiny chart table looking by the light of a small lamp at Hardin, who squatted against the moldy bulkhead, swatting at the bugs that were swirling in the lamplit space. It was the only private place in the ship where Wake could speak with Hardin.

"Don't ever embarrass me or this ship again with that kind of demeanor, Hardin. I don't care what you think of me or anything else. We have a job to do, and we will do it. Your insubordinate attitude just gets in the way. Do you understand me exactly?"

"Moore is an ass. Always has been. Toadying up to that ensign, and tryin' to get into our prize money. I know that kind, sir. They'll make sure they are there right after we get the schooner, holdin' out their hands for the money!"

Wake looked across the dim, smoky light into Hardin's eyes. He saw no sign of acknowledgment of what he had said to him, only anger.

"If they're in sight at the time of capture they will get some of the money. You know that. Now, answer me right here, Hardin. Your attitude will stop right now."

Hardin stared at Wake and said very deliberately, "Aye aye, sir. Am I dismissed?"

Wake, his own blood now warming, glared at the bosun. "Yes. We will speak of this no more."

Hardin immediately climbed the ladder out of the cramped cabin and left Wake thinking that the morning would be a crucial time for many reasons. He also knew at that moment that he and Hardin were going to have to settle the distrust between them. Wake sat alone in the dim light and thick air for a long time, sweating and thinking about where he was, and how in the world he had gotten there. He finally blew out the lamp and stretched out on the crude bunk, staying below in his own cabin, away from the men he commanded. In the sweltering air Wake finally drifted off to sleep.

He heard the whispers first. They intruded illogically upon him and Linda in his dream, a wonderful dream with her in his arms and the wind in the gumbo limbo trees around them. But now he heard Durlon's voice in the room quietly saying something to the effect of waking up the captain and letting him know something. He looked toward Linda, but she was gone. There was only Sommer, the boy, shaking him and saying, "Sir, they's acomin' down the river. The Rebs are acomin' down the river, we think."

Wake shuddered and sat up as Sommer climbed up the ladder and advised Durlon that the captain was awake and coming up. Wake sat in the dark and organized his thoughts while putting on his filthy trousers and shirt. Today was the day. Now was the time. It had all come down to this.

He saw as he came up on deck that the crews of the three boats were all mustered and ready. Everyone was staring forward, up the river, with the petty officers quietly hushing the men so all could hear. Then Wake heard the sound—a small creak followed by a swish, followed by another creak, and followed by the swish again.

The rhythmic sounds of sweep oars slowly moving a vessel.

"How far, do ye think, sir?" whispered Durlon.

"Don't know. Can't tell. Pass the word to Hardin to quietly get the anchor hove short and the sweeps ready."

Suddenly Hardin loomed up beside Wake and said that he had already done those things. All was ready. Durlon checked his cannon and its gun crew one more time while the rest of the crew got ready at their assigned sweeps. Wake looked at Moore's and Thorton's boats and saw that all appeared ready. He found himself wondering how Thorton would do if there was a fight and then thought of everyone in his own crew, wondering how *he* would do in a fight. The thought of his being in command of this whole thing made him shudder involuntarily. A bilious turmoil started in his bowels, and he took a deep measured breath to overcome it. A few seconds later it was gone, lost to the overpowering multitude of stimuli besieging his senses.

He heard Hardin telling Durlon to aim high and not hit the hulls with his canister load. Durlon replied with a brief and quiet acknowledgment. Others were starting to whisper until Hardin growled a low warning to "shut the hell up."

Wake glanced at his watch in the starlight and thought it indicated about four in the morning. The starlight gave a sense of depth to his eyesight, and Wake could even make out the men on the boats anchored on either side of him. Then his mind registered that the sounds were getting closer. To his straining ears it sounded like two vessels. Abruptly, a nighthawk flew by from the left shoreline and let out his high-pitched cry, startling everyone. Wake let out a breath and turned his focus back upriver, noting that the wind was coming down the river, muffling any noise his boats' crews might make from the sailors of the Rebel schooner and sloop.

Now they could get a bearing on the enemy sounds, coming down the southern shore of the river, to the right of the *Rosalie* and almost dead ahead of Thorton's boat. It sounded like the Confederates might be about a hundred yards away, coming downstream with the current. Wake looked over to the boat on his right. Thorton was staring ahead and whispering with a crewman. Wake knew he couldn't yell anything to Thorton, but just had to trust in the young man's judgment. A glance to his left showed Wake that Moore, in the other boat, had his crew hauling up the anchor and preparing to come over to the right.

Without warning, a blast exploded on the right, followed by a volley of more blasts, as the men in Thorton's boat fired at the enemy. The light of the musket blasts flared out over the water and illuminated the schooner for a brief moment. She was moving quickly under sweeps with the sloop right behind her. Men on all the vessels were now shouting and screaming. Blasts and flames were coming from everywhere. The stillness of the night was instantly replaced with a maelstrom of noise without logic or sense.

Wake, seeing that the schooner was now just about at the line of anchored vessels and was firing into Thorton's boat, stood up and yelled as loud as he could, "Fire, Durlon, fire!"

The roar of the twelve-pounder overwhelmed all other noise and action. The flame it spewed out carried for twenty feet and lit up the entire river, clearly showing the damage along the starboard side of the schooner from the dozens of small rounds that had been packed into the canister ammunition. The schooner, with no sweeps now working on her starboard side, suddenly swerved to her right toward the middle of the river and the *Rosalie*. The sound of the screaming and yelling and shooting from the schooner made it sound like a ship from hell as it continued out of control toward Wake's sloop.

Wake looked forward and saw that Hardin had gotten the anchor up and the men at the sweeps pulling. Durlon was yelling at his little gun crew to reload the gun faster so they could fire at the schooner again. Conner was at the helm and Wake told him to steer for the sloop, which was trying to get by the line of Union vessels, along the right-hand shoreline. He yelled over to Moore to board the schooner and then looked at Thorton's boat. Thorton was taking musket fire from the Confederate sloop now alongside him. It appeared to Wake that the sloop and Thorton's boat were about ten feet apart and firing continually into each other. As the *Rosalie* swung her bow over to the right, Wake saw the schooner coming up close ahead on the port bow. He pointed her out to Durlon and told him to fire when ready. Wake then kept his eyes on Thorton's boat and yelled for Hardin to get the men pulling hard so they could reinforce Thorton.

Another roar and eruption of light announced that the cannon had struck out again, this time over *Rosalie's* port side into the port side of the schooner drifting by. The nightmarish glare from the blast lit up the schooner in sharp detail, showing the carnage as it erupted along her decks at close range. Men aboard her were staggering, crawling, screaming for help. The main mast was canted over and the rigging was in chaos. Acrid smoke was everywhere in the hellish scene.

Durlon was jumping up and down, screaming for his gun crew to do it again, while Wake heard Moore yelling maniacally as his boat grappled the schooner on her other side and his men poured up and over her decks. Above it all he heard Hardin's deep voice, edged with anger. "Goddamnit, Durlon, you fool. You've holed her, you idiot!"

It seemed to Wake that everyone, including him, was screaming something to someone, and that no one was paying any attention to what anyone was saying. He found that he couldn't hear anything in detail, and he focused on getting his ship over to where Thorton was still battling the sloop. His eyes were blinded now, and he told Conner to steer for the musket fire since none of them could see in detail after the last blast of the cannon.

The musket fire now appeared to be moving down the river, and Wake realized that the fire was coming from the sloop and that she was probably past Thorton's boat. A moment later they surged past the ship's boat that had been commanded by Thorton. A sailor was still firing from her bow, but the rest of the crew was crawling or lying still. Another sailor called out to *Rosalie* that Thorton had been shot and that there were many wounded in the boat. Wake yelled back for them to row over to

Moore for help, that he was going after the sloop, which was dead ahead of the *Rosalie's* bowsprit.

Suddenly, Wake heard an explosion from close ahead and saw Smith, on the gun crew, clutch his left thigh and drop the rammer he was holding. Sommer, also on the gun crew, helped him to the deck as Durlon yelled to the helmsman, "Turn the bitch so I can get a shot!" Then a ragged series of explosions came from the bow, and Wilson, pulling the forward starboard sweep, doubled over onto Burns, who was pulling the after sweep. A yell came from the sloop ahead as Hardin fired a musket at them from his position at the mast.

Wake turned to Conners, told him to get a musket and start shooting, and pulled the tiller to turn the ship to the port, guessing that the Confederate sloop would then be exposed on *Rosalie's* starboard side. He yelled to Hardin to get all the men off the sweeps and start firing at the sloop, running forward to fire his own pistol at the unseen enemy who was cutting down his men in the darkness.

Rosalie was still turning when several bursts of light came from the Rebel sloop only a few feet away. Wake felt a stinging thud in the side of his head even as he methodically observed that the enemy was right where he had thought they would be. Swaying unsteadily on his feet, he tried to understand what had happened and what he should do next. Squinting his eyes to try to regain his night vision, he felt some sort of warm liquid covering them.

The night erupted again into an earsplitting explosion as the cannon belched out fire and metal over the starboard side directly into the sloop alongside. Wake, having stumbled close to the muzzle of the gun, was almost knocked over by the blast and went to his knees. He tried looking for the sloop, but he couldn't see it. He couldn't see anything but various blurs and patterns of light. He tried blinking and rubbing his eyes, but nothing would bring back his sight. He couldn't even see where he was on the deck or anyone around him. His hearing was gone too, replaced by a tremendous roar that filled his head and made him dizzy. Wake felt his blood pounding through his head with a growing ache of pain increasing by the second. He sensed that people were around him and something was happening close by but could not tell who or what. Blinded and deaf, Wake slowly sat down on the deck and held his ears, still blinking his eyes, and prayed aloud to God that this was only a temporary condition.

It could have been a moment, or several minutes, before his vision somewhat came back into focus. He still could not hear, but he now saw that Hardin was leading several men across to the sloop, which was right alongside. Wake staggered forward, holding his head and looking for someone to let go the anchor. When he found no one, he sat on the foredeck and cast loose the anchor himself.

Returning aft, he saw that the Reb sloop had no one but his own men standing on her deck. His own deck had Smith and Wilson rolling in pain as they held their wounds, tended by a terrified Billy Sommer, who was ineffectually trying to bandage them.

Wake then looked back upriver toward the schooner and saw a blur that was probably Moore, who had Thorton's boat alongside. Lanterns were showing men moving about on the deck. As his vision developed sharper detail, he saw Hardin and Durlon cross back to *Rosalie*, leaving Conner and Burns on the sloop holding their weapons on the Rebs who still lived. Lamar, the man who had been on the forward port sweep, was coming toward him with a smoking musket in one hand and a bandage in the other. A moment later Wake was sitting on the afterdeck with Lamar and the two petty officers squatting around him.

"Looks like a clean wound. Grooved alongside the ear," offered Durlon as he probed Wake's right ear, sending a searing pain like a hot fire poker through his brain. Durlon's hand came away covered in blood, and now Wake realized that the substance he had unconsciously assumed to be sweat or water all over him, not just his face, was his own blood.

"Looks like he can't hear or see. Get 'im to lay down. . . ."

Captain, lay down!" yelled Lamar into Wake's face from a foot away.

"Can you hear me, Durlon? Can you hear me? Can anyone hear me?" Wake glared at the men in front of him, angry at his own inability to hear what they were saying about him. Lamar and Durlon nodded affirmatively as they examined his wound.

"Lay down, Captain. We've got to dress that wound on your ear," Durlon said slowly into Wake's face. As he held Wake's head, Lamar wound the dressing around several times and tied it off tightly.

Hardin, watching Wake's wound with intense interest, now stood and turned to go forward. "He'll be okay. If he ain't dead by now, he'll survive. Let's see what happened to Wilson and Smith. And tell them Rebs to shut up over there, Conner!" Durlon guided Wake down to the deck and told Lamar to tend to him, then got up and went forward following Hardin.

Sommer, sitting there crying next to the now-motionless body of Wilson, scrambled out of the way as Hardin approached. Smith still lay doubled over and clutching his thigh, staunching the flow of blood from the large exit hole. The entrance wound on the back of his thigh was bleeding too, but not as badly. Smith's eyes were fixed on the exit wound his hand was compressing, as his wounded leg involuntarily trembled. His mouth was moving in a slow, never-ending stream of oaths that were directed at everything and everyone.

Hardin knelt down by Wilson, who had always been thought of by everyone else in the crew as his toady, and felt against his neck for a pulse. Feeling nothing, he looked into the dead man's eyes looking up at him. They were open but the lids were slitted, giving him a piercing expression. His face was tightened into a grimace with his teeth bared and clenched. The whole effect in the lantern light was one of malevolent intent. Wilson had been transformed in death from the subservient fawning pet into a rabid mongrel.

"Well, he's dead. Now, what about you, Smith?"

"Get the hell away from me, Hardin. Just get the hell away from me, you bastard. I don't want your hooks on me! Durlon, fer God's sake, get me a decent dressing and help plug this damn thing. The kid can't handle it."

Hardin moved back over to the Confederate sloop as Durlon assisted Smith in wrapping his wound tightly. Burns and Conners made way for him as he climbed over the human and structural damage that littered the decks of the sloop.

"Any still kickin'?" Hardin asked Conners.

"Yeah, a couple on the stern. They may make it. Can't tell for sure. That twelve-pounder shorely did do its work on 'em. Ol' Durlon showed 'em."

There were about half a dozen lifeless bodies on the decks of the sloop, and several more that were half-alive, crawling and squirming at the stern. The screams had turned into moans now. The end was near for some. Hardin ignored the wounded and instead looked about the captured vessel, checking her hold and cabin spaces, the rigging and hull. The rigging was cut to pieces, but the hull did not appear to be holed. Hardin yelled over to the sloop, "Well, Durlon, looks like ya at least didn't sink this one! Maybe five hundred, maybe more if we can get her fixed up afore Key West."

Wake's hearing was starting to come back now in his left ear. The entire right side of his head felt inflamed and throbbed with each rapid heartbeat. As he looked at the carnage around him, he made himself think about what he should do next. The loud pandemonium of the battle was over, replaced by quiet sounds of men crying and moaning, and ships' broken spars and rigging clattering. Wake was almost moved to tears as he thought of all that had happened since Sommer had awakened him. Then he thought of the time. It had been four o'clock in the morning when he climbed out of his dream about Linda. What time was it now? He dug into his pocket and found the watch his brother John had given him when he had left for the navy. By the lantern light he could see that it was still working, which gave him an illogical feeling of comfort, embarrassing him with the emotion of knowing that something was normal in this world of his that had descended into a hellish nightmare. Four twenty-two. Twenty-two minutes. All that happened had taken only twenty-two minutes. Wake sat there stunned. The mental effort to understand this profound fact overwhelmed his mind. He looked over at a sound from the enemy sloop and saw Hardin going through the pockets of the dead Confederates. It shocked him into action, and he stood up uncertainly on the afterdeck of his small ship.

"Hardin, leave the searching of the dead to Conner. Yell up to Moore to come downriver and raft up here. After the dead are searched, have Burns put them into the dinghy and take them ashore. And Hardin, as soon as Moore and his vessels are rafted up, I want a report on the men and the ships."

Wake felt a strength come into him as he took notice of Hardin's glare of anger upon hearing these commands. But he noted also that Hardin, watched by the others in the crew, moved to carry out the directions. Wake moved slowly forward to where Smith still lay swearing. Wilson lay next to him, the look of evil still stamped on his face. Durlon told Wake that it looked to him like Smith would survive the wound, if they could keep it clean and uninfected. Wake looked Smith in the eye and nodded silently. Smith stopped his swearing for a moment and made a grimace that was the best he could do for a grin. He then made an obviously tough effort and laughed. "I'll be all right, Captain. Ol' Durlon's an ugly cuss, but he's dressed me leg up rightly. Jus' gotta get to the surgeon and close it up. Hurts like a bitch though, sir, I don't mind tellin' ya'. Hell, Captain, ya' look worsen I do!"

"We'll both see the girls again, Smith, and this time we'll have a hell of a story to tell them, won't we?" Wake managed a laugh of his own and turned to survey the rest of the deck.

Sommer leaned against the twelve-pounder gun, his face aged ten years in the last thirty minutes. He was no longer distraught. He appeared now to be resigned to his fate and ready to handle whatever might come next. Wake nodded at him and turned to go back to the stern.

An hour later all the vessels had rafted up together. Moore came aboard *Rosalie* and made his report. Hardin listened and then made his own report for the sloop.

Wake listened as the "butchers bill," that quaint navy phrase, was given to him. Of the crew of the *Rosalie*, Wilson was killed, and Smith and Wake were wounded badly. Durlon had a cut on his arm that he did not remember getting, but it would heal. Of Thorton's boat that had ten men in the crew, Thorton and a seaman were dead. Three other men were wounded in limbs by gunshots. Moore thought they would probably live. Of Moore's crew of eight men, two seamen had cuts from their fight but nothing major. There were sixteen Confederate dead and two seriously wounded. They all had been taken ashore and left for their brethren on the river bank to deal with.

Wake now received the vessel report. The schooner's mainmast was gone. She had some holes below the waterline, but they thought that all were plugged. A mainmast, jury-rigged from the main boom, could be fished onto the stump of the severed original. Some rigging could be set up, enough to get her to Boca Grande, where the *Gem of the Sea* lay at anchor.

The sloop had her rigging and sails cut up, but the spar was still standing and she could be sailed. No cargo was found on either vessel. Evidently, what they had originally seen on deck had been unloaded in the night. A detailed search for papers or valuables would have to wait until daylight.

Thorton's boat was a mess from the human carnage, but serviceable. Moore's boat was in good shape. *Rosalie* was disheveled but in good working order.

The reports of the petty officers seemed to take forever, given in the monotonous dutiful way of the navy, with no emotion or clue as to the reporter's thoughts. It all served to drain Wake's strength and make him feel even more exhausted. He told Hardin to have all of their dead placed into Thorton's boat. The wounded would all come aboard *Rosalie*. Three-man watches would last until nine A.M., when all vessels would get under way separately for the mouth of the river. Thorton's boat would be towed by Moore's. Wake asked for questions and received none. He then ordered everyone off watch to get some sleep.

As the men trudged away to collapse somewhere, Wake heard the sound of a morning bird just upriver of the rafted boats. It seemed to be a peculiar kind of call, high-pitched and lilting. He thought it was mocking him for his weakness, and maybe for his leadership, in his first real battle in this awful war, which had led to the death and maiming of so many of his men for the capture of two Rebel craft that they had found to be empty of anything of real value.

Wake sat down alone on the transom board again and looked around him at the river, the jungle, and the vessels rafted together. His hearing had come back in the left ear, but the right side of his head still throbbed and stabbed him with pain. His eyesight had mostly returned, but his right eye was half shut from the swelling of the wound just behind it. That wound, along and through his right ear, had stopped its profuse bleeding. Now it was bonding with the dressing and stinging when his sweat rolled down into it.

Wake thought of the petty officers' report and knew he should put his own down on paper as soon as he could. He was exhausted but knew he couldn't sleep. He also knew that he couldn't bring himself to write the report just yet.

Thinking of the report stimulated him to remember the facts now for the report he would write later. He started with the logical beginning, the location where this nightmare of war had occurred, and to his immense shame he started crying. It was just a quivering lip at first, but it grew into muffled sobs as he realized he would have to also write the families of the men who died under his command in this forgotten place. The parents of a boy named Jonathan Thorton would have to know that their son, who tried to be a tough leader and was despised by his own men for his failure, was turned into a grotesque inhuman form by the ruthlessly efficient machines of war. Wake knew that vision would never leave his memory.

The sky gradually started to lighten into pinks and blues with the coming of the sun, bringing the beginnings of clarity out of the blurred confusion of darkness. Sounds of more birds transiting the sky, land creatures crunching around in the jungle growth ashore, and fish jumping in the coffee-colored waters brought back a false sense of normality to the river, as if the battle had never taken place, had not disturbed the routines of the animals living there. Wake imagined the animals were studiously ignoring the men and the ravages of their war, in the hope that they would soon leave this place to its rightful inhabitants.

When the glaring sun finally arrived in the river's sky, its uncompromising light shone on five small vessels rafted together in a jungle river far from the sea, their men strewn about their decks in attitudes of exhaustion or death. Three of the men sat barely awake with muskets across their knees, staring, without seeing, around the perimeter of their small part of the world. And a lone figure sat, head in his hands, on the stern of the *Rosalie*, overlooking the cruelly misnamed waters where he had finally known the ultimate burden of command in war.

In a place known as the Peace River. . . .

6

The Island of Refuge

Naval Master Peter Wake stood at attention. His body was as still as he could make it, but his mind was moving so fast that he had the impression that Admiral Barkley, seated before him at his cluttered desk in the hot room, could hear it whirring. The admiral looked up from his reading and unemotionally told Wake to sit. Barkley gave the impression that he was talking to a dog, a trusted dog, perhaps, whose obedience he assumed, but definitely a being of little consequence. Commander Johnson was already seated in a comfortable pose in the chair by the open window that overlooked the harbor. His feigned relaxation did not calm Wake a bit. Sitting at attention, or as best as the ex-merchant marine mate could imagine that position to be, Wake locked his eyes on the wall over the left shoulder of the admiral and waited.

Barkley finished reading the paper in his hand, looked up with a face of almost surprise to see Wake sitting in front of him, and glanced to Johnson on his left. Their eyes met and communicated, or rather confirmed some previous communication. Barkley turned his attention back to the obviously nervous young man before him.

"Well, Mr. Wake, it appears that you have demonstrated your tenacity in going up that river and bringing out those two Reb vessels. Three days up an uncharted, river, a victorious battle, and prizes brought back. Well done, sir."

"It further appears, Master Wake, that the papers found on one of those vessels have provided some very good intelligence about some of the activities of Reb sympathizers here at Key West. You just never know what you will find when you start digging, do you?" added Commander Johnson smoothly, his eyes surveying the junior officer.

Wake suddenly realized that he should respond to this apparently rhetorical question and stammered out, "Sir, I was just carrying out my orders. The men of the *Gem of the Sea*'s boats and my crew did their duty well. And I am glad that the papers were found helpful."

"And how are you, sir? Has your wound progressed well?" asked Barkley, with what certainly sounded like sincerity.

"Yes, sir, I am well. It has been a month, sir. The surgeon has released me. I would like to go back to my ship."

"Well, I am sure that you would. Let's see, your bosun has had her while you have been recuperating, right?" Johnson phrased carefully.

"Yes, sir. John Hardin. He is a very competent man." Wake said flatly, looking right at Johnson. The commander then interposed. "Your report was very interesting. Hardin has been very much involved in the exploits of the *Rosalie*. Must be pretty good. And evidently someone in Washington has connections with the Thorton family. They appreciated your narration of his gallantry."

"I wrote it as I saw it, sir."

The admiral watched the polite intercourse with a concerned look on his face. He regained control of the conversation. "Well, Wake, however it went, it ended well. Now we must discuss your next assignment."

Commander Johnson then rose, as if on cue, and walked

around the room to the chart on the opposite wall. He turned to the admiral and the master and began. "It is time to take the pro-Union men of the coast and go beyond transporting them to various islands for safety. Their use as guides and conduits for information," he was studiously avoiding the use of the word *spies*, "has been valuable. But General Woodbury believes that they are ready to rise up against the Rebels on the mainland. It appears that the time is right. From your activities along the coast, do you agree?"

Wake felt both of them staring at him, as he in turn stared at the chart on the wall and said, "Sir, there are some who could be trusted, I believe. But there are many I don't trust. The selection must be done with care."

"Well said, Wake." Admiral Barkley nodded. "Nevertheless, you will be *our man* on the scene. It's an army show, but the navy will transport them and support them if it comes to a battle near the water. By the navy, I mean the *Rosalie* and the *Gem of the Sea.*"

"We need a man we can trust when the operations of these units go in among the islands and up the rivers. A man who can make decisions. Do you understand what we mean, Mr. Wake?" Johnson questioned with his words and his facial expression.

"Sir, I believe you want me to be able to make the decision that the goal is realistic, and stop the operation if it appears wasteful or suicidal?" Wake ventured forth, not at all sure that is what they meant but trying to sound decisive.

"Precisely, Mr. Wake. But we want you to be tactful when dealing with the army." The admiral smiled. "Cooperation is essential in this area of the war."

"So, sir, I am to be tactful but firm when deciding that the army is getting us in deep trouble ashore."

"I believe that Master Wake has grasped the idea, Admiral. He will do well. The army will not get into too much trouble with him along," Johnson said as he gazed at Wake. "Master Wake, here are your orders, along with those for Lt. Baxter on the *Gem of the Sea.* I want you to set sail tomorrow morning on the tide. The army units should be meeting you in a week or so. The *Honduras* will bring them up."

Wake knew that he should wait until onboard the *Rosalie* to open his orders, but he couldn't help himself and asked, "Sir, where am I to meet the army?"

Commander Johnson made another communicative glance to the admiral, and then said cryptically to Wake, "You find out when you open your orders upon leaving the harbor, Wake. Too many Rebel sympathizers about, here on the island, for that information to be bandied around now. Not even the soldiers know where they are going."

"Aye, sir," replied Wake as he felt his face turn red and warm under the not-so-subtle reminder that he was just an underling and not part of the strategy planning by the commander and the admiral. As he saluted the senior officers and turned smartly to go, he was stopped on his course by Admiral Barkley, who uttered in an almost fatherly way, "Mr. Wake, your mission will have great consequence on the progress of the war for this squadron. You will understand that when you read your orders. Good luck, and God go with you."

Wake was surprised by this last statement and the manner in which it was delivered. Coupled with Johnson's eerie staring at him throughout the entire interview, Wake felt very uneasy when he thanked the admiral for his kind remark and walked out through the chief yeoman's office and into the waiting room. He felt even more uneasy exiting through the usual parasitic gathering of citizens, merchant captains, and army and navy officers in that room waiting for an audience with the admiral. They all scrutinized Wake with the demeanor of a jury deciding the fate of a defendant in the dock.

When he finally emerged from the squadron office building into the glaring sun and heat of midday, Wake's now-churning gut was convincing him that there was something very wrong with this whole thing. He walked along the harborside, then sat down on a shaded bench beneath one of the many coconut palms that dotted the grounds of the government buildings.

His mind went over the preceding conversation in detail and concentrated not only on what was said, but how it was said. He remembered the commander's constant survey of him, gauging him, testing him. But why? Why did Johnson stare at him so strangely when he talked of the papers they found on the captured ships with information on Reb sympathizers in Key West? The uneasiness turned into a sickening feeling as Linda's father came to mind. Could he be linked in some way to the Rebs up on the southwest coast of Florida? He gripped the bench and prayed that it not be so.

Wake's mind then methodically assessed the chances that the Key West authorities had linked him and Linda. It wouldn't have been too hard, Wake thought as his whole body seemed to deflate. Another complication of love, another reason why it was illogical, dangerous, and wrong for him to be in love with the most beautiful person he had ever known. All this time he had feared her father the most. Now he had to be concerned with his own side.

He felt an itch on his right ear and involuntarily reached up to scratch it. The wound was healed, but a mirror had already showed him that the scar was plain to see. His ear had been mangled and there was a straight line fore and aft of it that had healed as an angry red welt. He had never been a vain man, had never thought of himself as good-looking. But he saw the looks people gave that scar, and he felt somehow ashamed. He remembered the hospital and how he had hoped that the scars would heal into something less noticeable. But he was lucky he was not dead, and he knew it.

The big fear regarding his wound had been infection, and for the first week the nurses—male, sweaty, and unkempt—had tried to keep it washed each day. The pain of this procedure had been as bad as the initial wound. He finally had stopped them and done it himself. The hospital wasn't a very healthy place anyway. Even though it was located on the western side of the island by

Fort Taylor, where sea breezes were supposed to keep it disease-free, the breezes sometimes did not make themselves felt. It stank of urine and medicines and echoed with the constant moan of wounded and sick men, occasionally punctuated by the scream of a man undergoing a "procedure."

When he had felt better, he was allowed to leave the hospital during the day, and sometimes at night, and walk into the town of Key West. Several of these times he had met with Linda. These were always short, hurried affairs, with one eye on his watch and the other on the lookout for those who might see them. They were desperate moments that he frantically needed, that he lived for. She never mentioned his scar after the first time, when she held his head and so gently traced the line of the bullet, rocking him in her arms, softly telling him how much she loved him and quietly crying at the closeness of having lost him to the co-patriots of her father.

As he got up from the bench to walk to the officers' landing, he glanced back at the building housing the squadron's offices. The sun was now in the western sky, and as he looked against its glare he thought he saw a man, or men, in the window of the admiral's office on the second floor. He couldn't be sure. Were they surveying the ships at anchor or looking at him? Or was he perhaps becoming overly sensitive from his increasingly more complicated life? Wake shook his head clear of that unpleasant thought and looked to the northeast, away from the sun, where *Rosalie* swung on her anchor across the harbor. He would send word to her to be ready to sail at dawn. But now he had to be with Linda one last time, in the late afternoon hours of the day while her house was empty of her father and her uncle. He had to hold her one last time and memorize those eyes, and the smell of her perfume, and the touch of her softness, which had become the only normal part of his abnormal life. He made his way through the streets of the town to his lover, like a moth to the flame. . . .

His watch said that it was three o'clock in the morning, but his head told him that it was the end of the world. Never a large drinker, he had gone to a place quite different from the Russell House Hotel on Duval Street, where officers and prominent townspeople usually met for a drink. He'd found a bar that was little more than a barn in the eastern part of town back away from the nice areas. The hanging board out front declared it to be the Rum and Randy, and he thought a few glasses of what was known as "sailors' flips," concocted of rum, sugar, and beer, might cheer him up. He needed a bit of cheer after leaving Linda in the early evening just before her father and uncle were expected home. But the flips had not been what he expected. It was cheap rotgut rum from Cuba, two days away to the south, and the beer was stale. Soon a few drinks had become a few more. The atmosphere was alternately jolly or melancholy, depending on whether the officer singing a song was just making port or just about to sail from it. Wake recognized a couple of the officers from the schooners and other small vessels that *Rosalie* sometimes encountered. They compared experiences and memories of up north and eventually found a table to sit together. The others spoke of women they knew, with sometimes enough detail that the listeners knew that the narrator was talking of his fantasy and not of fact. But like sailors everywhere, they liked a good story, whether totally true or not—it made the time go by more pleasantly. Wake listened to the others' stories with a smile.

The unpainted, windowless room held tables for maybe twenty people but was now occupied by more than forty, not counting the girls who served and sat with the officers. Wake found himself feeling an odd, almost surreal appreciation of the people around him. He had the uncanny feeling that this was the last time that he would see this place and that he should have a good time here. It was not an unpleasant feeling, just an out-of-place feeling. So he joined in the songs and swilled down his flips and spoke lustfully with the others of the war and the way it should be fought, if only those in charge knew what they were doing.

And eventually he found himself at three o'clock in the dark of the morning with two ensigns, a lieutenant, and another master at the officers' landing. The master and the lieutenant were small-vessel captains like himself. They were starting to sober up with the knowledge that they would soon be aboard their ships with their men watching them. Both the two young ensigns were still at the height of their rum-induced silliness. Thinking that everything was funny, they were not listening to the lieutenant as he told them to pipe down. Then they made their rather considerable mistake. They told the lieutenant that he was just a gunboat skipper and that they were salts from a real man-o-war and didn't want to listen to a "small boat man."

Wake knew what would come next. It was the same whether you were in the merchant marine or the navy. It was the same in any port, with any nationality. You *never* insulted a man's ship. Seconds after the remark, both ensigns were crawling slowly away from the landing with blood pouring from their mouths and noses, and the lieutenant was peering out over the harbor for the duty boat, looking unconcerned, rubbing his knuckles where they had made quick contact with his targets.

The duty boat having arrived, the two masters and the lieutenant boarded and sat down in the stern sheets as the crew put their backs into it and made the rounds of the ships to drop off their passengers. Wake, his head starting to pound, concentrated on his mission, or at least what he knew of it. He looked over at the *Honduras* as they went by her at anchor. She appeared empty of troops and was quiet aboard, the duty watch on the foredeck talking in hushed voices as the launch rowed by.

Wake was the last to make his ship, and with barely concealed humor the boat crew made the signal to the anchor watch on deck that the captain was coming aboard. As he climbed up the side at the main chains, Wake glanced back at the boat crew, but the coxswain had already sheered off and was heading back to the landing. Probably to have a flip himself, thought Wake sarcastically as he made his way past an astonished Lamar on anchor watch. Wake looked once around the deck and then descended into his dark cave of a cabin, thinking of everything he had to do before making sail in three hours. Then he collapsed onto his crude bunk and mercifully lost conscious awareness of anything.

A minute later Wake woke up at six in the morning, three hours after he had fallen asleep. Young Sommer was shaking his shoulders and telling him that it was time to wake up. Wake very reluctantly rose up and adjusted his eyes to take in the starlight from the open hatchway. As he made his way up the ladder to the deck, he felt and heard the ship coming alive around him. Hardin spoke as Wake arrived at the tiller. "Mornin', sir. Anchor's hove short and mains'l's ready. Any orders, sir?"

Wake noted the neutral tone in the voice, then looked aloft to the wind and replied to weigh anchor and steer a course out the Northwest Channel. Moments later the sloop was moving away from the island on a broad reach as the eastern sky started to lighten. Wake breathed in the sea air and started to feel better.

With all sail set and a gentle easterly wind, *Rosalie* felt alive. Her easy motion and the sounds of the rigging whistling softly made Wake smile. Ol' Rosey was sailing again and she liked it. Like most sailors, he knew in his head that she was just wood and canvas, but like most sailors he couldn't help also feeling in his heart that she had a personality and a soul—sometimes forgiving, sometimes like a stubborn bitch, many times beautiful. She had been laid up at Key West for two weeks after the Peace River affair, having damage repaired and giving the crew liberty ashore. Hardin had taken her back to the coast only one time, and that for only a week's supply run to the various gunboat steamers offshore. As Wake inspected her decks and felt her rigging and sails, he felt glad to be away from the shore and free from the politics of landsmen.

One by one, the crew came up and welcomed Wake back, each in his own way. Even Hardin could not dampen his growing enthusiasm. Hardin reported to him that they were short a replacement man for the dead Wilson and another for the still-recovering Smith. Burns, who had lain in the same hospital as his captain, was on deck and moving slowly, having returned only the day before.

Wake noticed that all hands were looking at him frequently. They had all discussed his return to the ship and had decided that he had deserved a bit of a "rummed evenin' " after all he had been through. Hardin had not said a word to this conclusion of the crew, but had silently watched Wake and waited at the stern. Durlon, after greeting his captain's return, started to go over his gun and tackle, a ritual that was completed at least three times a day, every day. Of course, by now his faith in the gun and his own ability had been borne out in battle. The crew, with Wake mentally agreeing from the stern, had judged that Durlon and his gun had saved the day at the battle on the river. That those few well-loaded and well-placed shots had saved their lives as well was the consensus also.

As the sun timidly peeked up over the liquid horizon astern, Wake remembered that he had yet to know where they were going. With a glancing look at Hardin, he went down to his cabin and the envelope that contained his orders.

Below decks *Rosalie* was not quite as lovely. It was a pretty day on deck, but down in the cabin it was dark, dank, and smelly. Wake made a mental note to have Hardin get the crew to fumigate and clean the ship below deck. He rummaged in his bag for the envelope and finally brought up the large package, weighted to sink if the ship was in danger of capture and sealed in the blue wax of the admiral's office. His rigger's knife opened the waxed edges, allowing the lead bullet weights to fall out.

He pulled out three pieces of paper and spread them out on

his chart table. The first was a small chart of the area of Charlotte Harbor, the large bay with which he was now fairly familiar. He had never seen an official chart of that area—this was the first, and he realized that the chart had just been drawn and published a month ago by the navy.

The second piece of paper was his official orders. They directed him to meet with Lt. Baxter of the *Gem of the Sea* and advise him that offensive army operations were going to commence soon in that area of the coast and that all naval vessels were to assist their soldier colleagues to the best of their ability, as long as the object justified the potential losses. Commanding officers of ships were directed to provide boats, equipment, munitions, and manpower to secure landing places. Seamen were not to be sent long distances into the interior. Ship commanders were not to place their ships in a position of probable loss by enemy action or bad seamanship. Wake was directed to then go to the island of Useppa, located among the islands of Charlotte Harbor, and there render all assistance to the forces of the United States and/or to loyal refugees who may be at that place. He was to stay at that place until the army asked for him to escort them in their boats to the mainland for their operations, or for three weeks. Detailed reports of all operations were to be sent by the fastest means to the squadron at Key West.

The third piece of paper was addressed to Wake himself, but personally and not in the official language of the navy. It was from Commander Johnson and it asked him to ascertain from interviews with refugees and Rebel prisoners exactly what the possibilities were for an uprising among the inhabitants against the Confederate government in that area of Florida. It also asked for information from Wake on whom he suspected as disloyal among the refugees along the coast and at Key West. Johnson concluded in his letter that the response to these particular assignments was to be addressed to him in writing and given to his hand personally and immediately upon return to Key West.

Wake sat in his cabin stunned. His hand held the last memo

and his eyes looked at it, but his mind was seeing the expression of the commander during that last meeting just yesterday. The working sounds of the hull and frames of the sloop faded around him as he remembered Linda and their last rendezvous. The sick feeling returned to his abdomen as he realized that this communication meant that he was involved in a convoluted twist of conflicts on several levels.

Surprisingly, he felt a distant responsibility to keep Edgar Donahue, Linda's father, safe from the authorities. He rationalized this as an attempt to keep Linda safe from any harm and from being left alone should her father be arrested. But the feeling that he should shield her father from the authorities made him feel disloyal to the cause for which he was fighting, and for which his men had died and been wounded.

His mind progressed further from analysis of this communication to the very intense thought of what precisely the consequences were for him. Was this a way for Johnson to test his loyalty because Johnson knew about his relationship with Linda? Was this a way for Johnson to use him to get inside information on the Rebel sympathizers in Key West? Did Johnson think that he knew more than he did—that the Donahue family somehow divulged Rebel secrets to him? If Johnson knew of Linda's relationship with him and suspected her sympathies to be those of her father, did Johnson suspect that she was using him to ascertain information about the operations of the squadron and passing that intelligence along to the Confederate spies in Key West? That was ludicrous, he knew. But still, could Johnson suspect it? The answer was yes. Wake slowly sighed and shook his head in an effort to clear his mind of the thoughts that confused and hurt him. He had to stop building this up. He had to think this through and come to a logical conclusion. Johnson had only asked him to do what would be normally expected of him anyway. As a sailor he knew that you only reef down when the sea and sky showed you signs that a storm was coming. He saw no *real* signs that any storm was brewing with Johnson, and he would continue on his course and not reef until he did see those signs. But, sailor that he was, Wake decided that he would definitely keep an eye out to all points for any indication that he was in danger from any direction. He also decided, as he heard Hardin up on deck berating Sommer for being slow on the backstay hauling block, to reseal the orders and keep them placed well down in his bag. He memorized the location of the items in the bag on top of the envelope and returned to the deck, away from the gloom and doubt that had pervaded his cabin.

By the time he had regained the deck, *Rosalie* was fairly jumping the small beam seas. Her personality positively glowed, and the crew, satiated from another liberty in Key West, was moving about their business with the calm demeanor of experienced seamen. Maintenance was a never-ending routine aboard any vessel. But aboard a small naval vessel there were no idlers, and all hands had to turn to and handle various tasks that came up every day. For as happy as *Rosalie* was right now, she was a demanding girl, and failure to keep up her routine work would result in her reminding the sailors, at the most inopportune and possibly deadly moment, that they had failed her earlier when the work would have been relatively easy. As mean-spirited as Hardin was, Wake had to admit that the bosun was efficient at keeping *Rosalie* in good shape and ready for storm or battle.

Wake could see the eyes upon him and knew the question in their minds. He turned to Hardin and directed him to lay a course, after rounding the outer end of the Northwest Passage Channel, due north for Sanibel Island. He then walked forward to inspect the ship more closely, starting from the very bowsprit and working his way aft, as the men of the *Rosalie* exchanged looks and shrugs of resignation to their fate.

The next morning, as a colorful sunrise painted the sky to their starboard, they observed the coast of Captiva Island four miles to windward, just north of Sanibel, having made a good speed through the night and beating Wake's mental prediction of where the sun would see them first in the morn. *Rosalie* was still bounding along, heeled over with a beam reach, her wood and canvas and rigging combining their voices in a rhythmic song that sounded almost African on its arrival at Wake's ear.

The captain of the *Rosalie* couldn't help but stretch and smile at the sights and sounds that only sailors know and miss terribly when beached ashore for long periods of time. As exhausting and frequently frightening as the sea is, there would always be mornings like this for old sailors to remember when sitting in front of the fire on cold winter nights when they had finally come home from the oceans. And so Wake relished the moment and saw that many of the older men were in a similar revelation around him.

Durlon, who had the deck, asked if Wake wanted to tack the ship and turn back for Sanibel Island, since they had overshot it in the dark. His countenance changed for the worse when Wake replied that no, that was not necessary since they were heading to Boca Grande to speak with the *Gem of the Sea*. Wake did not go further, and Durlon did not ask with words the question in his mind. When his captain had returned below to his cabin, Durlon turned to Conner and whispered that he thought this voyage would end up at a bad spot since the captain had looked a bit concerned as he had spoken. There then began a whispered discussion of exactly what appearance did the captain's face have, and exactly what did that look mean, in terms of the likelihood of more work, or danger, or misery, for the men who sailed the *Rosalie*.

In the swaying dungeon of the cabin that was his sanctuary, Wake looked one more time at the chart that accompanied his orders. It showed the island of Useppa and the other islands in that area. *Rosalie* had been to the anchorage at Useppa before when Wake had dropped off supplies and refugees at the settlement there. It was a strange and unique island, Wake remembered, and he always thought that it had an ominous atmosphere. Perhaps that was because of the displaced refugees, who had lost almost everything on the mainland when they had fled their homes. Or perhaps it was because of the geography of the island, with its relatively high hills overlooking the surrounding waters, rising strangely out of its mangrove jungle shoreline.

Then there were the stories of the Calusa Indians, who had made those hills centuries earlier. Wake had heard that they maintained a vast and sophisticated culture on this coast, like the ones on the Spanish Main. He knew that the Spanish had never been able to totally subdue them. His sailors told him one night, while anchored off the island in the moonlight, that the hills had actually been temple mounds where sacrifices had been made during celestial events, and that the islands in this area still harbored descendants from that dark civilization. Just thirty years earlier, Seminole Indians had overrun the fishing settlement on the island in the night, the survivors being rescued days afterward, miles away huddled in a small boat. The whole island seemed to be a place where mysterious and dreadful things happened. He hoped that the future would not be consistent with the past.

By midday, the sloop had moored alongside the *Gem of the Sea*, which was anchored in her old spot off the island of Gasparilla, in Boca Grande Passage. Lt. Baxter welcomed Wake aboard and brought him into his cabin, which was small compared to those in regular men-o-war but much larger than that of the *Rosalie*. After asking Wake how his wound had progressed and what was going on at Key West, Baxter turned to the envelope Wake handed him.

Wake sat and had a drink of tea while Baxter read his orders. When he had finished, he looked at Wake and asked him if he had spoken with Admiral Barkley or Commander Johnson about their mission. When Wake related the conversation in the admiral's office, Baxter sighed and muttered that the fools in Key West were thinking up things to do so they could look useful to the senior fools in Washington. Wake, taken aback at this uncharacteristic attitude on the part of his friend, showed his concern on his face.

Seeing this, Baxter laughed. "I suppose, Peter, that this war has gotten to me, my friend. We sit here on the coast and try to stop their ships, we run up the rivers and try to destroy their depots, we transport the refugees to islands to try and make them safe. All of this, and we still haven't really stopped them, or even touched them. Meanwhile our men are dying of disease and Reb sharpshooters, one by one. . . ."

Baxter grew slower and sadder in his speech as he continued. Wake looked him in the eye and tried to sound optimistic. "Maybe now is the time to change all of that. Maybe this time we can actually gain some ground. Get these pro-Union people to fight for their country and rouse up the disaffected in the interior."

But Baxter looked at him and said, "As always, Peter, I will do my duty, and so will my men. It just seems that every idea that sounds good in Key West dies out here for lack of proper support or realistic expectations. I do not trust many of the people in these islands—nor the fools in the army either."

Wake had to agree with him there. Before he bade him goodbye, he asked for a ship's boat to meet him at Useppa Island in a week's time to exchange intelligence of the enemy and of the reinforcements enroute to them. Baxter laughed again and said that he would keep in touch and to have fun over there with those folks on that island. They parted on the main deck as friends and fellow captains, wishing each other well in the coming times.

Rosalie swung away with the tide and set sail close reaching to the east one hour after she had come alongside the *Gem*. In that time the crews of both ships had caught up on gossip, paid off debts, and made speculations about the future. The crew of the smaller vessel had told of their apprehensions about returning to this coast, as Wake had heard through the ports of Baxter's cabin. He was again amazed at how accurate the sailors' intuition could be on these things, with the scuttlebutt including various wagers on potential destinations. The conjectured possibilities narrowed as *Rosalie* came up toward the island of Bokeelia, with Wake himself steering the sloop past the shoals. When close to Bokeelia, Wake tacked the sloop and broad reached to the south down a broad swash channel past several small islands. With the bow pointed toward Useppa Island in the distance, the crew surmised their destination and began to discuss the reasons for it.

Hardin looked at the island ahead and turned to his captain, asking if they were going to anchor out or tie along the rickety dock that jutted out from the beach on the east side of the island. Wake's reply was to anchor out and that he would dinghy in to the island. Hardin shrugged and went forward to get the anchor ready, leaving Wake to survey the island, now with a new and more serious interest, for he would have to work closer than ever before with the people ashore.

The island was surrounded on its shores with mangrove jungle, except here at the landing beach. Relatively large in relation to its neighbors, it measured about a mile long by a quarter of that wide at the widest. Huts and crude shacks dotted the hills that came down to the water's edge. Several more substantial structures stood on a central hill, back from the water. The best-built structures on Useppa appeared to be the water cisterns that captured the rainwater and held it for the inhabitants to use. These were square and clinker-built, like small boats from New England, to be watertight. Fresh water was the most precious commodity on the islands, where few wells had been dug.

As *Rosalie* got closer to the anchorage off the settlement, Wake could see people waving to them and coming down to the boats drawn up on the beach. Most of the refugees, whatever their occupations had been before the war, were now fishermen. Fortunately, the fishing was so good in this area of the coast that even beginners could bring in enough to feed their families and sell some to the naval vessels that occasionally stopped. Wake made a mental note to buy some fish and gain some information while doing so.

About a hundred yards off the beach he rounded the sloop up into the wind and Hardin let go the anchor in a little over a fathom of water. As she fell back on the hook, sails thundering as they flapped in the wind with the crew struggling to bring down the large mainsail, two boats came off the beach and headed out to the ship. A moment later they were alongside and, without invitation, which faintly riled Wake, three men climbed up the side of the sloop and strode aft.

Before Wake could speak, one of them condescendingly introduced himself as a Michael Remus Horndum, leader of the settlement on Patricio Island, a mile away to the north. He stood about average height, was skinny like all of the islanders, and had a sneer on his face that gave the appearance of the man having a permanent seizure. His voice revealed his Northern city roots and was loudly overwhelming. His clothing evidently had once been fine, but age and weather had reduced it to a dull mockery of his present station in life. Wake, and most of his crew by the looks on their faces, instantly did not like or trust the man.

The other two quietly said that they were Harley Cornell of Useppa Island and Tom O'Clooney of Palmetto Island, just west of Useppa Island. Cornell gave the appearance of a school teacher, being of quiet manner and appearance, and reminded Wake that they had met before, about three months earlier when *Rosalie* had off-loaded some provisions for the islanders at Useppa. O'Clooney, a muscular man with a tanned and wrinkled face, smiled a great Irish smile of welcome that made him the instant friend of all hands. His large paw of a hand clasped Wake's with a good-natured strength that belied his pleasant appearance. A good friend or a bad enemy, thought Wake as he released his hand from O'Clooney's custody. The two islanders stood apart from Horndum and obviously shared the crews' opinion of the man from Patricio Island. Wake found himself wondering what the rest of the people on that island were like.

After the preliminary introductions were completed, Cornell invited Wake and his crew to the island for that evening's dinner and dance, a monthly affair that the islanders gave themselves to build morale and to keep an attempt at social intercourse alive in their sad situation. Refugees from all the islands would come by boat for these gatherings, and information as well as food, music, and drink were shared. Horndum echoed Cornell's invitation and told Wake that it was a good opportunity for him to meet the "important people" of the islands. O'Clooney laughed and said to come on over for a bit of relaxation for the captain and his crew.

Of course, all of this occurred in front of the crew, who were by this time doing their post anchoring duties with at least one ear and one eye taking in the conversation of their captain. Wake, remembering the pleasant sail of the last two days and trying to gain the confidence, and therefore the intelligence, of the islanders, accepted the invitation. He told Hardin, who was non-chalantly sitting on the gun and listening, that half the crew could have liberty ashore until midnight. The liberty party would consist of Hardin and four men, whom he could pick, with Durlon and the others standing an anchor watch. The response of the crew was instantaneous merriment for the liberty men and resignation by the others who had to stay aboard. Wake even felt cheered and thought that he might have been wrong about the island, mysteries and all.

With the departure of the islanders in their dories, the *Rosalie* returned to normal, some of the duty crew doing the ongoing routine work under the gaze of Durlon, and the others getting themselves ready for their time ashore. Wake gathered the liberty men at the stern and told them that they were not to cause trouble or give the ship a bad name. Hardin was told that he was responsible for watching over them, to which he actually smiled and stated that he would make sure the ruffians would not do anything "like they do in Key West." The last remark had worried Wake, but his mental preparation for dealing with the islands' leaders ashore diverted any serious misgivings.

The festivities started at six o'clock in the evening on the central hill that overlooked all of the surrounding islands. Wake had never been past the beach on the island before, and in the softening light he could smell the perfume of flowers blooming everywhere as he walked up the path through the settlement. Gumbo limbo trees stretched their clawlike limbs upward and outward, providing a wonderful shade and sense of grandeur. As he ascended the hill he could hear some stringed instruments playing a song that sounded familiar from his past, but his lack of musical ability prevented him from identifying either the song or the instruments.

At the top of the hill Wake was greeted by a small crowd of about fifty people, who grouped around him in a confusing whirl of introductions that left him dazed. Wake had a cup thrust into his hand and he absentmindedly took a swallow of it as he tried to handle his new-found position of high-ranking visitor and representative of the government for which these people had made such sacrifices. Just as he was thinking this thought, the contents of the cup went down his throat and he belatedly realized it was straight rum, and a powerful rum at that.

Coughing and sputtering, to the amusement of the men in the group and the sympathy of the women, Wake tried to regain his composure by complimenting the rum. After the laughter died down, Cornell said that dinner was served and they should all sit. The gathering was seated at a line of tables set up on top of the hill, with a magnificent view of the islands around them. The sun in the west was producing one of its most splendid displays of beauty, with changing colors that defied description diffusing throughout the sky and even touching the islands themselves. It was as if the sun was an actor who had saved his best performance for the last act of the day. With the natural beauty around him and the smells of the dinner tempting him, Wake had the pleasing sensation of actually being content. It was such a rare emotion in the last few months that he almost didn't recognize it. And as much as his constitution was against it, he felt himself starting to relax as he sat down at the position indicated at one of the tables.

Wake, seated at the position of honor next to Cornell, found the man Horndum sitting on his other side and the Irishman O'Clooney across from him. It seemed that the men all sat on one end of the table and the ladies at the other, which Wake found strange and a bit disappointing.

After Cornell said grace, the feast began. Wake, ever the sailor, noted that the wind had started to veer to the south but was still light. As the sun sank below the dark line of the Gulf of Mexico, dry "lighter wood" sticks were set afire as torches in pots and pans on the tables, apparently because candles were too dear to be used on this occasion, or perhaps they had none. A bonfire at each end, and two on either side, completed the lighting arrangements for the evening. Wake found himself impressed by most of the people he conversed with during the dinner of smoked and baked fish, roasted wild pig, and various tropical fruits. It seemed that many were former townspeople from all over the state, and their stories of how they came to be on this island had the common thread of sadness. Still, they were persevering, and several spoke of taking the offensive against the Rebels on the mainland.

Wake had heard stories like these before. While transporting families down the coast, or rescuing individuals on vessels or deserted islands, he had heard the stories of how they had fled, leaving everything they had built. The Confederates periodically attempted to sweep this area of the pro-Union refugees. The most recent planned attempt had almost come a month earlier, according to his hosts. However, the battle on the Peace River had thwarted that attack before it could be mounted. As the island men told Wake that piece of information, which he had not heard before, he noticed that the tables had gotten quiet and that everyone was listening. All eyes focused on Wake as Cornell stood with his hand out and solemnly said, "Captain Wake, thank you for all that you and your crew did. We don't have much here and cannot say or do more than that, but know that it is from the bottom of our hearts." A chorus of "here, here" broke out mixed with some "amens," and all the refugees applauded the now-embarrassed naval officer. He knew he would have to speak to these people and stood hesitantly.

"I did not know about the planned attack. We knew that they periodically would try, but I did not know that it would have come that soon. On behalf of my men and our ship, thank you for your kind words. Some day, God willing, this war will end, and we can all go back to our own peaceful pursuits. I wish all of you the most wonderful fortune in that endeavor."

Wake was not used to public speeches, in fact had never made one. His only speaking to a group of persons had been to a crew on a deck, and he hoped that he had sounded polished enough and not offended anyone. Cornell, sensing the young naval officer's predicament, thanked Wake for his words and mercifully suggested that they all now concentrate on eating dessert. This dessert, a pie made from the tart limes that grew nearby, mixed rather agreeably with the rest of the feast such that Wake found himself eating far more than he could remember in quite a long time. In his sated and slightly intoxicated state, with the stars now starting to appear in the indigo sky around them and someone playing the lilting song "Loreena" on a guitar, Wake thought of Linda and wished she were here with him to experience this.

As he looked around at these Americans who had been forced out of their homes in their own country, he saw that many of the men and women had grown very quiet while listening to the balladeer sing his story. Cornell and O'Clooney had taken pity on their guest and had steered Horndum off to some other victim who had to listen to his prattle about the way things would be in Florida when the war was over and it became "their turn" to run the state. Wake, lulled by all of this, was just starting to slip into a comfortable doze in his chair when he heard a girl scream down by the beach.

Another scream came, this time louder, longer, and more of an animalistic shriek. The girl and her screams seemed to be moving rapidly down the beach, away from the area of the dock. By this time, everyone on top of the hill had started down the path, some carrying the torches that had previously made the evening seem so gay. Wake looked around him for some of his crew but could find none. They had been seated much further down the table from him, and he had lost track of them after dinner.

The crowd made the beach in a short time and was confronted with a sight that instantly emptied Wake of any pleasant feeling. It was replaced by a rage such as he had never felt when he saw Hardin pinioned by four stout refugee fishermen. Hardin's shirt was missing and his trousers were down around his knees. He presented an almost lupine appearance, his mouth snarling at the fishermen and his hands frantically clawing at their arms. One of the refugee men, his face red with rage, came up to Cornell and Wake sputtering, "That navyman there ripped the dress of my girl. My girl is only thirteen. He tried to rape my little girl!"

Wake looked around for the other men of his crew and saw that Lamar, Sommer, and Burns were standing in the background of the very agitated crowd. He called them to him and told them to tie Hardin's hands securely behind his back and then guard him from escape. Wake then turned to Cornell and the fisherman and asked if the girl was physically harmed, to which the father said that she was bruised and had some cuts from the bushes.

"Sir, I don't know exactly what to say except that Hardin is under arrest and will be taken to the *Gem of the Sea* immediately." Wake said this to the girl's father but spoke loudly enough for all to hear. Cornell nodded his acknowledgment and tried to console his friend as some in the crowd made comments about taking care of "the animal" right there.

"Mr. Cornell, I am very sorry that happened. Tell me if there is anything that I can do for the girl or her family."

"Just get him off the island right now, Captain Wake, or he won't see the sun rise."

Wake strode over to the now-quiet Hardin and told the sailors guarding him to get the dory from the beach to take him to the sloop. When they had gone to see about the boat, Wake brought his face up close to Hardin's and breathed the words as calmly as he could. "What happened, Hardin? Tell me the truth." He could smell the rancid odor of the rum emanating from Hardin. He could see it in the eyes of the man. Hardin formed his words and spat them at Wake, as at a target.

"The little slut wanted it and said so. When her mother

came down the path, the girlie turned into a maniac and started screaming. That's it. Get me out of here and untie my hands. I can't stand bein' trussed up like this. If I ever get my hands on that little harlot, I'll make her never forget this."

Wake summoned all of his strength and turned away from the man. Sommer came running up and said that a dory was being brought up now to take the bosun to the ship and that Burns had gone in the dinghy to bring Durlon and other crew to assist. The crowd had divided, the women going to the home of the victim and the men standing on the beach watching the naval officer and his seamen. Wake could almost hear the calculations going on in some of their minds about whether they should, or could, take the prisoner by force and deal justice out right there. When Durlon jumped out of the dinghy with more men and the dory arrived from down the beach, all hands quickly turned to manhandling the still-resisting bosun into the dory.

On the row out to the sloop, Wake leaned over to Durlon and told him that at all times until they got to the *Gem of the Sea*, one of the two of them would be guarding Hardin from escape. Durlon nodded his understanding and glared at the bosun writhing on the floorboards of the dory. When they reached *Rosalie*, Hardin was fairly thrown up onto the deck, where Wake himself lashed him to the samson post on the foredeck. Wake took the first watch over the prisoner as the crew weighed anchor and set sail out of the anchorage in the gentle wind and the starlight, bound for the *Gem of the Sea* with their disgusting cargo.

When they at last reached the anchored *Gem of the Sea* and came alongside to raft up, Wake could see her captain on the quarterdeck looking concerned. An arrival at this time of night must mean an engagement with the Confederates, but Baxter had not heard any gunfire.

Instead he saw the bosun, trussed up like a pig to the slaughter, and a very quiet crew that ignored questions from the sailors on the larger ship. Baxter was looking very concerned indeed when Wake came aft to him and said in a low voice, "I had to come back now, my friend, because it seems my bosun has attempted to rape a young girl on Useppa during a dinner ashore there tonight. The whole island is angry, and I need to keep him in irons here. I have no irons aboard *Rosalie* and could not effectively guard against his escape. I want him in the Fort Taylor cells as soon as possible."

"I see, Peter. Well, perhaps we shall take him with us when we go in the next few days. I will need statements from all involved, of course. This is a serious offense and just may require a board of officers at the squadron."

"We could take him ourselves, but we must remain for the army next week. Besides, on our small vessel there are too many ways for him to cause mischief. Thank you for keeping him. I will get the statements tomorrow if I can moor alongside for the rest of the night and get some rest. This has taken it quite out of me."

"Certainly. Stay until morn, then get back and repair the relationship with those people as best you can. Hardin will do time in Portsmouth for this, and deserves all of it. Your report will have to explain it all, Peter. Now get some rest."

This last statement was broken by a howl from the *Gem of the Sea*'s foredeck where Hardin had been fastened with iron shackles to a ringbolt set in the deck before the foremast. He was kicking wildly at the crowd of sailors gathered around him, screaming the word "harlot" over and over. Baxter told one of his petty officers to "gag that child rapist animal on the deck. He will disturb our sleep with that howling. Should he by some means get out of the irons and try to escape, gun him down!" thereby ending any potential for sympathy among his crew. What little goodwill, if any, Hardin ever had with the sailors of the *Gem of the Sea* ended at that moment.

There remained one more thing for Wake to ask. He started formally. "Sir, I must beg to impose even further. This event leaves me more shorthanded than before. Could I take eight of your crew and the ship's cutter to assist *Rosalie* in carrying out her orders while you are gone?"

Baxter stood there staring at Wake. Eight men were a tenth of his crew. He shook his head, sighed, and replied, "Yes, I know that you'll need them. We'll detail them to you when you return from getting the statements on the island and submit your report of this incident. I will need the statements and report done by tomorrow night, so as to be free to leave whenever the wind serves."

Wake took a deep breath, looking at his friend, and sincerely said, "Aye, aye, sir. Thank you for your help. This has been a nightmare and I don't know how I will regain the refugees' confidence. I thought they were going to kill him right there on the beach."

"Twenty years in the Portsmouth Naval Prison will be worse than any death they could administer, Peter. Let them know his fate, get their statements, write your report, and get them back involved in hatred against the Rebs. That will turn them around. Get some sleep." Baxter turned to go below to his cabin, leaving Wake to look upon the creature lying alone on the foredeck.

Wake's return to Rosalie and descent to his own cabin did not lessen the nervousness in his mind. Sleep did not come easily as he went over in his mind what he could have done to prevent the heinous act of his second in command. He might have suspected Hardin of being capable of theft or fighting, but not an attack on a little girl. The memory of the look on Hardin's face was enough to make Wake cringe. The animal rage and obviously demented mind were frightening. Perhaps he should have let the islanders have their way.

His orderly mind returned to the problems he would face the next day. Working out those problems displaced his fearful memories and finally sleep came. Fear and rage had exhausted him, and Wake slid unexpectedly into slumber as he was working out the time of arrival of the sloop back at the anchorage. That island where he incongruously knew a brief contented peace, with the stars afloat in the sky above, atop a hill with kind refugees who had lost everything, had proven ominous indeed.

The morning afterward, Wake got his sloop under way early, not wanting to be near the thing on the foredeck of the other vessel any longer than necessary. His crew also seemed to want to flee the *Gem of the Sea*, though returning to the scene of the crime was not where they wanted to go. In the world of sailors, a crime committed against one of them was a crime committed against all of them, against their ship. The reverse was true also, though. Wake knew that "the tale would sail the fleet" and that he and his crew would hear about it for years. Fights would ensue in bars and brothels around the world, whenever his sailors would encounter that story and the narrator would ask if they were of the baby-raping crew of the *Rosalie*. Guilt by association was not the law of the land, but it was a rule of the seaports of the world. Wake knew that the only way to stop that evil reputation was to replace it with another, more respectful and overwhelming. A victory in war was what they needed now. And they needed the refugees' help to achieve that. Today would begin that effort, Wake knew.

Just before the daily meridian, *Rosalie* coasted into the anchorage off the beach and slid her hook into the mud. No crowds waved or came out to her. The settlement appeared almost deserted, with just a few shapes moving in the shade of the trees by the huts. Wake told Durlon to have young Sommer get the dinghy and row him ashore, that he would be back in a little while. Durlon was to stay aboard and not let anyone ashore except Sommer. Looking around the deck at the crew, Wake saw no enthusiasm to go ashore and felt the need to say, "Men, what has happened will be associated with us. We need to gain the confidence of these good people again. It may take awhile, but it will start today, with me. I know you understand and will do what you can."

The response was a nodded understanding from the men and a terrified look from Sommer, who clearly did not want to go back to the island. Wake descended the side of the sloop and sat in the dinghy, fending off as Sommer got it under way. They slowly made their way to the sparse dock without seeing anyone near the water. Wake told Sommer to stay with the dinghy as he walked ashore and tried to find someone from the settlement.

A voice from atop the nearest hill told Wake that he was acknowledged and asked that he wait a moment. This he did until Harley Cornell made his way down the path to the shade of a laurel tree where Wake stood waiting.

After initial polite greetings and another apology about what had happened, Wake explained that he had secured Hardin aboard the *Gem of the Sea* and had returned to Useppa Island to obtain statements to present at the court martial. He also asked Cornell if there was anything he could do for the girl and her family.

"Captain Wake, the islanders here have been horribly treated by the Rebel regime on the mainland, escaped with very little to their name, been ignored by the government in their time of need, and now attacked by a sailor who is supposed to protect them. They do not want anything to do with you or your crew."

"Sir, I understand their thoughts, and share them myself concerning Hardin, but I have to do my duty and obtain evidence against this man. The islanders," Wake avoided the word *refugees*, for they did not like it, "have sacrificed much for their loyalty to a system of democratic governing that includes our legal system. They must be made to understand that though it is not easy to make the statements, it must be done if we are to maintain our system of proof against those accused."

"Will they have to go to Key West to testify?" asked Cornell with concern.

"I do not know, but I shall certainly recommend that the court accept the statements in lieu of their travel to Key West," replied an equally concerned Wake. He did not know. He had never run into this before in his days at sea. He sought to reassure this man who had been initially so gracious and hospitable to him on his arrival at Useppa, less than twenty-four hours earlier. "Mr. Cornell, if I need to, I will personally go to the admiral and explain the reasons for the waiver of personal witness testimony at Key West."

"Very well, Captain Wake. I know that you cannot guarantee that they will not have to testify. I will do my best to persuade them to assist you. You have been a gentleman throughout this ghastly affair."

"Thank you, sir. I will wait here with my writing instruments until you deem it appropriate. The sooner we get those statements, sir, the sooner I can send Hardin to Key West."

Cornell nodded and then walked along the beach to a hut at the northern end of the settlement. Wake watched him go, wondering if that was the abode of the victim and her family, and then returned to Sommer and the dinghy to get his paper, ink, and pens. Sommer questioned his captain with his eyes, not daring to put it into words. Wake advised him that everything was good so far and to remain on the boat.

A few minutes later Cornell met Wake under the tree and bade him to follow as he walked back to the hut. The slow pace, silent guide, and baking heat reminded Wake of a long last march to the gallows. As he looked around him at the huts where the refugees lived and saw heads following him along the path, he remembered the ominous feeling about Useppa Island that he had had before landing here.

Upon entering, Wake was met by the victim's father, who ignored his offered hand and went outside. The mother was more polite and asked Wake to be seated at a very crude table while she got her daughter. The depressing atmosphere of the wood and palm thatch hut, accentuated by the demeanor of the parents and the daughter when she arrived, made Wake wish he could get through this excruciating duty faster. These people live like savages, Wake thought as he tried to gently ask the pertinent questions and record the girl's answers.

When he was done with the victim, Wake took a statement from the mother, the first person to see Hardin. She related hearing her daughter scream and then actually seeing a half-naked Hardin a moment later groping and restraining the girl on the beach. Wake paid particular attention to the sequence of events that seemed to invalidate Hardin's paltry alibi, for the girl's mother heard the scream even before she reached a position where she could see or be seen. The victim had echoed this information, having not seen her mother until after screaming.

Wake, not a lawyer or a lawman, thought that all of this was significant and would end any defense of the accused. He next took statements of the fishermen who apprehended Hardin, asking them to tell their recollections of his demeanor. When it was all done and six statements had been taken, he thanked Cornell again for his help. Cornell, who had stood by during all of the statements, acknowledged that this duty had to be carried out correctly and that Wake had done so.

And so, four hours after he had started taking the statements, Wake made his weary way back to the dock where Sommer waited. He turned to Cornell and explained that he had to get statements from his crew as well, and then he would send the perpetrator of this tragedy on his way in irons to the gaol in Key West. Before he shoved off in the dinghy, he turned to the island leader and quietly advised, "Mr. Cornell, this senseless crime doesn't stop the war, or the Rebels' wishes to eliminate this settlement. We are going to have to proceed with the preparations for your men to arm themselves and take action against the Rebs."

"I know. Some of these men were in the Rebel army, against their wishes, of course. Others fought the Indians here in the fifties. They know how to fight, and they will do well when the time comes. I think that the sooner your soldiers come to get them started, the better. We need to put this behind us."

"Aye aye, sir. We'll get them started soon." As Wake turned to tell Sommer to shove off, he heard Cornell say to him, "I hope the soldiers are better behaved, Wake. Our men will kill the next one who tries anything like that," and Cornell walked away slowly down the dock, leaving Wake staring at the man and the island, as little Sommer rowed him back to his ship.

Feeling the need to get away from the island, and its people and memories, Wake sailed the sloop out of the anchorage just before sunset. The departing sun was not putting on a show this time. High, thin clouds obscured the sun as it made its way down in a gauzy, gray sky. The only colors were the shades of the gray clouds, darker near the horizon. It was as if the sky were preventing the sun from seeing the island or its malignancy. An all-around gloomy day and evening did nothing to improve Wake's morale as he took statements from the crew on their involvement in the mess with Hardin.

None of them admitted being with Hardin when he approached the girl on the beach, but Sommer did state that he had seen Hardin "looking at her hard" during the dinner. All of them appeared genuinely shocked that he would do something like that, since they had seen nothing similar during other liberties ashore with him. Durlon told his captain later in the evening that he had always thought Hardin an odd character who was a bit rough with the bar girls in Key West, but had never seen him "pick on a nice girl before."

As the *Rosalie* crept along in the light air, all of the events of the previous twenty-four hours caught up with Wake. His head ached with shame and tension, and he felt that he had somehow failed in an endeavor of peaceful social interaction the night before, a failure that had cost a girl her innocence. He had failed to control the men under his command, failed in his responsibility. He fell asleep on the deck at the stern, wishing that this newest nightmare, for which he was totally unprepared, would have gone away when he woke up.

In the middle of the night *Rosalie* moored alongside her old friend, *Gem of the Sea*. This time there was no meeting of the crews, no exchange of information, just a silent handling of the mooring lines while the off-watch men of the *Rosalie* fell exhausted into their hammocks, after looking to make sure that the monster that used to be their mate was still securely bolted to the other vessel's deck. These men, who had feared Hardin as a bully even before his hateful crime, had now taken the voluntary step of testifying against him and feared how he might retaliate should he be somehow set free.

The crew of the larger vessel were also wary of the man chained to their foredeck. It was as if his mere presence provided a reminder that some among them might erupt as this one did, suddenly and without reason. The men of the *Gem of the Sea* were also angry that they should have to guard and handle this deviant for the crew of another vessel. Recollection of Hardin's less-than-thoughtful words and deeds in their presence after the Peace River battle several weeks prior, along with Bosun Mate Moore's remembrances of Hardin liberty stories that now came out in loud and detailed form, prompted the *Gem* crew to look upon the crew of the *Rosalie* with far less amity than before. It was if the men of the *Rosalie* had dumped some particularly foul-smelling refuse upon their holystoned deck and left it there out of malice.

The next morning at sunup, Baxter and Wake again met in the former's cabin and talked over the situation. Baxter informed Wake that he had decided the situation was such that it was necessary to leave that day for Key West and that no operations were to be done until his return, which might be in a week, depending upon Admiral Barkley. Baxter would pass along the report of Wake, which included the statements and his request for a waiver of requiring the victim and witnesses in Key West, and also pass along his own assessment of the situation of the refugees on the coast. When Wake related that Commander Johnson had once told him to be wary of Hardin after the affair with the *Betsy,* Baxter replied that Johnson may well have known something more than he had let on about Hardin. Neither Baxter nor Wake knew much of anything of Hardin's background, and Baxter vowed to find out what he could for his friend.

An hour later Baxter and his ship were sailing southwest out of the Boca Grande Passage, having left a boat and extra men for Wake as per their agreement the night Wake brought Baxter his new prisoner. The prisoner, still fastened as a part of the ship, made a final long and inhuman scream at the *Rosalie* from about half a mile away. All hands looked at Wake as the shriek assaulted them. Wake just stared at the diminishing form of the other ship. He then turned away from the sight and sound of his nightmare and set the men to working on the never-ending list of chores that their floating home required. He told Durlon to steer a course along the islands to the northward, in the direction away from their shame. They, and the small boat following under sail, coasted the islands' beaches in the Gulf of Mexico, with a sea breeze to clean their memories and a bright, hot sun to burn away the guilt in their souls.

A week later they were sailing along the inside passage by the island of Palmetto, having just left Useppa Island, where they had checked on the well-being of the refugees and for any intelligence of what the enemy was up to on the coast. Wake was the only one of the *Rosalie* to go ashore, and he met with Cornell again. The island leader told him that the girl and her family were getting back to as normal a life as they could as refugees on the island. Feelings were still tense though, as Wake could see by the looks he got from the other islanders. They no longer stayed out of sight when the sloop arrived, and some were polite to him, but most were cold to him and did not speak as he walked among them. Wake even went up to the father of the girl and asked how the family was doing and if there was anything he could do to help them. The man replied with a simple "no" and walked away.

Wake felt there was nothing he could do further and told Cornell as much. The older man said that the island men needed to feel that they were doing something. They felt helpless just sitting on the island. They were getting restless. Time was running short for patience to hold. Even getting information for the navy or guiding their ships along the coast was not enough for these men to feel that they were helping the country for which they had lost almost everything.

Wake's remonstrations that the navy and the army were preparing to get them fighting were met by Cornell's hand-wavings. "No more talking," muttered the man, who was old enough to be Wake's father.

Wake and *Rosalie* left shortly thereafter and began looking for a flatboat that the islanders said they had seen among the islands. They didn't know the men aboard her and thought she might be a Reb craft sent to spy on the refugee communities among the islands.

With *Rosalie* sailing southward through the small islands in the middle of the large bay, and the ship's boat sailing southward along the shallow coast of Pine Island that formed the eastern side of the bay, Wake felt that he had a relatively good chance of seeing the flatboat if it was being poled along in the open. He intensely wanted to do something positive for the islanders and show them a small victory. The crew understood and were intently searching the islands and coves for the suspicious vessel.

Off Chino Island, ten miles south of Palmetto Island, young Sommer heard a gun fire. It was the agreed signal between *Rosalie* and the ship's boat for the first vessel to find the flatboat. The ship's boat was a speck off York Island, to their southeast, which suddenly turned into a large tan butterfly as she tacked through the wind, spreading her old dirty sails as she came about and then disappeared around the corner of the island. Wake told Durlon on the helm to steer for her, and they set all the sail the Rosey could carry. With a broad reach and even the main topsail pulling, *Rosalie* went sliding through the waves toward whatever was happening on the other side of the island.

They heard more gunfire as they approached the island at full speed, centerboard hauled up to allow them to race over the shoals as the sailors speculated on what might be happening out of their sight. Wake ordered them to go to battle quarters and get ready. As Wake took the helm himself and Durlon ran his gun crew through the drill of loading the twelve-pounder, Conner turned out the muskets and cutlasses. Just as Wake was receiving his two loaded pistols, Lamar yelled out from the bowsprit that he saw the ship's boat around the point and that they were run up on shore next to a flatboat. As they came around the corner of York Island, they saw a group of sailors by the mangroves surrounding four men who were holding their hands up in the air.

Wake could see that the action was over as a sailor waved to the approaching sloop. He told the crew to stand down from quarters and douse the sails, no easy feat to do quickly. *Rosalie* came around up into the wind and lost her way amidst a thundering cacophony of sails luffing, men swearing, chain rattling out, and Sommer getting the dinghy ready to row his captain to the beach.

Upon Wake's arrival on the tiny beach carved by the sea out of the mangrove jungle shoreline of the island, he was met by Moore, the bosun's mate from the *Gem of the Sea,* who had command of the ship's boat.

"We got 'em, sir. Just started to talk to 'em. They tried to get into the trees here but we jus' ran the ol' darlin' ashore and went after 'em, quick as you please. Couple a shot stopped 'em in their tracks."

"What do you know of them and the boat?" asked Wake.

"They're not sayin' much, sir. 'Cept they're refugees who are runnin' from the Rebs and headin' to Key West, if ya can believe that, sir." The tone of his voice told what Moore thought of that story.

Wake decided to speak directly to the men and had them brought to him one by one. The first was named Thomas Jones, a young man who certainly looked the part of the refugee as his clothes were old and threadbare. But his demeanor was not that of the other refugees Wake had met. He was too enthusiastic about his loyalty. Most refugees were just plain tired and didn't have to show their loyalty—it came out in quiet narrations of their escapes and in the faraway look in their eyes. Jones quickly said he was a store clerk from Tampa, where he was scheduled to report for duty with the Rebel army but had fled to the wild country to the south instead, thinking that no one would find him there. There he met up with the others in the group at Punta Gorda, where they had a boat and invited him along. He immediately asked about how to join the Federal Army in Key West and was told by Wake that he could ask that when he got there. Jones was the kind of man who transferred his nervousness to others around him. Wake felt very uncomfortable.

The second man, a John Nelson, was an older man of maybe forty-five years, who had the strong look and calm demeanor of a fisherman. He quietly told Wake that they had all decided to go to Key West to join up for the Union side since the war had disrupted their livings and they couldn't fish or do their work anymore. He was from the area of Sarasota Bay and had made it overland from Fort Meade in the interior to the Peace River, where they had stolen a flatboat from the Rebs and gone down the river and along the coast. Wake knew he was lying from the first—didn't know how he knew but just sensed the story was wrong. Nelson had eyes that looked through you, not in an aggressive way, but in a passive stare that patiently waited for your response. Wake could almost see a smile in the eyes, as if they didn't believe the story either but were required by loyalty to act out the part.

The third man was also dressed in old clothes, had about thirty years to his credit and a badly healed scar on his left forearm. He called himself Roger Huntington of Hamilton County, in upper Florida, and he said he was released from the Nineteenth Florida Infantry Regiment after being wounded in Virginia six months earlier. He further related, in a voice that revealed some education, that he was tired of the whole affair and was ready to take the oath and fight for the blue. He said that he could read and write, was a sergeant before and wanted to be again. He had joined with Nelson up the Peace River and come down on the flatboat. His entire air was incongruous with the others. He was too calm, too quiet. The only emotion he showed was a constant sliding of his eyes toward the others in what looked to be an effort to communicate to them that everything was under control in the situation that they had found themselves.

The last one was a skinny boy of seventeen. The fear on his face was obvious. He gave a name of Oliver Dade, said he was from Punta Gorda and was running away from the Rebels there because he didn't want to die for them. Said he would take his chances in Key West with the Federal Army and that his mother, who lived alone, had agreed with his plan to leave the Rebel area and go for a new life. He explained that the situation among the few families at Punta Gorda had gotten worse since the navy had destroyed or captured most of the boats they had been using for fishing, and that many of them were moving into the interior to farm there.

Each of them said they thought the sailors in the boat were Confederates enforcing the conscript laws, and that was the reason for their flight. This sentence was the one constant detail in their stories. Pointing out the fact that the sailors wore Federal Navy uniforms and were flying an American flag brought no reply from the now-sullen suspects. Moore turned to Wake and said with an expectant air, "Well, what do we do with 'em, sir? Right off to Key West for the Fort Taylor cells?"

When Wake heard the phrase "Fort Taylor cells," the thought of Hardin and Useppa came into his mind. Instantly what was missing in the story of the prisoners came to him. Useppa! None of them had mentioned the island. Everyone on the coast knew there were refugees there. But these men didn't even mention the island where they could have been safe—or any other island in the area where refugees had set up camps. They had not stopped at Useppa even though they would have had to go close by on their way to York Island, where they were captured. Wake now realized that there was even more to the story than he suspected. He looked at Moore and managed to confuse the stalwart by ordering, "Moore, secure these prisoners and put two aboard the sloop and two on your boat. We will take them to Useppa Island immediately. Now, let's look at the flatboat."

The professed refugees were tied up with line and put aboard the two vessels while Wake and Moore examined the flatboat. It was a common type on the rivers of the coast that usually carried around a half a ton of goods and bales, with a crew of two or three, and propelled by poles and sweep oars. This one had no cargo and no items belonging to the men just seized. In fact, there was nothing on it. There was no way it could have gone to sea and made it to Key West. Wake wondered where the real destination might have been.

"Woulda gotten a bit hungry by tomorrow, I'd bet," offered Moore, who was starting to warm to the idea of finding out more about their prisoners.

"They tossed over their belongings at some point. I am curious about how long they have been refugees. I wonder if these men are some of those who go back and forth as refugees and Rebels. We need to find out more on them. Burn the flatboat and we'll get going while there is a good breeze." With that directive, Wake walked out into the water to his dinghy and told Sommer to pull for the ship.

On the sail back up the long sound between Pine Island and Captiva Island, the two vessels passed the open passage to the Gulf at Captiva Pass. As they sailed fast on the sea breeze up the inside passage through the islands, Durlon informed Wake that he saw the *Gem of the Sea* offshore of the pass, heading for Boca Grande. Wake nodded at the news, knowing that the information they'd hear from the senior ship would probably not be good. He and Durlon looked at each other and both men quietly sighed. Time would tell on that issue.

It was nightfall when they arrived off Useppa Island anchorage. Wake was rowed into the dock as the two vessels moored together at anchor off the beach. Cornell met him at the beach and inquired as to the nature of the visit. His manner was polite, but Wake noted an air of impatience about the man.

Wake explained about the capture of the men and that they said they were refugees. He described them and told Cornell their names. Cornell looked at Wake with a long gaze, saying nothing. Then he said that he believed that they were probably lying, and that he and some of the other island men would go and look at them to see if they could recognize them.

Accordingly, about half an hour later a dory put off from the beach and came alongside the sloop. Wake met Cornell and two other men from the island on deck when they climbed aboard.

The suspected Rebs were brought in front of them on the main deck and put in a row. There was no interaction between the islanders and the prisoners, but Wake sensed fear building in the captured men. When they were led away, Cornell spoke to Wake. "Captain Wake, you were right about them being Rebels. The boy we don't know, but we recognize the others. They ran cattle for the Rebel regime in the interior at Fort Meade."

Cornell continued, "Jones is really named Hartford and was in the militia at Tampa. He's in charge of enforcing conscription on this coast and is hated by most people in the area. Sort of a tax collector too. Throws his weight around with the simple folk up in those parts. Big man in his own mind.

"Huntington was with the Confederate Army and wounded awhile ago. We ran into him in Tampa telling all about his exploits with Lee up in Virginia, and that was a year ago. Last we heard, he had got some manner of waiver from regular army duty and was running cattle north into Georgia to the army. Occasionally he came down here looking for draft dodgers avoiding the Rebel conscription. Probably helping out Jones in that.

"That man Nelson has been 'sesesh' since it all started. He was one of the ones who was workin' the blockade runners out of Peace River. Surprised ya didn't see 'im durin' your fight. Musta got away." This last was accompanied by nods from the other two islanders, one of whom related that he had heard Nelson sailed to Key West periodically to make contact with the "sesesh" people there.

Cornell concluded, "The boy is not from Punta Gorda. There are only a few people there, and he is not from one of their families or James here," nodding in the direction of an older islander, "would have known him. He must be a new one that's come into the area. They're all liars and sesesh Rebels, Wake. Get 'em out of here, if you would please."

"Thank you for your help, gentlemen. We suspected that they were not what they were alleging to be. They will be sent to Key West as prisoners. I appreciate your assistance. If they were not heading to Key West on that little flatboat, I wonder where they *were* going in it?"

Cornell replied for the islanders, "Most likely Fort Myers or Punta Rassa. Hook up with the cattle and blockade runnin' people there. Maybe get a ride somewhere from there."

"Well, thank you again, gentlemen. When we can, we shall certainly check those areas again for Rebel craft. Let me know if there is anything I can do for you. Supplies may be here soon from Key West, and we can share some with Useppa."

Wake's last statement was met with indifference by the islanders, and they turned to get into their boat with no further word. As Cornell got into his position at the stern of the dory, he looked up at Wake and remarked, "I expect that we will have some word from Key West regarding recent events and our requests. One of our men spotted the *Gem of the Sea* coming to anchor at Boca Grande about an hour ago." His eyes surveyed Wake.

Wake, impressed one more time by the quiet but effective leader of the islanders and how much he knew, shrugged his shoulders and replied that he was sure that there would be some update on the various matters of importance in which they were interested. Wake bade the men goodbye and turned to Moore, who was standing with Durlon, watching and listening to the entire episode.

"Moore, get the prisoners into your boat and take them to Boca Grande right away. Give Lieutenant Baxter my respects and advise him that *Rosalie* will be over to him in the morning. You may give a verbal report of the events of this day. I will give him a written report. You did very well today, Moore."

Moore, usually reserved around officers, allowed himself a grin and replied that he would include in his report the fact that Wake had been smart enough to think of Useppa Island and have the men there look at the prisoners. He shook hands with Wake as he went aboard his boat, an unheard-of gesture for the man, and offered, "Good workin' with ya, sir. Hope to again. "

For the first time since the evening of the nightmare actions of Hardin, Wake felt positive about something. He felt that he had accomplished something tangible, that he had gotten some solid intelligence of the enemy, and that another veteran seaman had recognized his small victory. Something had gone right. He allowed himself a brief smile.

But as he lay on his bunk later that night after writing out his report of the actions of the day, he wondered what information Baxter would have for him from Key West. Trial. Embarrassment. Facing the Admiral and Commander Johnson about how he had undermined the grand plan to form offensive refugee army units by alienating those very people he was supposed to encourage. He cringed as he thought of how the news of Hardin's crime would have been received by both the navy and the army commanders in Key West. Admiral Barkley and General Woodbury had together put the plan forward in a demonstration of joint resolve.

And what of the promised army reinforcements and planned offensive action on this coast? He had stayed in the islands, with the boat from the *Gem of the Sea,* to be ready for their arrival. But days had come and gone and there was no ship carrying the soldiers and munitions needed. Wake knew by now the delicate state of affairs among many of the refugee camps and settlements along the coast. He had met men who were Rebels one day and loyal refugees the next. He had even seen the opposite happen, where refugees who had fled the Confederate regime on the mainland had returned when they could not make it work out in the islands. Some said that those people were Rebel spies from the beginning, sent to spy on the naval and refugee activities along the coast. But Wake knew that sometimes old enemies and failed crops or fishing adventures left the refugees no choice but to go back to the place and work that they knew. Like so many things in this awful war, there were no simple explanations. He hoped the soldiers and supplies would come soon, for it looked like Cornell could not keep his people together much longer, and Wake was wary of making any more promises about the future.

Wake felt that he was really onto something with the men captured at York Island. He just did not know what. But he did know that somehow, with or without reinforcements, he was going to have to explore that area in more detail, to try to uncover the answer to the riddle of why some relatively important men of the Rebel regime in this coast were in such a desolate area. Who were they meeting? For what purpose?

The gentle night at anchor did not allay his fears and help him sleep. Instead, the lack of any wind or waves, to make a distraction of noise or motion, allowed his mind to concentrate on his multifaceted predicament. Wake was finding his dilemma becoming more complicated by the day, and worse yet, he didn't know what to do about it since he was at the mercy of other factors that influenced his mission and his life. As he lay below on his bunk in his tiny box of a cabin, his mind floated images of Linda and he realized that his desire to be with her was increasing to an almost desperate need. She was his mental escape from the squalid life and hopeless assignment in which he found himself.

By noon the next day Useppa Island was behind them and the *Rosalie* was once again moored alongside her big sister, the *Gem of the Sea*. Baxter had a pensive look on his face as he led Wake aft to his cabin.

After the preliminary politeness, during which Wake could barely restrain himself from blurting out the burning question in his mind, Baxter came to the point.

"Peter, concerning Hardin. He never made it to Fort Taylor. He acted the part of a rabid dog the whole way to Key West. I thought it just a role for his trial, but then I found out it was real. As we were moving up the channel to the naval anchorage, he was released from the deck eyebolt to get him washed up before we turned him over to the army provost guard. Right then, like he had been waiting for the moment, still in his manacles and chain, he pushed his guard away and ran screaming like a banshee to the side by the stowed anchor and jumped overboard. By the time we got stopped and turned around he was down on the bottom in four fathoms. Never found him.

"None of the crew had any remorse, 'cause by that time they had had enough of his wild ravings and such. During the trip down the coast he was yelling and having such seizures that I have never seen. Like something inside him was giving him a fever and eating his guts and brain, making him twist and scream and beg. My carpenter's mate wondered if he'd had the 'syph' and it had touched his brain. You know how they go when they have *that* little gift. . . ."

Wake sat there stunned. Hardin was dead. Suicide by drowning. A raving sick maniac. The transformation of the man that night on the beach at Useppa Island had been so complete and shocking that Wake had wondered if he had really understood what it was he was seeing. Perhaps, he had thought at the time, he was misunderstanding Hardin and that his behavior had some explanation. Horrible, but somehow explainable. The thought of syphilis had entered his mind, but until now he had heard no one else offer it.

Baxter went further. "So when I finally got to the anchorage and went ashore to explain this all to the admiral, Commander Johnson said that he had heard something about Hardin that was a little odd.

"Johnson calls right away for the squadron surgeon, same one that worked on your head wound if I remember rightly, Morse is his name, and asks him about Hardin while I'm standing there. This Morse says that yes, Hardin was the one who went to a Negro healer woman on the outside of town, where those Bahamian people are, to treat him for an indelicate social disease. Never reported it to the naval surgeons, 'cause they would've put him on report. Had one of those old women treat him, God knows how, for his disease. Surgeon heard about those goings on with the sailors from the scuttlebutt and looked into it. Told the old lady to stay away from his sailors, tend to her own people."

Wake alerted to the fact that Johnson had heard of Hardin

from the surgeon. As nonchalantly as he could, he inquired, "When did Johnson know about this? Did he say?"

"Before you sailed, Peter. Don't know why he or the surgeon didn't tell you. Anyway, the admiral, who was also standing there for all of this, accepted my reports on the actions of Hardin and told me that it was over, thank God."

As Wake was digesting all of this information, Baxter excitedly proceeded. "Forget Hardin. I've news of the war that's important. Those orders you passed on to me are finally coming true. The steamer *Honduras* is coming up coast with a detachment of the Forty-seventh Pennsylvania from Fort Taylor. Should be here tomorrow. They are to go to Useppa Island and train those islanders to be soldiers. Going to form a new army regiment from the refugees around here and in Key West. That should be interesting! Both the admiral and the general at the fort are in on this. Seems a big push is in the wind. So get ready."

Without realizing it, Wake began to touch his scar, tracing the rough outline of the manifestation of his last encounter with Rebel bullets. Baxter, seeing this, joked that Wake had used up one chance and had better be more careful in the future.

"And I hope you have gotten the islanders around here back on our side, because Admiral Barkley still wanted *you* to be the liaison with the army. You are to handle any boat transportation in the islands that they need inshore here at this coast. He told me that it was a great opportunity for a young man. I am to give you any men or boats you need, and gun support if I can reach the location with my draft."

Wake just sat there and finally said, "Aye aye, sir," to this unforeseen confirmation of Admiral Barkley's support in spite of the Hardin affair. He took a hurried gulp of the water Baxter had given him and started to stand. "By your leave, sir. I should get back to *Rosalie* and sail to Useppa. The wind will serve at the present. I need to meet with those men again before the army troops arrive. Thank you for your hospitality and the intelligence from Key West." Baxter stood up, signifying the personal chat was over.

"Mr. Wake, one other thing. Commander Johnson sent out with us a replacement for Hardin. This one I know. Bit of a drunk and a problem. Name is Sean Rork, an Irishman from New York. Been in for about five years. I think he was merchant marine before on an Atlantic packet. He's been transferred from the *Dale*. Be careful."

"Personally sent by the commander, you say, sir?"

Baxter nodded and shrugged his shoulders slightly as he led them both up to the main deck, where Wake took his leave. When he got to the deck of his own ship, he was greeted by Durlon, who told him the new bosun was at the stern waiting to report into him, having crossed over from the *Gem of the Sea*.

The man Wake fixed his eyes on bore a superficial resemblance to Hardin. Both were stocky and ruddy-faced. Both were about mid-thirties. Both were keenly aware of their surroundings, as evidenced by the way Rork watched the men at work transferring supplies between the ships. But there was something about Rork that was different from Hardin. Wake couldn't put his finger on it yet, but he hoped that the man would turn out well. He could surely use someone he could trust completely. That would be a relationship he had never had with Hardin, who from the beginning had shown his disgust toward Wake in subtle yet real ways that were just short of naval insubordination. At any rate, the man could hardly be worse than Hardin.

As Wake approached the new bosun he saw the man stiffen and knuckle his salute. "Sean Rork, bosun's mate, reportin' in, sir," came the brogued voice. His face assumed the neutral aspect of the veteran seaman when addressing an officer, but his eyes contained a spark of life that Hardin's had not. I will try to salvage this man, thought Wake, as he bade the bosun below to his cabin for a chat.

Once in the hot cabin, they seated themselves on the bunk and the small sea chest. Wake began by asking Rork to relate his sea service. The man had started out as a boy seaman in Wexford, Ireland, on an Irish Sea packet boat from Dublin and Belfast to

Liverpool. That was followed by service aboard an Atlantic packet ship between New York and Liverpool. In the late '50s, he had joined the navy in order to become an American citizen, serving in the Mediterranean Squadron just before this war had broken out. Rising quickly to petty officer rank in the rapidly expanding navy, Rork had become a bosun of a naval schooner off South Carolina, but had then had a problem with a fight ashore at Port Royal with some soldiers who had "demeaned" him.

Rork had been transferred to the *Dale* in Key West and had sat on that ship in the harbor rotting away for a year. He said that he had hated it and was glad to get to sea on "a real sailin' boat that fights them Rebs ashore an' afloat," adding that he had had some trouble ashore in Key West with the "impolite-mannered folk" in one of the taverns. His brogue thickened a bit when he spoke of his troubles ashore, but he spoke without malice.

Wake thanked him for his recital and told Rork about Hardin, which resulted in an understanding nod from the bosun. He fixed his eyes on Rork and said quietly and seriously that he would tolerate no conduct that would bring disrepute upon the ship or himself. After Rork had agreed, Wake told a bit of his own history. They had been talking half an hour when Durlon called down and said the ship was loaded and stowed and ready to get under sail.

Wake and Rork went up the ladder to the deck just as Durlon gave the orders for casting off from the larger ship and setting the large mainsail. As he watched Rork get involved with Durlon in the evolutions for making sail, Wake thought that maybe, just maybe, Rork might work out. As with everything else, time would tell.

The wind served well for the sail to Useppa Island, and they made their arrival in only three hours. Rounding up into the westerly wind, *Rosalie* shook her sails down and the hook slid into the jade-colored anchorage in the lee of the large hill along the beach settlement. Sommer had the dinghy ready by the time Wake had come back up from below with the mail for the island from Key West. As he was rowed ashore, Wake spotted Cornell watching him from the stand of trees by the hut that served as his house. He noticed that the island leader did not come down to the dock to greet him but instead waited for Wake to come into the shade beneath the trees.

After politely greeting Cornell and handing over the twined stack of envelopes, Wake explained that he had information on the man Hardin. Cornell bade him to wait while he went into his home and gave his wife the mail to distribute, which she then proceeded to accomplish by a shout that seemed loud enough to reach all over the island. When the ensuing response from the islanders had calmed a bit, Cornell returned to the spot under the trees and asked what it was that Wake had to say about Hardin. Cornell projected impatience as well as resignation in dealing with an unpleasant subject from a man he would rather not deal with. Wake thought again how the demeanor of the islanders had changed so drastically after Hardin's crime, and how hard it would be to get their support again for mutual gain in the war against the Rebels.

As Wake delivered the facts surrounding the end of Hardin and the elimination of the problem of a trial, he could see Cornell nodding his head in approval at the outcome of the nightmare that had occurred on this very beach only a few feet away. Cornell said they should tell the victim's father right away. Wake agreed but first told him about the unit of the Forty-seventh Pennsylvania Infantry that was due to arrive the next day. Cornell left to tell the girl's father of Hardin's end and to call an immediate meeting of all the islanders to give them the news of the army's impending appearance on their island.

As he stood by Cornell at the islanders' gathering half an hour later, Wake was encouraged to see some smiles among the group. The men were standing taller and more confident, and the women seemed more animated than the last time he had seen them. Action was finally giving some meaning to their lives, Wake decided, as he also wondered which of the people standing there would be killed or wounded in the months to come.

Shaking off that morbid thought, he moved forward to speak when Cornell had finished. The crowd of refugees grew quiet as he began. "I want to say again how very sorry I and all of my crew are about what happened here. That man is dead and gone and will never pose a threat to anyone again. Please do not judge my men by what he did. They are good men, fighting a war far from their homes in a place foreign to them. We will help you all that we can and will help the soldiers all we can. All we ask is that you not judge us by the actions of that man and let us help you in the fight against the Rebels. All of us admire your loyalty to this country and our flag."

Silence greeted his ending, and Wake wondered if he had somehow misstated something. He looked into the eyes of the men nearest him and saw no hated or mistrust, however, just a grim acknowledgment of a job to be done and an acceptance of him as a partner in the effort. Several people were turning away to return to their activities when the father of Hardin's victim came up to Wake and shook his hand, quietly announcing, "As far as I am thinkin', that's over now. It twarn't your fault, and we all appreciate your help."

"Thank you, sir," Wake said, his heart and mind racing with relief, as a couple more men came up to him and shook his hand, most saying nothing but looking him in the eye and nodding their heads almost imperceptibly.

Wake felt a strong respect and appreciation for these people who had been through so much and who still had the grace to forgive in such a quiet and meaningful manner. He and Cornell walked back to the dock together without speaking, relief filling Wake's mind. When they had reached Sommer at the dinghy, Cornell put out his hand and told Wake that he thought "events might transpire more smoothly now."

As the young captain climbed up the side to the deck of his sloop, he saw the crew looking over to the island and followed their gaze. On the beach were several islanders waving to them, and they could hear some light-hearted voices from the island drift over the water. The sailors grinned as they waved back.

How strange, thought Wake, that the death of a crazed man and the probable impending death of many good men should bring a sense of joy back to people who had known little of it ever since this war had so changed their lives. Perhaps it was the influence of this tropical island, its hot and humid atmosphere pervading and distorting every sense. Perhaps it wasn't joy at all, thought Wake as he gazed out over the darkening water to the community by the beach, but a silent and steady envelopment of them all into a sense of complacent delusion.

Wake leaned his arm against the boom just above his head and shuddered as a chill went down his spine. He feared this island of refuge would soon be a field of war.

Revenge from Useppa

It was midmorning when Wake, writing in his cabin, heard the distant conch shell sound from Palmetto Island to the west. It was answered a moment later by a similar sound from Useppa Island and followed by another from Patricio Island. Rork put his head down the hatchway and informed his captain that the islanders had called over to the sloop that they had sighted the steamer carrying the soldiers coming along the coast and that she was probably nearing Boca Grande and the *Gem of the Sea*. A boat was approaching from the beach with Cornell in the bow. Wake thanked Rork for his report and thought about how the man was integrating into the crew. So far, Rork had been no problem. Indeed, he had been a generally positive influence on the behavior of the crew.

Wake ascended from his cabin and stood by the main shrouds to receive the delegation from the island. Cornell stepped up to the deck of the sloop without hesitation and turned to Wake in a formal, businesslike manner that was rare for the man.

"Captain Wake, the island leaders would like the honor of your presence tonight for dinner to complement the presence of the officers from the steamer and the army. Would you so honor us? I believe there will be much to speak of in preparation for our regiment's near future."

Wake, taken aback by the mention of the new refugee militia unit with the rather grandiose title of regiment, stammered, "Yes, of course, sir. It is I who will be honored."

"Excellent then. We shall expect you at six o'clock. We will be meeting with the army officers at that time on the island and would like your perspective included in the discussion. Dinner will follow."

Cornell's demeanor was positively commanding, thought Wake with a twinge of humor. Then he wondered how in the world the island leader could know when to expect the army officers on a ship that hadn't arrived at the island yet. The question must have formed on his face, for Cornell softened his tone and said, "We spoke with the ship when she was off Captiva Island. She'll be here by midafternoon. She's at Boca Grande now with Lieutenant Baxter."

For the hundredth time Wake marveled at the organization of the islanders and said so to Cornell, who smiled his response and handed over a filled burlap bag that another man had slung up to him from the dory.

"Here, this is for your crew. Some fresh fish caught this morning and already cut for your men to cook. We will also be sending some fruit over in a bit."

After Rork took the bag of fish and the crewmen standing close by expressed their thanks, Wake shook Cornell's hand and thanked him for the kindness. After Cornell left, Wake found himself wondering just who was in command of whom—appreciating the older man's quiet way of leadership that left room for another's pride. Wake figured Cornell would probably do well as a militia leader, and God help the Rebs if this group of refugees-turned-soldiers should fall on them with the passion of two years of wrongs to right.

The afternoon had a nice breeze and was discernibly cooler

than the day before, a sign that the oppressively hot rainy season was giving way to the windier and cooler dry season. The barometer supported this general optimism. And so, when the steamer *Honduras* rounded the point of land on Patricio Island and came straight for the anchorage where *Rosalie* sat comfortably pulling at her anchor, a scene from paradise greeted the sailors and soldiers aboard her. Before the steamer even let go her anchor, the dories of the islanders were clustered around her. The islanders came, as they had for Wake many weeks earlier, from all the islands close by with gestures of welcome.

The steamer's crew and passengers lined the railings, exchanging with the islanders news of the world as wells as pocket knives and tools and utensils—for fish and fruits from the islanders. Rork stood on the deck of the small sloop, a third the length of the steamer, and shook his head in bemusement at the scene unfolding two hundred feet away. Wake walked over to him by the samson post on the foredeck.

"It would seem our allies have arrived, Rork. The islanders appear pleased with them."

"Aye, that they have done, sir. And the islanders are actin' just like islanders the world over too. Somethin' new is always excitin' for them, ye know. Reminds me of when I saw me first Yankee ship in Wexford, those many years ago in me soft youth in Eire. Could not a stayed away from that strange ship, with her strange crew of men from the barbarous lands of the New World. 'Twas then that I made me mind to go to America. And so here I am with ye now, Captain," replied a grinning Rork as he turned full toward Wake.

"Well, we'll see if the islanders are as happy in six months, Rork. At least the weather has been kind today. For the work we're bound to do, a little cooler weather will be appreciated, especially by those Pennsylvania soldiers on the *Honduras* there."

Wake was referring to the dozen men in the blue wool of the army, standing at the railing and looking around at the jungle islands that were soon to be their home. It was a very far cry from

133

the hills of Pennsylvania, and the *Rosalie*'s sailors could see them pointing at Useppa Island and gesturing. Wake called away his dinghy and had Sommer row him over to the steamer, which was now completing her anchoring work and blowing off her steam.

On arriving at the side of the ship and climbing up to the main deck, Wake was greeted by the mate of this civilian steamer with a civilian crew chartered to the army for supply and passenger work on the coast. The difference between the crew of the large steamer and that of his small sloop was considerable. As the mate led him aft along the deck toward the captain's quarters, Wake remembered his days as a merchant marine mate as he surveyed the generally sloppy work done by the steamer's crew. He realized that his small crew was much more efficient and disciplined than this mob of derelicts. His impression surprised him since just a year before he had been one of this type of seamen and had despised the "puppetry" of naval seamen just as much as he imagined these men in front of him did right now.

An overweight and sweaty man of about fifty, wearing a faded brown jacket and stained grayish duck trousers, greeted him as he entered the captain's cabin. Standing next to Captain Sloan was an army lieutenant, younger than Wake, thin, pale and obviously nervous. The steamer captain made the introductions. "Lieutenant Vanding, this is Master Peter Wake, captain of the sloop *Rosalie*, anchored next to us. Master Wake knows these waters and coastline. I think you would be well served to use his knowledge and assistance. Master Wake, Lieutenant Arthur Vanding of the Forty-seventh Pennsylvania Volunteer Infantry Regiment, currently occupying Key West."

"My pleasure, Lieutenant. Welcome to this coast. Everyone has been looking forward to your force arriving and starting the offensive against the Rebels on the mainland. How many did you bring?"

Vanding stared at Wake without speaking, as Sloan filled the silence with barely concealed sarcasm. "Why, Captain Wake, the army has sent you all of twelve men with the good lieutenant here. Appears the grand invasion will be off to a grand start!"

134

Vanding glared at Sloan. "Captain, I have brought a cadre of regulars and enough equipment to supply one hundred men. More equipment and men will follow. I also have ten volunteers from among the Union civilian men at Key West. How many men do the volunteers have at this place?"

Wake looked at both men. Sloan he had met before in Key West and had not liked any better there. Vanding was an unknown. So far, the promised army reinforcement was not impressive. Wake hoped that the numbers of the "regiment" would increase once it got started and word went out among the refugees along the coast.

"Lieutenant, there are about thirty refugee men in these islands who are prepared to fight for our country. You evidently met some of them earlier today. We are expected on the island at six o'clock for a discussion of the future operations here. I will see you then."

Wake then turned to Sloan and said that he would have some of his crew assist with unloading the equipage to the island. Wake exited along the main deck amidst a clanging racket coming up from below decks and walked around the large, ungainly paddle boxes dominating both sides amidship. He was glad not to be on this ugly contraption of a vessel. With the unseamanlike hull lines, soot-grimed decks, surly crew, greasy smell, and generally poor condition, she was the very opposite of his pretty little sloop. To hell with her ten knots in no wind, he thought as Sommer pulled him across the rippled jade water to his own ship. As Wake settled back down into his small but private domain, writing his report on the chart table, he couldn't help worrying about the way this expedition was starting and about how the islanders might greet the paltry reinforcements sent to them.

At six o'clock Wake stood under the gumbo limbo trees on the beach and waited for the contingent from the steamer to arrive. Cornell stood by him, waiting with obvious anticipation for the meeting to get under way. Several other islanders had gathered a short distance away, apparently the secondary leaders of the "regiment" that would be formed, while others readied the table for the impending dinner.

An island dory eventually brought Vanding and Sloan to the rickety dock, from which they walked down the beach to the gathering and the introductions that Wake made all around.

The islanders were polite and hospitable, but Wake could see the surprise on their faces that there was only a lieutenant in charge of the army forces that had been sent to them. Cornell finally asked the question that Wake had dreaded. "Lieutenant Vanding, exactly how many men did you bring on the steamer to reinforce us and fight on the mainland?"

The answer was not what the refugees had expected, and Vanding's hesitant delivery did not help matters much either. Sloan said nothing, just stood there grinning at the pitiful joke that he saw unfolding before him. Wake couldn't stand it any longer and, against his better judgment, filled the vacuum of leadership. "Well, it's a beginning. As more Union men of the coast come to the colors, the regiment will grow. The lieutenant's men will provide a good training for the men of your regiment, Mr. Cornell."

Cornell, sensing Wake's efforts to help and Vanding's inept-ness, agreed with Wake and steered the small group up the path to the dinner tables on the hilltop. Cornell and Wake walked together up the path in silence until the top, when Cornell said to his young friend, "We will make it work, Captain Wake. You are right. It is a beginning and more than we've had."

The next day, as the sun rose over the Barras and Pine Islands to the east, Wake awoke to the sounds of men on the beach speaking crisply and condescendingly. Disoriented at first, Wake slowly realized that they were the men of the Forty-seventh Pennsylvania getting an early start at organizing the island volun-teers into a militia unit. Climbing up onto the main deck, he saw the crew of the sloop also stirring and looking to the west at the tragicomic scene on the beach.

There, lined up in a more or less orderly fashion, were the

revelers of the night before. Where just eight hours earlier men in tattered island clothing had been arm in arm with the neatly uniformed sergeant and lieutenant of the "famous Forty-seventh," singing songs and swilling jugs of quasi-rum and palm wine, there now stood the same soldiers in front of the same islanders, the latter a badly hung-over group of volunteers. It appeared that the sergeant and lieutenant had had some experience in overcoming alcoholic consequences, for they looked as if they had not even been at the party the night before. Wake smiled as he thought of how Key West had probably provided a lot of that type of experience for the men of the Forty-seventh. Indeed, the lieutenant on the beach this morning was not the nervous little Vanding of the meeting on the *Honduras.* The lieutenant's orders were clear and commanding, echoed each time by the sergeant. The young officer came alive on the drill field, leaving his lackluster personality behind. Wake wondered how that officer would behave if and when he heard bullets filling the air around him.

Wake noticed that the men of his crew were not laughing at the proceedings on the beach. Instead, they were quietly discussing the training evolutions and pointing out which of the volunteers was doing well. Wake saw that Rork was leading this discussion. It somehow made him feel more confident to know that his men were professionally evaluating the militiamen rather than just mocking them. One sign of veterans, he thought, is not making fun of anyone they may have to depend on in the near future.

Later in the day the volunteers, organized now into a ranger company, began their shooting drill. Almost all of them knew how to shoot, but the sergeant taught them the standard army loading drill. He then marched them down the beach a safe distance where they could fire at buoys floating off the island away from any vessels or other inhabited places. This the crew of the *Rosalie* watched very intently, with Rork providing commentary and Durlon setting up small wagers on the results. Wake watched the men on the beach going through the drill and firing volleys at the buoys and realized that his men had only been drilled at firing individually, not as a group. But they had held their own at the battle up the river, and Wake decided that he didn't have to drill them the army way.

While the men of the volunteers were going through their paces, the children and many of the women watched from atop the hills of the island. That the militiamen were conscious of their families watching them was obvious, as they would chance the wrath of the sergeant and glance smilingly over at their loved ones on the hill after they had done something particularly impressive. Wake, occasionally watching throughout the day from the deck of the sloop, felt a pang of regret that these men would someday soon have to face something far worse than the sergeant's words. He hoped that they would be far better prepared in that event than they looked at this point.

That night he went ashore and met with Vanding and Cornell at the latter's home, a hut made of some ship's woodwork, tree limbs, and palm thatch. As they sat on crude stools in the "parlor" room and discussed the day's events over a jug of palm wine, Cornell stopped his small talk suddenly. He looked at Vanding, then at Wake, and carefully told them that his men were ready. They were ready now to strike at the enemy they had feared and fled from for the last two years. It was time. He welcomed the Forty-seventh to come along with them, but the Rangers were going to attack the Rebels with or without the Forty-seventh.

There was no doubting the sincerity of Cornell's statement. Wake knew that the man meant what he said, and even Vanding sensed the intense force of his words. Vanding sat there and nodded slowly as Wake said to Cornell, "We are with you, sir. Any day there will be more reinforcements from Key West and we can go forward with an attack."

Cornell smiled and intoned, almost like a preacher, "Gentlemen, as the elected captain of this ranger company, I am telling you that we are going forward, alone if necessary, in one week against the Rebels on the mainland. The army and the navy are most welcome to come along, but this is our time, our duty. I know you both will understand."

"But we have no final orders yet, sir," stammered Vanding. He looked toward Wake for assistance with this militia leader who was not willing to go slowly and carefully. However, Wake understood Cornell and the refugees by now and replied to Cornell, "You will have my assistance, sir. My men and I are with you." Then, grinning, he turned to the young army lieutenant. "Mr. Vanding, I think your men can manage to keep up with the Rangers on the mainland. I propose a toast to the success of the Florida Rangers!"

All three men raised their coconut-shell cups of palm wine and drank. Vanding, still nervous about acting without orders, went along with the other two and put on a brave show of confidence, which started Cornell and Wake laughing. By the time Mrs. Cornell had come back into the room, all three men were laughing over the ironic improbability of their situation. There they were—a sailor, a refugee, and a soldier on a jungle island grandly sipping palm wine out of coconut cups and toasting to the imminent defeat of the enemy by a band of ragged civilian refugees. The tension of the preceding weeks disappeared in the camaraderie and preposterousness of the moment.

The palm wine jug managed to last several hours into the night, and by the time Wake was walked back to the beach where Sommer lay sleeping in the dinghy, the three men had become well aware of each other's histories. For the first time in a long time, Wake felt positive about the future.

Two days later the *Honduras* left to go further up the coast to Tampa, leaving the Forty-seventh's soldiers on the island. Wake had taken his sloop each day through the islands of the area, look-ing for Rebels and/or information on their whereabouts. At sun-set on the second day, with *Rosalie* anchored off Useppa, Rork called out that a steamer was coming round an adjacent island. It was the tug *Honeysuckle*, come up from Key West. As the ship came closer, Wake could see her decks crowded with blue coats.

Half an hour later he was on board the anchored steam tug and speaking with a volunteer lieutenant from the Florida

Rangers company at Key West. General Woodbury at Key West had sent another twenty refugee militia men who had volunteered to serve the Union. These men, assembled from up and down the Florida Keys, were to be under the command of Captain Cornell and to commence operations as soon as possible. Vanding and the regulars of the Forty-seventh would be under Cornell's direction also. Wake thanked the lieutenant and hastened ashore to give the good news to his compatriots.

When Cornell and Vanding received the information, gone was the palm wine laughter. Cornell looked thoughtfully at Vanding, who in turn swallowed hard and said, "So now we can go. The Forty-seventh Pennsylvania will be honored to serve you, sir."

Later that night the militia lieutenant from the tug, a very young man named Thompkins, who was from St. Augustine, came ashore and talked with the other three officers. A plan was suggested by Cornell and refined by Wake, with Thompkins and Vandings listening. The plan was to go up through the Charlotte Harbor area, then land a force of men at the mouth of the Myakka River. From there they would reconnoiter to the northeast and try to find out the disposition of the Confederate militia forces and the cattle herds that were destined for the main Rebel armies in Tennessee. Once ashore, they would attempt to recruit Union loyalists to the regiment. They would embark on small boats from the *Gem of the Sea* and the surrounding islands, sailing through the night to get to Myakka. The gunboat would go with them and provide support for the beachhead the sailors would man until the soldiers returned to the boats. The mission would take at least three days once they landed.

Each man knew that the time had come. There was no turning back. Grimly, they discussed how to handle difficulties that might occur. Cornell, a veteran of the Seminole War, knew the worth of surprise and did not want to squander it. He reminded them that they needed to get each man in their units ready, for they would leave the next night. Wake returned to his ship to prepare a report on this impending action. *Honeysuckle*, due to leave the next day to go back to Key West, would take their plan back to the general and the admiral.

The next morning was one of hurrying, as the sloop sailed for the *Gem of the Sea,* lying off Lacosta Island. Wake went aboard and spoke with Captain Baxter. His recital of the plan of action met with Baxter's approval, after which, with no time for pleasantries, Wake and the *Rosalie* sailed back through the islands to Useppa with three of Baxter's small sailing boats to help transport the soldiers to the Myakka River.

By the time of their return in the late afternoon, the island had been transformed into a depot of sorts, with supplies and munitions piled on the beach and soldiers from the Rangers and the Forty-seventh milling about waiting for their vessels to arrive. Cornell was having a discussion with Vanding and Thompkins when Wake came up to them and advised that the boats were ready to be loaded. The officers turned their men to the task of wading out to the boats anchored in waist-deep water and heaving the supplies up into the waiting arms of the sailors, who then stowed them in such a fashion so as not to ruin the sailing trim of the vessels. Petty officers from the *Gem of the Sea,* who were commanding the boats, were also getting the armament ready for action. By sunset, all the gear was stowed aboard the three small boats and the *Rosalie.*

Wake suggested that all hands eat their evening meal and then sleep for an hour or so before sailing through the night northward to their destination. This suggestion proved to be practical for only the sailors, however, as the families ashore were emotional and long-winded with their goodbyes to the soldiers grouped on the beach. In the end, Cornell started embarking his men earlier than planned, just to get them away from the families, who were now starting to realize the seriousness of their final words to their loved ones.

A chorus of apprehension and anticipation came from the shore as more than fifty soldiers, both militia and regulars, said goodbye to the islanders. As the almost full moon rose in the east, the sloop and the smaller craft hoisted their sails and glided away from the island of Useppa in a gentle northwest breeze. The vessels were just barely lit from the moon, and the stars appeared everywhere in the convex ceiling of the clear night sky. After they had gotten about a mile from Useppa Island, it grew quiet on all four craft, with only the soft call of the lookouts and the leadsman on the *Rosalie* disturbing the thoughts of the men of the expedition.

Busy as he was with the navigation of the flotilla, Wake took time to think of these men he was delivering to possible death—proud men, both young and old, who were now about to see the face of war that the rest of the country had endured for the last two years. These were men who were as ready as they could be to do their duty. Cornell was on the sloop, standing aft by the stern and looking back toward the three cutters sailing astern. Wake heard the militia leader sigh and turn away from his view to face forward.

"Captain Wake, I want to thank you for all of your assistance on this matter. You and the navy have been our salvation these last few years. Now we get to have our revenge and stand for ourselves. I fear that it may go on for a long time, but at least we can help now, and not sit and wait for something to happen."

"Sir, we are here to help. Your refugees have been invaluable to the navy during the last years with their information on enemy movements and local knowledge of the coast. But I should not call them refugees any longer, I believe. No, sir, they are now militia and are fighters for the cause. They'll do well, sir. Don't you worry."

"Well, son, it's not a few renegade Seminoles we're going after this time. No, it's going to be tougher than that. I know many of them over there on the mainland personally. It's going to be damned tough." Cornell sighed again. "I'm going to lie down now for a while and try to get my people to do the same and stay out of your crew's way. Good night, sir."

Wake felt a chill go up his spine on hearing Cornell's remark about the people on the mainland. He remembered that the war on this coast was different for the refugee Rangers. Unlike the soldiers from the Forty-seventh Pennsylvania or the navy's sailors, the militia men knew many of their enemies here, knew their families and homes. Once again, Wake found himself thinking about the refugees, what they had gone through and what they would have to endure in the near future.

Dawn found them off the mouth of the Myakka River, carefully sounding their way up through the shallows of Charlotte Harbor. The cutters led the flotilla in under oars, the sloop slowly following under sail in an almost nonexistent morning land breeze. Every eye was focused on the shore as they got closer, looking for signs of movement in the mangrove jungle and straining to hear any shot that might be launched from the green walls of the river.

Cornell chose a sandy spit of land that protruded from the eastern shore as the landing site. The *Rosalie* anchored off the shore by about one hundred yards in a fathom of water, while the cutters were run into the shallows as far as they could be floated. The disembarkation of men and supplies evolved into a scene of laughing and yelling and confusion as the sailors and soldiers attempted to get the beachhead set up as quickly as possible.

Wake didn't like all of the noise and sensed that Cornell didn't either. A quiet and surreptitious landing it was not, in spite of the angry threats of the sergeants and petty officers. The larklike atmosphere was at odds with the reality of the situation, and it seemed forever before the beachhead was set up and secure.

Finally, in the heat of the midday sun, Cornell said goodbye to Wake on the beach. "Well, goodbye and good luck here. We will be back in three days. The password will be 'Barkley,' in honor of your admiral," Cornell said with a mischievous smile. "And we will be very sure to call it out as soon as we get close to your picket line. Please have the kindness to alert your sailors not to shoot us."

"We will do our best to shoot only the enemy. Or at least whoever we think is probably the enemy," replied Wake, with the tensions of the moment broken by the nervous humor of overstated politeness. "Good luck to you, sir," called out Wake to his friend as the column trudged off the beach and into the mangroves.

After the expedition had departed, the beachhead sailors, under the command of Bosun Moore from the *Gem of the Sea*, started to clear brush from the picket line they had formed. Piling up the brush and tree limbs to form crude breastworks, the sailors began the work of making a defensive position out of the depot on the beach. Moore was very serious in his endeavors, and so Wake left him alone and went back to the sloop to check their dispositions for fighting, should it come to that.

Rosalie, at Rork's suggestion, was anchored fore and aft with spring lines bent to the anchor rodes so that she could be rotated to bring her gun to bear at various locations. He explained to Wake that this was a trick he had learned from a discussion with a bosun in Key West who had served on the James River Squadron in Virginia. Durlon had gotten canister ammunition ready for the twelve-pounder and had a ready locker of pistols and muskets on deck. The crew spent the afternoon drilling in the loading and firing of the deck gun, as well as getting some sleep.

A position this close to the enemy would require half the crew to be awake, alert, and armed. Wake was concerned that the Rebels might try to board his ship in the night, especially after his victory over them on the Peace River, just a few miles away to the east. Wake was very uneasy with his role of providing static gunfire support for the beachhead. He was used to being able to move at will on the water, not being trussed up along the shore.

That night was cloudy, with some rain and a wind from the south. The signs told of a nor'wester coming the next day or so, the first of the winter season, and Wake was concerned about his powder and his men in the chilled, wet weather. Cold weather in December in Florida wasn't comparable to that he had seen in New England, but could still be miserable to a man exposed to the elements out on the deck. Tarpaulins were stretched over the main boom, ready to be cast off if necessary, in an effort to keep the men dry and therefore more alert. Periodic shouts of alarm from the sailors ashore hearing things moving around in the jungle just ahead of them would send the entire flotilla into battle quarters. Each time it took at least ten to fifteen minutes to calm everyone down and get them back to the watch on watch routine of half the crew at rest and the other half instantly ready to fight.

Just after midnight, a sailor on the beach fired at a buttonwood tree that he had been staring at for an hour and had just seen move. That ignited several other shots at the buttonwood tree from the startled and scared sailors on the beachhead. Wake was grateful that Durlon had not fired his gun too. Durlon had been about to fire when Moore called from the beach to say it was just a nervous sailor shooting at a tree and not an enemy attack. The loud guffaws from the vessels and the beachhead were a little too quick and jittery and showed that all hands were just as nervous as the poor unfortunate who had started the shooting.

Wake thought back to his meeting with the admiral. Barkley and Johnson had told him that they had confidence in his ability to use judgment about what to do in operations with the army. And here he was with a flotilla of four small vessels and twenty-five sailors defending a beachhead, waiting for fifty untried soldiers to return from a march into the midst of enemy territory— completely surrounded, without any communications, anchored close to a lee shore with a storm pending, and very vulnerable to attack. Wake started to think that this might be the very situation that he had been warned not to get into. Looking around in the gloomy night, he could see only the lanterns on *Rosalie* and a few lanterns on the beach. The enemy could be upon them before they knew it. He stayed up all night, sitting and waiting. . . .

Dawn came very slowly. Clouds kept the sun from lightening the area until two hours after sunrise. Moore sent a patrol of five sailors up the narrow path from the beach into the mangroves to see if they could find any sign of Rebels in the area. The others on the beach divided their time between standing guard duty and organizing the supplies piled there.

A lookout in the crosstrees of the sloop gazed around the horizon to see if any vessels were approaching from upriver or out on the wide expanse of Charlotte Harbor. When the land patrol came back, Wake sent eight men in one of the cutter boats upriver with the flood tide to check the shorelines for signs of Rebel activity.

By midafternoon Wake started to worry. No sign of the cutter had been seen or heard. As he was debating whether to send another cutter after the first, a bang was heard from the river bank on their side, downstream. Instantly a small geyser reached up from the water between the sloop and the beach. The lookout cried out that there was rifle smoke from the mangroves about a hundred yards down the shoreline. No orders had to be given, for the crew of the gunboat sloop and the sailors on the beach immediately went to their quarters for battle.

Durlon had the twelve-pounder slewed around in seconds. He and the rest of his small gun crew looked at Wake for permission to fire. But Wake decided to wait. He knew that he had to conserve ammunition in case they would need it later. The gunboat did not carry much and resupply was not near. He shook his head at Durlon and said, "Durlon, I know you want to blow him out of there, but we may need your little darling for more numerous targets if they rush the beach. I want to save her for when she can do the most good."

Rork nodded his head and added, "I agree, Captain. We do not have much ammunition for the gun and should spend it wisely. Like the liberty in New York Port on half pay, Durlon! Ye find the good places first and then spend your money!"

"Thank you, Rork. Couldn't have explained it better myself. But I do think that a musket shot in that direction might be in order. Durlon, could you attend to that, please. It might keep our little Rebel friend put off for a while. And with any luck you might even hit him!"

Durlon, laughing now, started to take wagers on the coming target practice as he rose to the challenge of getting a .58 caliber musket ball accurately into the area of the sharpshooter from a hundred yards. Wake was glad to have the diversion for the men and not to have to sit there and take sniper fire without firing back. Personally, he didn't think Durlon would hit anything, but he entered the betting as well, placing a penny on Durlon's skill and hoping for a cry of wounding from the Rebel in the mangroves. A penny was the most he would allow for wagering on the sloop, which was more than naval regulations would allow. Regulations from the Secretary of the Navy in Washington disapproved of any form of gambling at all. Wake reasoned, however, that the Secretary of the Navy was a very long way away and was not being shot at, and therefore that little rule could be dispensed with for the time being.

Durlon shot three times into the tangle of mangroves at different places along the shoreline. They saw no sound or movement afterward and Wake ended the contest and paid his penny to Rork, the main bettor against Durlon.

Wake ordered more men to watch that shoreline and all hands to stay as much under cover as possible. His thoughts were returning to the problem of the missing cutter when the lookout, now the most unwanted position because of its vulnerability, called down to say that he saw it coming downriver. As the sailors afloat and ashore stared upriver at the approaching cutter, a commotion could be seen among the men rowing the small boat. As they got closer, one of the cutter's men yelled that a sailor was snake bit and fever ridden.

Wake met the boat as it grounded ashore, and the unfortunate boy was pulled to the lone sail tent that was set up. The stricken sailor, named Fox, was bitten in the hand. He was convulsing, and his hand was swollen and turning red.

Wake could see two bite marks and heard Fox tell of how he had put his hand down to sit on the ground after they had gone ashore far upriver. Fox said that the snake was where he had planned to sit, and that it was dark brown and about five feet long. The mouth was a grayish white with large fangs that sank into his hand as he tried to get away. The boy was terrified and breathing heavily. Moore quickly told a sailor to get water and douse Fox's head to try to cool him off as well as divert his attention. Then Moore took his sheath knife and cut open the hand where the bite marks were. As he worked, he looked up at Wake.

"We've got to get the poison out, sir, quick like. The boy's hand'll rot if we don't get it out. Seen it before. Got to bleed it out. Lie still, son."

"Rork, get some men to help Moore hold Fox down." Wake wished he could do something to help Fox, who was now crying with the pain as his hand trembled out of control. "And, Rork, get something to give Fox. Is there any rum or whiskey?"

At this last comment, the attention of the men surrounding the boy turned to Rork, who replied, "A wee bit in the medical chest, sir. I'll get it now for the lad."

Then Wake heard a thud and turned to see Fitzhugh, coxswain of the cutter that had gone on the patrol, pulling his fist back after he had pounded it into the side of Fox's head. Moore looked up and said to the astonished officer, "Sir, the boy's in pain that even rum can't help. Fitz's punch took care of that. Boy can lay still now while we bleed him."

"Very well, Moore, if you say so," muttered Wake as he stood looking to see if Fitzhugh had enjoyed his hit. Seeing no joy in that weathered face, Wake turned and made his way back to the water's edge to be rowed out to the *Rosalie*. As he got in the dinghy, he called out in a level tone to Moore and Fitzhugh to come out to the sloop and give the patrol report after they were done with Fox.

Awhile later the three were squeezed into the captain's cabin.

"Well, Moore, your man can give his report now on the river patrol. Include why they went ashore and why they were late."

Moore, who had stayed at the beach camp during the patrol upriver, prompted his man and told him to be clear. Fitzhugh cleared his throat and said, "Well, sir, we started upriver and got about five mile with the flood tide. Saw a landing place on the starboard shore and went close aboard to see if they was any signs of Rebs there. Saw none standing around and decided to look at a camp we saw just inland by about fifty yards, sir. Looked fresh to me. Fire pit looked 'bout a day old or so. Had some stumps sittin' around the fire and some bones layin' round there too.

"Crew was tired and I knew they would be having to fight the tide some on the way back so I told the lads to lay down if they wanted. Young Fox there sat himself down and shot right back up again. Started screamin' 'bout snakes. That set the other lads to prancin' around, and I ordered the lot of 'em to the cutter. Then we got in and shoved off an' came back, but the tide was still aginst us. Had a hell of a row, shorthanded and all. Had Fox down, and another man holdin' him. Took a bit to get here. Sorry, sir, for Fox. Us Yankee boys don't know 'bout these damn Southland creatures. Goddamn this place. Don't know why anybody would want it. That snake serpent was right in the middle of a camp!"

Wake sighed and told Moore to write up Fitzhugh's report. He finished the meeting by saying, "Gentlemen, we cannot go wandering off into the jungle of this coast with green sailors. There's more than just snakes out there. You were lucky, Fitzhugh. Fox may lose his arm or his life, but you might have lost your whole crew. You were supposed to stay in the boat. If you had to go ashore, you should have been more careful." Wake turned to the coxswain. "Moore, try to keep Fox quiet tonight, but without hurting him any more. His screams will alert the Rebs and unnerve our boys."

He indicated that they were dismissed. After they were gone, Wake lay down on his crude bunk, thinking of the many ways for a man to die on this coast and hoping that no more examples would appear. Wake knew they would have to spend at least another night in this dreadful spot, as he prepared to go up on deck and present a confident appearance for his crew. He took a deep breath and sighed, then climbed up the ladder.

The afternoon was fading and the wind was definitely turning cooler and more northwesterly, more signs showing that winter had arrived. Wake looked around and saw nothing but the sailors, both afloat and ashore, eating their evening meal early.

Rork came up to him on the afterdeck and saluted.

"Boy was lucky, sir, that the snake bit him in the hand. Lose the hand, or lower arm maybe, but live through it. Heard that a sailor lad up by Tampa lost a leg, the rot was so bad."

"Thank you for that anecdote, Rork. Fox has just become an object lesson for the rest of the flotilla here. One they won't soon forget. But I expect the petty officers to lead, and not allow their people to become object lessons!"

"Aye aye, sir," replied an astonished Rork, who had never seen his captain raise his voice at anyone. "Sir, Fitzhugh ain't the brightest man I've seen. But he's not too bad neither. He's a bit shaken by it too. Tough place, this . . ."

Rork drifted off without finishing his sentence. When Wake turned to see why, his gaze followed Rork's to the shoreline in the gathering dusk. Downriver by quite a ways, there was substantial movement in the mangroves.

"Durlon, lay a musket round in that clump of tall trees over there," ordered Wake, as he pointed out the suspicious area to the gunner.

Bang! All hands strained to see the musket's results, though none appeared.

"That will do, Durlon. Thank you."

With a very studied attempt at nonchalance, Wake then said to Rork, "I believe that I have not eaten yet, and I am famished. Will you join me for supper?"

"Why, you do me an honor, sir. I would be pleased to share a meal with you," replied the smiling bosun.

The two men sat on the deck of the sloop and ate the salted beef junk that had been boiling in the cookpot set on the charcoal box just forward of the mast. As they ate, they discussed the probabilities of an attack that evening against the beach camp and the sloop. That they were being watched by Confederate pickets was obvious. What was unknown was what had happened to Cornell and his contingent and when the Rebels would attack the beachhead camp. Rork opined that the camp would not be attacked until Cornell's soldiers were returning, exhausted and not alert. Wake thought that there would be two attacks. First, one on the sailors to cut off retreat, then one on the soldiers inland to destroy this first attempt to push Union forces into the interior of this coast.

After the supper, Wake told Rork to get some sleep since from now on one of the two of them would be up and alert all night, watch on watch. Rork dutifully went below to cocoon himself in his swaying hammock. In these now-cool nights, the berthing area below decks was no longer hot and miserable. Rork was glad to get out of the rising wind with its cutting moisture.

Wake sat on the stern watching Moore on the beach arranging his night positions. All of *Rosalie*'s crew on watch were alert and under cover. Another night of waiting began. Four hours of peering into the darkness for any sign of the enemy took its toll on Wake and his men. Keeping them awake and alert was paramount, however, and no one was allowed to doze even for a moment.

Having been relieved at the end of his watch by Rork, Wake had been asleep for about an hour when he heard the first bang. Then he heard another and then a rattle of pops and bangs and voices yelling loudly about where and who. Wake jumped up on deck from his scuttle hatch. He saw Rork standing by the twelve-pounder, pointing at the beach and telling the men, "Slew her around ta there, laddies. There they are, lads. Gun the bastards down, now!"

The flame of the gun illuminated the night and the sound of the explosion enveloped them. Wake saw ragged-looking men with long guns jumping over the small brush defensive line the beachhead sailors had erected. The men were yelling and whooping at the top of their lungs, their gunfire smashing into the sailors, who were trying to form a line to fire a volley. No Reb uniforms were apparent, but none were needed, for everyone not in the blue of the navy was an enemy. The blindness caused by the gun flash and the noise of dozens of small arms going off in all directions on the beach caused confusion among the *Rosalie's* sailors. Fear of hitting their comrades in the melee on shore slowed the rate of musket fire from the sloop's sailors, as they tried to identify which of the forms in the chaos on the beach were the enemy.

Only Durlon and his gun crew were in rapid action, sponging out and loading the wadding, canister, and more wadding, as the gunner called out the cadence of the official navy gun drill. Like a machine, the gun crew worked through the drill until moments later when they were ready for another shot. Wake saw that Durlon was aiming at the mangrove jungle just in front of the beachhead sailors in an effort to miss the Union men and hit any Rebels who were reinforcing the attack.

Boom! Again the gun flew back on its slides as the mangrove treeline was shredded by the canister, this time closer to the hand-to-hand fighting. The wall of lead fired from the gun leveled the trees beyond the breastworks. Some men had been hit by the hail of deadly balls, but not many.

While Durlon was reloading, Wake yelled over to the beach, "Moore! Get your men back to the water so we can fire into them! Get back to the water!"

The flashing chaos of the beach provided no answer that Wake's instructions had been heard or followed. The din of yells, screams of pain, and firearms shooting made any exchange of words impossible.

"Rork! Get over there right now and have them get to the water. Swim out here if they have to. We've got to get the gun to bear on the enemy!"

Rork immediately understood Wake's plan and jumped into the dinghy, not waiting for a crewman to assist. The bosun then rowed as fast as he could to the shore, ducking each time a bullet shot a geyser up close to him. As soon as he got to knee-deep water, he got out and yelled, his loud voice transcending the pandemonium, "Boyos! Rally on me that the Rosey can gun 'em down, lads! Come *here* now!"

Durlon's loading drill cadence gave an eerie background to the noise of the shore fight, while Rork's manhandling of the sailors back into the water added another movement into the riot of action on the darkened beach. Once several of the sailors saw what Rork was doing, they urged their crewmates back into their familiar element and away from the shrieking Rebels.

The beachhead shrank to the water's edge, bodies lying around the camp in various stages of wounding or death. In the darkness the bodies of friend and foe were indistinguishable. Wake could tell the difference only between those standing and those lying on the ground. The sailors in the water were now trying to get into the cutters and row off, at Rork's urging. Wake saw his opportunity.

"Durlon, fire onto the beach now, man. Fire now!"

Boom! Noise and light took over as the canister shot flew in a cloud of death over the beach. In the moment that the flash lit up the Confederate troops lined up on the beach and firing at the gunboat, Wake saw the last defiant volley launch from the muskets, rifles, and shotguns of a dozen men. The screams he heard from the beach were matched by those of Sommer and Lamar of his own crew, hit by the Rebel volley.

Now with less enthusiasm, Durlon continued his monotone cadence of the gun drill, stepping over the wounded boy on the deck even as he pushed Burns to get around to the muzzle and sponge out the gun. Wake leaned over to check Sommer's wound, glancing to his side to tell Durlon, "Fire again, gunner. Fire again at them."

"Aye aye. That we'll do, sir," replied the exhausted gunner.

Rork suddenly appeared on deck, having climbed up the main shroud chains on the side of the hull, and seeing the damage to ship and crew, moaned, "Oh, Lord above, bless us and protect us now."

He joined Wake in an examination of the thirteen-year-old's

wounds. There were holes in the thigh, front and back, as well as entrance and exit wounds in the extreme left side of the abdomen. The boy was curled up on the deck, crying and screaming unintelligibly, his body jerking in spasms of pain. The thigh wound appeared survivable, but Wake was unsure of the severity of the gunshot to his side. It looked bad.

"Rork, tend to Sommer here. I'll check Lamar."

Boom! Another mind-numbing shock of sound and light engulfed the deck as Durlon fired again. This round of packed missiles swept the beach and the water's edge, but without return fire from the enemy.

Wake made his way through the men and equipment on the crowded deck to Lamar, who was up forward by the mast holding his left arm and swearing. Wake's mind registered that there was less noise coming from the land and more coming from the water around the gunboat, where sailors were swimming over to the ship for safety. Lamar's arm was wounded below the elbow— a gash through flesh that could heal if infection was kept out. The bleeding was under control and the wound less critical than Sommer's so Wake turned his attention to the beachhead.

It was not what he saw that shocked him, for he could not see a thing. All the lanterns were out on the beach, and not another light yielded any clue of the situation there. The sound, however, was eerie. All firing had stopped, and moaning, screaming, and pleading from the beach and the foreshore had taken its place. The wounded of both sides mingled their cries. The battle was over, but the pain was not.

He could hear people starting to move among the wounded on the beach, and Wake assumed that they were Rebels trying to rescue their wounded comrades. He let them go without ordering any more firing. It was over, and he had to rescue his own sailors, who were scattered, dead, wounded, and dazed, on the beach and in the water. He suddenly realized that he did not know what time it was. He reached in his pocket for his watch and found by the lantern light on deck that it was four in the morning. His mind jumped back to that other battle on that other river. Wake's hand subconsciously went up to the scar on his head as he remembered the aftermath of *that* battle.

This one was different. And not in favor of his side. The Rebels had pushed them off their beach position and scattered their men and equipment. The only thing that had saved many more from dying here was the twelve-pounder of the *Rosalie* and Durlon's skillful use of it.

Wake also realized that he still had soldiers depending on him who were inland on their mission. He had no idea what had happened to them. No sounds of battle had been heard from their direction, so he had to assume that they were still in good shape and active.

As he surveyed the carnage around him, he knew his first job was to get the wounded aboard and the still-effective ones into some type of organization in the cutters. He had to struggle to concentrate with all the noise of the suffering. When he saw Rork coming toward him, he knew it would call for more decisions.

Rork stood quietly, waiting for his captain to recognize him. When Wake finally did, Rork gave the report Wake had been dreading.

"Sir, butcher's bill is bad, but old Rosey saved it from being a worse un. Dead are six men, including little Fox and Bosun Moore. Fitzhugh is among the fourteen wounded, three of 'em bad, including the little lad Sommer. I don't know about that wound of Sommer, sir. Through an' through, but we've got to keep that thing clean for certain. After all of them are counted off, sir, we have in the way of nine men not wounded. Countin' the lads not wounded too bad to fight, includin' Lamar there, we have about thirteen men effective for fightin'. Damage to one of the cutters makes it too bad for using. Between the Reb bullets and Durlon's grape, that boat is done for. Leavin' us two cutters and the *Rosalie*, sir. Old Rosey is ready for action or sailin' though, sir."

Wake exhaled a deep breath. The list of wounded and dead

had almost made him sick. There was another question to be answered.

"Rork, did any of them say how this happened?"

Rork scowled and spoke in a low tone.

"Aye, Captain. Fitzhugh told me the Rebs said the proper password and walked forward until they were almost within the camp. Opened fire at point blank range. Our lads didn't have a chance till the Rosey saved 'em."

"They knew the password? Then there's a traitor or a fool involved in this endeavor, Rork, and we'd better find out who it is quickly. You heard no firing from the direction of the army expedition?"

"Just the odd shot now and again, sir. No sound of any battle. Further orders, sir?"

"Very well, Rork. Make sure the wounded on the beach are taken off immediately to the boats and the sloop. Leave the Reb dead and wounded for the Rebs to get. Keep a strong watch tonight till dawn. At that time, we'll get under way and take the wounded to the *Gem of the Sea*. We will have to come back for the soldiers as soon as we can."

"Aye aye, sir. 'Bout two hours till light. I'll put half the men down till then, once we make sure of the wounded boys ashore."

"Rork, what do you make of the weather?"

"Nor'wester later today or tonight, for sure, sir. Winds veerin' now and risin', sure as hell."

Wake told the bosun to carry on and stood there looking aloft at the clouds, worrying about the impending storm. Wounded men covered the open areas of the deck. Wake felt suddenly so tired. But now Rork was back with something else.

"Sir, what about our dead lads? A burial on the beach in the morn, or take with us when we leave this place?"

"We will take *all* of our men away with us, Rork."

With those tired words, Wake sat down at the stern and looked about him as Rork turned away to lead the working parties. The men were finally all back aboard the sloop and the two remaining cutters. Wounded were laid out on the deck of the sloop and were being tended to by Durlon and Burns. Wake, feeling useless and wanting to do something, went to help them.

The watch indicated six-thirty in the morning when Rork came to his captain and advised him that all vessels were ready to get under way for Boca Grande and the surgeon's mates aboard the *Gem of the Sea.* Extra sailors from the cutters were on the sloop to help work the sails, and Rork soon had them hauling away on the main and jib halliards to set the reefed sails. Other men were weighing the anchor, and soon the *Rosalie* spun around and downwind to the mouth of the river. The cutters set smaller sails and followed along in the path of the larger ship. The wind had picked up considerably during the remaining dark hours, by dawn becoming enough that sail area had to be reduced to dampen the roll of the vessel for the safety and comfort of the wounded, who still lay on the deck of the gunboat.

Wake set the course to the south. As the flotilla left the mouth of the Myakka River, the wind and seas picked up even further, as did the speed of the advance. Wake could see that all hands were exhausted and told Rork to set watch with a skeleton watch and send the rest off watch to get some rest. Though he was exhausted himself, Wake sent Rork off for a couple hours of sleep also.

Several hours later, now on a broad reach that sent them racing along the coast of the Turtle Bay islands, they saw the *Gem of the Sea* anchored off the island of Gasparilla in the Boca Grande Passage. When they came alongside and rafted up to the *Gem,* Wake could feel the eyes of the other crew on the men on the deck. An unusual quiet settled over both crews as the wounded were transferred and the cutters rafted. Wake went aboard the other ship to make his report to Baxter.

In the cabin, after a large glass of rum had steadied his nerves and facilitated his voice, Wake told his superior what he had pieced together of the battle. Baxter listened with concern as Wake explained that so many of the *Gem of the Sea*'s crew had been caught unaware on the beach because the enemy had known the password and deceived the sailor pickets on the breastworks. Once inside the perimeter, they had opened fire with devastating results. Lt. Baxter calmly refrained from any comment until Wake had completed his report. He bade Wake to sit and rest as he said, "Peter, you've been through yet another confrontation with the Rebs and have come out of it in good order. Your luck holds, my friend, and I owe the lives of so many of my men to you and your men. Without your gunfire, they would have all been killed on the beach. It is a wonder to me how more were not killed. I am glad that you were not wounded again."

"Durlon did terrible but effective work, sir. He knows what he is doing with that gun."

"Yes, Mr. Wake, he does. But someone else did not know what he was doing. Something went horribly wrong. I want to know how the Rebels knew our password. And I want to know as soon as possible. I want the man who is responsible for this. There is a spy somewhere and I want him."

Baxter's voice had gone low and cold. His eyes leveled on Wake and the silence after his last statement was deafening.

"Yes, sir. We'll find out. We will get the man who did this."

"Very good, Peter. Now get under way as soon as possible and get back to that place to take the Rangers off and away."

"Aye aye, sir." Wake saluted and left the cabin. He felt a chill as he left the other man standing there gazing vacantly at the deck beams overhead. Baxter had never shown this side to Wake before. The death and wounding of so many of his men by treachery had affected the lieutenant strongly. Wake had no doubt of the will of his friend, and left the ship quickly to attend to the departure of his sloop.

The sail back to the Myakka was not nearly as fast nor as calm as the sail downwind from the river had been. The course back to the beachhead was upwind and against the seas. Tacking back and forth up the twenty-five-mile length of Charlotte Harbor was a laborious process that took a full night and much of the next day. The wind, which had been strong before, was now at gale force. *Rosalie*, without the cutters this time, slogged into the tempest with animal force. Everything and everyone on her was wet and cold, for the temperature had plummeted as the wind had risen. Gone were any sensations of the tropics as the storm delivered its northern-born fury. It reminded Wake of the New England weather that he had known for so long, and he bent down in his foul-weather slicker and held onto the binnacle box as his sloop crashed into wave after wave.

When they finally arrived at the beach, upriver from the mouth of the Myakka, they found it deserted of equipment or people. When they had last seen the beach, as they had sailed away with the wounded, it had been covered with strewn boxes, rifles, and supplies. Movement had been seen and heard at that time in the tree line upland from the beach, and Wake had departed with the wounded without chancing more casualties to remove the abandoned equipage.

In the short time since then, the beach had been picked clean. The contents of that area were now probably serving the Confederate soldiery, suggested Rork as he stood next to his captain, surveying the sand where so many men met their fate in the darkness and chaos.

The *Rosalie* was anchored midstream with spring lines bent to enable her to swing her bearing in a wider arc. Wake and his men sat and waited and listened for any signs of the volunteer Florida Rangers and the Pennsylvania troops who were dependent on the sailors to transport them away from here.

They waited for two days, then, hearing them long before they saw them, the sailors greeted the soldiers as they shuffled down the path out of the jungle onto the beach. Wake was rowed ashore in the dinghy, leaving Rork to get the gunboat into shallow water so the troops could just walk out to her and climb aboard. When he got to the beach he found Cornell and Vanding. For a moment no one said a word, then Cornell said, "Thank God you're safe, Peter. We heard the shooting several days ago and knew it was a bad one when we heard the big gun firing. Where are the rest of the sailors and boats?"

As several of the soldiers formed a rear guard defensive position in the trees just in from the beach, others trudged past Wake and stood in the shallows, waiting for the *Rosalie* to anchor close enough to shore for them to wade out to her. Wake told the two army officers about the battle and the aftermath. They stood there stunned. He then inquired about their mission and its results. For a moment they did not react, still contemplating the events that had taken place right where they stood. Then they told the story of their expedition. Vanding spoke first and related to Wake how they had marched for two days in a skirmish line to find the Confederate cattle supply. When they finally found some scraggly-looking range cows, they made camp and spent the night without fires to conceal themselves from the enemy. During that night some of the men slipped out of the camp and had not been seen again. The men who had left were some of the Key West volunteers who had come up the coast to Useppa Island and joined the new militia regiment.

Cornell now broke into Vanding's narrative and continued.

"Peter, I am ashamed to say that I believe that those men—there were three named Brown, Liter, and Simmons—were probably spies. Every day and night thereafter we had sharpshooters firing at us. Four men wounded but none killed, thank the Lord.

"I further believe, Peter Wake, that they gave the password to their brethren, which allowed the Rebels to attack you through the treachery you've described."

"Captain Cornell, what do you know of these men? Their origins, families, anything?" questioned Wake.

"All I know is that they were from Key West and that they kept themselves quiet and apart. They had been in Key West for some time apparently, having come over from some island in the Bahamas after they were stranded there on a vessel as refugees. They were all friends and did not take kindly to inquiries about their past."

Vanding added, "They looked a surly bunch from the start,

but I had no experience with Florida pro-Union men and kept my impressions to myself. I wish now, Captain Cornell, that I had spoken with you about them."

"'Tis all right, son. I should have deciphered them early, but I did not catch them either. Captain Wake, I cannot tell you how very sorry we are this has happened to your good sailors, sir. We will find those men and hang them when we do."

"Sir, you mentioned they were from the Bahamas? Something about being stranded there as refugees? Then Key West?" asked Wake.

"Yes, Peter. Can't remember the island, but it was in the Bahamas. Evidently the Rebel spies in Key West had sent them on this mission to gain intelligence of our plans and movements. Everyone knows that Key West has spies in the town. I am just shocked that they were allowed to join our group of patriots."

"Yes, . . . well, gentlemen, let's get the men to the sloop and get away from this place and back to your island of Useppa, sir," said Wake. But even as he said those words, he was thinking of Rebel spies in Key West and Confederate spies from the Bahamas. Could it be connected to Saunders, from Abaco Island in the Bahamas. And what of Linda's father? Was he the Rebel spy master in Key West? Was he involved with all of this? Could Commander Johnson have known or wondered about any of this? Wake felt suddenly ill in his bowels with the enormity of what he was considering. His confidence now faltering, he turned to the job at hand and urged the weary soldiers to wade out to the sloop for their ride homeward.

As he was standing on deck an hour later, taking a last look at the shoreline of the river while the sloop was weighing anchor, Cornell came up to him and said nonchalantly, "Well, at least they won't call us refugees anymore. We are on the offensive now and have drawn our first blood. Started our revenge."

Wake looked at his older friend with surprise and queried, "I thought that you had no opportunity to fire back at the Rebs, Mr. Cornell. That was my impression, sir."

Cornell gazed at the shore and said, "You are right, my

friend. We didn't shoot any Rebs. Never saw them. They just occasionally fired from long range and then disappeared. No, Peter, we killed the cows. Killed them all where they stood. That was our battle. Against . . . cows . . ."

Wake became oblivious to the sounds and bustle all around him as the crowded sloop set sail. He just stared at his friend and muttered, "Cows . . ."

Cornell regarded the man who had been through so much in the last days, and had lost so much, in order that the Florida Rangers could finally fight like men against the enemy who had humiliated them for so long. "Some revenge, wasn't it, Captain Wake?"

8

The Shoals of Havana

The room appeared the same, but something was different. Wake had been in the squadron offices many times before and could tell that this time changes were in the air from the way the yeoman was looking at him and the way the other officers glanced at him in the reception room, where they all waited for a meeting, an audience, or orders from the chief of the admiral's staff. Even the marine guard had looked at him differently when he entered the building.

Of course the weather was far more pleasant these days than in the summertime. The southeast trade winds blew fresh across the island of Key West, the sun warmed the air to just the right degree but without the pervasive humidity of the summer, and even the people and animals of the island seemed to be more pleasant and efficient in their interactions with each other. Wake had decided that in the month of December Key West was not all that bad.

The staff yeoman did not call out this time for "Master Wake!" Instead, he walked over to where Wake was standing by a window and quietly invited him to enter the admiral's office.

Wake, who had been summoned from his vessel to see the chief of staff, Commander Johnson, was surprised by both the manner and the destination of the invitation. He tried his best to appear calm in front of his brother officers at this turn of events and slowly walked through the offices of the yeomen and the chief of staff to that of Admiral Barkley.

Barkley was with Johnson at the window overlooking the harbor. The admiral was looking out past Johnson's pointing arm and confirming something as Wake walked in and stood at attention. The yeoman announced, "Master Wake of the sloop *Rosalie* has arrived, sir."

"Ah, Wake," said the admiral, "good to see you again. Another brush with the enemy up there at Charlotte Harbor, I've heard. The report of the militia commander and of Lieutenant Baxter was that you saved the day on that river up there. General Woodbury is very appreciative of your help to the army. I believe that he mentioned as much to Washington."

"We were very lucky, sir. And I have a gunner's mate named Durlon who did good work and saved a lot of sailors' lives that night."

"Yes, Mr. Wake, so you said in your report." Barkley now sounded less pleasant. "But the important thing was that the enemy had a thrust into their previously safe areas, and their counterattack was prevented from becoming a disaster. That was not luck. That was good planning on your part with the gunboat and the men. And good execution by your gunner too."

Johnson chose this moment to start in before Wake could reply to the unaccustomed compliment by the admiral. "You justified our confidence in you, Wake. You used your head and prevented a disaster. Now we have another assignment for you and the *Rosalie*."

Wake waited for a while to reply, thinking more was forthcoming from the commander. But nothing more was said. Instead the admiral and the commander exchanged glances, Barkley finally saying, "Mr. Wake, I am sending you to take dispatches to Havana. I am sending *you* because your vessel is small and unobtrusive, because you have a head on your shoulders that can make adjustments as things go along, because you have powers of observation."

Johnson went on. "Your primary mission will be to take communications to the consul there and wait for return dispatches. It may take several days in Havana for the return dispatches to be made up. You will spend those days ascertaining intelligence of Rebel shipping and their apparatus in the city for controlling ship movements and dealing with the Spanish authorities."

"Sir, with respect, doesn't the consul do that already? Won't I be in his way there? And if I go ashore and try to gain intelligence in that city, couldn't the Spanish consider that as spying, sir?"

"Ah ha, Johnson, I told you he would get to windward of that point early on! Good deductions, son. You're right. Absolutely right. But the consul, even though he tries to gain information for us on the enemy vessels and their shore establishment, has not a speck of experience for this type of work. He evidently is some former mayor of an Ohio town who did sterling work for some political warrior in Washington and got appointed consul to Havana as a spoil. And *we* pay the price in shoddy intelligence from the closest port to our country with the enemy shipping in the open!"

Johnson followed his admiral. "Of course, Mr. Wake, these comments are not for dissemination. But, yes, we are sending you to do the job the consulate there obviously hasn't. It will be potentially very tricky. The admiral," at this point the commander's monotone revealed no trace of his own opinion, "believes that you are the man for this mission. There will, of course, be no written orders other than those for a communications courier."

"Aye aye, sir," Wake stammered, as he could think of no other words to say.

"Wake, you'll sail in another day. I expect you'll be in

Havana for several days. I will see you in about a week. I want to know what is really going on in that port. We are hearing rumors that some Reb vessels are being fitted out with guns. I want to know where and how. Also, and this is most important, are they communicating in any way with the Rebel spies on this island? Now good luck to you, son."

"Thank you, Admiral. I'll get you the knowledge you seek, sir. I understand the difficulties."

Commander Johnson ushered Wake smoothly out of the office and into the reception area. At the outer door Johnson stopped and for a moment looked Wake in the eye. The moment seemed an hour to the younger man. Without another word, Johnson then turned around and returned to the admiral's office, leaving a numbed and silent Wake standing in the middle of the room with a dozen officers staring at him.

The chief staff yeoman approached Wake and stood at attention. He handed Wake a large envelope and a wrapped box. Both had the familiar seal of the squadron on the blue ribbon tying each package tightly.

"Your orders from the admiral, sir. And might I be so bold as to say good job on that river fight, sir. We all heard about it."

After the extraordinary previous few minutes Wake was a little slow in acknowledging the chief yeoman, a man of about fifty who had seen a lot of officers come and go in his time. Finally Wake came to his senses and realized that the chief yeoman and all of the other officers in the room were awaiting his reply.

"Very well, Chief. Thank you for your kind comment, but the good job was more done by my gunner, Durlon, than by me. It *was* a close run thing . . ."

"Well said, sir. Durlon's a good man, and you're an even better one for remembering him. There are those officers who don't."

Wake was taken aback by this unusual familiarity on the part of a petty officer until he realized that this man, as the chief yeoman of the admiral's staff, probably knew more secrets and opinions than any other, including the admiral. The man had more influence than most of the ship captains and all of the junior officers like Wake.

The other officers in the room started conversations among themselves after the exchange between the master and the chief yeoman, as they were as impressed by the chief's statement as Wake was. Some were nodding in agreement, and others were obviously at variance with the chief's opinion. Wake became aware that he was the topic of discussion in the room and he did not like it. Feeling the palpable jealousy among some of the officers, Wake ignored them and continued with the chief yeoman.

"Thank you, Chief. The envelope contains my orders, of course, but what is in the box?"

"Dispatches for Havana from the admiral, sir."

"Very well, thank you. I'll be on my way."

"Sir, one more thing, if I may. Beware of the shoals of Havana, sir. I've been there myself. Seen many a man fetch up on one that he never saw till it was too late. They are everywhere, and not a damn one charted, sir. Even a few of 'em out in the *water*. . . ." At this last the chief yeoman looked Wake in the eye, just as Commander Johnson had moments earlier. "Would be sad to see a good man end his career like that. Be careful, sir."

Both men turned to go off in different directions, the chief yeoman back to his desk to write out the orders of his superiors for the governing of the squadron, and the young officer outside to think about all that had just happened to him.

The sun was shining and the breeze made the air seem clean as Wake walked out past the marine guard to the front gate of the naval station. In spite of the beautiful weather, he felt uneasy as he recited to himself the various comments from the admiral, the commander, and the chief yeoman—uneasy about the meaning of what they said, uneasy about what he was about to do in a foreign country, and very uneasy about the outcome of the pending mission.

His first priority was to get the envelope and the box back to his cabin. This he did in the next half hour since the dinghy was standing by at the officer's landing. Once aboard the *Rosalie* and safely ensconced in his cabin, Wake opened the orders from the envelope.

They were standard navy orders and betrayed none of the information that had been imparted in the admiral's office. They appeared almost boring in comparison to the intrigue and innuendo to which he had just been privy. And then it hit him like the impact from a gun recoil. His verbal orders were not supported in these written orders. Wake now realized that he was engaged in a very dangerous game, one that had many unforeseen "shoals," as the chief yeoman had said. Of course, the chief yeoman had probably been the one to write out these orders for Admiral Barkley and Commander Johnson. This new insight into his immediate future made Wake even more uneasy than his ignorance had earlier. He had better think out every move on this mission. The consequences were enormous.

Wake returned to the deck and observed Rork speaking with the new men. *Rosalie* had been given a draft of new seamen to replace those of the original crew who had been killed, wounded, or had their enlistments expire. It struck Wake as sad that he had lost the entire crew of "Roseys" except for Durlon and Rork. Several had been wounded and a few killed at the engagements at the Peace and Myakka Rivers. Hardin's fate did not cause any grief, but still he was one more of the original crew who had gone. The *Rosalie* had gotten the reputation for being in action and for getting things done, but the price was not to be dwelled upon. Wake knew that he and his sloop were being talked about in the East Gulf Blockading Squadron, and he didn't like that any more than he'd liked the scene with the other officers at the squadron offices. He felt a new pressure that he feared might silently undermine his life.

"Rork, I am going ashore now. I shall return by the end of the day. Present yourself at the yard victual and supply officer and make up provisions for two weeks. They should have received authorization from the squadron. We get under way at dawn. Full ammunition load."

Rork grinned at the last sentence of his orders. He knew that Wake had something special up, and he was ready for whatever the young captain had in mind. "Aye aye, sir. Full ammunition load and provisions for two weeks. Old Rosey's going to be busy yet again!"

"And, Rork, you may exercise the new men today after resupplying from the yard. I want everyone *steady* on this voyage."

Several of the new men were standing close by and couldn't help but hear the orders. They nodded their heads at the information but their expressions showed confusion. Rork turned to them, smiled, and gave loud encouragement.

"And steady they'll be, sir. Won't you, boyos!"

Wake was rowed ashore by Durlon, who was going to obtain some accoutrements for his beloved gun from the chief gunner at the yard. When he was disembarked at the officers' landing, Wake muttered a brief goodbye to the gunner's mate and walked through the naval station and out the front gate into the town.

He had not seen Linda in several weeks and then only briefly on the street, where they could not embrace and speak of the feelings in their hearts. He wondered if it was not more painful to be this close to her and see her yet not be able to hold her. He had to be very careful now. The repeated inferences he had received from various sources about Confederate operatives working in Key West seemed, to his distressed mind, to be warnings about Linda's father. And so, particularly in light of his new mission, he had to be discreet in his behavior. He was still wary of Commander Johnson and the cryptic meaning of his words. As he walked along the streets of the town of Key West to Whitehead Street on the gorgeous December day, Wake mused that were it just war by fighting the enemy, it would be hard, but clear.

The houses and establishments of the town had not seen a fresh coat of paint since the war deprived them of such luxuries. Key West always seemed a bit tense under its apparent facade of toleration of the occupation by Federal forces. The formerly gay house fronts were now faded from bright blues and greens to powdery neutral shades as if in silent protest to the dampening of the traditional free-enterprise atmosphere of the island. These images crowded Wake's mind as he strolled under the cool shade of the banyan trees on Whitehead Street to the alleyway that led behind the Donahue house.

Once there, behind the cooking shed that was detached in the backyard from the main house, Wake waited. It was near time for the midday meal, and he knew that with the cook now gone and buried, Linda would be doing the cooking for her father and uncle. Smells from the kitchen were making him very hungry. He heard humming in the kitchen and knew that Linda was there, just a few feet away.

As he entered the narrow kitchen, she was startled and almost dropped the hot pan she was carrying from the oven to the table. As quickly as it was put down on the table, she was in his arms.

"Peter, I knew you would come today. I heard at the store that *Rosalie* had come into port. How long do you have?"

"About three hours, maybe four. Go serve the family. I'll wait out here for you. Maybe help myself to your cooking! It's good to know that you can fill my stomach as well as my heart! I've missed you more than you'll ever know."

"I won't be able to even eat knowing you're here so close. I've missed you so much I can't stand it, Peter. And now today, Father is in a very bad mood. The newspapers from the North have come in this week, having nothing but bad news for the South. The Mississippi is under Union control, Lee is going backward, and some general named Sherman is in the mountains by Chattanooga. The Union people are all dancing with joy, but many islanders are depressed about it all. You should hear the talk at the store. This town is full of spies and toadies for *both* sides. It's disgusting, Peter. And you, my poor darling, are in the middle of all of the danger up on that forsaken coast."

Their conversation was ended by her father calling from the

house, wanting to know when his meal would be ready. Wake stayed hidden in the bushes for half an hour, glancing continually around to see if anyone was watching, until Linda returned.

"Now I must clean up the kitchen from the noon meal and ready the evening one. I think that will take me all afternoon out here. What do you think, Peter Wake?"

"It will be a very busy afternoon, ma'am. That is what I think."

With an occasional rattle of pots and pans, Linda stayed in the cooking house all afternoon with her young naval officer. With one eye looking out toward the main house, they caught up on all the events in their lives that had occurred in the last month. That Christmas was coming, with all the joy that season usually brings, was not mentioned. The Donahue family would be having a subdued Christmas, their first without Linda's mother. And Wake would probably be back from Cuba, but on duty somewhere else.

The talk gradually lessened and the embraces lengthened along with the shadows of the trees. An hour before sunset, Wake realized that he had overstayed and was bound to go. He hated these moments. He left her as he always did, trying to lighten the heartache for both of them. His departure was quick, with a laugh and a kiss, but the pain was still there. Then he was gone back down the alley, this time out a different way than his ingress, lest anyone connect his location in that part of town to Linda's family. It was only after he was away from her alluring power that he sensed again the danger in their rendezvous. Danger from both sides.

Shoals of Havana! If only the chief yeoman knew of the shoals in Key West that I have sailed around and through, thought Wake. For the thousandth time he wondered if he and Linda would ever be found out by either side. Disaster would result either way, he knew. The walk back to the officers' landing was not nearly as pleasant as the walk from that place.

Early December mornings were lovely down here, especially

when contrasted with those in New England. Wake had seen his share of tough winter storms and knew that right then in New England there were men who would give a lot to be where he was, danger and intrigue or not. Up there, the wind would be bitter and wet and could kill a man merely through too much exposure. But here, in the tropics of Florida, the trade wind blew on its daily ritual, fresh and sweet, a nice sailing breeze from the southeast.

The drill of weighing anchor and setting the mainsail was done with a minimum of fuss, thanks to Rork's leadership with the new hands in the crew. Of the six new men, three were seasoned, able seamen and the others were brand new. Of the new ones, only one had grown up on a coast and knew what he was about. Rork and Durlon led them through the procedures patiently but firmly, and Wake was impressed that they did as well as they did. Evidently the practice the day before had paid off.

The reddish brown walls of Fort Taylor were close aboard for the departure of *Rosalie* from Key West, for this time she was sailing south. Wake looked at the soldiers on guard detail on the parapets and thought back to the May morning seven months ago when he had defended a young girl named Linda from an obnoxious lieutenant at that very fortress. It felt like seven years instead of seven months.

Rork was initially curious about the orders to set a broad reach out the main channel to the Straits of Florida, but he kept his thoughts to himself as the sloop bounded along through the jade and turquoise waters by the reefs that guarded the channel. In the daytime you didn't need channel markers, for the water was so clear and the colors of the various depths so bright that anyone could steer a course through the shoals from the island. The reefs did their evil work at night and on cloudy days, when sailors fell victim to them, often fatally.

As they heeled over with the breeze, Wake was thinking about how many a man in Key West had been made very rich by these reefs. According to Linda, her father had made money from wreck salvaging over the years also. Odd that nature and man should combine in an enterprise and make such riches off the unfortunate who struck these reefs. An excellent warning for the mission about to begin, he thought as he appreciated the breath-taking view of the sea and coral reefs below that only sailors who sailed these waters were privileged to know.

The wind from the southeast, opposing the tremendous ocean river of the Gulf Stream, made a course to the southwest the best track. Once this order had been given, every man in the crew soon knew the destination. Havana. It was one of the most mysterious ports in the Caribbean, especially now with the war making it a center of enemy activity. Rork grinned again upon hearing this directive and turned to leading the crew in setting up the trim of the running rigging with a vigor that matched the speed of the *Rosalie* in the freshening wind.

Upon clearing the reefs, *Rosalie* rode the great ocean swells that had traveled five hundred miles through the Old Bahama Channel from the island of Hispaniola to break on Florida's off-shore islands and reefs. Driven by the trade winds, they became seasoned, old moving hills by the time they reached the sloop sailing toward Cuba. The rhythmic motion they created became the basic time measurement for the crew of the small ship. It took two swells to reach the foredeck from the stern. Three to climb aloft to the crosstrees for the lookout. Only one to walk athwart the beam of the sloop by the gun.

The greater time period was the half hour strike of the bell. The new men grew into this world of time and speed and undulating motion rather quickly. Wake was grateful for that. He had seen whole crews get sick and incapacitated only hours out of port, in his earlier life as a merchant officer. Perhaps this would be a good crew, and their mission would be far less difficult than apparently everyone with experience seemed to think. This beautiful day was a day for a sailor to remember. Wake was determined to approach his coming mission in Havana with optimism.

Wake's optimism was echoed by the weather, which stayed fair for the entire crossing of the Straits. By morning they were off the Cuban coastline to the west of Havana. On sighting the island in the early light, Wake gave the order to close-haul as far upwind to the east as possible. Soon the mountains of the interior behind the coast were in view as *Rosalie* flew over the swells and occasionally dropped into the troughs. Her heel increased to the point that they were sailing under double-reefed main and jib only, making seven knots with no effort.

The chart and information provided in his orders envelope showed that a guard cutter usually patrolled the coast off Havana and would be the pilot vessel as well. The lookout spotted the cutter in the midafternoon, and the *Rosalie* came close aboard the Guardia Costa vessel about three hours before sundown. The officer on the cutter spoke broken English and was able to understand Wake's request to enter the port on official duty for the consul.

During this intercourse Wake found out that a crewman aboard spoke Spanish. Sampson, a veteran navy sailor, spoke up when the conversation across the water to the cutter commander seemed to fall apart. He translated into Spanish what Wake was trying to convey. The Spanish officer then continued on to Sampson, who told Wake that the officer said the *Rosalie* was too small for him to bother with piloting into the harbor and to go ahead themselves with no escort.

Sampson continued, adding his own estimate of the officer and his motives. "The dago officer says to go into the harbor and anchor under the guns of the fort until the morn, sir. Says there will be a revenue officer to clear us in the morn. He also says to make sure we render respects to the fortress, doin' a gun salute to looward. Anything else and the fortress will sink us, he says, sir. I'm thinkin' the little bag o' bilgewater is tryin' to show who's who here. Bit a bragado, if'n ya ask me, sir."

"Thank you, Sampson, for your report. Rork, bear away for

the entrance to the harbor. Durlon, clear away the gun for a salute to the fortress when we come abeam."

Both petty officers acknowledged their orders and went about their business of getting ready for entering a foreign port. This was Wake's first foreign port of call since becoming an officer in the U.S. Navy, and he relied upon his number two to make sure events would transpire properly.

The little sloop passed between the headlands into the passage to the harbor. Fortress El Morro was to windward and stood like a giant guardian over the city and port. Unlike the brown brick of Fort Taylor at Key West, El Morro had very old, gray stone walls. It gave a much more formidable impression than any American fortress Wake had seen. On the leeward headland there was another fortress, Castillo de Real Fuerza, smaller than El Morro but impressive in its own right. As she passed under the towering walls of El Morro, *Rosalie* lost some of the steady wind that had propelled her for the last hundred miles. Wake was impressed that just as she lost speed, the sloop passed into an area where dozens of the fortress guns would bear. It would be a slaughter if they ever had to fight their way into or out of this place under sail.

After rendering the gun salute and receiving a rather dilatory one in return, *Rosalie* proceeded a short distance further and dropped her anchor into the deep waters of Havana harbor. She was still not in the regular anchorage of the port, but she was in calm water and secure. Wake could see officers on the walls of the fortress looking at the sloop through telescopes. He imagined the speculation that would be going on there.

Every hour while they were anchored under the fortress, the harbor patrol rowed by and inspected them. The harbor patrol consisted of a twenty-foot rowing launch with eight men, only four of whom were actually rowing. Some minor officer in an apparently Spanish navy uniform was sitting in the stern, with two men armed with muskets sitting in the bows. A coxswain of sorts completed the crew. Most had no uniform and were obviously not enthusiastic about their duties. However, they did manage to pass the American sloop gunboat every hour on the hour.

The sounds of the waterfront continued well into the night, drifting across the water with piercing screams, soft laughter, and loud threats creating a constant background of noise in several languages. Wake kept a watch on watch for the whole crew throughout the night. When the first beams of sunlight illuminated the buildings of the harbor, he called for the whole crew to be on deck and working. He was nervous about being in this port, and he was also nervous about his crew being subject to the many vices for which the port was infamous. Wake reasoned that with many crewmen on watch at any one time the chances of a sailor being taken by one of the various evils of rum, women, or gambling was lessened.

Three hours past sunrise the government revenue cutter came alongside. The inspector of customs was an aging and overweight bureaucrat of the crumbling Spanish Empire. Sampson provided an interpretation of the sweating man's monologue, which increased in length once he found that he did not have to use his pidgin English.

The inspector, Señor Caldez, took great pains to explain to Wake and his listening crew that he was not a Cuban but a Spaniard, sent out to this island to further the government of the empire and bring these heathens into civilization. Sweat gave way to spittle as the man progressed into a speech that was beyond Sampson's powers to decipher.

Rork had his hands full maintaining discipline among the snickering gathered crew and finally had to order them aloft on a chafe repair chore that was more discipline than work. The final straw had been when one of them had made a disparaging comment about Señor Caldez and one of the inspector's assistants said something to Caldez about it. The bureaucrat went on in his speech, to Wake's relief, but Rork preempted any further problems with his direction to replace the baggywrinkle at the backstay and shrouds.

After the inspector's comments had finally ended, Wake was

astonished to find the inspection had also ended, with no inquiries as to the mission of the sloop in Cuban waters. The heavy Spaniard descended into the cutter with the flourish of a courtesan and said a few final words to Sampson as he was rowed away.

"Sir, the head man there, Señor Caldez, he says that you may anchor in the main anchorage by the waterfront over there. Says if you need anything, to call on him. He stressed the word *anything*, sir. I think he means women, sir."

The laughter from above was immediate as Sampson reported the last. Rork's roar for silence was greeted with sheepish grins aloft and a look of concern on Sampson.

"I'm sorry to be forward, sir, but that is what he said."

"Never mind the fools aloft, Sampson. You did well and I appreciate it. I will probably be using your services other times while we are here. In the meantime, Rork, let us weigh anchor and practice the men who are aloft down on the sweeps. They can spend their nervous energy rowing us across the harbor to the main anchorage. Sampson here can be the helmsman for this exercise."

An hour later the *Rosalie* was anchored with the other vessels right in front of the city itself. An amazing assortment of ships and boats filled the harbor. Flags from a dozen countries flew from the various ships, including, to the amazement of the crew of the *Rosalie,* a ship flying the flag of the Confederacy. Wake had never seen a flag like that so far in the war. He knew that international and Spanish law permitted it but was still aghast at actually seeing it.

The ship with the Rebel flag was a small, fast-looking screw steamer. Maybe a hundred feet long, with no guns apparent and no crew on deck. Wake was determined to find out what the consulate knew of her and whatever else he could ascertain. There were no other American naval vessels in the harbor and only one on patrol in the Straits of Florida, so *Rosalie* was the sole representative of the United States Navy. Wake turned to Rork and told him to gather the men aft.

"All hands turn to and lay aft!" Rork bellowed. Wake noticed that even Rork was a bit on edge in these surroundings. His normally calm and humorous Irish wit was not in evidence since they had come to this port.

When the small crew had assembled by the tiller, Wake started to talk.

"Men, over there is an enemy vessel. We cannot touch her here. Everyone knows that we are the only United States ship in the harbor, and everyone will be watching us to see if we do anything against international or Spanish law. Do not give anyone any offense while we are here. Do not allow anyone to come aboard *Rosalie*. This is a very dangerous place. Follow your orders, and we will leave in one piece. Disobey them, and some or all of us could be killed or wounded. I know that some of you do not understand the reasons for my caution. It is enough that you understand my orders. Do not violate them."

Speech completed, Wake looked at the men for signs of comprehension. They just stood there with no reaction. After a moment of silence, Wake ordered Rork to get the men working again, this time under the direction of Durlon, who had them clean his deadly beauty to his satisfaction.

When the men were fully engaged in their tasks, Wake had Sampson row him in the dinghy to the Spanish navy landing, where Señor Caldez's cutter was moored. After obtaining permission to leave the dinghy there under Cuban guard and rudimentary directions to their destination, Wake and Sampson started their journey through the city to the American Consulate.

The walk took them six blocks along the harbor to the Plaza de San Francisco, where a large, ancient church with a towering steeple topped by a saint holding a cross provided them with a turning point to head west three blocks. They joined throngs of people, busy and self-absorbed on commercial or personal endeavors, striding purposefully along the boulevard. Wake and Sampson viewed the merchants' houses and offices as they walked, eventually passing by the consulates of Britain and France, with their magnificent fronts.

Havana was a dirty city like any other seaport, but with an

international air flavored by the many languages heard everywhere, a product of the maritime enterprises that went on both in public and behind closed doors. The streets of the old city were laid out in a large grid pattern running back from the shore, with mazes of alleyways running in between them. The buildings were of various ages and structures, but most were of stone block, with ornate facades that belied the shabby interiors that could be seen through open doors. Once away from the harborside, the breeze disappeared and the malodorous effect of the habitations, refuse and sewage, rose until it felt like you could almost touch it. The indistinct sounds coming from shore that were so exotically foreign out at the anchorage were now obnoxious in their raucous detail, with prostitutes shouting, families arguing, drunks coughing and gagging, and street vendors yelling above it all. The consulate was in the business part of the city, not far from the commerce of the docks. It was an area that had once been exclusive and was inside the defensive walls that ringed the western part of the port. But now the neighborhood had lost its glamour and was merely productive. The city of Havana was unlike any other place Wake had ever been. It intrigued and repulsed him at the same time.

The loveliness of the city as seen from the deck of the *Rosalie* entering from seaward was a false beauty, Wake decided as he spotted the American flag hanging in front of a building a block away and headed for it. Havana reminded him of the painted harlots he had seen in seaports up and down the New England and Canadian coasts—once you got close you realized their age and their disposition were quite different from their first appearance. You also learned that they were very dangerous and unpredictable.

Turning right at a major cross street, Wake spotted the American consulate office a few doors to the north, its flag hanging limp in the fetid heat. A quarter mile further in the distance he could see the lovely Catedral de Habana, with its two mismatched bell towers overlooking the central plaza. Off farther to the right he could see the imposing Castillo de Real Fuerza, one of the fortresses that he had had to sail past in order to enter the harbor. As Wake turned to enter the consulate, a glance down the other way on the street revealed some sort of argument between a uniformed Spanish official and a crowd of Cubans. Sampson's linguistic ability was not equal to the task of fully translating all that was said, but he was able to infer that the crowd was berating the official, who apparently was a tax collector of sorts, for the corruption in his organization. The scene in the street enhanced Wake's impression that Havana, indeed probably all of Cuba, was a giant façade that was maintained for the ego of the Spanish Empire.

Once there, Sampson waited in the reception area as Wake went upstairs, where he was shown into the office of the consul. Wake presented his box of communications from Key West and Washington to an assistant and then studied the consul himself. Garrison Mason was a heavy, middle-aged man of pale complexion and was dressed in a business suit that did not improve his image. He gave the impression of being a man more at ease at a party than in an office dealing with the large issues that loomed everyday in this place. Wake could smell cigar smoke everywhere in the room, which was furnished in a surprisingly spartan fashion. A long way from Ohio, Wake mused.

The assistant began opening the box of documents as the consul spoke with Wake about events transpiring to the north. The consul stopped abruptly when he saw the assistant hold up an envelope with the White House seal embossed on it. The assistant quickly opened it and started reading.

"Collins, is that for me, from President Lincoln? Why, give it to me, man! It might be a reply to my request to get out of here."

"Yes, sir, it is from the president, but I fear not what you wanted. It says to stay until next summer, sir."

Consul Mason grabbed the presidential letter and left the room, ignoring Wake and muttering about lack of appreciation from people who should know better. That left Collins and Wake looking at each other. Wake was the first to speak.

"Mr. Collins, could you give me an assessment of the situation here in Havana? Admiral Barkley desires to know what is what here and directed me to find out."

Collins replied, "Excuse old Mason there. He hates it here, didn't want to come. Thought that it would lead to a soft position in Washington if he came down here for a while. That was two years ago, and I am now of the sad opinion that he was sent here to keep him out of Washington. He is a good man at heart, but this last letter dashed his final hope of political resurrection. I suspect he will resign now and return to Ohio. Ah, but the situation here in Havana. Not what it seems, I'm afraid. Let me fill you and your admiral in on the situation."

Collins, who had been the assistant to the consuls in Havana for the last ten years, began to give Wake a picture of the hopelessly convoluted state of things in Havana. His narration took half of an hour, but it was invaluable for Wake. Collins explained that Havana was actually two cities, the grand one that symbolized the most glorious period of the Spanish Empire, and the other that symbolized the squalor that the empire had become. The two Havanas existed together in the same space, one beautiful and exciting, the other lethargic and aging. The old quarter around the port was 350 years old, the empire's crown jewel of the Caribbean. The buildings and fortresses there were magnificent monuments to the Spanish Empire. The Spanish bureaucracy was still one of the primary owners of these great structures, and the proud Spanish clung to these buildings as shields against the rude reality of a Cuba that was changing.

The other city of Havana was the Cuban city. These quarters had none of the grandeur of the old Spanish city. This part of Havana had problems and people that the Spanish had ignored for the last two hundred years. The Cubans had been seething for revolution, the Spanish barely maintaining control of the island since the great Latin American revolutions of the 1820s.

In addition to the dangers of the Confederate enemy here from his own country's civil war, Wake learned about the civil war between the two great factions on the island that was smoldering just below the surface and about to ignite. Revolutionaries, emboldened by democratic ideas just a day's sail away to the north, were everywhere despite the efforts of the Spanish-run secret police to eliminate them. Some of the revolutionary groups had United States sympathizers supporting them. Other groups had Confederate supporters. Cuba was still a slave island, and the Confederates emphasized this when dealing with the Spanish and the Cuban upper class in the hopes of forming a common cultural bond. Wake's New England blood chilled at that thought. Men as animals? Bought and sold like beasts of burden? He had seen freed contraband blacks, former slaves who were now under protection of the Federal forces, but had never seen an actual slave. He wondered how he would react. He wondered what the slaves would think of him, a Yankee officer of a country that was freeing blacks. The whole issue of slavery made him uncomfortable, and he shivered in the heat.

Collins cautioned Wake against accidentally getting involved, or even in contact, with these groups. The consequences could be large for an American who blundered into the simmering chaos of Havana politics. One perceived infraction could sway the Spanish government toward granting the wishes of the Confederate States. He also cautioned him against making abolitionist comments.

Wake thanked the assistant consul for his insight into the political situation. He then asked specifically about the Rebel shipping organization in the city. Collins stated that the Rebels had a group of Anglo and Cuban merchants who doubled as quasi-official representatives of their government, but that not much was known about them. He counseled Wake against reconnoitering for intelligence of the Confederate liaisons in Havana, stating that it might play into their hands and offend the Spanish authorities by flaunting their sovereignty.

Collins continued by calling Wake's attention to the Rebel vessel lying in the harbor. He said that the word in the harbor was that she was due to sail in four days with a rumored cargo of rum and merchant items for a port in the upper Gulf of Mexico, probably Mobile. She had not flown the Rebel flag until the *Rosalie* had arrived and apparently was doing so out of defiance and a desire to impress her Cuban friends. Collins concluded by saying that he thought that she would probably be caught in the blockade anyway and warned Wake not to try to do anything against her in Spanish waters.

After this long discourse on the Havana state of affairs, Wake was getting fatigued by the bewildering swirl of information and personalities. He expressed his appreciation to the assistant consul and left the consulate building with Sampson alongside. As they walked down the Malecon, the great boulevard by the sea that was the cultural and social center of the city, Wake asked Sampson if he had been to this port before.

"Never been here, sir. Been mainly to Mexico and the Middle America coast. This place makes me a bit uneasy though, sir. Completely unlike them other countries. Odd, seein' the Spanish flag and grandees around here. Don't see 'em at the other places. Somethin' about this port is no damn good. Beg your pardon for bein' so bold with my words, sir."

"Quite all right, Sampson. I agree about it being very strange. Strange indeed. Tell you what, Sampson. When we meet a Spanish speaker, do not covey to them that you have the ability to converse in their language. Let them speak their lingo and later contrive to let me know their conversations. We must be very guarded while here."

"Aye aye, sir. Listen in Spanish but speak not!"

"Precisely, Sampson. And I want to find out about that Rebel steamer too. Keep your ears open on that account especially."

Wake stopped and turned to look out over the extraordinary view of the harbor and sea that the Malecon afforded. He noticed that an average-looking man dressed like the other Cubans on the boulevard stopped also about fifty feet behind them. Wake began an animated conversation with Sampson about the size of the guns in the fortress of Morro across the channel, confusing

Sampson but enabling Wake to get a better look at the man. After a minute Wake resumed his stroll and explained to Sampson about the man, who had continued his following, for that is what it now certainly appeared to be.

"Should I go about and conk the bastard, sir? We can take him off and talk to him private like."

"No, Sampson," laughed Wake, "I am afraid the Spanish would not like that, especially here on the boulevard, and I am sure that the consul would disapprove. Though I must admit that it is tempting. No, we will continue our walk to the naval landing."

The sun was high by the time they got to the naval landing and found their dinghy among the raft of small craft at the dock. The short trip to the sloop was made with Sampson rowing and watching the surveillance man over the stern and Wake watching the Rebel steamer over the bow. When they got alongside the *Rosalie*, Sampson advised his captain that the man in question had watched them for some time as they rowed out to their ship. Then he had departed the dock and gone into a tavern of some sort on the great boulevard just outside the naval dock area. He confirmed to Wake that he could find that tavern again when next on land. The seed of an idea started to germinate in Wake's mind. To bring it to fruition, he would need some good luck that very night.

After sunset Wake gathered Rork and Durlon in his cabin. By the dim light of the chart lamp he explained what his plan would entail.

"All right men, here is what we are going to do. Sampson and I are going ashore and will not be back until much later, probably until two bells in the middle watch at least. Rork, you have the command until then. In the unlikely event that I do not make it back by daylight, you will make it ashore and inform the consul that Sampson and I must have been taken drunk in a pub and are worse for the wear. Upon that report, you will depart Havana with dispatches and sail for Key West. There you will report in person to Commander Johnson or Admiral Barkley what has transpired. Am I understood?"

"Yes, sir," said Durlon and Rork. Rork continued, "Beggin' your pardon, sir. Not to be out of my place, sir, but what will ye be doin' ashore?"

Wake smiled and replied, "Well, Rork, Sampson and I are going for a drink tonight in a certain tavern by the waterfront that may contain further information on what exactly the Rebels are doing in Havana."

Durlon laughed quietly at the thought of his captain having a drink with Sampson in a Cuban tavern, but Rork kept his eyes on Wake and leveled his voice. "Captain, this sounds to be very dangerous and not the kind of thing for just the two of you. I should come along for some . . . added influence, sir."

Wake knew what kind of "influence" Rork wanted to add.

"Rork, thank you for your concern, but Sampson and I can handle the evening. I need you to handle *Rosalie* in my absence and in the unlikely event I don't return by daylight. Durlon, I need you to assist Rork. That is all I have to say on the subject, men. Sampson and I will leave directly."

"Aye, sir," acknowledged Rork, who still had a look of concern in his eyes. "An' may the wisdom of Saint Patrick be with you, sir."

An hour later Wake and Sampson, both dressed in the nondescript clothing of American merchant sailors, stood by the crude bar, drinking cheap rum in the tavern the mystery surveillance man had entered. The room was dark and dank with gray stone walls that had to be at least two hundred years old. Dim lanterns attempted to light up areas of the room, which appeared to have two doors set back into the shadowed far wall by a corner. The noise was deafening, several languages competing for loudest and a desultory guitar player singing a mournful song in the corner. Among the rough men of the place were equally rough-looking women who were plainly bargaining for payment in exchange for the theoretical pleasures they could offer. Several were eyeing Wake and Sampson, since Americans were known to have more money than the other sailors of the world, particularly with the war raging just to the north of the island and the U.S. government chartering ships at top dollar to transport supplies for the army and navy.

Making small talk and occasionally laughing loudly, Wake and Sampson surveyed the room and its occupants for the man from the afternoon. The other men in the room noticed the two gringos but did not speak with them. It was apparent to Wake that all in the room knew they were there, but no hostility was apparent. The woman behind the bar was watching them very closely and obviously trying to listen to their conversation, which, according to plan, was that of merchant seamen looking for another ship.

Two more wooden cups of rum went down their throats, and Wake decided to engage the prostitutes in talk to occupy time while he and Sampson continued their perusal of the room and its occupants. A girl of young but indeterminate age sidled up to Wake while an older-looking woman rubbed against Sampson. The young one had not been ravaged by her lifestyle yet, and Wake felt slightly attracted to her despite his better judgment telling him otherwise. Wake prayed not to get drunk on the rotgut wine. He knew this was one of those places where a man could get killed in a moment, and it would be nothing but a spectacle for the others to watch.

It seemed the price, negotiated in gestures and simple seaport English since Sampson was not letting on that he could understand Spanish, was fluctuating. Both men and the two females started laughing at the comical gesturing that they had all resorted to in order to communicate. While acting the drunk seaman and laughing with the others, Wake suddenly saw a glow of light enlarge at the back of the room. What he saw took him aback completely.

One of the doors in the dark recesses of the tavern had opened as a barmaid emerged, allowing the brightly lit room beyond to fill the dim void and illuminate the area. Through the doorway Wake saw a well-dressed man standing in the distant room pointing his finger at another man. Wake instantly recognized the man being pointed at.

It was Saunders, John Saunders from the sloop that Wake had let go up near Sanibel Island many months ago.

Wake stood there staring, remembering that day when Hardin had warned him that Saunders was a Confederate engaged in blockade running, remembering how he had let the man go because he did not have absolute proof, remembering the humiliation when he had finally gotten proof afterward but had already lost the Rebel blockade runner. First he felt a sickness in his stomach. Then he felt a cold anger and focused on the Confederate who was so close but untouchable.

Finally Sampson, who of course knew nothing of that prior incident, nudged Wake and said, "Well, mate, they've come down to our station in price! A half dollar each." Beside him the females looked eager for his affirmative reply.

"Ladies, uno momentito. Sampson and I must talko. Must talk. Moneda!" Wake said to the surprised prostitutes and the equally surprised Sampson. The two women stood there mutely waiting while Wake quietly explained to Sampson that he had no intention of going into an alley with some "poxy trollop" and then having to visit the surgeon repeatedly later. Wake further explained to a chagrined Sampson that the object of their mission was in the room beyond and told him briefly about the incident with Saunders and the box that was later found that proved him to be an enemy. A very dangerous one at that.

While Wake was explaining all this to Sampson, the barmaid was putting tankards of rum on a tray for a girl who had emerged from the room in back. Sampson was attentive to his captain but also listening to the servant talk about her customers. Sampson interrupted Wake as the servant girl returned to Saunders' room with the new drinks, and said to him quietly, "Sir, I do believe that the bar women were talkin' about the men in that room. The little servant girl said that the men had Confederate paper money that she thought was useless, but they promised her gold later to pay for their lodging and refreshments." He raised his voice and said, "And that's what methinks, sir, I mean, mate. Sorry for the mistake."

"That's all right, Sampson, you son of a whore," Wake laughed loudly in the seaman role again for the benefit of the prostitutes still standing next to them, then quietly added, "but we must get more information on what they are about. You go with one of these girls and ask about those men. Find out what she knows. I will stay here and watch that room. Sampson, be back in ten minutes and be careful, man. Do you understand me?"

"Aye, matey . . . sir, careful it is and back to me moorin' in ten minutes. 'Tis rough duty I shall do, but I'm not a man to shy back."

After showing the other woman that he had no money and her wait would be fruitless, for the next few minutes Wake stood there and watched the tavern and the door in the dark corner. He was starting to feel the effects of the rum and reminded himself to be careful. On Sampson's beaming return, after more than the agreed-upon ten minutes, he ordered two more rums. Sampson was looking sheepish—certainly out of character for the man.

"Sorry I was a bit tardy, sir. Couldn't be helped, honest, sir. Had to play the part, as it were. Well, that little one, Rosa Elena, was a pretty good time, and she talked a bit afterward. She said there are always ships with Southern confederados here looking for men who know the coast. If we want to ship out on one, we just go to that back room and ask. She also said that the important-looking man in there comes to the tavern every couple of months and stays for a week, then leaves again. That is the sum of it, sir. She's just a whore and doesn't know that much."

"Very good, Sampson. We'll stay here for a bit further. Mind the drink does not take you over," ordered Wake as he continued his survey of the tavern.

An hour later, after midnight and many rums each, Wake turned to Sampson and told him they were leaving. Saunders had just walked out of his room, followed by two other men, and they were heading for the front door of the tavern. One of the men with Saunders looked familiar to Wake, but the dim light did not serve to clarify his identity. Wake and Sampson walked out onto the street a moment after the three men.

They could see Saunders and his cohorts walking along the Malecon. They were having an animated conversation and apparently were not aware they were being followed. Wake and Sampson walked along until they saw the men come to a bumboat dock, where they watched Saunders embark on a dory and disappear out into the dark harbor beyond. When they lost sight of the small boat, it was heading for the general anchorage where the Rebel steamer was moored. The other two men walked away to a dark side street. When they turned toward Wake for a brief moment, he could see them more clearly. The recognition of one man did not surprise him and he shook his head. Sampson recognized the man at the same time and muttered, "Well, I'll be damned if it isn't that ol' bag o' bilge water, fancy man himself, Caldez. Looks as if this is gettin' stormier by the minute, Captain. Wonder who else is in cahoots with the Rebs."

At this new twist Wake told Sampson that they would return to their dinghy landing and have a trip around the harbor.

While rowing from the landing to the *Rosalie,* they went alongside the Rebel steamer. The watch on deck studied them as they passed fifty yards off. No obvious signs of imminent departure were apparent, and the lights were out except for the quarterdeck lamp. No sign of Saunders could be seen. Tired and more than a little drunk, the two returned to the sloop to find Rork waiting on deck. Both went below and collapsed without saying anything to anyone.

At the consulate the next day Wake found the consul in a very good mood. He did not apologize for his abrupt departure the day before, and Wake, a junior officer, knew enough not to press that issue. Mason's conviviality continued until Wake presented him with his new-found knowledge of Confederate activity in Havana, omitting the method of gaining the new information.

"Wake, that is really nothing new. The Rebs are all about here. The Spanish are making money off them hand over fist. Everyone is corrupt here."

"Sir, it appears that the Spanish officials are doing this in the open. Perhaps a diplomatic protest?"

"Doesn't do any good, Wake. Anyway, I will be gone from this hellish place soon. I am resigning and taking the next packet to Philadelphia, and it will be the next fool's problem. And don't tell *me* how to do the job of consul! I am tired of idiots telling me how to do my job!"

"Aye aye, sir. Meant no disrespect, sir. Just passing on my information," replied Wake in the neutral tone of a subordinate who has angered a superior. He backed away and made his way out of Mason's office as the consul turned and stared out the window, as if looking for the very ship that would allow his escape from this place.

Collins met him on his way out of the building. Wake, by this time wary of everyone in Havana, did not relate his information to the assistant consul. Instead he listened as Collins invited him to a function that night at the consulate in honor of the new Spanish naval commander of the Havana region. Wake's attendance, as the only American naval officer in Havana at that moment, was mandatory, Collins explained. He added that the *Rosalie* would only be needed one or two days more until the dispatches from consular officials around the island were gathered. Then she could return to Key West.

After spending a day at anchor watching the various vessels of the Caribbean pass into and out of the harbor, Wake got himself ready for the event that night. When Sampson, who had heard his captain was going ashore again that night through the scuttlebutt of the small crew, offered to assist him with translating, Wake laughed and told him that his services would not be needed.

By the end of the second dogwatch Wake was at the consulate in his best available uniform, which wasn't saying much. He had never been to a formal affair in uniform and felt very much out of place. The dinner and entertainment afterward were Spanish and Cuban, showing him a side of the Hispanic culture that he had not seen. Wake was enthralled with it all. The women were very beautiful and the food was indescribably delicious. When the dancing music started later, he could not help himself from being taken over by the African-Latin Cuban rhythm. He knew he could not actually perform the dances but sat there next to the Consul entranced as dozens of couples moved to the sounds of the Caribbean.

Mason was jovial again during the evening, as if he had no recollection of the afternoon's anger in his office. He introduced Wake to various officials and their ladies throughout the night, always acting as if Wake were the captain of a large man-o-war instead of a small sloop. The perfect politician, thought Wake as he endured the endless polite conversation. Another of those "shoals of Havana" they warned me about. The new Spanish admiral, resplendent in full dress uniform and medals, had not spent more than a few seconds with the junior officer from the United States, clearly not impressed by Wake's rank or his ship.

The evening was nearing an end when Wake somehow found himself dancing a waltz with a very beautiful woman. The wife of the governor of Havana Province, she had classic dark Spanish looks and charm. He found himself comparing her to Linda, and while she was undeniably beautiful, she made him feel very uncomfortable. He decided that she was a symbol for all that Havana stood for to him: beautiful but most definitely not a place to be comfortable.

When the affair came to a close very late in the evening, Wake found himself near the door listening to the drone of good-byes when he heard Collins speaking to a man by a carriage outside. The conversation was muttered, but Wake recognized the word "Saunders." By the time he had maneuvered over to the assistant consul, the carriage, and Collins' friend, had departed.

Wake wondered if he was surrounded by incompetence or malintent as he looked at Collins with new suspicion. He knew that Collins really ran the consulate in Havana, as Mason was clearly a noneffective figurehead.

Rork was waiting for him again on deck when the Spanish navy pinnace arrived with Wake aboard. This time Wake was not tired or affected by drink and stayed up late sitting on the transom with Rork going over all that had been learned while in Havana and trying to decipher the meaning of it all. Not much time was left to get the intelligence that Admiral Barkley needed. Tomorrow might be the last day they would have in Cuba.

All morning Wake pondered what to do, whom to confide in. He went over in his mind the facts as known: Saunders was engaged in a blockade-running scheme that encompassed Florida, Cuba, and possibly the Bahamas. Mason was incompetent, to be charitable. Collins was intelligent and just might be an opponent. Caldez, and probably other Spanish officers as well, was involved with Saunders and the Confederates.

But all of these facts just made for more questions and did not answer the main question about Saunders. He was the one Wake was determined to defeat. Saunders was one of the men who, through his supply of munitions, allowed the damned war to continue on and on, dragging more and more men to their deaths. Wake cursed himself that he'd let him go, that Hardin had been right and he'd been wrong. How many men were killed by the guns Saunders had brought in after that? Wake knew about Saunders now, and somewhat of how he operated. His new self-assigned mission was to stop him. It had become personal.

A message from assistant consul Collins arrived at *Rosalie* in the afternoon by a harbor messenger boat. In the note Collins advised Wake that the communications and reports for the United States were all gathered and he could get them that day and depart the next. The short note contained no other clues as to what Collins was thinking, and Wake determined to go back to the consulate offices immediately for the dispatches and any further intelligence he could obtain. With little delay, he retraced his steps through the city from the naval landing to the offices.

Once at the American Consulate, Wake met with Collins, who related that he had heard disturbing information that Wake had been frequenting places in Havana that he should not have. Collins' demeanor was that of a school master to a disruptive pupil, and Wake did not like it. He felt his blood start to boil, and it took all of his restraint to be respectful, for young junior naval officers did not act anything but respectful to senior diplomats from the Department of State.

"So I am forced to acknowledge, Mr. Wake, that you did not act accordingly with my warning and instead chose to act directly against my wishes by going into places that are known to be centers of revolutionary activity. I am very much upset, sir, and want you out of this port as soon as possible before you create some incident that I will have to deal with after you have departed. You appear to be incompetent, and I don't need any more complications of our position here. Why they employed such as you for this assignment I do not know. The navy must be very busy indeed to send someone as junior as you."

"I am very apologetic, sir. I did not know that I had visited a center of revolutionary activity, sir," said Wake as he suddenly realized that Collins did not mention Rebel activities at the specific tavern he and Sampson had visited. Could it be that he does not know of them? And if the Rebs are there, could there be Cuban anti-Spanish revolutionaries there? And are they in cooperation with each other? Was there a way to end Saunders' operations in Havana? And then it came to him as if a veil had been lifted from his vision. A plan so obvious that he wondered why he had not thought of it earlier. But first he had to deal with Collins and calm him down.

"Sir, I will take the dispatches and do as you order. *Rosalie* will leave on the morning tide. I am sorry for misunderstanding your wishes, sir. I did not mean to make your position more difficult," Wake said with as much remorse as he could portray.

"Well, Wake, perhaps you did misunderstand. You are young, and ignorant in your own way. Be on your way then. And learn to listen to men who have experience. . . ."

"Aye aye, sir. Thank you for your patience, sir."

Wake kept his bearing submissive as he left Collins' presence and received the official pouch of dispatches from a clerk in another office. Sampson, who had been assigned to help him guard the dispatch pouch while in transit to the sloop through the dangerous streets of Havana, rejoined him in the lobby and together they left the building. They walked to the Malecon, where Wake gazed out over the harbor and thought over the idea that had come to him while enduring Collins' humiliating remarks. A moment later Wake turned to Sampson, whose curiosity about the reason for his captain's pensiveness was obvious but silent.

"Well, Sampson, I may need your Spanish directly. We are now going to visit an admiral, the new one at the Spanish naval yard here. Let's get under way."

"An admiral, sir? I've never even seen an admiral, much less have I met one, sir. And a Spanish grandee admiral at that! Aye aye, sir."

The long walk along the harbor front offered Wake time to figure out how he would handle the conversation he was about to have. By the time they had made their way through the gate and to the admiral's offices, he knew how he could get an admiral to listen to a junior foreign naval officer and act upon that officer's information.

Sampson's Spanish was not eloquent, but he was able to convey to the staff officer that it was of vital importance that the American officer speak directly and immediately to the admiral commanding the Spanish Navy in Havana. After a few minutes Admiral Don Cesar Rodriguez y Lafitte passed the word to the American officer that he would receive him. No Spanish officer could speak English, so Sampson was retained to translate.

While walking through the ancient rooms of the castlelike building, black men in an equally ancient style of livery were seen attending to the service of Spanish naval officers.

Slaves . . . these men are slaves, Wake realized with a start.

Even though they were not dressed in rags and treated like dogs, but were sophisticated and acting as servants would elsewhere, they were slaves nonetheless. The officers being attended by the black men were seemingly unaware of any impropriety, neither arrogant nor condescending in their demeanor toward their servants. Wake wondered if this was the way it was in the Confederate Navy. As he walked into the outer offices of the Spanish admiral, he found himself curious about how the slaves in livery felt about their plight, wanting to ask them, until he forced his mind to return to the paramount business at hand.

Wake, with Sampson behind and to his left, stood at attention after they were ushered into the admiral's ornate and musty office. The admiral's aide introduced them in his language to the admiral, whose manner was remarkably like Admiral Barkley's. Wake had a fleeting thought that possibly all admirals were similar since they all had similar responsibilities. Then he cleared his mind to concentrate on the importance of his next words.

"Sir," Wake started slowly as Sampson translated, "I am the American naval officer who was so honored to pay our navy's official respects to you last night at the reception at the consulate. Once again, I offer our congratulations on your new command and our total cooperation in matters that concern us both. The Navy of the United States of America has much respect for the Navy of the Spanish Empire."

Admiral Rodriguez acknowledged with a nod what Wake had said and assumed a look that expressed a desire to expedite the interview. Wake did not need Sampson to translate that, and he continued.

"Because I know of the admiral's fine reputation for professional competence," this part Wake was trying not to overdo but knew that he must say something of the sort, "and his well-known regard for honesty, as well as his personal devotion to the crown of Spain, I knew that I had to come immediately to the admiral upon coming into intelligence that affected him directly and personally, as well as the empire of Her Most Catholic Majesty of Spain.

"I am concerned about a situation that involves life and death, with an immediacy that demands my imposing upon your hospitality and patience, sir. Things are happening as I speak that will influence your situation here in Cuba."

Now the admiral was listening and made no attempt to conceal it. Wake took a breath and plunged ahead. "Sir, it has come to my attention that there is a threat to your new command, and to the Spanish Empire, in Havana. It involves Cuban anti-Spanish revolutionaries, Confederate spies, and a corrupt Spanish official, all right here in Havana."

The look of impatience on the admiral's face had changed to one of concern. Wake noticed him glance at his staff aide, who looked equally serious. They both listened carefully as Wake continued.

"The situation is this, sir. The Confederates who are in rebellion against the national government of the United States are using Havana as a supply depot for their blockade runners. They have an officer in the Confederate Army here in Havana and I believe are doing this through cooperation with Cuban anti-Spanish revolutionaries, who are working to bring down the government of the Spanish Empire in Cuba and elsewhere in the Caribbean."

Now came the most difficult phase for Wake. He was already in a very dangerous situation by even going to the Spanish admiral in the first place. Low-ranking officers did not do what he was doing. The consequences of this meeting were enormous. Now came the part that might evolve into the destruction of Saunders and the Rebel organization—or the destruction of his own career in the U. S. Navy. He knew he could rely on neither Consul Mason nor Assistant Consul Collins.

No, the only hope for decisive action was to apply to the sense of Spanish honor the new admiral was reputed to have, and count on the fact that he was new and therefore maybe not part of the entrenched corruption. In addition, the Spanish were desperate to retain Cuba, and everyone in this part of the world knew it.

"I have exact locations and names, sir. The organization also has a corrupt official in the port. The guns that are brought in for trans-shipment to the Confederates go through the port. The official and Cuban revolutionaries are undoubtedly both involved. I would not be surprised if some of the guns are diverted for use against the Spanish authorities in Cuba. There may well be an alliance of the Confederates and the Cubans for the expulsion of the Spanish and future annexation in return for cooperation now. They share much common thought about rebellion against national governments. This entire situation is sinister and can end only badly for the men of the Spanish Navy and the empire."

Most of this last was supposition, but it had the desired effect. The admiral, silent to this point, now spoke without emotion as he gazed directly into Wake's eyes. Wake was intimidated by Rodriguez's glare as Sampson translated.

"You say you know where these men are located. Please give me that information now. Also the names that you know and whatever else you know."

Wake told him the location of the tavern and the names of Caldez and Saunders. He did not include his suspicions about Collins. The object of this meeting was to eliminate the Rebel organization and Saunders personally. If Wake could not accomplish that himself in a neutral country, he had no compunctions against getting that country to bring action to that end in a mutual satisfaction of goals. He had gone to the edge of honor with his ruse de guerre but felt justified by the results he hoped it would gain.

After the aide noted the information, Admiral Rodriguez thanked Wake for his assistance. The admiral seemed to have no illusions about why Wake had come to him. Significantly, he did not ask if the consul knew or had told the civil authorities of this information, and Wake did not broach the subject either. They both knew there was no reason to involve people who might intentionally or accidentally alert Saunders' organization.

"Master Peter Wake, on behalf of the navy of Her Most Catholic Majesty, I thank you for this timely assistance. It shall not be forgotten. We shall take steps to eliminate this threat to the sovereignty of our government. The Spanish Navy will do this immediately, since the threat appears to be naval in nature. Can we assist you in any way?"

"Sir, there is something you can do, or rather omit doing, that would assist me. This conversation has been rather delicate for a junior officer to conduct in a foreign land, as you may imagine, sir. It would probably be better if it stayed confidential, and therefore you did not alert anyone as to the the source of your information. As for my assistance to you, sir, it is my honor to assist a country in retaining her land and culture against the scourge of rebellion, particularly our brothers in the famous Spanish Navy, for whom we have high regard."

Wake could see Sampson actually wince as he translated and hoped that it sounded as sincere in Spanish as he had tried to make it in English. Suddenly, he had the irresistible urge to rub the scar on the side of his head, which began to itch. He successfully willed himself not to touch it, but it bothered him that it was choosing this moment to aggravate him. Damned thing won't ever go away, and it pipes up at the worst times, Wake found himself thinking as he put on a face of respect for the Spanish officers.

A flurry of Spanish confused even Sampson as the admiral proceeded to give orders to the staff aide. Within moments another two officers arrived and received more orders from Admiral Rodriguez. Things were progressing rapidly indeed. Finally, during a lull in the noise of the room, Wake told the admiral that he was bound for Key West on the morning tide and thanked him for his assistance. Rodriguez stopped his commands, turned to Wake and said in a tone heavy with meaning, "By the time you leave, Master Wake, both of our countries will have fewer rebels in Havana, Cuba."

Wake stood to attention and replied in an equally meaningful tone, "Aye aye, sir," and left with Sampson. In the outer office, he breathed a sigh of relief and led the sailor out of the building as fast as decorum would allow. Sampson, having witnessed something few, if any, sailors ever got to see, was enthusiastically congratulating Wake on the outcome of the meeting.

"Sir, in all my days I never seen anything like that. Just a pure rare thing, sir. A Spanish admiral an' all. You got 'em to do in that Reb and all the Cuban scum too. Well said and well done, sir. Never saw nothing like it. Them boys on the ol' Rosey been a bit put out and all 'cause they ain't been ashore. Thought they been left out of the fun. But they'll surely love hearing 'bout this. Jes' wait till them Rebels find they got no warm home here no more."

"Sampson, you will not tell anyone of this. You know why you can't. That is an order that you violate at your direct peril. Do you understand exactly what I mean? No one!"

The sailor stopped grinning and realized that he had overstepped his bounds. He quickly reversed course.

"Aye aye, sir. My mouth is sealed on all that happened. I can keep a secret, sir. Not even the devil rum can get it if'n I wanna keep it inside. Not to worry, sir. "

On that Wake had considerable doubts, but as they walked to the naval landing and the dinghy he decided to hope for the best. He had done all he could do and had put himself in considerable jeopardy by doing so. He hoped Admiral Barkley would approve, for he knew that Mason and Collins would not if and when they ever found out.

The sun was descending as they rowed out into the harbor toward the anchorage and their *Rosalie.* While admiring its glow on the steeples of the cathedral, Wake saw a steam vessel coming at speed up the channel from the naval docks. Spanish marines with rifles ready were crowded onto her decks and she was heading right for the dinghy. Other doubts started to form in his mind as he realized that there was no place to hide or run and that the oncoming vessel would be there in seconds. Sampson also saw what was heading their way but said nothing, set his jaw tight and kept rowing. As the vessel neared, Wake observed the officers aboard looking at him closely. She did not slow down, however, and proceeded past the dinghy, throwing a wave that threatened to swamp the small boat.

Moments later Wake saw her come alongside the anchored steamer with the Confederate flag flying. Even at their distance from the scene, Sampson and his captain could hear the protests in English and the threats in Spanish as the marines and sailors seized the vessel. The flag was jerked down the halliard, and a Spanish one appeared at the peak in replacement. Soon the sounds of protest ended.

Wake and Sampson stared at each other smiling and then turned together and looked over at the tavern. The sight there held them spellbound enough to stop Sampson's rowing.

Marines from the docks were forcing men outside and into two different lines. Bayonets were freely used to encourage the men, who were now marched back down the boulevard toward the naval dockyard. One line of men were light-skinned and the other darker. Other marines were entering doors along the streets in that area, and other people were being herded out of the buildings. Pedestrians started to vacate the streets, and suddenly some screaming could be heard from inside the tavern itself.

Wake was too far away to be certain, but he thought he saw marines coming out of the tavern with a tall, well-dressed man who certainly appeared to be their old nemesis, Saunders. This time, of course, he would be hard-pressed to talk his way out of his situation, Wake knew. This time, he was grouped with the anti-Spanish Cubans and would not be dealt with lightly by the government, especially Admiral Rodriguez.

Sampson could not help himself, and his impressions emerged. "Well, sir. Never met an admiral afore this. Wonder if a Yankee admiral coulda got all this done so quick like? Hate to have that grandee Spaniard admiral for a enemy, sir. That's for certain."

"Sampson, I do believe I agree with you on that," replied

Wake, laughing, though more than a little shaken at the turn of events.

The next morning's ebb tide allowed them to coast past the walls and guns of El Morro Fortress. Once past the headland, they caught some of the easterly breeze and heeled over on the starboard tack, bound for Key West. As they cleared the land, Rork said to the sailor at the helm, "Come up three points to windward, Hewlitt. There's a fathom-deep rocky shoal over there that'll kick up the seas off that lee headland called Sotaventoo, or somethin' of that nature. An' we surely don't want to be the ones who get it renamed for us, now do we, lad? Ain't many of them, but them that are hereabouts are bad indeed. Got coral rocks that will cut the guts out of a good ship and crew. Don't know about 'em till you've found one the hard way!"

Rork, you don't know the half of it, thought Wake as he stood by the starboard running back stay and let his eyes take in the beautiful coastline of Cuba. He now knew that the shoals of Havana appear in many forms, all of which are deadly. Wake turned and looked forward along the deck toward Key West, far over the horizon. Sampson was working on lashing down the anchor when he glanced up and saw his captain looking in his direction. He smiled at Wake and shook his fist at the coastline receding astern. Wake took a deep lungful of clean sea air and nodded back to the crewman who had shared the Cuban dangers with him ashore.

"Steady on, Rork, and mind we steer small in these swells. You may set the watches. We are clear of the shoals at last."

Late in the afternoon the next day, immediately after coming to anchor, Wake found himself in Admiral Barkley's office explaining the details of what had transpired in Havana. Commander Johnson and the admiral listened intently and did not interrupt the narration of events as the three men sat around a chart table.

When he had concluded, Wake sat there waiting for the official reaction to his decisions in Cuba. Admiral Barkley was first.

"Peter Wake, you did very well in a difficult situation. You accomplished your mission of finding out what is what with the Rebels in Havana and then took action to end their operations. I particularly enjoy how you got the Spaniards to take care of our problem and our enemies. Must have been quite a sight to see that Saunders' face when his supposed allies took him away. Commander Johnson, I like a man who seizes an opportunity! God hates a coward, Mr. Wake, and he helps them that help themselves."

Commander Johnson allowed himself a rare smile.

"It appears, sir, that Mr. Wake has done well and made the correct decisions. It also appears that this man Saunders will be incapacitated by the Spanish Navy for at least some time, although it would have been more suitable to find out all his connections in this area. I still wonder who is who on this island, sir."

Wake hoped his heartbeat was not audible as Johnson stated the last. They looked at each other as Barkley went on.

"True, Commander, but Wake did the best with the least. I appreciate your good work, Mr. Wake. It's good to know I have a man the commander and I can trust to use his head. On this station I may have further use of your talents. Now, turn in your ledgers and reports and get your vessel alongside the dock for reprovisioning. You'll have priority. I'll give you two days."

"Aye aye, sir."

Wake left the spartan, whitewashed room, as different from that of the Spanish admiral's as it could be, and walked out to the front of the building. As he stood in the sunshine feeling that at last he had accomplished something tangible and had lost none of his men's blood doing it, Commander Johnson approached him.

"Mr. Wake, you were very lucky in Havana. Nothing wrong with that, of course. Good commanding officers recognize luck and capitalize on it. Still, you were very lucky. There were many ways for that plan of yours to go afoul."

"Yes, sir" was the only reply Wake could think up, startled as he was by this informal meet with his superior.

"I hope you are as lucky on this island, Wake, and use your head to keep off the shoals around here. There are rumors among the officers that you are in dangerous liaison with some of the island's more undesirable people. Perception can be taken as reality, Wake. Watch your course."

And with that Commander Johnson walked away to the docks of the naval station's boiler shop, leaving Wake standing there and staring after him, with a tightening feeling in his guts.

The feeling of accomplishment was gone. . . .

9

Ghosts of the Martyrs

Christmas was coming soon, although you could not tell from the weather in Key West. It made Wake a bit nostalgic about his New England Christmases when he looked about him and found no resemblance to his memories. He missed the sweet warmth and smell of baking coming from the kitchen of the family's home after coming in from the cold, crisp air outside. He missed the gatherings of his seafaring family when the menfolk, at least those who were in port at the time, told sea tales to an enthralled group around the fireplace. The women would prepare a sumptuous feast and all would clan together for that special day. Churches would be filled during candlelight services, and the joyous reason for celebrating that day would transcend all other influences.

His memories were called up short, however, when he was summoned again to the admiral's office. It had been several weeks since he had last seen the admiral and the commander after his return from Cuba. In that time he had been busy doing the mundane work of the small vessels of the squadron, in particular assisting the schooner *Chambers,* which had replaced the *Gem of the Sea* at Boca Grande Passage. Patrolling around the islands of those bays had revealed some Rebel activity, but most of the blockade runners seemed to be dormant.

Now, on one of his infrequent returns to Key West, he had suddenly been summoned to appear in front of the admiral with all speed. As he entered the squadron office building he wondered what could bring this haste. He prayed it had nothing to do with Linda or her father. He entered the office after the staff yeoman announced his presence.

Admiral Barkley was in a pleasant mood and smiled when he saw Wake. "Ah, Wake is here. Very good. Mr. Wake, please sit at the chart table. There is something the commander and I want to show you."

Commander Johnson smiled and gestured to a chair at the table. "Hello, Wake, we have another special assignment for you. Sit down and look at this."

Wake did as he was bid and looked at a chart of the Florida Keys spread out on the table. Johnson was pointing to an area by the middle of the hundred-mile-long chain of reefs and islets. Wake saw there an island noted as Lignumvitae Key, bounded to the south and east by the Matecumbe Keys. A small island named Indian Key stood beyond the Matecumbe Keys among the treacherous reefs that abounded in that area. Wake noted the curious names, but he'd become accustomed to strangely named places in this part of the world.

Commander Johnson started. "Mr. Wake, we need a small sloop to search this area for the reported remains of a Rebel steamer that went ashore there. We are not certain of the validity of this report but need to have it verified or discounted. The report came in today from a schooner captain who sighted a wrecked steamer with what he thought was a Rebel flag inshore of what is known among the locals as Alligator Reef."

Barkley added, "The water there goes from ten fathoms to less than one, in one hundred yards, I am told. The Rebel survivors may be among these islands adjacent. Odd names. Lignumvitae, Matecumbe, . . ."

"Lignumvitae is a type of tree with heavy wood, sir," Johnson offered. "The locals say the island is covered with it. Matecumbe is some sort of Spaniard name, I should think."

"Yes, whatever. Well, Wake, I want you to sail there right away and report what you find. Do not try to bring them back. If you find the ship or the crew, return here for help. The chances of rescue by their compatriots are slim and I do not want the Rebels overpowering your small crew and getting themselves a gunboat sloop."

Wake replied, "Aye aye, sir."

"Normally I would send a steamer with a crew large enough to handle any contingencies, but that I do not have at this moment. Speed in containing this situation, if they are Rebels, is essential. I'll not have a bunch of damned piratical Rebels operating from islands right around the corner from this station." Barkley fairly spat out this statement with his anger.

Johnson continued. "I believe that you understand the consequences, Mr. Wake. Go this afternoon. The wind should serve, and you could arrive by first light in the morn. Remember, observe and report back."

Wake acknowledged his orders and stood to leave. On his way out of the room he turned as the admiral spoke one last time to him. "Oh, and Wake, mind you, don't end up shipwrecked next to the Rebels. That would not do well at all."

Another acknowledgment and he was on his way. Johnson had said nothing else, and Wake had not detected any further suspicions on the commander's part. As he walked past the sentry and down the shoreline to the officers' landing, Wake wondered for the hundredth time if he was just imagining Johnson's hostility enlarged by his sense of guilt over Linda and her father.

Wake had been exceptionally careful in seeing Linda since his last meeting with Commander Johnson. He had seen her only twice and had watched his path both times for sign of a witness who could betray his affair. Linda told him that she thought he was imagining things, but she had no idea what kind of man

Commander Johnson was and the power that he held over Wake and Linda. At any rate, she had agreed to be more careful in their rendezvous. Each one lasted only an hour or two, always ending far too quickly. He felt sure that Johnson could have no more recent information on his relationship with Linda since he'd been too careful for that.

Rork was on the foredeck with Holmes, showing him how to splice, when Wake returned to the sloop. Wake related their orders to Rork, and the bosun called the crew on deck and had the sloop under way in five minutes. The wind, southwesterly and wet, foretold a storm coming in a day or two out of the northwest. But for now it would serve, and the *Rosalie* set off down the main ship channel to the south toward the Atlantic side of the chain of islands.

After close-hauling down the channel and passing the outer reefs of Key West, the sloop eased her sheets and bore off to the east on a broad reach that fairly flew them through the seas. Even with only a reefed mainsail and jib showing, *Rosalie* was making such good speed that Wake knew they would sail the seventy miles and get there before sunrise, necessitating a beat back and forth until dawn could show them the deadly reefs. Finally, against his wishes, for no sailor wants to slow his ship when she is performing so well, Wake ordered Rork to furl the mainsail and run under the jib alone.

The night was spent rolling her gunwales under, for the wind veered to the west as anticipated. With only the jib drawing she had slowed and rolled with the wind and seas astern. Even with the centerboard down she rolled. The newer hands aboard were unaccustomed to this motion and it took its toll among them. The smell and noise in the gyrating lower deck combined to influence even the most senior veteran's internal constitution. Everyone slept on deck after lashing himself to some secure location. Durlon, of course, lashed himself to his beloved gun, while Wake chose the quarter cleats at the stern. It was a long and miserable night.

At sunrise they were off an island, which the log run indicated should be Long Key. The islands they were looking for were soon seen coming low over the horizon on the port bow.

All hands were called to look out for the reefs, smoke ashore, or a shipwreck. They were still in deep water by the cast of the lead, but Wake knew that sooner or later he would have to enter through the barrier reefs and sail along the channel known to be inside the reefs.

According to the simple details of the islands noted on his chart, he should go northeast until Lower Matecumbe Key lined up with the shore of Lignumvitae. With the wind now blowing, and a northwester coming very soon, that anchorage under the lee of Matecumbe would be the best location to anchor if wind should increase to storm strength.

Just as the wind veered further and went to the northwest, the lookout clinging aloft in the crosstrees called out that he saw something in the water by the small island, presumably Indian Key, on the port bow. It was something dark and obviously not part of the island. As they got closer it started to take the elongated shape of a vessel. Slowly, a broken-off mast and a shortened smoke stack became identifiable against the dark green of the island's jungle. A ragged cloth was on the mast about halfway up. Wake found himself staring at the shipwreck, not paying attention to his seamanship, and suddenly realized that he was now amongst the reefs that had claimed the steamer lying there ahead.

"Come up and steer for the middle of Lower Matecumbe Island, Rork. About due north, I should think."

As Rork passed along the order to Seaman Nelson on the helm, Hewlitt and Schmidt, the new boy seaman, hauled down the sheet as the sloop went from a reach to close-hauled on the port tack. She was now smashing through the seas and heeling over till her gunwales were sloshing green water. The crew, all holding onto a spar or rigging, were staring at the shipwreck and the surrounding islands searching for some sign of survivors. It was then that Durlon, holding onto the gun, turned aft to say something to Wake and stopped before he could say a word. He just stared over the port quarter and raised his hand, pointing in that direction. His eyes opened to the size of half dollars and a creak came out of his mouth.

"Oh Lordy, Captain. Look at that!"

Rork and Wake turned around together and saw something that was almost unreal. To the northwest was a solid black wall of clouds that stretched over the entire horizon. The clouds in the front edge of the wall were churning and boiling, with the water ahead of the wall whipped into a frothy frenzy of dark gray. It was as if the cloud wall had evil intent. It was breathing and moving like a giant monster that had found a minuscule prey and was about to devour it. Wake and the bosun, and all the rest of the crew, stood swaying with the motion of the ship, staring at the beast coming for them. Only Nelson on the helm looked ahead, with occasional horrified glances over his left shoulder.

Wake looked at the island on the port bow and the lee it would offer. It was about three miles ahead. The storm front looked to be about eight miles distant, closing very rapidly. Wake couldn't believe how fast it had appeared and how close it had gotten without anyone seeing it. He had never seen anything like it in all his years at sea.

"Rork, all hands secure the ship aloft and alow for the storm. Make ready the anchor to let go at a moment's notice. Send a man to the shrouds with the shallow lead line. I want to know what the bottom is at all times now."

Rork was in his element now. Every inch the bosun, he took over the crew and got them moving in response to the captain's commands. The deck now heeled over even further as the first gusts of heavier wind started to reach out to the *Rosalie.* Solid water was now coming knee high aboard the lee deck, and the crew were struggling to keep their footing.

Wake glanced over at the steamer wreck, now obscured by a blurring mist from the seas breaking over its hull. The wreck appeared to have settled down onto the bottom in the shallow water by Indian Key, listing over severely, the deck houses smashed, and the spars and stack about to fall. He could see no sign of life on the wreck and could spare no further time to check, for the storm was gaining even more rapidly on them than he had previously calculated.

The wind made the rigging shriek in an insane chorus. The shrouds had the bass while the running rigging of the halliards and topping lifts added a crazy fluctuating tenor. Hearing became impossible, forcing the crew to communicate solely by gesture.

All hands knew that this was a very serious and deadly peril they were facing, and even the stalwart Rork's face contorted in severe concentration as he manhandled the anchor from its deck lashings for letting go quickly in an emergency. Rork looked aft at Wake and said with his face that all was done that could be done and that the Rosey was as ready as she could be for what would soon descend on them.

"Three fathoms!" called out Seaman White, half under water by the shrouds on the lee side.

Rosalie, who had been through so much in the last year, was straining herself in an effort to stay upright and moving. When Wake turned, he saw the boy Schmidt, a look of abject terror in his eyes, crawling along the deck toward him screaming something. When he reached the captain, he yelled into Wake's ear.

"Captain! . . . there's water atop the bilges. Everything's floatin' down there. Water is in the powder store. We're takin' on water, sir!"

Wake screamed back at the boy's face, "Tell Durlon to throw over the gun's round shot. Now! Go forward and tell him, boy!"

Wake could see relatively calmer water a mile ahead where the low island formed a poor lee from the wind, which was increasing to a constant roar. No longer were different sounds distinguishable. The wind had become a cacophony of raw noise that physically assaulted a man. Wake had trouble thinking. He just wanted it all to stop. The black swirling clouds of the wall were now almost above them. Underneath to the northwest Wake saw only black clouds meshed with the black sea, no horizon to be found. The entire world had become the storm, with the only other color the gray of the wave tops as they blew off.

"One!" screamed the leadsman in the shrouds as another wave smashed into the weather bow. Wake didn't understand how the canvas of the jib had stood up so far to this wind, now at full gale strength and gusting higher. Nelson on the helm, assisted by Sampson, could barely stop the sloop from rounding up into the wind. Wake knew that the end was near, and he looked forward to the bows where he saw Rork gazing aft with a strange, comical grin on his face. Rork's eyes met Wake's, and the Irish bosun let out a deep-throated Gaelic scream that pierced the storm itself. It was a scream that surely came from centuries of the Irish going into battle, a scream that, combined with the crazed look on his face, gave Wake a new sense of strength, as if at least he had this crazy man on his side in this battle to the death. Wake lifted his fist against the clouds, and his father's words came back to him. *Be a navy man, son. At least if you have to die, you'll die clean and not in the mud.*

Seconds later they felt a crunch as a wave let the sloop down into a trough and then lifted her up again. The crunch was a solid feeling as if they had hit a reef. The leadsman was trying to say something, but it all was lost, blown far away on the wind. The front wall of the storm passed over them and swept off to the southeast, casting a shadow over the sea. The blackness of the clouds within the storm turned the day into darkest night and all visibility disappeared.

Attuned to every movement of his ship, Wake was relieved to feel that at least they were still under way. Durlon, Schmidt, and Holmes were still trying to do the impossible job of jettisoning the ball shot in an effort to lighten the ship, forming a line from below and handing the rounds to each other and then over the side. The men on the helm were still trying to steer due north though they could not see the island, now somewhere ahead of the sloop.

Wake felt something odd in the motion of the sloop and tried to determine the source of this new threat. Then he realized that it was not a threat but a blessing. The motion was a bit easier, not much, but discernible. Were they starting to get under the lee of the island? Then he heard a loud crack and saw the jib explode into tatters from the sheer force of the storm wind.

"Set the second jib! We must get farther up into the lee of the island!"

His hand gestures told more than his lost words, and Rork, who had already decided on the same thing, got the men to set the larger second jib sail in an effort to move further under the lee of the island to windward, before it too inevitably blew out. In the moments of pandemonium while they got the jib up, the sloop pitched wildly, tossing the men on her deck with a violence that made all tasks, even simple ones, take much longer to complete. Finally, after sliding off to leeward a hundred yards among the unseen reefs, they got the jib up and sheeted, and *Rosalie* took off again for the island's lee.

Out of the black mist ahead came a frothing horizontal form. Wake realized that the island was close by and he dared not go any further toward the shore. The wind and seas had decreased slightly when he gave Rork a gesture to let go the anchor, which was done without delay. The jib sheet was also let go, and it quickly began a gunfire of snapping as it was hauled down on deck. The men let the chain and then the rode pay out with some tension on the line. The turns around the samson post forward started to groan as they bit into the wood.

Then Wake saw two things come into his eyes' focus. In his immediate fore he saw Rork, muscles straining, take the strain on the rode and bend down several more turns on the post. And beyond Rork, on the beach of the island, he saw several men standing and pointing at the *Rosalie*.

With a tremendous jerk, the sloop stood up to the taut anchor rode and spun around into the wind. She instantly started to pitch violently on the bow, and Rork pushed his men aft as a wave came over his position. Wake called for all men to come aft, and they collapsed around him, clinging even to rigging and deck bolts.

Every third or fourth sea came over the bow, but even with that, they were relatively safe and could survive if they could keep her afloat. Wake told Rork to have half the men work the pump for fifteen minutes while the other half rested, then switch. Durlon reported that the water below had stopped coming in as fast, and he thought it was seams that had worked free in the bending of the hull while sailing in the storm.

By this time the wind had diminished enough that speech could almost be heard, and the first words that Wake heard from Rork were "Now just who would those lads be?" as he pointed to several more men on the beach who had joined the earlier ones.

Wake shouted back, "Doesn't really matter now, does it? We've got to save her first and worry about them later."

But worry did start to make its way into Wake's mind as he tried unsuccessfully to figure if the shipwreck was close enough to this spot that those men could be from her. He couldn't tell at this point, so he settled for dealing with the more serious problem of keeping his ship afloat.

The wind shrieking, the sloop pitching, and the men groaning from pain and exhaustion produced an almost overwhelming desire in Wake to just go to sleep, but he knew they were all in deathly peril if the rode should part. He and Rork conferred and decided to get the jib ready to set again if they should start to drag.

As the day wore on, gray and wet, the men worked at the pumps or rested as best they could on the pitching deck. After several hours the wind decreased to a near gale. The seas receded to the point that they no longer washed over the bow, and the motion of the sloop relaxed just enough so that the men could move about. The storm continued, however, and as the day progressed into evening the temperature dropped further than Wake had felt in this area of Florida before. With the wind and the wet clothes, the men began to suffer from the cold as they still lay on the deck.

Durlon reported that the seams were probably not working apart as much as before since the water in the hull was now starting to stay level and possibly fall. Wake ordered the men to continue on the pump, and he took his turn along with everyone else. The men off watch lay huddled together on the afterdeck with a sail over them as the men on watch working the pump struggled to stay awake. It was the worst night Wake had ever spent at sea, and he wondered if they would make it to see the dawn.

The dawn they did see was misty with a blood-red sun rising out of the east like the devil himself. The wind had finally calmed down until it was strong and constant from the northwest. As the light gradually grew around them, Wake looked over his command.

The bilges still had water, but Wake at last had given in and let all his men rest. Every man had wounds sustained during the fight with the storm—cuts, gashes, and bruises. There seemed to be no broken bones, but most of the men had legs and arms that seemed leaden, muscles that refused to function. The eyes impressed Wake the most. All the men had a look in their eyes he had never seen before. Was it the look of men who had seen death and did not fear it anymore? Even little Fritz Schmidt appeared ten years older this morning.

Wake walked slowly over to where Rork lay on the deck. He sat down next to him and looked where Rork was staring. The air had cleared so that they could see not only the wreck a half mile away by mangrove-covered Indian Key but also the beach nearest the wreck on Lower Matecumbe Key. And on that beach they now could see a camp of lean-tos made from sails draped over oars and pieces of broken spars. A few boxes and pieces of shattered wood dotted the beach. Nearby they also saw men lying on the sand surely staring back at them on the sloop, anchored a hundred and fifty yards off the beach. It was obvious that the men on the beach were from the destroyed ship in the shallows. But are they Rebels? Wake wondered as his body rose more slowly than his mind willed. He hoped to find his telescope intact somewhere in his cabin.

Rork was wondering too. "Don't see a Rebel flag, sir. But that cloth we saw yesterday before the tempest descended upon us could have been their banner. Torn away now, by the power of God, sir. Those boys don't look much better than our lads."

"You're right, Rork. They probably are Rebels. And they probably are pretty desperate by now to get away. We must be on our guard. We need to assess the damage to *Rosalie* and get her in sailing condition before anything else." With that goal in mind, Wake began to function at more normal speed. "Durlon! I want you to immediately check the weapons and make as many ready as you can. Rork, check the hull first, then the rigging and sails. Get all ready for sea as soon as possible."

Slowly at first—from exhaustion, not insubordination—the men of the crew started to follow the orders. Every movement exacted its toll of pain. Every man was needed, however, and every man did his duty to make the sloop seaworthy again. Rork reported to Wake as the captain stood holding onto the mast, watching the beach camp.

"We can manage the water in the bilge, sir. Durlon was right. It was from the seams working open, and they look to be tight again. Everything everywhere is wet though. By Jesus it is a mess down there. But fortune smiled on the lads' possessions in their hammocks. They were lashed up properly afore the storm and stayed intact. Everything else is soaked."

Abruptly, a thought came into Wake's mind. It had been so long since he had thought about food that he had forgotten a basic factor.

"What about our provisions?"

"Ruined, sir. The lot of it. Some fresh water in the scuttle-butt and some of the new biscuits in the tins. That is it."

Wake looked at the now-calmer waters around them. Farther offshore of the island the seas were still rough, but here it was starting to lie down a bit. "What about Hewlitt? Wasn't he a fisherman in New Jersey?"

"Right you are on that, sir."

"Well, let's see how good a fisherman he was and is. Set him to fishing for dinner. Use whatever you have to get something to eat." The talk of food had made Wake hungry. Rork smiled and almost laughed.

"Very good, sir. By the power of Saint Patrick, we'll have fresh fish for dinner today!"

Durlon was next with his report on the weapons aboard. "Powder is completely useless, sir. Not even able to dry it out. The water also got into the special dry-wrapped charges they just issued us. Dissolved the whole bunch, includin' the musket charges. I found a canister round completely broken apart. All the shrapnel strewn about. All we've got left is the cutlasses, I am sad to say."

Durlon looked completely demoralized. Wake had never seen him this way. "Very well, Durlon. Help the others with the sails and rigging. I want her ready to weigh anchor in two hours."

With the crew now up and working, Wake found a moment to ponder his next move regarding the shipwreck and the men on the beach. What should and could he do? There was no dinghy to row ashore. That had been washed away at some point during the wild ride toward the beach in the storm. He decided to sail close along the beach and hail them to determine if they were a Northern vessel that had gone to ruin on the reefs, or the Rebels they suspected. Meanwhile, Wake could see the men on the beach beginning to stir. There were almost twenty men there, watching him look at them. He could not hear their voices but could tell that they were discussing the sloop.

Several of the disheveled men on the beach walked down the sand to a point opposite the sloop and yelled out to Wake. The wind was still strong enough to impede voices and he could not make out what they were saying. They raised their arms and waved repeatedly, obviously asking for help and beckoning him to come to the beach. No sign of their nationality could be observed, and the crew of the sloop could still not be certain where they had come from or with what side of this war they were affiliated.

Finally, two hours after they had started to make repairs, Rork reported to his captain that she was as ready as she ever would be. Wake thanked him for the efforts and granted a half hour rest for all hands. At the end of the rest period, during the meridian of the day, the sun came out, fitfully at first, then stronger as the clouds started to thin out. The effect upon the men was energizing and they fell upon the anchor rode with a will as they walked away with it up and down the deck

The cable was up and down when Rork hauled away on the mainsail halliard himself, assisted by Sampson. Up went the gaff and then the great mainsail. When the gaff was topped off, the main showed a double reef, for Rork did not want too much strain on the rig. *Rosalie* then tried to sail the anchor out, but the hook would not budge. Wake thought this would happen but had prayed it would not. The storm had put such a tremendous load and strain on the anchor that she had buried far down in the sand. Wake knew what was next.

"Shall I leave it, sir? We'll never get it up," Rork admitted as he shook his head.

"Yes, leave it. Buoy it and leave it. Another report for the navy I'll have to make, Rork. Another hook to be replaced by the supply officer at the yard. They'll not like to hear that when we return."

"Well, sir. At least we're all alive to make the report!" Wake smiled because he knew the bosun was right.

Rosalie came back to life as she swung off the wind and surged along the beach. Wake steered her himself at first, turning the great tiller over to White when she gathered way. As they sailed close into the beach he called out to the men there.

"Are you from that wreck!"

The men nodded and yelled back. "Yes! We have no food left and little water. Can you help us! Take us off here!" They were coming out into the water now, arms outstretched. Some started to swim out.

Wake ordered Rork to luff the sloop up into the wind so he could speak further with the shipwrecked sailors. He called out again. "What ship and where from?"

The answer came back from an older, balding man standing waist-deep in the water.

"The steam schooner *Agnes* of Nassau! Five days out, bound for Key West for sponges."

Immediately Wake was on guard. A sponge steam schooner? He had never heard of such a thing. Spongers sailed their own cargo to Nassau and none used steamers. None had this many men either. And that man in the water had a Southern accent. Something was odd about that man's voice . . . something familiar but negative. The luffing mainsail above his head was making a regular drumbeat of noise as Wake stared intently at the man who had just spoken. Then it came to him, nearly knocking him over with the shock. Wake did not want to believe it. It was too awful to be true, but it was true!

Rork interrupted his horrified thoughts. "Sir, that story doesn't sound right to me. Not at all, sir. I'm thinkin' that those men are not what they say they are, and we best be gettin' back to the squadron for help, sir. Sir?"

Wake turned to his bosun and said the words as if someone else were saying them. He knew that he would remember this decision for the rest of his life. He had to leave the men on the beach and report them as Confederates, to be captured later if they were still alive. He said it slowly, but he said it. "I agree, Rork. We will leave them and sail for Key West to report. Steer close to the steamer as we leave so that we might get some information on her identity."

As the sloop turned off the wind again and sailed away from

the beach, the men on the sand and in the water began to scream, begging to be taken away with the sloop, begging for food and water the *Rosalie* could not spare. She couldn't even get close to them for fear they would attack the crew of the sloop and overwhelm them, as the admiral had warned him.

As they sailed over by the wrecked steamer, Wake forced himself to concentrate on her instead of her crew. He carefully noted the characteristics of the hull and spars for his report. The seas were still too rough to be able to go alongside and look into her and find out what contraband she carried. She appeared to be of new construction and was probably fairly fast. It was a shame to see her there, a dead and mangled ship that was once a beautiful work of man's creation. But such abstract thoughts did not last long as Wake glanced forward and saw his whole crew staring at the men far behind on the beach, who were still waving at the sloop and probably still screaming even though they were far out of earshot by now. The sloop's crew all understood why they had to leave the Rebels stranded. But that common bond among all seamen still made them desperately want to go back and try to help them, in spite of the logic.

After making their way out through the maze of reefs, they tacked *Rosalie* and settled down on a starboard tack broad reach under mainsail alone, bound for the squadron back at Key West to report what they had seen and what they had done. Now the wind was from the northeast, a fair wind for sailing to Key West but a foul one to sail back to the shipwrecked Confederates. It might be days before a ship could get back and capture them—if they were still alive.

Wake wished they were headed for some other place, any other place. His report to Admiral Barkley and Commander Johnson would be difficult, but his next rendezvous with Linda would probably be the last once he told her what the circumstances of war had just forced him to do. He did not expect that she would understand. How could she ever understand? For that older man in the water who had given the false information was none other than her pro-Rebel father, William Donahue. He had obviously been engaged, like other Key West Rebel sympathizers, in guiding a blockade runner through the islands. And now he must be treated like any other enemy.

They arrived back in the harbor of Key West the next morning after an early breakfast of Hewlitt's freshly caught and grilled fish. Catching the fish, difficult in the still-windy conditions, was a feat that had increased his stature among the crew. After berating him for taking so long to get enough fish aboard to feed the entire crew, they all expressed grudging gratitude to Hewlitt as they devoured the first food they had eaten in a day and a half. The fact it was Sunday registered on Wake as the sloop sailed slowly up the channel under the mainsail only, passing close aboard Fort Taylor, where he could hear the singing at the Sunday morning services inside the fortress. It also dawned on him that Christmas was only five days away. He felt so very tired in this last month of 1863. It had been a long year. And it wasn't over yet.

He sailed her directly up to the repair yard dock, without the normal permission required by the repair officer, and moored alongside smartly. Leaving Rork in charge, he quickly went to the squadron offices to report on his mission. Once there he found the duty yeoman, who advised him that the admiral and the commander were not there but at their personal quarters. Wake finally found Johnson at his sparse quarters above the officer's mess and, with dread, reported in. Johnson listened to the narrative, waited a moment, and then spoke.

"Hmm . . . Wake, we do not have a steam vessel or even a schooner to go to capture those Rebel survivors. Our vessels are otherwise employed right now. A steam tug is due from Charleston any day now though, and we can send her with enough men to handle the assignment. You did well to follow your orders and not land on the beach. They would have overwhelmed you certainly. I know that was difficult for you to do, but this is war, and they are the enemy."

"Yes, sir," replied Wake in a monotone.

"And I see that William Donahue was among them. We have known of his sympathies for some time and suspected he was in active assistance to the blockade runners during his absences from this island. His stories of running down the islands to the Bahamas for trade goods coincided too many times with our intelligence of Rebel steamers coming through this area. And I, of course, have heard of your involvement with his daughter. I warned you about that. Perception is reality, Mr. Wake. And the perception among many of the officers of this squadron is that you have been cavorting with the daughter of a Rebel who would do anything to inflict harm upon this fleet. Your relationship is openly discussed and is embarrassing for the squadron."

"Sir," Wake could feel his face turning red and his blood getting hot, "I resent the word 'cavorting' and I demand to know who is making such a dishonorable slander upon that good lady's reputation!"

"You can't demand anything, Wake! What you can do is stand there and listen! Listen to what you are doing to your reputation and to that young lady's. We are at war, Wake. We are at war with her family. Men are dying because her family is helping the enemy. They are the enemy, man! And I am not convinced that she is entirely innocent!"

Wake was stunned by the sheer anger in Johnson's voice. He had never seen the man lose control in the slightest. He also was stunned by the power that the man in front of him had over both himself and Linda Donahue. He could send either of them away—to exile or prison. It was war, as he had said. Wake tried to calm him down.

"Sir, the lady in question is a decent young girl who dreads this war like everyone else. Her father is a Confederate sympathizer, but that does not prove anything against her. She is embarrassed by her father's attitude toward the national government and does not support it. I have lost men on my own ship, sir, to battle against the enemy. I know the loss of war. But Linda and I are in love, Commander Johnson, not in conspiracy."

Johnson's voice returned to its normal manner as he said, "Wake, I know that too. So does the admiral. But it doesn't make it any less trying. We are in an endeavor of massive war that makes no allowances for two young people in love. I do not know what I will recommend to the admiral concerning you and this problem, but something will have to be done."

"Sir, I know that your responsibility is not to me, or to Linda. It is to the squadron and the navy as a whole. But, sir, I have carried out every task assigned to me. Not once has my affection for Linda swayed me from my duty or provided the failure of a mission. I hope to marry her once this awful conflict has ended. I hope you can see your way not to make our lives any more difficult than they are."

"Mr. Wake, I hear your point. I hope you heard mine. You will have two days to refit and then you will rejoin the *Chambers* at Boca Grande. I will send you your written orders as soon as I can. You are dismissed."

"Aye aye, sir." Wake turned on his heel and left the building. Outside he found himself walking directly to Linda's home, without any sense of how he was going to tell her what had happened. His usual route by way of the cook shed out back provided no way for him to know whether she was home. He found himself illogically listening for any sound of her father's presence, and then remembered that her uncle might be home. Carefully he waited for some sign of his lover. Finally she appeared on the back stoop of the house, carrying some laundry to a line between two trees. A whistle stopped her, and his hand movement caught her eye. She was with him in the cooking shed in an instant. After a long embrace and kiss, he sat her down on the stool by the fireplace and told her he had something very grim to tell her.

"Oh, Peter, it's Daddy, isn't it. He's back from Nassau and done something foolish, hasn't he? Has he been arrested? What did he do now? He has been so very vexed lately over the way the war has gone for his Rebel friends. He's been just crazy with rage. Tell me he didn't do something to the army provost guard patrol!

He's threatened to do something to them for so long now. He's even made mention of being a martyr for the cause. Lord have mercy upon us. I've been so fearful for him."

"No, not that. He wasn't on the Nassau packet boat, and he isn't back in Key West. He was on a Confederate blockade runner that shipwrecked in the upper Keys. He and the crew were stranded on a small island close by. I saw them. I had to leave them there because they are the enemy and we were afraid they would try to overwhelm my small crew and capture *Rosalie*. I am sorry I could not rescue them, Linda. I had to do my duty."

She sat there staring at him as if seeing him for the first time. He could see in her eyes that she was imagining the scene as he had sailed away from her father and left him to his fate. She didn't cry, just stared at him.

"You just left him. Left the crew there. Even the worst wreckers of the Keys would rescue the people from shipwrecks. I can't believe you just left him, knowing he was my father. No one abandons shipwrecked seamen."

"It's the war. He was with the enemy. They are going to send out a ship to get them as soon as they can."

"Yes, Peter, it is the war, and look what it has done to us. Oh God, please let this all stop! When men can't help other men in need because they fly another flag! A piece of cloth. It's barbaric—that's what it is—it's barbaric, Peter. Look what this war has made us all."

"There is more, Linda. The squadron commander knows about us. Apparently, we are the talk of the officers' mess. I didn't know that until Commander Johnson told me just now. He is very upset. Thinks that you may have an involvement or interest in your father's Rebel sympathies. He is worried about the effect upon the squadron. He has a point, dear."

Now the tears came. Quietly, trying not to lose control, Linda sobbed as she struggled to tell him, "Oh no, not that. I've always been most afraid of that. Even more than what my father would do to get arrested again. You have been through so much.

I have made your life more dangerous than it already is, my darling. I'm so sorry. I am not the kind of girl a young naval officer should be with, Peter. Especially not now. This damnable war has ruined my whole life. . . . It's taking everyone away from me."

"I love you, Linda. We will get through this. We will survive this. We won't let them win. None of them, from either side. We are better than that, and we need each other."

"I love you too. I know I shouldn't, but can't help it."

"That's the girl I love. Be strong. Your father will be brought back. We will all be reconciled one day after this war is done. You know that I have to go now. I must reprovision the sloop and I don't have much time. They are watching me now for any failures and I've got to be careful. I will see you on my return, dear. We will get through this."

The goodbye was wrenching on both sides, and Wake almost ran out of the backyard when it was done. He had to get back to the sloop and immerse himself in his job, forgetting all the other people and events that were crowding in on him. But the image of Linda crying would not leave his mind.

As he walked down Duval Street, he remembered what Linda had said about her father talking about becoming a martyr. Wake recalled Sampson explaining the original name the Spanish had for the Florida Keys. *Islas de los Martires.* Islands of the Martyrs, named after the men who had been shipwrecked and died among the reefs and small islands when the Spanish first arrived in this area. Their ghosts supposedly still haunted sailors who ventured too close. Rork greeted him as he neared the sloop at the dock.

"Captain, the chief yard matey says his boss man says that no vessel can be alongside without permission and we have to shove off. The chap has been a very disagreeable sort about it. Somethin' about job orders and requests and gettin' in line. Said a mere wee sloop could wait behind the important ships. Can you believe it, sir. More pompous than a bishop at a celebration, sir!"

"Okay, Rork. Let's go and get this straightened out." Wake

was finally able to displace the previous thoughts from his mind and plunge into this new problem that had suddenly entered his never-ending list of challenges.

10

Her Majesty's Wishes

The year 1864 started out with bad weather—not the kind of bad weather Wake had known in his years on the New England coast, but bad enough for the Gulf of Mexico. The storms, however, had not stopped the increasing rate of operations. Raids along the coast were ceaseless as the navy improved its strength in ships and men, and its ability to project that strength ashore.

The *Rosalie* and the *Chambers* supported the army in a push up into Confederate territory when General Woodbury brought troops from Key West and ascended the Caloosahatchee River, capturing Fort Myers. The fort, long abandoned by the army after the Third Seminole War had ended in 1858, was occupied by Wake's old friends in the Forty-seventh Pennsylvania Infantry, the Hundred-tenth New York Infantry, and the previous Useppa Island Florida Rangers, now formed into the Second United States Florida Cavalry. Wake had the impression that finally the prospects for the Union victory were getting better after seeing all these successes, and that perhaps 1864 would be the last year of this war.

These efforts made the first month of the new year a busy one for Wake and his crew. No new actual fighting was undertaken by the little armed sloop, but the work of a small ship in the squadron was never-ending. It mainly consisted of the mundane duties of supply and dispatch runs, with an occasional penetration up a bay or river to try to find Rebel vessels.

He had seen Linda only once, for a very brief hour, in that month. She told him that her father and the other men from the shipwreck had been captured several days after Wake had left them. Three men had died on the beach from exposure to the elements. The survivors had all been made prisoners of war and sent to Fort Warren up north. Linda had not been able to see her father before he was sent away. Her uncle had taken over her father's small store, but the authorities had been making frequent visits to inspect the merchandise, apparently in an effort to find contraband. The searches had been crude and thorough, leaving no doubt to Linda and her uncle that the provost marshal thought they were the enemy and not wanted on the island.

On a port call in early February, Wake was summoned to the admiral's offices, the first time since the assignment to go in search of the Rebel shipwreck two months before. He went with trepidation of his reception. Johnson had been promoted to captain and retained his position as flag captain chief of staff for the admiral. He had not spoken to Wake since the last heated meeting in his quarters. Wake knew what Johnson thought of him but wondered what Admiral Barkley's thoughts might be.

"Master Peter Wake of the sloop *Rosalie* reporting as ordered, sir."

Admiral Barkley put down the report he was reading and looked at Wake standing there before his desk.

"Wake, haven't seen you since the shipwreck assignment. Heard you were involved with General Woodbury's expedition up the coast. Evidently all went well or Woodbury would have been quick to advise me. Captain Johnson, I believe we have another interesting mission for young Wake here, do we not?"

"Yes, sir. The British problem, sir, combined with the intelligence gathered earlier by Mr. Wake made him the logical choice. Also, his vessel is relatively obscure and easily forgotten by observers in the islands there."

Wake had no idea what they were talking about, except that he was going to be involved in something. His trepidation mounted as he tried to be quietly patient.

The admiral continued. "Wake, you have proven yourself as a resourceful young ship commander. I have come to trust that you can accomplish missions that others would wallow in because you can make decisions. I am going to send you on another matter, but first I want to tell you something."

A significant pause ensued as Admiral Barkley glanced over at Captain Johnson.

"Wake, it turns out that you have no judgment at all in your personal life. You have had the bad sense to become involved with a lady of a Rebel family. The whole island knows of it. I am disappointed, sir. Straighten out your personal affairs, Wake, before it is too late."

The junior officer stood before his seniors, not knowing what to say or do. His silence provoked Johnson to fill the void.

"Admiral, I have had a talk with Mr. Wake about this already. He has been duly warned, sir, about the consequences of his decisions. May I suggest we give him his verbal orders and some background on the situation in the Bahamas?"

By this point the admiral was staring at Wake, obviously trying to fathom something about the young man from his eyes. He acquiesced to Captain Johnson at last.

"All right, Captain, let us delve into the paramount matter before us and leave the foolish one behind, hoping that Mr. Wake here will also. Give him the intelligence known so far."

Johnson walked over to the chart table, sat down, and bade Wake to do likewise. On the chart of the upper Bahamas spread out before them, Johnson pointed out the Abaco Islands, along the northern edge of the colony, and New Providence Island, where the capital of Nassau was located. Wake nodded his comprehension and Johnson continued, now with Admiral Barkley standing behind Wake's chair.

"We have intelligence, some of which came from your own operations off southwest Florida, that blockade runners into Florida, Georgia, and South Carolina are coming from the Abaco Islands, here." A bony finger struck the chart with force at the place with the odd name of Man-O-War Cay. "And that the leader of the organization that has been effecting those transgressions is none other than your very own John Saunders. Saunders, it is said, has strong ties in the colonial administration in Nassau. He evidently has relatives among the former loyalists in those islands who fled the United States after our Revolution. Recently the colonial administration has become very vociferous in demanding that all United States warships vacate the area of the Bahamas and stay out of British waters, saying we are violating their neutrality. Are you with me so far, Wake?"

"Yes, sir," said Wake, not really understanding what course this tack was taking.

"Now Saunders, as far as we know, is hopefully in a Spanish dungeon in Havana and not able to direct his group. Possibly we even may have the good fortune to learn of his execution at the hands of our friends in the Spanish Navy for plotting to overthrow the government there. But still, we are getting advice, from persons who should know, that the trafficking in contraband from these Abaco Islands is continuing even without Mr. Saunders. The fact that we cannot obtain any definite facts because our navy is banned from the waters there is most distressing. Civilian intelligence seems also to have come to an end, most particularly in the Abacos, where our informant was forced by circumstances to leave rather precipitously. We need to know what is going on at those islands, in the least obvious manner possible. I am sure you are comprehending the situation. Correct, Mr. Wake?"

"Yes, sir." Wake did not like the way this one-sided conversation was headed.

"You and the *Rosalie* are the least obvious method of gaining a true appreciation of the situation in the upper Bahamas, and most particularly at this Man-O-War place." Admiral Barkley leaned over the chart and turned to speak to Wake from inches away. "Go there as a small trading sloop. Find out what ships are there. What type they are. Where they have come from. Where they are headed. Do not take action while in British waters. Do not let the British even know that you are there officially. Do not give anyone any reason to suspect your mission. Can you understand all this, Mr. Wake?"

"Yes, sir, I believe I do. When, sir?"

"As soon as you are provisioned and ready, Mr. Wake. Put some cargo on deck to disguise your twelve-pounder gun and let your crew wear some clothes from the slop chest for this voyage."

Johnson added, "Wake, if you are chased by a British naval vessel, dump the deck gun overboard and continue the façade of being a cargo lugger just sailing through the islands from the Florida Keys. Do not advise them of your true identity. They will let you go; don't worry."

Wake did not believe that the powerful Royal Navy would let a suspicious vessel go, but held his tongue.

"Now, you will receive your written orders from the yeoman clerk in the outer office. Get that information on these blockade runners, Wake. We need it to stop the munitions from getting to the Rebel armies. We also need it to shut those British government bastards up with solid evidence of their cooperation with the Rebels to use the Bahamas as a trans-shipment point and base of operations. Any questions?"

"Ah, . . . well, no, sir."

"All right. Wake, this will be a very important assignment that has not been decided upon lightly." Admiral Barkley was looking very serious as he spoke. "It is being given to you because of my trust in your professional judgment. Do this well, son. We might be able to end this war sooner if we can reduce their supplies from coming in. You may go now."

Wake stood and said his formal respects and goodbyes. They wished him luck, never taking their eyes off his eyes. He felt devoid of strength as he emerged from the building and walked over to the waterfront. This was going to be very difficult.

Upon returning to the *Rosalie* he invited Rork into his cabin and told him they were going on another mission to gather information for the admiral, without telling him the destination. Rork did not look pleased but replied, "Aye aye, sir" when told to disguise the deck gun and crew. Wake advised him that he wanted the sloop under way the morning after next, fully provisioned for a month. If anyone at the commissary or the supply shops was not completely cooperative, then Rork was to let Wake know his name. Wake's demeanor told Rork that his captain was nervous about this coming cruise and that everything had better be done correctly and quickly.

On the appointed morning, before sunrise, Wake brought Rork and Durlon into his cabin and told them the details of the destination and the mission. They reacted by asking questions and making suggestions on how to conduct the cruise to increase their chances of success. Wake was very proud of the way they took on this new assignment: no complaints or recriminations against the admiral, just a professional assessment of how to do it well.

Two hours later they were sailing in the deep water outside the fringing reefs of the Florida Keys, close-hauled on a starboard tack with the trade wind out of the southeast. The *Rosalie* was enjoying the moment as she bounded along in the deep blue water, heeled over by the press of the full mainsail and jib. It was definitely a wonderful day to start a cruise to a foreign destination, with a few puffy clouds in a powder-blue sky. Wake allowed himself a little smugness, thinking how in New England right now they were hiding in their houses from the bitter weather. Perhaps he didn't miss the north as much as he thought, certainly not on a January day like this.

Three mornings later they were broad reaching in light winds under the same canvas somewhere off the island of Grand Bahama. The lookout spotted it on the port bow about noon. All hands crowded onto the foredeck to see the low-lying island come over the horizon. In the past day they had seen various vessels sailing or steaming in the Straits of Florida, but none of them had been British warships. Most were trading schooners, and one time they had seen a United States naval steamer in the distance.

Wake chose to round the island's western end by a wide berth. He did not want to call attention to *Rosalie* by sailing close in to the shore, even though it would have decreased the distance sailed. He needed to get around the end of Grand Bahama Island, come easterly and sail close-hauled along the fringe of islands that line the northern edge of the Little Bahama Bank. As he would get more easting, they would sail along the islands offshore of Great Abaco Island. Among those islands, where Great Abaco turns from a southeast trend to one to the due south, they would find the place called Man-O-War Cay. They would stay offshore until reaching that island, then turn into the shallows and reefs and make their way into the maze of small islands. Wake estimated two more days to arrive at their destination.

Since neither he nor any of his crew had ever been in these waters, they would proceed with caution. The last thing he needed was to wreck his ship. The reefs would be as dangerous as the Confederate blockade runners. His orders stressed the need for secrecy and discretion. Admiral Barkley himself had added an addendum to his orders advising Wake to actually trade some of the goods loaded onto his deck to complete his disguise, and to allow only the petty officers ashore to "guard against accidental discovery from rum-loosened lips."

In spite of the extremely tense feeling in his stomach and mind, Wake had to smile at the admiral adding that proscription. He was, of course, exactly correct. He knew that the ways of the navy, and its sailors, had not changed much since he was a young officer. Wake chuckled aloud. Rork looked over at his commander with concern since they were entering waters filled with dangerous reefs and enemy sympathizers, and attention to detail was needed. As he turned back to overseeing the men replacing the chafing baggywrinkle on the shrouds aloft, Rork guessed that his captain was probably thinking about that young lady of his in Key West.

On the fifth day out of Key West they tacked inshore at Man-O-War Cay. Sail had been reduced as they were now close-hauled on the other tack, the wind holding steady in the southeast. The *Rosalie* passed the large rock off the eastern end of the island, through water even clearer than that of the Florida Keys. As they approached the island, the crew saw a dozen native sloops in the three-mile-wide bay between the outer fringe islands and the large island of Abaco. One was entering the harbor at Man-O-War Cay, and Wake decided to follow her in. In for a penny, in for a pound, he thought as he listened to the leadsman call out the depths. A fathom and more took them into the harbor, where there were no large vessels of either steam or sail, only small native sloops and a schooner of the same size as the *Rosalie*. Rork gave Wake an inquiring glance.

"Rork, we shall anchor here and I will go ashore to ascertain any intelligence of the Rebel ships or their sympathizers. Stay aboard and alert. Tell any bumboat that comes along that we are only here for a while and will be leaving soon. And remember to keep the crew below decks. Only you and Durlon will be seen. This is a trading sloop and not a naval vessel. No need for all those men, right?"

"Aye, right ye are, sir. Jest a simple lot o' traders we are, back in the midst of the damned English occupiers of my beloved Eire."

"Try not to start anything unpleasant in my absence with these 'damned English,' Rork," Wake said as he prepared to row himself off in the dinghy to a crude jetty close by.

When ashore, Wake went to see the local commissioner of the island, who functioned as the government representative and therefore was the customs official also. Wake was nervous about his mission and wondered several times if Admiral Barkley had authorized it alone, or if Secretary of the Navy Wells in

Washington had approved of it. He also wondered what it was exactly that had made their informant "precipitously" leave the area. Many scenarios crossed his mind on that subject—all of them very unpleasant. The young officer was acutely aware of how the British would view the mission of the *Rosalie* if they ever found out the truth. He was directed to walk up the hill to the house of the commissioner by a quiet man in a boat building shed who regarded Wake with undisguised curiosity.

The limestone and shell walls of the commissioner's home were washed with a faded pink pigment from seashells, which added a gay atmosphere, especially when combined with the beautiful flowers that abounded in the yard. The house itself, set upon a hill overlooking the small harbor, was not substantial in size or elegance, but had enough added details of construction and personal touch to make it the home of the leader of the islanders.

Wake stepped up onto the verandah and spoke loudly to announce himself. "Hello! Commissioner Williams! Anyone home?"

"No need to yell too loud, young man. I am right here in my home," came the reply from the middle-aged man who showed at the main doorway. He was short and slightly built, with fading reddish hair and a face that was made almost blood red by either the broiling sun or strong drink. He stood looking at Wake without offering his hand and continued, "Commissioner Albert Williams of Her Majesty's Government of the Colony of the Bahamas, West Indies Station, Man-O-War Cay. Now, I know that you are from the United States by your accent, probably from a New England state, but that is all I know. Would you please introduce yourself and state how the commissioner of this small island can be of assistance to you?"

"Sir, I am Peter Wake, the captain of the trading sloop just come to anchor in your harbor. I have my manifest and bill of lading and am here to complete my entry into the colony. I am four days outbound from St. Augustine."

"I see. And what brings you to *this* island?"

"I've heard there is trade to be found among these islands. I have not been among them before and am looking for new places. I have some cotton by the bale, molasses, turpentine, cloth goods, and some sundry items. If anyone here needs a cargo to be run into Florida, or a pilot to run a vessel to Florida, I can furnish that also."

The commissioner was watching him very carefully. Wake was hoping his story was holding water with this man, who had control over the islands in this immediate area. After a moment the commissioner replied.

"Mr. Wake, your accent does not support your proposition. A Yankee who wants to run the blockade? Please explain that, if you would."

"I am born and bred a Yankee sailor. But I'll be damned if I'll die to keep the South in the country against their will. If they want to go, I say let them go. I think this war is trumped up by the New York merchants, Commissioner, and I will not be a party to it. I am a sailor and a trader and want to stay free. I guess some would say I am absconding from the conscription. I say I am a free man of the sea and want to practice my trade. I know the coast of Florida and can take cargo there if I can find some to be taken. That is all there is to it, sir."

"A free man of the sea? Well, even a free man of the sea must pay the Queen's shilling in these waters, Peter Wake. You have your papers? I will inspect them and sign them. You will have one month here in the Abaco Islands to trade. Should you not pay the Queen's excise upon the trade you have completed prior to departure, you will be gaoled in Nassau. And *that*, Peter Wake, will not be pleasant, I assure you.

"Now let me see your papers of pratique, lading, crew, et cetera, and get this business completed. You just might find some transactions to your satisfaction here in these islands. Also, we have very strict laws here. *Her Majesty*," Williams said this with exaggerated importance, "wishes that you follow them, and the instructions of her officers, both civil and naval. Keep your men and yourself in good behavior, Mr. Wake."

"Thank you, Commissioner. I will be sailing throughout the Abacos and probably won't stay an entire month. I want to leave if I can't get any trade to Florida. If you would be so kind, sir, let anyone know who is interested to contract with me that he can communicate with the *Rosalie* whilst I am here."

As the commissioner was signing the papers, Wake continued on his rhetoric with an inquiry.

"By the way, Commissioner Williams, will I have to worry about United States Navy ships molesting me in your waters? I have heard they intrude here."

"Not anymore. The governor in Nassau put an end to that. They were getting damned arrogant and inspecting ships in British waters! No, they will not molest you or anyone else here. It would appear that you have already met them, or at least someone unpleasant, by that scar on your head. A bullet or a blade, sir?"

Wake's hand came unconsciously up to the side of his head where the scar still traced the wound from the battle that night on the river. His fingers ran along the line by his ear as he replied to the observant commissioner. "Aye, sir. Riggin' knife on the mess deck of the warship *Vandalia*, Commissioner. Had my fill o' the navy after a month, and that was three years ago. Decided I didn't like their ways, especially the ways of a certain toady officers' steward who had a bosun as a protector. Bastard of a bosun, was a brute all right. Knew I had to leave when he didn't quite kill me and we were both on the same ship. Woulda killed me certain, but I made my freedom. Took French leave and went back sailing as a free seaman."

"I see, Captain Wake. So you definitely have no reason to love the American Navy. Should I hear of any cargo needing a run to Florida, I will remember you. Good luck, sir."

As Wake descended the hill on his way back to the island's quiet waterfront, he breathed deeply and tried to look as unconcerned as possible. He had made up the *Vandalia* story on the spot and did not know if the commissioner believed him. He figured it would soon be obvious either way. By a storefront along the docks, he said hello to a severe-looking woman who openly stared at him. Wake noticed that these islanders were very quiet and almost fearful of strangers. He had uncomfortable thoughts as he came back aboard the sloop minutes later and spoke to Rork.

"We will stay here until tomorrow morn and then sail for Nassau. Trade some small stuff with the bumboats. But no rum. Not a drop! Fruits, yes, get us some fruit. How are the men below, Rork?"

"Hot, sir, but the wind sail is funneling some air below, and the awnings help."

"Good. I want to get out of here as soon as I can for their health, but we must get the information we came for."

Rork looked at his captain with curious but respectful eyes and said nothing but nodded his acknowledgment. An hour later he came below to Wake's cabin and told him of a trade he had made for bananas that had included some useful information in addition.

"Captain, the man who sold the bananas asked if we were the new American pilot coming to the island from Nassau. Said they had heard a pilot was coming to steer the runners through. When I said that we didn't come from Nassau, but that we could take a cargo to Florida, he shut up like a clam. Handed over the fruit and rowed off for the little dock down the way as fast as you please."

"Coming from Nassau, eh? So they have an American pilot coming here? To meet blockade runners. But this harbor isn't deep enough. Ocean ships can't get through the reef. Anything over a fathom in draft would have a hard time in these waters."

Durlon came up to the captain and bosun standing by the mast and contributed to the conversation.

"May be just an old gunner, sir, but I was thinkin' that maybe they meets them offshore of the island. No need to come inshore, just sail out by island boat and go off from there to the Southern coast."

Wake pondered that while the petty officers looked at him. He turned toward Durlon.

"You may be a gunner, but, by God, I do think you have a point. This is no seaport. Nothing here for a runner except knowledge. Knowledge of a pilot. If this bumboatman was right, and they are expecting a pilot to come here and rendezvous soon with a runner, we may be in some sort of luck. Keep your eyes open."

"Aye, sir. This old muzzle-lover may just be right, though 'twill be a rare thing!" offered Rork as he punched Durlon's arm and smiled the wide Irish grin that made him a favorite among the Key West barmaids.

As Durlon turned to go aft, he punched Rork back. "Ya Irish rogue! Ya love me plenty when the shootin's goin' on!"

The rest of the day passed slowly as the small boat work of the island went on around them. No other boats came alongside. The three men waited under the awning doing the usual chores required every day aboard every vessel, large or small.

In the late afternoon they heard a commotion by the government dock. A large schooner with the peculiar long-boomed rig of the Bahamas sailed into the anchorage and glided up to the dock. Commissioner Williams and a few other islanders met the sloop as she made fast to the dock. Wake could see Williams go aboard quickly and converse with several men at the stern, then lead them ashore and up the hill to his house. Meanwhile, the islanders had set about unloading the cargo heaped on her decks. Wake turned to Rork.

"Rork, I want you and Durlon to keep watch on the hill where the commissioner's house is located. If you see any of those men come down the hill, let me know immediately. I believe that our Rebel pilot may be among them."

Rork acknowledged and went back to his business, glancing frequently over at the hill above the waterfront. In the dusk of the late afternoon he woke his captain up from a nap, informing him that the men from the schooner were back aboard and that

Williams came back with them. Wake nodded and said to keep watch for anything unusual.

Wake heard it before Durlon told him—an odd mournful sound that he occasionally heard in Key West. It was a conch shell being blown, with a plaintive wail stretching out the sound. After the initial elongated blast, several loud, short ones followed. Wake, Durlon, and Rork looked ashore where a gathering had formed on the dock by the large schooner.

Activity swarmed on the schooner and the dock in the last light of the day after the sun had gone down. People came out of their homes, and men around the shore stopped and looked over at the schooner as the crew aboard bore a hand at the halyards to raise the huge mainsail. Other crewmen were casting off dock lines, while still more were backwinding the jib to get her turned around and headed down channel. It was as if the conch shell sounding had stirred a mound of ants into some frenzied action. Everywhere on the island people were taking notice of the schooner. Some were yelling encouragement, and now Wake could make out Commissioner Williams standing on the dock, pronouncing in a loud voice that did not seem to go with his small body, "God speed to you, and may your return be with success! Give Captain Dunbarton our good wishes!"

Wake turned to Rork and Durlon. "I believe that conch shell sounded an alarm that a runner is near the island. We can't hope to catch up with the schooner over there or get close to the runner, but maybe we can get some intelligence from that crew later about what ship they met and where she was bound."

Both petty officers nodded agreement as they all watched the schooner quickly gather headway and sail out of the anchorage, with the shore entourage still shouting encouragement.

Rork suggested moments later, "Perhaps I could have a drop of rum with those lads later, if they return tonight, sir? Nay tellin' what I may be hearin' if they are feelin' good enough."

Wake regarded Rork in the dim light. He had come to trust and rely on this man. Rork had an easy way with other sailors, an instinctive basic bond. He seldom had to raise his voice. He could be trusted and would be the one to get the information better than Wake could.

"All right, Rork. Upon their return I'll let you gauge the moment to go and get the information. Durlon and I will remain aboard. Don't stay too long. I presume I don't have to warn you about the obvious, so I won't."

Durlon, mute through this dialogue, could be still no longer. "An' don't you do any stirrin' of their limey blood, Rork, ya Irish rebel!"

Rork took all of this approval and assistance in stride. "Aye now, me Captain. I'll not partake o' too much as that wouldn't be very sociable like, sir. And you, Gunner Durlon, know well that I am the picture of politeness even when with difficult people. Why, I'm an Irish gentlemen, I am, sir." This comment was accompanied by a smile and a glance into the eyes of his friend.

It was well past midnight when Rork came to Wake's cabin and told him he was off to have a drop with the schooner's crew. Throughout the next four hours Durlon and Wake stayed on deck and listened as the drinking and carousing went on a hundred yards away aboard the large Bahamian vessel over at the dock. Occasionally they could hear an Irish ballad rise up as the other noise fell away. No sound of argument or discord was discernible and they relaxed their vigil but still stayed awake to listen if their crewmate might need help.

At dawn a very exhausted Wake greeted a very gleeful Rork as he came over the side at the shrouds after handing Durlon the dinghy's painter. They all retired below to Wake's cabin to hear the intelligence that Rork had gathered.

"What a wonderful bit of sailors those boyos are, Captain. Not a bad one in the lot. Well, not a really bad one anyway. They are mainly from Nassau and don't like the perfidious English any more than I do!" Wake smiled as he listened. Rork's brogue was thicker than usual with the rum inside him.

"It turns out, sir, that you and ol' Durlon here were right on the runner meetin' up with them offshore. They took a pilot from

Savannah out to a runner about three miles offshore. The pilot had just come into Nassau from Charleston. They don't have the runners go into Nassau nowadays prior to goin' through our navy's blockade. Now they have them come to these islands and meet up with the coastal pilot offshore, then go into the Confederacy. The little buggers're doin' this at least once a week! Makin' a nice little bag o' gold, real gold, a fee for bringin' mister pilot from Nassau to the runners out by this island.

"See, sir, Mister Governor of the Bahamas can say that no runners are comin' in from across the ocean to Nassau and the American Navy should not be a-worrying about Bahamas waters. 'Course they still come in on the short haul from the Rebel mainland and put off their cargo and pilot quick like. Merchants of Nassau are very happy with that. These boyos I met with are delighted with the way things have worked out!"

Wake wanted to get the specifics before Rork passed out, which looked imminent.

"Rork, what was the name of the ship they met? What was her cargo, and from where was she?"

"Well now, sir, they was a bit quiet about that, sir. Took several more turns at the jug to get 'em to speak on that. But the rum loosened them all after a while." Durlon looked at Wake with a grin as they both thought of their Irish friend loosening someone else's lips with rum. Rork appeared pretty loose himself.

"She be the *Mary Anne*, screw steamer two weeks out of Bristol with manufactured merchant goods and some rifles, they think. Not sure on the rifles. They just hear from the crews what is aboard. Last night it was calm and they came alongside of the steamer for mail and small stuff. Got to talk to the crew. Crew of the steamer said their captain was . . . oh well, sir, they did not like their captain. Some unpleasantness aboard of her evidently. Anyway, they say they do this once a week and get good money for it from a merchant in Nassau."

"Anything else, Rork?"

"That you're *able* to remember?" added Durlon, laughing.

"No, sir. Oh, exceptin' one little thing, sir." Rork ignored his friend and turned to stare rather blankly at Wake. "It would seem, Captain, that your friend, the English gentleman named Williams, of Her Majesty's Government of the Bahamas and the Honorable Commissioner of these particular lumps of sand in the sea, is not following Her Britannic Majesty's neutrality orders. In point of fact, he is assisting the Rebels in some disturbing ways. For it turns out that a man named Saunders, aye, sir, I said Saunders, has come here before and is the man who used the island for the pilot rendezvous in the first place, two years past. It further seems, me good Captain, that the man in question, Mr. Saunders, is from Virginia with relatives around here and was recently in Cuba arranging some other shipping for the American Rebels." The grin was gone from Rork's face now as he continued in a low and menacing voice. "And that particular bastard was last seen here on this island not more than a month ago. A month ago! Sailed up from Nassau with me boyos over there and got aboard a runner bound for the coast by Savannah a fortnight back."

Wake and Durlon sat there staring at Rork. He was a little drunk, yes, but not enough to misunderstand or imagine that intelligence.

"Rork, they are *sure* it was a man named Saunders? *Our* Saunders?"

"No doubt, sir. He was a friend of the commissioner and stayed at his house until the runner arrived offshore for the rendezvous to get the pilot. Not more than a month ago. Captain, I am thinkin' that our enemy Saunders is more lucky or more skilled than we ever thought, sir. Must definitely have a bit o' the Irish in his bones, that one."

"Well, I'll be damned." It was the only thing Durlon could think to say as Wake tried to decipher the meaning of what Rork had said. There was no good meaning to it. Saunders had either escaped from the Spanish or bought his way out through friends in the bureaucracy or through some other relationship. How? How did he do it?

"Permission to retire to me hammock, sir. I'm a wee bit tired, sir."

"Very good, Rork, get some rest, for we will weigh anchor by noon and sail for Nassau. You did well."

Wake thought about the information that Rork had gathered. Saunders out of Cuba. And *that* quickly. He wondered why the admiral didn't know it in Key West. Then he remembered that the admiral had said that the civilian intelligence had dried up in the Abaco Islands of the Bahamas. Evidently even the consulate in Nassau had not been able to find out how the runners still got their Confederate pilots to steer them in through the blockade. Now, however, they had that information and knew the Havana operations of the enemy were tied to the Bahamas. But why hadn't the Havana consulate passed on the news of Saunders' departure from that city? This was more complex than anyone had imagined. He thought that perhaps one more visit to the commissioner ashore might be beneficial and yield additional facts. Besides, he still wanted to know if anyone had heard of John Saunders in these islands and what, if any, connection he really had here. He remembered Saunders explaining, that day when Wake had decided to let him go free, his family's post–Revolutionary War Loyalist connection here. The memory caused him to burn with humiliation.

Midmorning Wake again ascended the hill to Commissioner Williams' house. Williams was polite and inquired how long Wake was planning to stay among the Abaco Islands.

"I am under way today, sir, with the tide for Nassau. Maybe there will be a cargo there for me since not much seems to be available here. I was told though that there might be some small cargo here to sail to Florida, which is why I came here. I guess my friend was wrong."

"And what friend might that be, Captain Wake?"

Wake plunged in and hoped he would not betray his feelings when he said the man's name. "A gentleman who said he was from these islands, sir. Man named John Saunders, whom I met on the west coast of Florida. I assisted the gentleman and afterward he advised me of the situation here in your islands."

"John Saunders, you say? And how is John?" Williams was looking directly at Wake now.

"Don't rightly know, Commissioner. It's been a year since I saw him. Have you seen him since?" Wake was using all of his willpower to remain calm.

"No, Mr. Wake, I have not seen Mr. Saunders lately. I have heard that he has been busy with other obligations in other places. Saunders told you correctly. There are opportunities here for a man knowing the Southern coast. But none at the present, I am afraid. Good luck on your voyage to Nassau."

Wake bade his respects and departed. He could not ascertain any more intelligence from the commissioner's words than what he had heard, and he knew what he had heard was a skilled lie. The man was inscrutable and more than a little unnerving. Wake decided that it was definitely time to leave the anchorage. Things were getting complicated quickly.

They made sail at noon, Rork seemingly none the worse for wear and waving goodbye to his friends from a few hours before. The wind was fair for leaving the island but promised a rough hundred-mile voyage to New Providence Island, where Nassau was located. As they left Man-O-War Cay, Wake noticed none of the enthusiasm among the population that had accompanied the departure of the pilot's sloop the evening before. In fact, the people along the waterfront barely appeared to register that fact that they were leaving. Wake had the vague feeling that the people of this island were different from any other people he had ever met. In fact, the entire situation in these islands, from the commissioner's demeanor to the islanders' behavior to the undercurrent of Confederate blockade-running operations, made him feel very uneasy. But navigating out through the reefs soon fully occupied him.

Wake had only the jib set. Even then, *Rosalie* still moved at a brisk pace on the full reach, heading northeast. Once she rounded the reefs and was in five fathoms, they hauled up close to the wind with a fully reefed mainsail and slogged into the southerly wind.

The wind was steady and strong as the sloop, centerboard down, tried to make long tacks in the beat to the south along the islands skirting the Abaco coast. Wake had heard that the wreckers of these islands were related by blood to some of those in the Florida Keys. As *Rosalie* passed Elbow Cay, he saw that the British government was building a lighthouse there. He had heard while ashore on Man-O-War Cay that the lighthouse on Elbow was to protect ships that came upon the island in the dark after crossing the ocean from the east. It was the first land seen since leaving Europe, and frequently the last since so many wrecked there. But when the islander had told him about the lighthouse, he had spoken with contempt of how it would deprive so many islanders the living their families had been making for generations. Wake shook his head at the memory, thinking that many a sailor considered them little better than pirates, in spite of some spectacular rescues of stranded crews that had been made by these very same men, in both Florida and the Bahamas.

The rest of the day was spent smashing into the confused seas by Ocean Point on the east coast of Great Abaco Island itself. The sloop was trying to point as far as she could into the wind, but that was at the expense of speed. Wake knew that it would take a long time to get his little ship south to New Providence Island, but there was nothing he could do about it.

By nightfall they were still fighting their way to the south. No lights shone on this coast. The deep water came all the way up to the cliffs lining the shore. Wake dead-reckoned his way along the coast, doubling the lookout in the pitch-black night, hoping that he had kept far enough off. Making a long tack offshore to the southeast and a short tack inshore to the southwest, *Rosalie* pounded her way through the dark ocean, repeating the maneuver with all hands called many times.

When the eastern sky lightened enough that a dim horizon line could be discerned, both lookouts saw a shape in the western gloom and shouted together.

"Broad on the port bow! A steam warship!

The entire crew of the sloop gathered on the cold and wet deck to peer out at the large ship coming at them. It came from the direction of the southeastern point of Great Abaco labeled curiously on the chart as "Hole in the Wall." The lookouts were correct, she was a warship. And she was heading for the sloop from about five or six miles away.

Wake started to do the geometry in his mind. He calculated that the steamer would be upon them in several minutes, what with the wind behind them and smoke pouring from her funnel. He did not know if they would try to stop and inspect the small sloop, especially in these seas, but he looked over to the cliffs of Abaco to see if there was any way to escape to the east or south if they did attempt to force him to stop.

He turned aft to find Rork eyeing the distant ship. The bosun swayed easily with the rolling deck and just as easily asked Wake what they were going to do. Wake was impressed by his calm demeanor.

"Well, she'll be here very soon. No time to turn and run. Just make sure the deck gun is hidden but ready to go over in a moment."

"Aye aye, sir. We'll slide the little devil off the lee side, should it come to that, no fear, sir."

"Very good, Rork. Keep her steady on this course. We should make the point with room to spare. Once around we can bear off a bit."

As Rork acknowledged the order, Wake gauged the imaginary triangle again. The point of intercept for the two vessels would be in about a mile, and it would take just a few minutes. The steamer was getting closer very fast.

"She's the *Peterel*, sir!" cried out Chestnut from the foredeck. "I saw her in Key West last year. Took a message to her and saw her close up. Gunboat with a barque rig. Does only about seven knots 'cause her bottom's foul and they haven't careened her lately. Limeys were complainin' about her bein' slow and all. Said she leaks like a Bahama fish boat, sir!"

Rork was quick on Chestnut's comment. "Louis, me boy, you say she's slow? Her own men say it? You heard them say it? No time for the tales, son. This is a bit of a serious time."

"Aye, Mister Bosun. That's what I heard them say, without no doubts."

Rork looked at Wake with a gleam in his eye. "Well, Captain. Old Rosey will do seven off the wind on a day like today. Once we double the point yonder there, we can show her our heels. Even if they set sail they can't point like us. Either way we may have a chance to confound the English bastards. 'Tis always a touch o' fun to do that, I can tell ya, sir!"

Wake found himself, against his better judgment, infected with the bosun's enthusiasm. He made his decision in an instant.

"Right you are, Rork. Looks to me that we will pass close aboard of Her Majesty's steamer and then be able to bear off. When we do, shake out the reefs in the mains'l and set the jib too. Remember, we're a trader. The crew can pretend to be passengers. We'll show her how to fly!"

The ships got closer and Wake could see the figures of the men on the Britisher's bow pointing at the sloop. The men set to their tasks with the enthusiasm of a race crew, but Wake knew the consequences of failure were far worse. All hands held on as she continued close-hauled toward the point at the end of Hole in the Wall, plunging into the seas coming over the port bow.

Then he saw the brilliant spot of color in the steamer's rigging catch the first rays of the sun as it started to boil up out of the horizon. It was the Red Ensign of the Royal Navy, the navy that had made, and now protected, the British Empire, which spanned the globe and made the American Navy seem puny in comparison. A golden shaft of light lit up the blood red of the flag as it ascended the peak halyard of the mizzen mast on the Royal Navy ship.

"She's showin' her colors, sir!" volunteered Chestnut. "Doesn't that mean for us to heave to, sir?"

Now Wake wasn't feeling so enthusiastic. He was in a very

dangerous situation. "Steady on, boys. We will not heave to in these seas. Rork, please send up our ensign and stand by to slack away on the sheets."

A small American flag, of the type a coastal sailor would have aboard, was hauled up to the peak of the mainsail. Afterward all the crew waved at the oncoming ship in the most innocent way they could imagine, all the while preparing to ease away off the wind and set more sail.

As the *Peterel* passed within a hundred feet to windward of the *Rosalie*, Wake heard a man call out through a trumpet, "Ahoy to the sloop there! Your name and last port?"

The rumble of machinery and the loud swish of the steamer's bow wave became almost overwhelming as Wake answered with cupped hands, "*Rosalie!* Two days outbound from Man-O-War, bound for Nassau!"

"*Rosalie!* Heave to in our lee! Heave to!"

The officers on the stern of the steamer were examining the small sloop and her crew with telescopes, giving Wake the feeling of a bug being eyed by a predator prior to being eaten. That feeling was heightened by the close-up look at the armament of the British warship. Modern weaponry was very much apparent, including pivot-mounted, breech-loading Armstrong guns. Wake glanced at Durlon, who spoke quietly to his captain.

"Aye, she may be slow but those Armstrongs can reach out and hurt us, Captain. Those look like twenty-pounders, and that one there," he nodded in the direction of the largest gun on the steamer's deck, which was partially hidden by the bulwark, "looks, by God, to be a forty-pounder! "

Sloshing along downwind, the steamer slid past them quickly and was soon astern. Her officers were still eyeing the American sloop. They became more animated as the distance between the ships increased. Now they were yelling something, but no words could be made out. The moment had come for action, and Wake was thinking that it had to be done correctly and quickly.

"Ease away on the sheet! Set the jib and shake out those mains'l reefs!"

Instantly the pounding gave way to a rolling swoop over the beam seas as the *Rosalie* heeled over with the lee rail awash. The added press of sail served to dampen her motion a bit, and the increase in speed seemed even more pronounced as the sound of the bow wave increased in tempo. They were positively flying along, almost passing out of the water at the crest of a wave. Hole in the Wall slid by to leeward.

Wake stood at the stern, still trying to look innocent by waving to the warship heading away to the northeast. As he waved he felt a change in her motion, and Holmes at the great tiller interrupted him. "Sir, bit of a wind shift. We're getting headed, sir."

With that new development, Rork let out a string of Irish oaths that impressed even Wake. Quickly the crew hauled the sheets in again to conform to the now west-of-south wind. It was back-breaking work, for the sloop with all sail set was creating a tremendous force to haul against. Just then Chestnut and young Schmidt yelled in unison, "She's coming round!" as they pointed aft. Wake turned to see the other ship, astern by a mile now, slowly turn up into the wind and come round on their heading. With none of her barque-rigged sails set, *Peterel* could turn around fast. Now time would tell who was faster. Wake looked at Great Abaco Island again to gauge whether he could round the last remaining headland, Southwest Point, and then fly off to leeward on the west coast of the island.

"Stream the log, Rork. As soon as we round that point we shall run off close along the shore. Maybe we can make them timid among the reefs!"

The log showed the sloop was making eight knots, with surges even faster. She was smashing along in the seas and the strain was evident in her standing rigging, with the leeward shrouds sagging off and the windward ones taut and moaning in the wind. Rork was watching everything at once, directing preventer lines to be set up and putting an extra man on the helm to help with the steering. Wake knew she was being overpowered by the wind, but he also knew it was her only chance of escaping the steamer, now dully colliding with the seas astern of them and heading for the Americans.

The set and drift of the sloop carried her down to the leeward shore, and soon they could hear the crash of the surf less than a mile away. In a few minutes Wake judged that the time was right, even with that wind shift, and that they should now head west close aboard the rocks at the base of Southwest Point.

"Bear away and ease the sheets! Mind your helm and steer small for the west, close on the shoreline!"

This order was punctuated by the sight—for the sound had been carried off to the northeast—of a plume of water that erupted a quarter mile ahead of the bows. Wake was stunned at first and came out of his shock finally when Durlon came up to him and yelled into his ear, "Damned good shot, sir. Probably can't do *that* again though! Sheer luck, if ya' ask me!"

There was nothing more to do than what they were already doing. The distance between the little sloop and the shore narrowed rapidly as they passed Southwest Point very close and slewed around to run off on a broad reach along the coast of the island. Wake estimated that they were still about a mile and a half from the steamer, and the British were not gaining much, if any.

He could tell by the buildup of the seas that they were getting close to the reefs along the shore. The wind was also building. The chart indicated a bay far ahead with reefs and islands in it. If they could make it to the safety of the shallow water, where the steamer could not go, they might just force the enemy, for that is how Wake now thought of them, to give up the chase.

Boom! . . . The sound was coming along the wind, since the steamer was now astern and upwind of the sloop, steering farther out around the point than the Americans, as the next plume of water erupted far out ahead of them. Durlon pointed out to his shipmates that he had predicted that wild shot, and started to make wagers concerning the next one. Somehow this calmed everyone, including Wake, enough to face the next few shots with academic interest. None of them came close.

Cedar Point was a headland coming up several miles ahead and, with *Rosalie* on a broad reach, would be easily rounded. The chart indicated there would be enough water for the sloop to cross the gap in the reefs, but the two-fathom bottom would bar the steamer from the entrance.

For the next half hour the chase continued as before, but without further shots from the British ship. The distance between them was difficult to gauge but definitely was not diminishing. The coast prior to reaching the bay ahead was straight and without off-lying reefs. All they had to do was hold on to their lead and make it through the reefs of the bay they were quickly approaching. Soon they could see the waves rising up along the reef, then the foam became visible, and soon they could hear the crash of the heavy seas as they broke down upon the coral rocks.

The wall of exploding surf had a quiet space showing a quarter mile off Cedar Point and the sloop headed for that. *Rosalie* was sailing faster now than Wake had ever experienced since joining her. Surging down the waves, which were building as they got closer to the bay and the bottom shallowed, the sloop was on the verge of broaching several times. The sheer strength of the helmsmen and their intuitive knowledge of how to steer through the following seas was what kept them from veering out of control and ending up a wreck on the reefs to leeward. Rork and Wake stood quietly next to them, not wanting to distract the men who had the lives of all aboard in their hands. Every man in the crew intensely watched the men on the tiller and the Royal Navy steamer astern of them. Wagers and jocularity were gone as they all hauled or slacked the sheets and tried to hold on and not fall on the pitching and rolling deck.

The reefs ahead now showed with terrifying clarity. Even the razor-sharp coral could be seen below the crashing surf. The sound of the seas smashing into the reefs was a constant rumble occasionally interrupted by much louder thuds as a larger wave fell heavily onto the coral formations. Faster than Wake had predicted, they found themselves within the maelstrom of noise and spray, with the seas lifting them high and throwing them forward. The die was now cast and they could not turn around or to either side but had to hope they could get through the apparent gap in the teeth of the coral they were steering for. *Rosalie* rose higher and held there for a moment, then fell down the front of the wave, her bow wave making a rushing sound that overwhelmed all else.

The men at the tiller were struggling to keep her under control as the sloop raced forward at speeds faster than Wake had ever seen any ship under sail make. The log was now uselessly skipping astern of them but Wake estimated that they must be making at least twelve or thirteen knots, possibly more. It would be instantaneous death for all of them if they hit a reef at this speed. The two helmsmen were barely able to stand from exhaustion and their arms and legs were shaking uncontrollably from the effort. Wake and Rork relieved the seamen and held the straining tiller, steering through the opening in the brown coral walls that were plainly visible in the breaking seas on either side of the sloop. It was all they could do to keep her on course.

"Hold on and pray for forgiveness, men!" he shouted with a smile as Rork bore a hand to help on the tiller. All hands held onto anything substantial as they entered the narrow channel.

"All right, ya limey bastards! Lay off and belay!" the bosun yelled as he fought the helm to help Wake counter the twist of the seas trying to slew *Rosalie* around. He even held the tiller with one hand to shake the other in a great fist at the steamer, which was periodically disappearing behind the huge seas thrown up by the rising bottom.

"By the mark, two!" cried Sampson from the leeward shrouds as he was knee-deep awash in the green water. "By the mark, four!" he cried again as he cast the lead line again and found the depth increasing inshore of the reefs.

And in a moment the water was amazingly calmer and the sloop much easier to steer, with the tempest of the reefs behind them. Rork and the captain were relieved at the helm by White and Hewlitt. Wake collapsed onto the deck, gasping for breath and looking out to sea. The steamer was continuing north past the reefs and the bay. A final shot came their way and exploded in the top of a wave along the reef to windward of them. Durlon winced, and Sampson and Nelson asked for their money since it had come much closer than he had predicted in his wager.

Wake shook his head in disbelief and stood, helping an exhausted Rork up from deck where he was resting from the ordeal.

"White, steer for that small island there ahead. Durlon, if you could spare the time away from your gambling endeavor, kindly drop the mains'l immediately. I want to reduce our visibility to them as much as possible."

Wake was duly acknowledged by a grinning Durlon and a serious-faced White, and the sloop sailed through the shoaling water to a point of land at a thin island ahead of the bow. By the time they had reached the point, *Rosalie* had only the jib pulling and they had slowed to a couple of knots. Soon they had drifted around and under the lee of the point into flat water. Wake felt exhausted and sat on the stern rail.

"Anchor and get the sail down. I want a man aloft to tell me what they are doing. Schmidt, that will be you."

The rest of the crew stowed the gear and sails as the boy climbed the shrouds to the crosstree spreaders and stood by the topmast, peering out to sea through the mangrove trees of the island that separated the Americans from the British. He called out from aloft.

"They've come about, sir. The steamer is headin' back along the reefs real slow into the wind. They's makin' heavy weather of it, sir."

"Continue, son. What are they doing now? Are they lowering a boat?"

"No, sir, they haven't stopped to lower a boat, sir. Looks to be they're goin' away to windward, back the way we all come from, sir. That's good, ain't it, sir?"

Wake, a slumped and exhausted form on the deck among the other slumped forms of his crew next to him, started laughing.

He was joined by Rork and Durlon and soon all the rest of the men. The boy up on the mast looked confused.

"Yes, young sailor Schmidt. The fact that they are going away would be a good thing. A very good thing! Stay up there for another hour and keep your eyes peeled for any sign of the steamer or one of her boats. Our fate is in your hands now, son."

Rork spoke up from his seat on the deck by the binnacle. "They won't be launchin' a boat to go through *that* surf, sir. Even the crazy limeys won't be daft enough to do that!"

Rork got a quizzical look on his face as he thought of what he had just said, then started laughing again. Wake joined as he pointed to the bosun.

"You're right again, Bosun Rork. Nobody but a damned fool would go through that reef in that surf! Certainly no seaman worth his salt that I know."

Soon all hands on the Rosalie were laughing at the bosun and his unintended comment on their sanity. And with that the exhausted crew of the sloop *Rosalie* slept, many of them on the deck, anchored behind a mangrove island hidden away from their pursuer. Remembering the words of Commissioner Williams regarding the wishes of Queen Victoria that he and his crew should be well behaved, Wake laughed in his thoughts. Oh, if Her Majesty could only know how badly her wishes have been ignored! He did not know what they would do next, but he did know that they would soon have to escape the waters of the Bahamas. Her Britannic Majesty's Ship *Peterel* was bound to return when the weather piped down in order to capture the insolent Americans who had flaunted her authority. Nassau was no longer a part of the plan. Now they had to make the safety of Florida.

Two days later the wind veered to the north and blew fresh and cold. The seas no longer crashed in from offshore against the reef, but instead small waves rolled out from shore. The sloop sailed downwind out through the perilous cut in the reefs when the sun was high and the coral was easily seen in the clear waters. Lookouts, who had watched the horizon for the last two days and found nothing, doubled their efforts, for all hands knew that by now there might be several ships of the Royal Navy bound for this bay in an effort to trap and capture the cheeky Americans. Wake sailed with just the jib drawing in order to reduce the sight of his ship on the horizon to any others.

That night they set all sail and raced along the Northwest Providence Channel to the west. No other ships were seen, but at dawn the next day they reduced sail again as they had come into the trade route and saw many island sloops and schooners. Occasionally they sighted a full ship-rigged vessel or a steamer, but none came close enough to be recognized.

On the third dawn after leaving the bay, they saw the coast of Florida, low and sandy, and closed inshore with sails wing and wing on a gentle breeze from the east. The men of the *Rosalie* were cheered by the realization that they were safely out of British territory. Catching the countercurrent along the beach, *Rosalie* sailed on a broad port reach until they saw the familiar sights of the Florida Keys stretch out before them, curving southwest and then due west into the Gulf of Mexico. Wake felt a mixture of emotions. He was glad to be back in the relatively safe waters of his home area, glad to return to the arms of Linda, and glad to be able to rest himself and his men. But he dreaded having to tell Admiral Barkley the intelligence he had found out, that somehow his plan in Cuba to rid them of Saunders had been thwarted and that the blockade-running operations of the northern Bahamian islands was far more extensive than thought previously. He feared that this damned war would drag on and on if they were not even able to stop blockade runners like Saunders from their operations.

On the other hand, Wake was fairly certain that their identity had not been compromised and that the British probably thought the sloop was just another trading vessel smuggling items into or out of the colony. If the *Peterel's* crew had been able to board the *Rosalie*, the bad news for the admiral would have included the nightmare of an international incident as well.

Wake touched his scar as he watched Fort Taylor pass by to

starboard on their return to Key West harbor. It was by the sheerest luck that he and his men were not in the dungeons of Fort Charlotte in Nassau for violating Her Majesty's wishes. As he had rapidly learned in the last six months, of such things were success and failure determined in war.

Even in the heat of the noonday calm, the thought of what could have happened made him shudder.

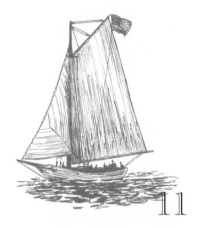

11
Course Made Good

It had been almost a year of war for Wake. Vicksburg, Gettysburg, Chickamauga, and the Wilderness were the newest locations of the bloody battles on land, seizing the attention of a terrified nation. The navy had fought all along the country's coastlines and rivers as well. Sensational accounts of the new Confederate submersible weapon at Charleston and Rebel torpedo bombs in Virginia had filled the newspapers and dominated the talk in the taverns of Key West. It seemed that the insanity would never end. Just as another Union victory would be announced, with the accompanying toll of dead and maimed, the Southerners would somehow fight their way to one more innovative success, doing more with less each time. Wake was alternately depressed by the Union inability to decisively end the carnage and awed by the Confederacy's ability to prolong it. It was all so different from what he had expected a year ago.

It had been a very long year since Peter Wake had left New England and the merchant marine for this life of a naval officer in the East Gulf Blockading Squadron at war in a tropical world of islands and jungles, a life and world that he could not have imagined before his arrival. The year had presented him a series of difficult problems with no easy answers. And it was truly beyond his comprehension that he had grown accustomed to living in this world of sailors and guns and danger. It intrigued him to think of what challenges might rise over the horizon in the near future of his life.

These impressions and conjectures swirled about in his head as he walked into the squadron's offices on a hot, windy April afternoon in Key West. The rainy season was still months off, and the trade winds were sailing across the island unfettered in their passage from Cuba. The young officer waited respectfully, but with obvious tension, in the outer lobby as the staff clerk informed the chief yeoman that Master Peter Wake had arrived for his meeting with the admiral.

It had been two months since Wake had returned from the mission to the Bahama Islands. In that time he and the *Rosalie* had been assigned support duty to various vessels along the coast. It was a dull routine of supply and dispatch compared to missions where they had been independent with responsibility for important results. But he had to admit it was better than the duty endured by those poor souls who just sat on their ships on the blockade and seldom got to leave at all. At least *Rosalie* was able to get under way and move about, with an occasional return to Key West.

When he first returned from the Bahamas, Wake had immediately reported to the admiral and Captain Johnson. It had not been pleasant to make that report, but Wake had been surprised at their reaction. Instead of rage, they had expressed admiration for the way he had gathered the intelligence and then eluded the Royal Navy gunboat challenging him to heave to. They understood his frustration at Saunders' apparently being at large and in operation again. Even Captain Johnson, not someone Wake considered sympathetic to his situation or future, had been restrained. In the end, the admiral, who was looking very sickly at that briefing, had told Wake that it was a difficult job done well and sent him back to routine coastal duty.

And now they had suddenly summoned him to the offices upon his return from Sanibel Island. The chief yeoman of the squadron, a man even the officers treated with deference, ushered Wake into the outer office of the admiral, where the personal yeoman of the admiral announced his arrival.

Wake was shocked when he entered. Admiral Barkley, a robust man a year ago, looked like death itself. He had become emaciated in the last two months, his color was almost transparent, and his demeanor was of a very old and frail man. The uniform hung in drapes from his frame and did nothing to conceal the sad fact that this man whom Wake respected was dying. The admiral tried to speak but produced instead a gut-wrenching cough. Captain Johnson spoke while the admiral tried to regain his composure.

"Mr. Wake, it is good to see you, sir. The admiral has asked you here to advise you of a new assignment. And also of the results of your examination."

Wake saw the smile form on Johnson's face and knew that his examination for lieutenant, completed in front of the review board the previous month, had been successful. At the time he had felt somewhat at ease with how it had gone, but one could never be sure on those things. He knew that he had fulfilled the necessary duties and sea experience. He was confident that he had written his examination essays as well as any other candidate. The steamship maneuvering category had given him pause since he had no practical experience in that, but he had used common sense in his reply and had received signs of affirmation from the interview board in return. He knew that he had a problem with his reputation among some officers in Key West, but had taken heart when he had found the board composed of captains from several vessels that had just reported in to the squadron from up north with no previous connection here. It was almost more than he could do to wait for the admiral to try to speak again. Finally he spoke, his voice barely audible.

"Peter Wake, you have justified my confidence in you. I am

proud to announce the Navy Department's confirmation of your promotion to the commissioned rank of volunteer lieutenant. You have earned it."

Admiral Barkley held out a thin hand, and Wake shook it gently, looking into the admiral's fading eyes and remembering his father far away in New England.

"I don't know quite what to say, sir, except thank you. It has been a true honor to serve under you. I have learned so much about so many things."

Wake felt moisture come to his eyes and an uncomfortable lump in his throat. He stopped speaking even though there was so much more he wanted to say. Once again Captain Johnson broke the lull.

"Wake, you did earn it, I will say that. I have not approved of some of your behavior and associations, but I know that you are a good seaman and commander. Congratulations."

The admiral was still staring at now-Lieutenant Wake. He seemed about to say something, and both of the other officers waited for him.

"I am dying, Lieutenant. They say I have the consumption. That the yellow jack I had last summer weakened me to the point that this damned thing will kill me. Imagine that! I will die like a sick dog on this godforsaken island!"

Wake did not know what to say. Johnson looked at his commander with tenderness but said nothing. Barkley went on.

"I know that I am an old sea dog. Fought for this nation in three wars and so many other damned places along the way I have forgotten half of 'em. Just always wished I could die on a deck, not in some sickroom. If it had to be this way, then I should have gone with Essie those years ago in Charleston when she passed on. But I am not here to speak of me, Wake. I want to speak of you. Of our navy. Of your future."

"Yes, sir" was the only thing for Wake to say.

"This war will be over, probably by the turn of the year, or at the latest next spring. It seems to drag, but the Rebels are losing their strength steadily now. The army fools in Virginia will probably bungle it for a while longer, but time is against the Rebels now, and the Union will win for sure. Afterward, things will change. The navy will be dismembered as the politicians and pundits take over from the admirals and captains. The navy, the one we fight in and for, will be a tenth of her size. Officers will beg for berths aboard anything that will float. The volunteer officers will be trying to get regular commissions, but just a few will succeed. Only those with respect among the fleet or influence in Washington will get those positions.

"You will have both, young Lieutenant Peter Wake, because you have earned the former, and I am giving you the latter. It is something I need to do for my navy before I go."

Wake found Johnson looking him in the eyes as Barkley gasped out more words in a gravelled voice.

"And so I want to know, Wake, and know right now! Do you intend to stand up and be a real naval officer? Not just for the duration of this conflict, but for the navy after this war? Do you have what it takes to be a commander when the times get lean? Will you stand by this navy and make it better over the years? Think well your answer, young man, for it will contain your future."

"Ah, . . . sir, I *was* thinking of staying in the navy for a career. I was thinking of that very thing today, sir."

"And what do you say? Aye or nay?"

A silence filled the room as the old man looked up into Wake's eyes. Emotions overshadowed the conversation, and Wake knew exactly why the admiral had asked the question. It was a question of life: afloat or ashore, naval or merchant, with meaning or with mere existence. His answer was the only one he had seriously considered in the last several months, a very different one from what he would have answered a year ago.

"I have become a navy man, Admiral. Never thought that I would, but I have lived a lot in this last year. This navy is my home, which is more than a merchant sailor can say. If the navy will have me, I will stay as long as they want me, sir."

The old man lit up with positive glee. Johnson smiled as the admiral proclaimed, "See, Johnson. I knew he had it in his heart! Damn it if I didn't know *that!*"

"Admiral, that you did, sir. Young Wake here answered as you thought he would."

"Wake, Johnson here will give you your orders. You're getting a schooner. You may take two petty officers and two seamen with you from *Rosalie.* Make me proud, son. Now go before I drop in front of you. . . ." Barkley was again seized with coughing. He fell into a chair, clutching his chest. Captain Johnson motioned for Wake to leave the office and called for the clerk to come and minister to his dying chief. Johnson met Wake outside a moment later.

"I know that was difficult, Lieutenant Wake. He feels that you have adjusted to naval life and would make a good career officer for the navy. He feels it would be the best for you and for the service."

"Captain, I had thought it over prior to this and made my decision. I meant what I said to the admiral."

"And he meant what he said to you. You may have friends you don't even know about, Lieutenant. The admiral doesn't have long, I fear. He asked for a sick leave, but they haven't sent a replacement, so he stays on at his post. The man will probably die here." Johnson then handed Wake the familiar envelope with the blue trim that contained orders for ship commanders. "Your orders are in here. You're getting the two-gun schooner, *St. James.* She is lying at anchor off the repair docks here. Brought in a week ago, captured off Pensacola and adjudicated to us yesterday. You will take command immediately. Get her armed and manned and ready for sea. The orders for the yard are in there as well. You will have priority over the other small craft. Your station will be the Florida Keys, and also down to the Cuba coast when ordered."

Captain Johnson then handed Wake another envelope, much fancier than the first, with the seal of the Secretary of the Navy on the flap.

"This is your commission as a volunteer lieutenant from

Washington. Good luck, Lieutenant. . . . And, Lieutenant Wake, though I am glad for your promotion, I am still concerned about your associations. Stand clear of those shoals, for you now carry the weight of Cantwell Barkley's blessing. Don't disrespect that man's honor. . . . Carry yourself accordingly for the good of the service."

The captain shook his hand with unexpected sincerity, turned, and went back into the office where the admiral was still gasping and swearing. The door closed and Wake was left alone feeling stunned and bittersweet.

After he left the building, he was inexorably drawn through the familiar streets toward the back alley he knew so well. Against the will of Captain Johnson and "the good of the service," but by an inexplicable will of his soul, he moved toward the one constant factor in his life that was soft and caring.

Treading among the hibiscus bushes by the cooking shed behind the main house, he looked for Linda, finally catching a glimpse of her in a window by the parlor. Not knowing who was in the house with her, he waited for a few minutes in the bushes, hoping she would come within hearing so that he could call out to her. He knew this was unseemly for a grown man, and a lieutenant especially. He vowed that they would make the decision to bring their relationship into the open.

Linda made her way onto the back portion of the verandah that circled the house and then walked across the growing shadows of the afternoon in the small backyard toward the kitchen. She stopped abruptly when Wake called out softly to her. He pulled her into the bushes and held her closely, willing himself to breathe in as much of her scent as possible as he stroked the softness of her beautiful auburn hair. But as he held her, in the same way he had so many times before, he felt a difference in her behavior.

Linda kissed him on the cheek and disengaged from his arms.

"Peter, . . . so you're obviously back in port. I was wondering when you'd come again. It's been so long since I've seen you."

"Linda darling, it's not that I didn't want to, but I couldn't come to you. You know they don't give me much time in port."

"Yes, I know that, Peter. And I think I know why now. They all know about us and hate the thought of you and me together. They are trying to *save* you from me. I know that now. Peter, no one on this island thinks that a love can survive between a Yankee sailor and the daughter of a Rebel. I hear the twitters of the 'ladies' at the market when I walk in. They are so smug they don't even care if I hear them make their little comments about me. My uncle hasn't confronted me yet, but I know he soon will. The navy thinks it's bad for you, and the islanders think it's bad for me. I don't know what to do. Peter, I have an awful feeling in my heart about this. About us."

"Look, it has been difficult, and it will be difficult. But this war won't last forever. At the end the country will have to mend and heal these attitudes. Even here. Linda, even the Rebel sympathizers in Key West appreciated it when Colonel Good of the Forty-seventh Pennsylvania rescinded that ridiculous order to send away families with men in the Confederate armies. There *are* some decent men and women here. We have to hold on till this thing is over."

"Peter, yes, of course we were glad not to have to suddenly leave on a ship and be sent to the swamps of Carolina to fend for ourselves. But when does the next order come from the authorities? And will there be a decent man like Colonel Good here to stop it? You just don't know what it is like here. You come and go. You are busy on your ship and have other things on your mind. For me, this place is a prison, and I have to survive among the other people here. It is horrible. You just don't know."

Wake felt unarmed against this argument. He didn't know what to say or do. He tried to hold her once more, but she moved away and looked up at his eyes without saying anything. He tried a change of topic.

"Dear, I do have some good news. I have been commissioned

a lieutenant! Admiral Barkley told me personally just an hour ago. I will get a new command. A schooner, like I used to sail up north." As soon as he said it, he realized it was a feeble attempt to brighten her mood. He sensed that something was happening that he could not stop.

"That is wonderful for you, Peter. I am glad for you. But it doesn't change our situation, does it?"

Wake took in the change in her voice. It had become neutral and without emotion. They stood staring at each other, their eyes communicating. Her lovely green eyes showed determination, though her chin quivered slightly. He couldn't believe it. Was he losing her because of this damned island and its strange people? And this damned war?

"I don't know what you mean, Linda. Say it plain."

"I can't take it any longer, Peter. I can't play the role any longer. I am tired. I am so tired of it all, and I can't carry on waiting for those few surprise moments when you can get some little time to steal away and see me.

"And it isn't good for you either, Peter. 'Consorting with the enemy' is what they call it. Admiral Barkley is a good man and has done what he could for you, but when he dies you will have no defender. The other officers think of the Southern girls here as playthings and look upon you as a fool to fall in love with one of us. You know that because you have heard them say as much among themselves in the taverns. I've heard these things too."

"What do you want, Linda?"

"I want us to have a normal life together, openly. That is what I want, but that is not what I can have. I need to go back inside now. Uncle will be wondering. Peter, when you can come in the front door for me, come back. Until then, my heart can't take the ache of living this way. Goodbye, Peter. I will always love you, even though I know now I can't have you. . . ."

With that final statement she walked into the kitchen, picked up a pot off the fire and returned to the house without looking back. Wake stood there, eyes misting over until he couldn't see anything. He stood for several more minutes, a naval officer first reduced to seeing his lover in secret and now crying uncontrollably, in uniform, because she had had the courage to face the fact, and tell him, that their love was doomed from the start. He didn't know what to do. He couldn't move. Wake slowly sat down with his head in his hands, trying to regain his composure and think, but he couldn't make sense of this.

The sound of the provost patrol from Fort Taylor finally shook him out of his melancholia. He heard the soldiers as they turned the corner and marched down Whitehead Street, the crunch of their boots in unison making a rhythmic statement about the reality of life in Key West, an example of what Linda had tried to explain to him. These troops had come from Pennsylvania and New York to prevent the island from aiding the Confederates on the mainland. For the people of the island, the troops were foreigners. He was a foreigner, part of an occupying power on this island. Linda was right, of course. He was one of the wardens, and she was one of the prisoners.

With a sigh Wake stood and brushed himself off. He made his way out of the alleyway and back to Duval Street. Walking down to the harbor, he watched as sailors on liberty walked out of some of the "authorized" tap rooms on the side streets, arms wrapped around the girls of the establishments. No false pretenses there. It made him feel worse, and he hurried back to the waterfront.

When he reached the *Rosalie*, by way of the harbor boat, he went immediately down into his cabin and stretched out on his crude bunk. An hour later he took off his uniform and sat there looking at his insignia. Tomorrow he would have to get new insignia from the chandlery where officers' uniforms could be bought.

Opening the envelope from Washington, he looked at the commission. The much-sought-after document meant he had a decent chance for a professional home for the rest of his life with at least half-pay security. He felt no emotion as he stared at the paper, however. It wasn't as important now.

Next he opened his orders and found that the *St. James* was a seventy-ton schooner built just five years ago, even newer than the *Rosalie*. She was to be armed with two six-pounder boat howitzers and manned by a crew of twenty-five. The yard was ordered to "take all care to provision, supply, and equip her for naval usage." Her length of eighty-five feet and draft of six feet meant she could go almost anywhere she might be needed. He found himself wondering if his cabin would be more spacious.

A voice calling him to supper brought him on deck, where the crew not on liberty ashore were starting to eat their salt pork. Rork stared at Wake as they sat on the deck and ate their food. He could sense that something was bothering his commander and finally spoke up.

"Sir, how did it go ashore today? I saw you had some orders with you when you returned. Do we have another go at the Rebs? Or more of the same work?"

Wake was glad to be able to finally speak of positive information. "Rork, the day was eventful. I found out several things that may interest you."

"I'm all ears, sir! I'd be much obliged to find out just what has happened among the esteemed leadership on this fine day!"

Wake smiled at Rork's reply as Durlon came over and sat with them. Wake continued with a lighter tone. "Well, men, first I found out that I have passed the examination for lieutenant and have been given my commission."

"Excellent, sir! Well done and well earned, if I do say so meself," said Rork with a huge Irish grin lighting up his face.

Durlon put down his plate and extended his hand. "I'll be damned, sir. So the powers that be actually knew talent when they saw it. Congratulations, sir. We're all glad for ya."

"Thank you, men. I must admit it surprised me a bit, but it is very welcome. I've decided to stay in for a career, even after this war is done."

Both petty officers nodded their approval of this decision and looked at him for more revelations.

"Also, I have been given command of a schooner just taken into the service, the *St. James*, which is lying at anchor over there by the docks. Spent many years on schooners up north. Haven't gotten to see her myself yet, but she sounds like a good vessel." Wake held up his hand as Rork and Durlon were about to congratulate him again. "And, I have been given permission to ship two petty officers over to her from *Rosalie*. So that would mean you two, if you want to come with me."

"Honored, sir," said a suddenly serious Rork.

"No sense in not going with ya, sir. So what are her guns, sir?" said an equally serious Durlon. He was always serious when he spoke of cannons.

"Good, I'm glad you'll both be with me. We can take two seamen also. Rork, you can recommend which to me later. Durlon, she'll have two twelve-pounder howitzers. Close-in weapons."

Durlon pondered this news and replied, "A schooner with twelve-pounders. That will do, sir. We can make some mischief with that."

Rork looked at his gunner friend and laughed. "Mischief, me old son? We could make a bit of *hell* with those two darlins'. I do believe, sir, that my friend here is startin' to speak with a bit o' understatement. He must be gettin' old."

"Be that as it may, Rork, we will go over in the morning and see our new ship and make plans for getting her fitted out and under way as soon as we can."

The pleasant period lasted for another hour as the three men spoke of their new ship and her area of operations. They talked of which crewmen to bring along and how to get the most from the yard and supply clerks. As dark descended with the completeness of the tropics, Wake wandered back to his cabin and thought about gaining a new ship and losing the love of his life, all in one day. It all was happening so fast that he couldn't fathom the meaning yet. He collapsed in his bunk in the tiny, musty cabin and fell asleep exhausted from the emotions that had drained him.

The next five days proved to be as physically wearing as the last had proved emotional. Wake and the two petty officers had to turn their beloved *Rosalie* temporarily over to a newly arrived bosun's mate from the steam gunboat U.S.S. *Tahoma*. He had stories to tell of serving under the famous Alexander Semmes, cousin of the notorious Rebel naval officer Raphael Semmes, who was making news around the world as he scourged the American merchant marine. The Semmes of the East Gulf Blockading Squadron was equally as active in bringing the war ashore and afloat to the Confederates of Florida, and had recently been sent north to command a new monitor gunboat. Wake had heard of the man, and once had met him, but was impressed when the bosun told them of the *Tahoma*'s exploits. After spending time with the new interim commander of his old sloop, he felt that Old Rosey was going to be in good hands, which made him feel better, for he had come to love the little ship that had carried them through so much in the last year.

The *St. James* did indeed have a larger cabin for the captain. She also carried a tall rig for her length, a valuable asset when the summer doldrums would come. Since her hull drew more water and was more voluminous, the crew berthing area made out of the former hold was more habitable also. Wake and Durlon noted with approval that her magazine was far more secure and that the two twelve-pounders would not impact her center of gravity as much as on the *Rosalie*. Rork was very impressed that her rigging and canvas looked almost new, which was very unusual for a blockade runner at this point in the war. He surmised that she must have been refitted at Nassau lately and wondered if their old nemesis Saunders had been part of that effort.

All in all, Wake was pleased with how things were progressing. The new crew was signed aboard and consisted of a few veterans, like Sampson and Hewlitt from the *Rosalie*, but mostly new recruits. These young men were in awe of Rork and Durlon and absolutely fearful of Wake. In their short time in the navy they had already learned the power of a naval officer over their lives.

The one distressing factor was, as always, dealing with the yard and supply petty officers, who seemed to be greatly disturbed when anything disrupted their personal plans and schedules. The crew had to resort to threatening, cajoling, inducing, and openly bribing in order to get the equipment, supplies, and provisioning that the *St. James* needed to make her a fighting ship.

Finally it was done and the day came for Wake to assemble the crew on deck and read his orders for command and the official commissioning of the vessel into the United States Navy. Afterward, they set sail and made their way south down the main channel past Fort Taylor toward the Atlantic Ocean, Wake thinking again of the day he had met Linda in the guard room there. He was trying to block any sadness from his feelings, however, since they were sailing outbound on a gorgeous day with a fair southwesterly breeze and the brilliant colors of the reefs lit up the waters all around them. The various blues and greens, with an occasional purple or yellow, reminded him of how far away he was from New England and his previous life. He turned away from staring at the walls of Fort Taylor and looked out to sea, where indigo blue signaled deep water beyond the reef.

He had not even tried to see Linda again after that last meeting. Her words had burned into his mind, and he relived that moment again and again. Though he knew that the blame lay with the war, he could not help feeling in his heart that he was responsible for her sadness, that he had somehow failed, that he should have done something, said something. He was trying to come to terms with his new reality, that he was empty except for this ship, this crew, and this mission.

They turned eastward at the outer reef and ran on a broad reach out to the Gulf Stream. The patrol orders were to sail to Salt Key Bank, or Cay Sal, as the Spanish had called it for four hundred years, between the Bahamas and Cuba, and search there for any suspicious ships. Then they would turn northward and proceed to Cape Florida, thence back to Key West by the inside channel among the keys. It was a simple plan, with some intricate navigation required among the reefs at their destinations, but Wake welcomed it as a mind-consuming exercise that would overwhelm the memories haunting him. Rork and Durlon knew something was still bothering their captain, but did not know that the Rebel girl, whom they both knew about, had broken his heart.

On their second day out they saw a native sloop from the Bahamas and hailed her. She reported that there was a schooner in the Cay Sal area flying a British flag but appearing American built and manned. The black spongers aboard the sloop added that the Americans in the schooner didn't look like they were there to trade with the other spongers and turtlers who sailed those waters. Wake was intrigued and decided to investigate the schooner.

With the wind still out of the southwest, Wake sailed the *St. James* around to the northeast end of the chain of barely visible islets known as the Double Headed Shot Cays. Neither he nor any of his crew had been to this place, but Wake had heard plenty of stories about shipwrecks in the area. The depth rose from many hundreds of fathoms—no one knew exactly how many—to only ten fathoms in the space of a hundred yards. He could just imagine trying to approach from the west with the ocean swells coming onto the shallow banks. They reduced sail and steered northeast for a day, then tacked her back round and sailed slowly under just the jib due south, looking for some sign of the islands. The last thing Wake wanted was to find the reefs with his keel.

After a day of slow sailing, they tacked back to the north in the dark of the night. Now the new lieutenant was worried about the effect of the currents in the area. He had heard stories about those too. The next morning they sailed south again, with double lookouts in the bows.

First they sensed the change in the seas on the starboard beam. The swells started to lump up and make crests, disrupting the regular pattern they had been sailing through. Now all hands were called to look in all directions forward of amidships. They crept forward to the south, rolling with the increased wave action, until at midmorning a young new crewman by the name of Lawrence cried out that he thought he saw something in the distance on the port bow.

Rork scrambled up to the crosstrees and stood next to Lawrence. He searched the scene with a telescope, a valuable instrument not entrusted to a mere youngster. Soon he was calling down to his captain that the sailor was surely correct and the reef islets were some few miles ahead. Wake luffed the jib to slow her speed to a crawl as the bottom started to show underneath.

Sampson swung the lead line. "Nay on to seven!" "By the deep five!" "Now under four!" He called out from the port shrouds as he swung the line up and ahead and down into the water. The bottom was showing in stark clarity, terrifying for the new hands, but Wake knew how to "read" the waters of this part of the world by now and was calling the steering by the colors he saw. They drew closer to the line of reef islets and observed no vessels among them. Steering around the huge coral heads that rose up brown and menacing from the sandy bottom, they finally came around the end of the easternmost islet and anchored in two fathoms under its small lee.

Rork was sent with the launch to the closest islet to see what he could find ashore on the coral and sand rocks that rose only a few feet out of the sea. The launch was a luxury compared to the dinghy they had used with *Rosalie*. Rork was able to take five men with him and covered the short distance quickly. A few minutes later he returned, explaining to his captain that no sign of a camp or any people could be seen. Wake then decided that they would have to go the length of the chain of islets, searching each one for any sign that sailors had been there. These islands had been used for rendezvous by pirates in the previous century, and he surmised that the blockade runners could be using them as such now.

The wind was on their bow as the *St. James* weighed anchor and tacked under jib and reefed foresail along the southwesterly line of small islands. At each cay they repeated the procedure of anchoring and rowing ashore, but always they returned without any sign of their possible enemy. They sailed until midday, when the sun was high enough for them to read the colors of the water, and thus stay off the jagged reaches of coral rock that threatened to maroon them in this desolate place.

After anchoring for the afternoon and evening, they got under way again the next day, following the same routine of Wake making detailed sketches of the area while Rork, Sampson, or Durlon read the water and steered the schooner through the dangers. After three days they reached the westernmost end of the chain, and Wake gave the order to let her run away to the east, along the path they had come.

After days of fruitless search he became concerned about water and other provisions. There was no further reason to stay at Cay Sal, and Wake determined that they should make their run north to Cape Florida before the food and water situation should become urgent. It took only two days to make the run easterly, but by the time they turned north the wind had gone into that direction also, making the course another very close haul.

Emerging from the shallows of the Cay Sal Bank under reefed fore and main with a small jib showing, *St. James* heeled over to shoulder her way into the building seas and wind. The confused seas became large swells and the schooner fairly swooped along in the rhythm of the ocean. By the end of that day, after the sun had sunk into the haze of the horizon, Wake could tell that they were in the Gulf Stream again. But this time was different. The wind and current were now opposing each other, and the seas upon the surface of the great swells were starting to rise and curl. He had seen this before on *Rosalie* and was very glad to be aboard a much larger vessel that could handle the potential peril with more ease. As they smashed their way along to the north, the night was wet and cold on deck and seawater found its way everywhere below, making the crew's spaces even more uncomfortable.

Watch after watch they slogged into the next day, wondering

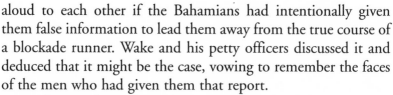

aloud to each other if the Bahamians had intentionally given them false information to lead them away from the true course of a blockade runner. Wake and his petty officers discussed it and deduced that it might be the case, vowing to remember the faces of the men who had given them that report.

By the next day Wake had new navigational decisions to make. With the sky overcast he had not been able to take a sight for a position and had been relying on his and Rork's dead reckoning since leaving the shallow islets behind. The difficulty was that the great ocean river of the Gulf Stream had greatly influenced their course. But how much and in what direction?

The lieutenant decided to make a tack to the west, running until he could see the Florida mainland, then sail south to Cape Florida. After conferring with Rork and getting his estimate of the Stream's effect upon their course, Wake made his announcement and the schooner was borne away with the sheets eased on a starboard tack. The crew, even the newcomers to the ways of the navy, knew that a miscalculation could result in their sailing to the west on a latitude too far south that would end them on one of the Florida Keys' reefs before they ever saw the land ahead. Wake knew their fears—indeed, he shared them within himself— but he also knew that a decision had to be made. Rork's estimate did not seem to be enough to the east and north, and he rejected it as probably wrong. He went with his own estimate. Either he had made his calculations correctly about the course made good, or he had not and they would pay the price for the mistake.

All hands watched ahead as the *St. James* slid through the seas on her beam reach. It was her best point of sail, and it seemed as though they were almost going to lift up into the air at times when coming off a wave. Despite the anxiety, Wake found himself smiling in appreciation of how his new ship sailed. She was fast warming into his heart with her ways.

By dusk the sun had fallen through the sky to become a flaring beacon for the helmsman to steer by. Wake, not wanting to close the land in the coming darkness, was just about to give the order to tack back to the east when the lookout aloft yelled with such glee that he almost fell.

"Land! I see land ahead there. See it? The big tree off over there." His arm pointed to two points off the port bow.

"Lookout aloft! Give a proper report or I'll have ye stand the next watch up there with the birds, damn ya," came booming up from the deck as Rork took a telescope from the binnacle rack and, winking at Wake, swung into the ratlines to climb upward. "Captain, he probably saw a cloud, but I'll be checking up on the lad anyhow."

Moments later, the entire crew stood swaying on the main deck of the schooner, every eye focused on the bosun.

Rork roared down, "By the saints in heaven! Lord Jesus, Mary, and Joseph! The boyo here is right enough that he sees something ahead, Captain. But it ain't a cloud or a tree, by God. It's the lighthouse at Cape Florida itself, sir! Dead on exact landfall, sir."

A ragged cheer went up from the crowd on the deck as Durlon made his way over and shook Wake's hand. All hands watched as the gunner's mate grinned at his captain.

"Damned good navigation, sir! Never saw it done like that afore."

Wake thanked him for his kind words as Rork came down the swaying backstay hand over hand, landing on the deck next to them with a thud.

"Well, Captain, you was as right as the misty rain on a Irish day, sir. You've done right for all of us lads."

With all of the crew beaming at him for his navigational victory and the sun turning into a fiery display of luminescent colors ahead of them, suddenly Wake felt illogically sad. His eyes were seeing the happy crew in front of him, but his mind was looking at the images of the war he had fought for the last twelve months in this alien tropical world. The faces of men, his men, killed in battles, came flooding into his senses. He knew the crew was expecting him to say something—a profound or witty saying, at least an order. Something.

But he stood rooted to the deck as the memory of Hardin lashed to the gunboat's foredeck, screaming his inhuman shriek, swept over him with a cold chill. Then came Linda's father, waving to them for help as they sailed away from the shipwrecked survivors on the beach. And Saunders came into his mind, smiling—or was he laughing?—from the deck of the schooner *Victoria* as she sailed away.

As his men started to sense that something was wrong with their captain and Rork moved closer to shake him out of whatever dream he was in, Wake saw Linda. He saw her in the bed of her quaint little room. He saw her crying in front of the army lieutenant at Fort Taylor, begging for her father's freedom. He saw her sobbing out the story of her family's deadly fight with yellow fever. He saw her on their last day together, and her final words echoed through his mind. She overpowered all the other images and floated before his eyes, staring at him.

"Sir, are ye all right?" The tenderness in Rork's voice came through the fog in Wake's brain. "You've had a bad bit o' tension, sir, with all the navigatin' and all. Perhaps ye can go below to rest now, and we'll heave her to till daylight. Then we can go inshore to the lighthouse. Don't worry about a thing, Captain. Me and the lads will take her now."

Wake turned to the man he had become closest to in this mad world of death and danger and spoke for the first time since the ghosts from the past had overcome him. Rork leaned close to hear as Durlon ushered the crew away and back to work.

"Rork, so many men dead. Mistakes made. Things I should've done and said. People dead because of my decisions. This year has been a hell of one damned impossible situation after another."

Wake's hand traced the scar on the side of his head while his body slumped as though physically assaulted. He looked at his friend, silhouetted against the sun boiling down onto the Florida mainland.

"Peter Wake," the bosun said quietly, "you have done all that anyone could do. And more. Many men are alive because o' your decisions. Many more are living through this awful war with some wee bit o' dignity because o' your caring. The lads know what you've done for them. You're the kind of man this navy needs. Ye not need to be shamed or doubtful o' your decisions in the past, sir.

"Ah laddee, your own life has not gone well ashore, I can sense. But know that your life among us *has* gone well. You've stood the test and steered a course made good, against all that's come our way."

Wake studied the face of the bosun and found no mockery, only concern. No one was near them now. Even Durlon had given them their space on the deck to talk. Darkness was filling the air around them, and no sound save that of the sea could be heard.

"Rork, I just feel so damned alone, and I wonder if the next time the mistake will be paid for in blood."

"Aye, Captain Peter Wake. 'Tis the way of a captain. The best kind o' captain, the kind that cares. An you're never alone, not as long as you've got us lads."

Wake smiled and realized that the big Irishman was exactly right. His home was here now. He could not go back to the family's shipping business in New England. The decision to stay in for a career in this navy was the correct one. He knew he could not go back to a dull but safe life.

"Ye've got some more of those decisions to make in the morn, Captain Wake. You get some rest, and I'll get the old girl tacked an' hove to for the night. Ye know, sir, this old paddy is rightly honored to serve with ye, and I know the future'll be lookin' up with the sunrise."

Wake turned to descend to his cabin, grasping Rork's leathered hand.

"Sorry for the moment of doubt, Bosun Rork." His eyes locked onto Rork's as Wake's voiced firmed. "In the morning we will go ashore and speak with the light keeper. Perhaps he just may have some vessel for us to hunt. I do believe there's a fair bit more to do in this war, so there's no sense in wasting time dreaming about things that aren't. . . . And Bosun Rork, . . ."

"Sir?"

"The honor is all mine."

The commander of the United States Naval schooner *St. James,* a much different man from the one who had been rowed to *Rosalie* in Key West Harbor a year before, descended to the sanctuary of his private cabin and stretched out on his bunk. Sleep finally came in the darkness, providing a respite from those unsolvable dilemmas that had haunted his mind and taken him to the edge of honor.

Peter Wake's past was far behind him, and his future was decided. Now it was time to get on and live it.